PENGUIN BOOKS

RUSKIN TODAY

Kenneth Clark was born in 1903. He was educated at Winchester and Oxford, and worked for two years with Bernard Berenson in Florence. He was appointed Director of the National Gallery at the age of 30 and remained there until 1945. During the war he organised the war artists' scheme, and with Dame Myra Hess was responsible for the National Gallery Concerts. He was Slade Professor of Fine Art at Oxford from 1946 to 1950. Lord Clark was Chairman of the Arts Council from May 1953 to 1960, and was appointed Chairman on the setting up of the Independent Television Authority. He is widely known for his television programmes on art, especially the series on *Civilisation*. His first publication, written at the age of 22, was *The Gothic Revival*, and many others followed; four of them, *Leonardo da Vinci* (1939), *Landscape into Art* (1949), *The Nude* (1956), and *Civilisation* (1969), have been published in Penguins. His later works are *Rembrandt and the Italian Renaissance* (1966), *A Failure of Nerve* (1967), *Looking at Pictures* (1972), *Westminster Abbey* (1972; jointly), *The Artist Grows Old* (Rede Lecture; 1972), *The Romantic Rebellion* (1973), *Another Part of the Wood*, the first volume of his autobiography (1974), *Henry Moore Drawings* (1974), *The Drawings by Sandro Botticelli for Dante's Divine Comedy* (1976), *Animals and Men* (1977), *The Other Half*, the second volume of his autobiography (1978), *An Introduction to Rembrandt* (1978), *The Best of Aubrey Beardsley* (1978) and *Moments of Vision* (1981). Kenneth Clark was knighted in 1938 and made a Life Peer in 1969. Among other honours conferred, he has been made an Honorary Fellow of the Royal Institute of British Architects and an Honorary Fellow of the Royal Academy of Arts. In 1970 he was awarded the U.S. National Gallery of Arts medal and in 1976 was awarded the Order of Merit.

RUSKIN TODAY

CHOSEN AND ANNOTATED BY

KENNETH CLARK

PENGUIN BOOKS

Penguin Books Ltd, Harmondsworth, Middlesex, England
Penguin Books, 625 Madison Avenue, New York, New York 10022, U.S.A.
Penguin Books Australia Ltd, Ringwood, Victoria, Australia
Penguin Books Canada Ltd, 2801 John Street, Markham, Ontario, Canada L3R 1B4
Penguin Books (N.Z.) Ltd, 182-190 Wairau Road, Auckland 10, New Zealand

—

First published by John Murray 1964 by
arrangement with Penguin Books Ltd
Published in Peregrine Books 1967
Reprinted 1982
Reprinted in Penguin Books 1982

—

—

Made and printed in Great Britain
by Richard Clay (The Chaucer Press) Ltd,
Bungay, Suffolk
Set in Monotype Bembo

CONTENTS

PREFACE

This selection from Ruskin's writings was begun many years ago solely in order that I might re-read passages which had given me particular pleasure. When it was decided that this personal choice should be published as an anthology I felt that, in fairness to Ruskin, I ought to include the expression of certain opinions by which he set great store, however much I disagreed with them; and that his chief interests, or, perhaps I should say, his ruling passions, should be exhibited in his own words, if only by a sentence or two. This raised the difficulty of how much space I should give to the sheer nonsense which occupies a great part of his later works. I had not forgotten that *Unto this Last*, in many ways his greatest work, was considered nonsense by his contemporaries. But there is a difference, clearly perceptible after a century, between controversial opinions and intellectual chaos; and the few examples which I have included of Ruskin's mind out of control will I hope convince the reader that I have not been unduly severe. In spite of my efforts to give a balanced picture of Ruskin's thought, I know that my first impulse has been to choose passages that are beautifully written. This would have annoyed him because, as he wrote to an earlier anthologist, 'It is the chief provocation of my life to be called a word painter instead of a thinker.'

But, on the whole, authors write best when they are interested in their subject, and Ruskin's style may be a clearer indication of his real convictions than he would have cared to admit. In one respect, however, my anthology is misleading. Ruskin, all his life, was deeply preoccupied with religion. I am not capable of understanding this branch of his thought, and have therefore omitted it, except for one superb sentence (in no. 309).

The arrangement of this selection was an insoluble problem. Ruskin disliked systems, and allowed his mind to pass from one

subject to another without a break. I have begun with a 'Self-Portrait'
because anyone coming fresh to the subject must first of all make
allowance for his strange and fascinating character. Then comes
'Nature' because, as he frequently said himself, the love of nature
preceded and dominated his love of art. Nevertheless, the section on
'Art' is the longest in the book, because, when all is said, our fathers
were right in recognizing Ruskin's responsiveness to certain works of
art and architecture as his rarest endowment. In the section on
'Society and Economics' I have included some of his thoughts about
life in general. Finally I was left with a quantity of famous passages
which did not fit into any of these categories. I hesitated to class them
as 'fine writing', since nearly every piece quoted in the other sections
is finely written. I have called them, rather lamely, 'Poetic Description', conscious that this, too, could apply to more than half the
quotations in the book. Within each of these sections I have tried to
arrange the extracts in such a way as to make the book readable,
aiming at contrast and variety rather than consistency and logic; and
I have resisted the temptation to split up a quotation into its appro-
priate categories, in order to preserve those surprising transitions
which are so characteristic of Ruskin's thought (e.g. nos. 26 and 57).
Finally I have included the whole of the section in *Modern Painters*,
Vol. v, known as 'The Two Boyhoods', in order that the reader may
have some idea of how Ruskin's mind moved at a longer stretch.

My work has been done from the great edition of Ruskin's
works, prepared over a period of ten years, with incredible industry
and a noble devotion to truth, by E. T. Cook and Alexander Wedderburn. These thirty-nine volumes, in my school library, were my
first introduction to Ruskin, and I have continued to use them ever
since with increasing admiration. I therefore began by giving all
references to the Cook and Wedderburn edition. But if Ruskin is
ever read again it will probably be in less bulky volumes and I have
ended by using the system prepared by Ruskin himself, by which
in all the books published in his lifetime, the paragraphs were numbered. These references are sometimes rather cumbersome (especially

in *Modern Painters*) but in the end they should prove an advantage. For work not published in his lifetime, such as the very important appendix to the second volume of *Modern Painters*, I have referred to the Library edition thus – C. & W. Vol. o, p. oo. Two exceptions are *Fors Clavigera*, where I have simply given the date of the letter, and the letters, where the date and name of the recipient seemed adequate.

The introductory notes to some of the sections are intended to provide a background for the reader who is not familiar with Ruskin's work. I have kept them short, as it is time people read Ruskin's own words, instead of reading about him. Between 1929 and 1953, at least seven full-length biographies of Ruskin were published; but his own works were almost entirely unread. In 1942 I mentioned to my friend Bill Williams that I was making an anthology of passages from Ruskin, and believed that it might be worth publishing. He received the idea with an enthusiasm which would have surprised me in anyone else, and ever since, with a mixture of tenacity and tact, has urged me to complete my selection. I now offer Sir William Emrys Williams this anthology, in memory of twenty years' work together.

K. C.

Saltwood
Christmas 1962

INTRODUCTION

No other writer, perhaps, has suffered so great a fall in reputation as Ruskin. Throughout the whole second half of the nineteenth century he was accepted by all thoughtful people as one of the impregnable figures in English literature. His fame passed through several phases, each of which netted a new band of admirers. In 1845 the first volume of *Modern Painters* had won him the support of the intellectuals; *The Seven Lamps of Architecture* had extended his appeal to the serious minded; *Unto this Last* (1860), and his other studies in political economy, although they shocked many of his earlier readers, made him the prophet of a new social consciousness. Then came his volumes of lectures, *Sesame and Lilies* and *The Crown of Wild Olive*, which made him, for the first time, a popular writer, and a selection of descriptive passages from *Modern Painters*, called *Frondes Agrestes* (1875). Those volumes, bound in vellum or limp leather, were to be found lying beside the *Idylls of the King* on the tables of those who did not normally read, but wished to show some evidence of refinement. For almost fifty years, to read Ruskin was accepted as proof of the possession of a soul.

But his literary reputation was far more serious than this. From Wordsworth to Proust there was hardly a distinguished man of letters who did not admire him. Austere critics like Leslie Stephen believed him to be one of the unassailable masters of English prose, and, on the death of Tennyson, Gladstone (whom he habitually insulted) wished to make him Poet Laureate, and was only prevented from doing so by the fact that he was out of his mind.

Nor was his reputation confined to literature. Tolstoy, Gandhi, and Bernard Shaw, to name only three, believed him to be one of the greatest social reformers of his time. His writings on economics became a spur to action. Ruskin Societies sprang up all over England; a college in Oxford for working men was named after him, and when, at the first meeting of the parliamentary Labour Party, members were asked what had been the determining influence on their lives, almost every one answered 'the works of Ruskin'.

Now, in the middle of the twentieth century, what is left of this towering reputation? Practically nothing but a malicious interest in the story of his private life. Ironically, but not exceptionally, the decline in his fame seems to have coincided with the publication of a superb library edition of his works, one of the most thorough and devoted pieces of editing ever undertaken.[1] It is sometimes said that the size of the edition acted like a tombstone on Ruskin's reputation, but in fact a popular edition of favourite works, which appeared at the same time, was equally unread, and is still in print; and some of the volumes in the London Library set, which was bought on publication, are uncut. This indifference has increased, so that his works, which thirty years ago could still be seen in the upper shelves of second-hand booksellers, are now hard to find. Mention Ruskin in a popular bookshop, and you will be offered books *about* him, but never books *by* him. I have been told that when his works are bought in a mixed lot, they are simply thrown out, like sprats or dogfish. They are not worth the shelf-room.

What has brought about this catastrophic change, which goes far beyond the ordinary pendulum swing of fashion? The first answer is that Ruskin was a popular moralist and a preacher. We all hope to improve, and we like writers who try and improve us – on our own terms. We will even put up with a scolding if the teacher is saying the sort of thing we want to hear. But the moment his message doesn't suit us we turn from him with indignation and contempt. Ruskin was a moralist and preacher born. His first recorded utterance at the age of five was a sermon, which began with the words 'People, be good'. And throughout his life he felt bound to consider every subject, from architecture to mineralogy, as a branch of morals. He had been brought up as a 'Bible Christian' and although

1. *The Works of John Ruskin*, Library Edition, edited by E. T. Cook and Alexander Wedderburn, London, 1903 to 1912.

in middle life he shook off the evangelical temper of his youth, the assumptions and the cadences of weekly sermons still controlled his thoughts, particularly when, as in the first Oxford lectures, he was impressed by the importance of an occasion. Our ancestors enjoyed a sermon, and looked forward particularly to the peroration (what is known in Welsh oratory as the *hwyl*) in which the preacher was carried out of himself in a mounting spiral of eloquence. So the soaring rhythms and crowning quotations from the Bible, with which Ruskin, in his own words, 'rounded off' each section of *Modern Painters*, seemed to them his most admirable accomplishment. Today we find them embarrassing and incredible, and I must confess that in making this selection, whenever I have seen a biblical quotation in the offing, I have begun to lose interest, because I know that at this point Ruskin will cease to use his own powers of intelligent observation, and will rely on holy writ to save him further thought.

The second reason why Ruskin is hard to read is his inability to concentrate. This was part of his genius. In his mind, as in the eye of an impressionist painter, everything was more or less reflected in everything else; and when he tries too hard to keep his mind in a single track, as in the second volume of *Modern Painters*, some of its beautiful colour is lost. Still, it must be admitted that after the age of about thirty his inability to stick to the point becomes rather frustrating, and in his later writings, where literally every sentence starts a new train of thought, he reduces his reader to a kind of hysterical despair.

His sense of analogy was corrupted by a real weakness of character, which may be described as a mixture of self-indulgence and arrogance. It was sheer self-indulgence for him to give his opinion on every single topic – natural history, botany, geology, mythology, and public affairs – as well as on matters with which he was more directly concerned; and arrogance to suppose that his opinions were not only worth expressing, but were infallibly correct. This irrelevance is often said to be a symptom of his mental decline; but it appears when he was at the height of his powers and was part of the action of his mind the moment words began to flow from his pen.

He had a curious inability to relate the expression of his opinions to his knowledge. He knew a good deal about geology and took trouble to learn about ornithology and botany: but when he came to write on these subjects all his researches were forgotten and fanciful etymologies took the place of facts. As often as not the subjects themselves were hardly mentioned after the first two or three paragraphs, and there boiled up in him a desire to dogmatize which could not be satisfied by mere exposition.

The third reason why we do not read Ruskin is our mistrust of eloquence. From childhood he was gifted with an astounding fluency. At the age of fourteen he wrote to his father:

> I would write a short, pithy, economic, sensible, concentrated and serious letter, if I could, for I have scarcely time to write a long one. Observe, I only say 'to write' for as to the composition 'tis nothing, positively nothing. I roll on like a ball, with the exception ... that I have no friction to contend with in my mind and in consequence have some difficulty in stopping myself when there is nothing else to stop me.

This fluency was accompanied by an exceptional command of language, and the result was the highly coloured prose style which so much delighted our grandfathers.

There are good reasons why this kind of writing is no longer admired and, by younger critics, actively despised. It introduces an emotional appeal into matters which should be the concern of reason, and even the emotions it arouses are inflated by the pressure of words. It is commonly used to conceal the truth, to stir up hatred, and to promote war. A rhetorical style intoxicates the writer and seems to generate a particular state of mind, so that Ruskin will suddenly indulge in a tub-thumping justification of the Crimean War[1] or a violent incitement to go out and seize colonies[2] (although in his quieter moments he knew that both war and colonialism were

1. *Modern Painters*, Vol. III.   2. *Lectures on Art*, I, § 29.

wrong), simply because the mounting rhythm of his style carried him in that direction. Today the suspicion we feel for degraded rhetoric extends to elaborate writings of all kinds. We find it hard to believe that anyone who is sincerely anxious to tell the truth will do so in long and well-contrived sentences, rather than in a series of monosyllables and grunts. And so the marvellous eloquence which, to his contemporaries, seemed to guarantee Ruskin's immortality, has become one of the principal reasons why he remains unread.

These are some of the reasons why Ruskin's *Collected Works* remain unopened, and personally I believe that posterity will continue to find a great many of these thirty-nine volumes unreadable. Many authors, of course, are remembered for a small fraction of their output. Library editions are like icebergs, where five-sixths of the total bulk is submerged. The trouble is that most authors have managed to put their inspiration into one or two volumes, whereas Ruskin scattered his throughout his works. Patience and tenacity are needed to discover it. I will now give some reasons why the effort is worth making.

*

The first reason for reading Ruskin is that he was a poet. In saying this I am not thinking primarily of his elaborate descriptions of nature, beautiful as they sometimes are, but of the many passages in which his accurate perceptions and marvellous sense of analogy are used under the impulse of what Wordsworth called 'a passion and an appetite'.

> I don't think myself a great genius [he wrote to his father], but I believe I have genius; something different from mere cleverness. . . . There is a strong instinct in me, which I cannot analyse, to draw and describe the things which I love – not for reputation, nor for the good of others, nor for my own advantage, but a sort of instinct like that of eating and drinking[1].

Of course his perceptions gained by being the focus of his very

1. 2 June 1852.

active and far-ranging mind. Ruskin's poetry was not purely perceptual, any more than Wordsworth's was; there are comments on every subject, from immortality to taxation, in which his imaginative grasp gives his thought a poetic wholeness and intensity. But as a rule it is the thing seen, whether in nature or art, which stirs his emotions to the point at which thought, feeling, and language are one, the point of incandescence which we call poetry.

The language in which he conveyed these moments of heightened perception was an instrument of great range, flexibility, and force. The vocabulary is rich and precise. The rhythms which, in his rhetorical outbursts, have an almost Swinburnian redundancy, become, when mind and eye are at one, extremely subtle and varied, and seem to reflect exactly his emotion as he contemplates a scene or develops an idea. In fact many of his descriptions were, so to say, painted direct from nature, written on the spot in a kind of ecstasy, without grammar or punctuation; and, even when they are worked up, they retain a closeness to the original emotion rarely combined with mastery of an elaborate style. Again and again in compiling this anthology I have held my breath with astonishment and delight at his sheer technical accomplishment. Even the 'set pieces', such as the falls of Schaffhausen or the approach to Venice, are amazing performances; and when the tone is a little quieter and more personal only the most puritanical enemy of eloquence could object. When he wished to write simply, as in *The Elements of Drawing*, *Unto this Last*, and *Praeterita*, he achieves a beautiful transparency of language, without ever becoming flat, or losing flexibility. Later, under the influence of Carlyle, he developed a more wayward rhythm, as of the spoken word, which allowed him to surprise the unwary reader with a sudden, savage bite. But even then he remained a poet, piercing through the surfaces of things, seeing similars in dissimilars, and illuminating the familiar by some flashing analogy.

A second reason for reading Ruskin is that he was a character of great fascination and complexity, worthy of a novelist of the genius of George Eliot. He was made up of contradictions: intelligence and silliness, puritanism and a refined sensuality, selfishness and extreme generosity. The central drama of his life, that of the pampered aesthete who gradually becomes aware of social injustice, and as a result sacrifices his reputation, his wealth, and ultimately his sanity, is as moving as anything in fiction. This drama can be read in Ruskin's works. He loved to talk about himself, either directly as in the pages of *Fors Clavigera* and in *Praeterita*, that disarming account of his youth; or indirectly, in his books and lectures. He had a keen eye for character, including his own, and he manages to convey some of the fantasy, impulsiveness, and delicacy of feeling which enchanted his contemporaries; also, it must be admitted, an archness, a dictatorial egotism, and a self-pity which are less attractive. Even in the years when he has been out of favour distinguished authors have continued to write books about Ruskin. But they have not improved on the self-portrait which he drew in his books and letters with such uncanny detachment.

Being answerable to no one, he could allow himself the luxury of saying exactly what was in his mind. He cared nothing for consistency or system, only for the immediate impact of some newly perceived truth. As a result, his works are full of surprises which must have kept his original readers in a state of delighted suspense and still give us a slight shock today. Who would have expected to hear him praise sculpture primarily for its abstract qualities, or attack Sir Joshua Reynolds for snobbishness, or prophetically warn his country against entering an arms race? Who could have foreseen that he would admire with passion Swinburne's *Poems and Ballads*, and tick off Tennyson for writing the *Idylls of the King*? In each case we should have expected him to hold exactly the opposite point of view.

Because he wrote so much nonsense, posterity has underrated his intelligence. The fact is that when his mind was in working order it was remarkably powerful, and cut through contemporary humbug with great precision. His passion for beauty, whether in art or in nature, was combined with a power of analysis which he himself rated most highly of all his gifts. It is extremely rare for anyone who is capable of the intense and dream-like joy which we call aesthetic emotion to do more than utter cries of satisfaction. But when Ruskin was moved by a Gothic window or a cloud, a Turner or a Byzantine capital, he could analyse its structure and recognize the relationship of the parts without losing his delight in the whole. In his analysis of colours, that most evasive element in all the arts, he goes further than any preceding writer. I should add that this applies only to works in which he has absorbed the total visual impression. Often, in writing about a painting, he goes no further than the subject, and his full powers of mind are not brought into play.

Finally, we should read Ruskin for the very quality of his mind which, when abused, makes him unreadable: his refusal to consider any human faculty in isolation. This characteristic, which produced the intellectual chaos of his later works, also allowed him to make his most important and original discoveries. In art it led him to reject theories of beauty founded on taste or rules of proportion. He saw that these concepts were only abstractions, made up of an amalgam of lesser faculties. For example, he insisted on the importance of sensibility: 'the whole function of the artist in the world is to be a seeing and feeling creature' (no. 122); and no one has written more passionately about the supremacy of colour. But his sense of the wholeness of man allowed him to recognize that these two elements in art, which writers on aesthetics had docketed away, to their satisfaction, in the department of sensation, are equally connected with man's moral and imaginative life. 'Colour is the type of love.' As we read his comparison of a Turner watercolour with a Persian miniature (no. 119) we are gradually persuaded that the quiet and tender colours of the Turner really do involve a range of moral feeling, and what Arnold called 'a criticism of life', which the miniature lacks. The same conviction of human wholeness which exposed the hollowness of 'aesthetic man' led him later to turn with horror from the concept of 'economic man'. Today we have, on the whole, accepted the notion that social and economic problems cannot be separated from moral issues. No politician would care to say in public (although I have heard it said in private) that a large pool of unemployment is desirable, although from the narrowly economic view of capitalist society this is incontestable. In art, however, a belief in a 'pure aesthetic sensation' still lingers on the air; and for this reason Ruskin's best writings on art may enlighten and surprise where his more acceptable writings on society only promote complacency. Ruskin's moralistic theories of art are not Ruskin for today; but they may be Ruskin for tomorrow.

I

SELF-PORTRAIT

A NOTE ON RUSKIN'S LIFE

John Ruskin was born on 18 February 1819, the only child of John James Ruskin, a Scottish sherry merchant resident in London, and Margaret Cox, his wife. His parents were cousins, and his mother entered the Ruskin family as companion-housekeeper to John James's father. This strange character, Ruskin's grandfather, was a successful Edinburgh grocer, who, after a life of wild extravagance, returned to Bowerswell, near Perth, where he went mad and finally shot himself in 1817. Margaret Cox was then free to marry John James, who had been paying off his father's debts and waiting for her for nine years. She was thirty-eight when her son was born, and, like Hannah, devoted the child to God. She was deeply religious in a narrow Sectarian manner, and Ruskin's early life was dominated by Bible readings and by the swelling, minatory cadences of low-church sermons. In his fragment of autobiography, *Praeterita*,[1] he describes the narrowness and austerity of his upbringing (cf. nos. 3 and 4). The parents had gone to live in a solid suburban house at Herne Hill, in south London, and there suffered from the social uneasiness common to many prosperous middle-class people in the nineteenth century, which led to their living in almost total isolation. This was compensated for by travel. Mr Ruskin liked to visit his customers, and twice a year the family set out on coaching expeditions which took them through the most picturesque scenery of England. Later they made an annual journey to France, Switzerland, and Italy. These were the formative episodes in Ruskin's youth, and in a sense he never took roots in England. His spirit burned most brightly, whether in perception or in exposition, when in Chambéry, Rouen, Venice, or Pisa.

1. *Praeterita* was first published in twenty-eight paper-bound parts between 1885 and 1889. Ruskin's mind finally collapsed before he could finish the third section, but the account of his childhood and youth, written with the help of notes and diaries, is remarkably clear and accurate.

His parents did not send him to school, but allowed him to attend lectures at King's College, London. They also arranged for him to be taught painting by a fashionable water colourist, Copley Fielding. In 1836 they so far relaxed as to let him go to Oxford, where his father procured for him the status of a Gentleman Commoner at Christ Church, but he did not escape from parental supervision, as his mother came to live in rooms in the High Street. At Oxford he spent his time drawing architecture and writing poetry, and succeeded in winning the Newdigate prize, with a poem on Salsetta and Elephanta. Many of his poems were published in collections such as *Friendship's Offering*, and together they fill a volume in his collected works. They are in the conventional keepsake style, and are rightly forgotten.

During the years 1836 to 1839, his peace of mind was shattered by his love for Adèle Domecq, the eldest daughter of his father's Spanish partner (cf. nos. 13 and 254). He was too shy to propose marriage, which would, in any case, have been impossible, as Adèle was a Catholic. His disturbed emotions were thought to have affected his health, and he was removed from Oxford before taking a degree.[1] Here it should be noted that throughout his life Ruskin suffered from alternating bouts of exaltation and depression.[2] All his best work was written in a state of euphoria, which accounts for its tone of messianic self-confidence; and these periods were succeeded by months of hypochondria and gloom, during which he was not only incapable of creative work, but lost his responsiveness to beauty, both in nature and art.

During the last year of his frustrated love-affair, his unhappiness was compensated for by a growing passion for the work of J. M. W. Turner. Ruskin had first become aware of it through the microscopic steel engraving in Rogers's *Italy*, and shortly afterwards he

1. He was subsequently awarded an honorary fourth, and so was able to publish *Modern Painters* under the pseudonym 'A Graduate of Oxford'.

2. R. H. Wilenski (in *John Ruskin*, 1933) was the first to state clearly that Ruskin was of the type known as manic depressive. This is one of the few cases in which genius is made more comprehensible by a medical diagnosis.

saw original water colours in the collection of a retired coachmaker named Godfrey Windus. On 22 June 1840 he met his hero, and recorded his impressions in his diary (cf. no. 12). That summer the family set off on a tour of France, Switzerland, and Italy, which, to judge from the references to it in his journals and in *Praeterita* (cf. no. 15), was a decisive event in his life. His depression and supposed ill health were maintained as far as Rome and Naples, although his Journal[1] shows no falling off in his power of observation; but on his way home on 2 June 1841, sight of the Alps produced in him a complete change of heart: 'I had found my life again; – all the best of it. What good of religion, love, admiration or hope, had ever been taught me, or felt by my best nature, rekindled at once; and my line of work . . . determined for me '(no. 20). Love of Alpine scenery, combined with love of Turner, thus became the dominant influences on his mind.

Ruskin's first defence of Turner was a letter to *Blackwood's Magazine*, written in 1835, but never published (cf. no. 211). In 1842 a further attack on Turner in the *Literary Gazette* fired him to undertake the more sustained apologia, which was published in the following year as *Modern Painters*. This was followed by a long period of depression; then, in April 1845, he was, for the first time, allowed to take a tour abroad without his parents. This was another turning-point in his life. In Pisa and Lucca he discovered Italian romanesque and Gothic architecture, and his interest switched from landscape painting to figurative art, whether of Fra Angelico or Tintoretto. The immediate results of this journey were the second volume of *Modern Painters*, written in 1846, and *The Seven Lamps of Architecture*, written in the winter of 1848.

Meanwhile there occurred that unhappy event in Ruskin's life which, after being almost entirely omitted from his early biographies, has now become a focus of curiosity, his marriage. His bride was a Scottish girl named Euphemia Gray, whose father, a distant

1. Large portions of his Journal are quoted in the prefaces to C. & W. Two volumes of the complete Journal have now been published: *The Diaries of John Ruskin* edited by Joan Evans and John Howard Whitehouse.

relative, had bought the old Ruskin home at Bowerswell. He had known her since she was a little girl and had written for her a fairy tale called 'The King of the Golden River'; and left to himself his feelings would probably have remained on this level. But his parents, alarmed at his nervous symptoms, were anxious to see him married; and her father, who was in debt, thought that he could make a useful arrangement. Between them they worked up their children into believing that they were in love. Ruskin wrote her a number of breathless love letters, more hysterical than passionate; Effie was flattered by the attentions of this strange being, whom everyone said was a genius. They were married in April 1847. No doubt Ruskin was a most unsatisfactory husband. He had a boy-ish notion of femininity, half kitten, half fairy queen, and when confronted with the real thing he shrank back in horror. And then, unfortunately, his fundamental selfishness asserted itself. Since his wife was not the fairy kitten which he had anticipated, he could not be bothered with her. She became simply a nuisance. The marriage might have dragged out a long, unhappy life, if Effie had been a self-effacing girl, ready to fit in with the quiet middle-class ways of the Ruskin household. But she was a girl of spirit who loved society, and was not at all content to stay at home with old Mrs Rus-kin, making jam and counting the linen. Moreover, the strain of her situation gave her nervous headaches and other indispositions, irritating equally in a fairy queen or a mother's help. With some notion that they should look like a young married couple, Ruskin took a house in Park Street, and Effie went into society, where she appears to have shone; but Ruskin hated it, and whenever possible slipped back to work in his old study at Denmark Hill.

After almost six years of increasing neglect, he pushed her into the arms of his brilliant young protégé, John Everett Millais, and his marriage was annulled. Meanwhile Ruskin had gone abroad with his parents, and found himself 'stronger in health, higher in hope and deeper in peace' than he had been for years.[1] Nevertheless this

---

1. *The Diaries of John Ruskin*, ed. Joan Evans, Vol. II, p. 500.

episode harmed his reputation. Effie's supporters, like the formidable Lady Eastlake, campaigned against him, and Ruskin (perhaps to his relief) was never again accepted in the smart intellectual society of London.

During the six years of his marriage Ruskin's mind was probably stronger and clearer than at any other period. *The Seven Lamps of Architecture* was written in the winter of 1848, *The Stones of Venice* in the autumn and winter of 1852. He also made the acquaintance of Carlyle,[1] Denison Maurice, and Rossetti. After he returned to London in October 1854 he taught at the newly opened Working Men's College, an experience which greatly enlarged his sympathies and confirmed the interest in social problems already shown in *The Stones of Venice*. During the winter he was at work on the third and fourth volumes of *Modern Painters*. Such intense activity was inevitably followed by a reaction, and in the spring of 1855 he had another of the illnesses which (in Dr Joan Evans's words) 'everyone was thankful to regard as physical'. By 1856 he had recovered. He wrote the admirable *Elements of Drawing*, and shortly afterwards was invited to catalogue the twenty thousand or so watercolours and drawings which Turner had bequeathed to the National Gallery. Turner had died in 1851, and Ruskin was named as one of his executors. It was assumed that Ruskin would write a full-length monograph on his hero, but he declined to do so, partly, no doubt, because he had already written so much, partly because his feelings about Turner had changed. Some indication of the change is perceptible in the fifth volume of *Modern Painters* which was written immediately after his work on the Turner bequest.

In 1858 Ruskin again took a continental tour without his parents. It began with a short period of depression, but a month in Turin produced a mood of intense exaltation, associated with Paolo Veronese, and the pleasures of the senses generally. I describe elsewhere (p. 129) the effects on Ruskin's art-criticism of what he called

---

1. He had first felt the impact of Carlyle when reading *Heroes and Hero-Worship* on the grassy slopes of Chamonix in 1842. (C. & W., Vol. III, XXIV.)

his 'de-conversion'. It removed the last trace of protestant bigotry and, although fifteen years later he was again to feel the need of religious conviction, his outlook remained tolerant and catholic.

1858 was probably the last happy year of Ruskin's life. By the end of 1859 two factors had begun to unsettle his mind, his love for Rose La Touche and his wholehearted engagement in social and economic problems. The first was pure misfortune. Ruskin, who seems to have been incapable of normal relations with a grown-up woman, had a passion for little girls. As a man of forty he used to stay in a girls' school called Winnington, where he joined in the games and talked to the girls about history, geology, and morals, conversations which he polished up into a book called *The Ethics of the Dust*. This diffused passion was focused on Rose. Her mother, who was in love with Ruskin, had asked him to teach her ten-year-old daughter painting, and in the spring of 1859 Rose visited him at Denmark Hill. Ruskin soon realized that this was to be the all-consuming passion of his life, and set his heart on marrying Rose as soon as she should be of age. The miserable drama that ensued lasted for over fifteen years. Rose changed from a clever, self-conscious child into a morbid young woman, painfully religious and, in the end, mentally unbalanced. Mrs La Touche's love naturally changed to hatred and she used every dishonourable means of turning Rose against Ruskin, destroying his letters, and even writing to Effie Millais for a testimonial of his impotence and cruelty, which, of course, Effie was delighted to provide.[1] Ruskin kept alive a flicker of hope which was unwisely fanned by well-meaning friends. Finally Rose died, on 26 May 1875, after sending Ruskin word that she would see him if 'he could tell her that he loved God more than herself'. The whole episode is pitiful and, when followed in detail, unbearably tedious; but unfortunately it has a bearing on our estimate of Ruskin's work, not only because it probably hastened his mental collapse, but because a worship of Rose influenced his aesthetic judgements. He

1. Ruskin always believed that it was this document which finally sent Rose out of her mind. Cf. the letter to Mark Pattison quoted in Joan Evans's *John Ruskin*, p. 353, n. 4.

identified her with Ilaria di Caretto and with Carpaccio's St Ursula; he conceived a passion for the *Roman de la Rose*, and the very words Rose and Rosey came to have a special meaning for him. However, one must admit that, given Ruskin's peculiar characteristics, something of the sort was bound to happen to him, and if he had married Rose, or any other little girl of his adoration, the result might have been equally disastrous.[1]

If the Rose La Touche episode shows Ruskin at his weakest [2] the other crisis of 1859 shows him at his best. This was the determination to put aside his work on art, and devote himself to exposing the wickedness and stupidity of *laissez faire* economics. I describe elsewhere (p. 263) how he came to write the papers later published as *Unto this Last*, and mention the effect they had on his reputation. For a time he was almost ostracized and from 1861 to 1863 spent a great part of the year at Mornex, in Switzerland. The saddest result of his noble and courageous protest was a growing estrangement from his father. Ruskin's curious relations with his parents are described in *Praeterita* with ostensible candour, but we can tell from letters that his feelings went far deeper than is shown in the delicate summary of no. 1. In them we find the accumulated resentment of a man who throughout his life has subjected his will to others, combined with the knowledge that although he has adopted this filial posture in the name of duty, he has actually done so as the line of least resistance. His bitterness towards his father was quite unjustified, for his early letters show that a touching confidence existed between them. But when old Mr Ruskin died, in March 1864, his son could dwell only on some obscure grievance connected with Turner, whose works the father had bought for him so generously, and who had, in fact, preferred the father to the son.

1. Even after this heart-breaking episode, Ruskin occasionally conceived sentimental passions for young girls, and as late as 1887 he proposed to marry Miss Kathleen Olander who, like Rose, hoped to convert him to orthodox Christianity.

2. 'Ruskin himself is a very simple matter. In face, in manner, in talk, in mind, he is weakness pure and simple'—Henry James, after a visit to Denmark Hill in March 1869 (*Letters*, 1, 20).

Ruskin's mother, who had been the real drag on his life, survived for another seven years becoming progressively more difficult. Ruskin treated her with deference, but escaped abroad when he could, leaving her in the care of a dutiful cousin named Joan Agnew.

Ruskin inherited from his father a considerable fortune. The greater part of it he gave away in an impulsive and disorderly manner, but he still felt uneasy at the possession of unused money and his principles would not allow him to invest it. He became convinced that he must not only write in condemnation of the capitalist system, but must take some positive action. In *Fors Clavigera* [1] for May 1871 he outlined a scheme for a sort of agrarian communism; he himself would make the chief contribution, and he asked others to give a tenth of their possessions. The scheme aroused little enthusiasm; but Ruskin persevered and, in *Fors* of November 1874, gave fuller details of the new community which was to be called St George's Company. It was later named St George's Guild.[2] Ruskin was the Master, and produced every year an annual report and some very unconvincing accounts. He was completely devoid of practical sense or even common prudence, and the affairs of the guild ran into every sort of trouble. Yet so great was the hunger for idealism in that material age, that his most preposterous plans were supported. Just as he induced Andrew Lang, Oscar Wilde, Alfred Milner, and Arnold Toynbee (foreman) to work on a road at Hinksey, so he managed to enrol several hundred members of St George's Guild, some of whom left their jobs and their homes and gave up their savings, to receive in return five acres of barren land. No wonder a few poor people felt that they had been swindled, and even his staunchest admirers were dismayed.

By following to the end the catastrophes of 1859 I have, perhaps,

1. For his monthly Letters to the Workmen and Labourers of Great Britain, called *Fors Clavigera*, see p. 266.
2. The only durable outcome of St George's Guild was the building and installation of a small museum in Sheffield.

given too gloomy a picture of Ruskin's life. After three years the panic aroused by *Unto this Last* began to subside; as so often in England, people felt that his disturbing opinions did not need to be taken seriously, and that to keep a tame revolutionary was really rather nice. He was therefore invited to lecture by the most respectable bodies throughout the country. The best of these lectures were printed in *Sesame and Lilies* (1865) and *The Crown of Wild Olive* (1866), the first books by Ruskin to reach a wide public. They touched on every topic – education, religion, patriotism, war – with Ruskinian inconsequence, but the mind was still in control. They contain much sentimental rhetoric, which made them popular in their own day, and has become distasteful to us; but, as the reader of the following selection will discover, they also contain some of Ruskin's boldest thoughts and most magical pieces of writing.

In 1869 he was appointed Slade Professor at Oxford, and took pleasure in the large audience of young people who hung upon his words. He was also greatly pleased to become an honorary fellow of Corpus Christi College, and be given rooms looking over Christ Church meadow. Many of his letters and numbers of *Fors* were written in this room (cf. nos. 57 and 58) and give one the feeling that, for the first time, he felt at home in England. Perhaps as a result of this escape from south London (also from his mother, who had died in 1871) he decided to have a home of his own, and bought, without having seen it, a tumble-down villa on Coniston Water named Brantwood. After the necessary repairs, he went to live there in September 1872, although he kept on his old house at Herne Hill to the end of his life. Visitors to Brantwood have described its unequalled combination of ugliness and discomfort. Ruskin says in *Praeterita*, 'We had not set ourselves to have a taste in anything. There was never any question of matching colours in furniture or having the correct pattern in china'; and it is perhaps a strength of his criticism that he disregarded the dubious concept of 'good taste'. But his indifference to his immediate surroundings does suggest a limitation of his critical faculties, that same preference of the part to the whole which cramped his judgement of architecture. His rooms were full of Turner watercolours and other works of art, but he was so intent on looking *into* them that he did not look *at* them, or relate them to their surroundings.

As noted elsewhere (p. 131) the quality of the Oxford lectures fell off after 1872. He became incapable of concentration, and, in so far as his mind could be directed at all, it was towards birds, plants, and minerals rather than towards works of art. In 1874 his old interests were to some extent revived by a visit to Assisi; he spent much time in the Sacristan's cell, and often referred to himself as a lay brother of St Francis. This was perhaps his last period of calm. In the next three years he became increasingly agitated and confused and in February 1878, soon after writing the touching sentence quoted in no. 80, his mind collapsed altogether. His attack of mania lasted about six weeks. After his recovery he accepted, with perfect candour, the fact that he had been mad, and seems rather to have enjoyed describing his symptoms to his friends;[1] but the attack left him much feebler, and he only gradually regained his ability to write and draw. Later in the year he was vexed by a libel action brought against him by Whistler; and the verdict, one farthing damages to Whistler, was a blow to his prestige. He made it a pretext for resigning his professorship. He was lifted out of his despair by a visit to the great French cathedrals, Rouen, Beauvais, Amiens, and Chartres (he always hated Rheims), and once more felt the need to impart enormous truths about history, architecture, and religion. Under a general title *Our Fathers Have Told Us*, he planned to write ten volumes, in each of which a cathedral would be taken as a type of christian and historical witness. One of these volumes was actually written, *The Bible of Amiens*, and through drifting clouds of allegory and allusion one can still discover some of his old poetry of perception. It appealed so strongly to the perceptive genius of Marcel Proust that he translated it into French. Early in 1881 he was again out of his mind for a month and during the next two years he

1. Cf. no. 70, also letter to Charles Eliot Norton, 23 July 1878.

had several more attacks, each of which left him weaker and more irresolute. Then in the autumn of 1883, and for the last time, he was elated by the sight of the Alps, and believed that he was fully restored. 'Ruskin flourishes', wrote Burne-Jones, 'and looks well – really looks stronger than for many years past. The hair that he has grown over his mouth hides that often angry feature, and his eyes look gentle and invite the unwary, who could never guess the dragon that lurks in the bush below.'[1] His friends in Oxford, with mistaken kindness, reinstated him as Slade Professor, and in the spring of 1883 he gave a series of lectures entitled *The Art of England*. But it soon became all too evident that he had not recovered his mental powers. Instead of talking about Giotto and Botticelli, or even about Sir Joshua Reynolds and Gainsborough, his astonished audiences heard him cry out in ecstasy over the drawings of various harmless ladies – Francesca Alexander, Lillias Trotter, Mrs Allingham – of whom only one, Kate Greenaway, is remembered today. Kate Greenaway was, indeed, the chief solace of these miserable years, and the pages of *Fors Clavigera* which had once crackled with his bitterness and indignation, were now illustrated by her pretty, mob-capped children. 'The sight of them', he said, 'alters one's thoughts of all the world.'[2] Finally a lecture called the *Pleasures of Truth*, in which he introduced Bewick's engraving of a pig as a type of protestantism, convinced his friends that he must be persuaded to resign. He left Oxford in March 1885, never to return.

In the next four years his attacks of madness recurred at shorter intervals, but between them he still had the wits to write *Praeterita*, that enchanting record of his youth, which by its charm and humour offset the melancholy impression of his letters. He was looked after by his mother's former companion, Joan Agnew, who had married the son of Joseph Severn, Keats's friend; and Ruskin intended that the last chapter of *Praeterita*, entitled 'Joanna's Care', should be a tribute to her devotion. Unfortunately by the time he came to write it even her patience was exhausted, and there were frequent

1. C. & W., Vol. XXIX, p. xxvi.   2. C. & W., XXIX, p. xxvi.

quarrels. At least once he turned her out of the house. But gradually he ceased to be aware of immediate experiences. The chapter was put together from notes and diaries, no doubt with the help of friends, and Joan Severn remained with him till his death. For the last eleven years he lived on at Brantwood in a silent coma, unable to write, scarcely recognizing his friends, frequently photographed, a national institution. He died on 20 January 1900 and was buried at Coniston.

1

ANALYSIS OF HIS UPBRINGING

I never had heard my father's or mother's voice once raised in any question with each other; nor seen an angry, or even slightly hurt or offended, glance in the eyes of either. I had never heard a servant scolded; nor even suddenly, passionately, or in any severe manner, blamed. I had never seen a moment's trouble or disorder in any household matter; nor anything whatever either done in a hurry or undone in due time. I had no conception of such a feeling as anxiety; my father's occasional vexation in the afternoons, when he had only got an order for twelve butts after expecting one for fifteen, as I have just stated, was never manifested to *me*; and itself related only to the question whether his name would be a step higher or lower in the year's list of sherry exporters; for he never spent more than half his income, and therefore found himself little incommoded by occasional variations in the total of it. I had never done any wrong that I knew of – beyond occasionally delaying the commitment to heart of some improving sentence, that I might watch a wasp on the window pane, or a bird in the cherry tree; and I had never seen any grief.

Next to this quite priceless gift of Peace, I had received the perfect understanding of the natures of Obedience and Faith. I obeyed word, or lifted finger, of father or mother, simply as a ship her helm; not only without idea of resistance, but receiving the direction as a part of my own life and force, and helpful law, as necessary to me in every moral action as the law of gravity in leaping. And my practice in Faith was soon complete: nothing was ever promised me that was not given; nothing ever threatened me that was not inflicted, and nothing ever told me that was not true.

Peace, obedience, faith; these three for chief good; next to these, the habit of fixed attention with both eyes and mind – on which I will not further enlarge at this moment, this being the main practical faculty of my life, causing Mazzini to say of me, in conversation authentically reported, a year or two before his death, that I had 'the most analytic mind in Europe.' An opinion in which, so far as I am acquainted with Europe, I am myself entirely disposed to concur.

Lastly, an extreme perfection in palate and all other bodily senses, given by the utter prohibition of cake, wine comfits, or, except in carefullest restriction, fruit; and by fine preparation of what food was given me. Such I esteem the main blessings of my childhood; – next, let me count the equally dominant calamities.

First, that I had nothing to love.

My parents were – in a sort – visible powers of nature to me, no more loved than the sun and the moon: only I should have been annoyed and puzzled if either of them had gone out; (how much, now, when both are darkened!) – still less did I love God; not that I had any quarrel with Him, or fear of Him; but simply found what people told me was His service, disagreeable; and what people told me was His book, not entertaining. I had no companions to quarrel with, neither; nobody to assist, and nobody to thank. Not a servant was ever allowed to do anything for me, but what it was their duty to do; and why should I have been grateful to the cook for cooking, or the gardener for gardening, – when the one dared not give me a baked potato without asking leave, and the other would not let my ants' nests alone, because they made the walks untidy? The evil consequence of all this was not, however, what might perhaps have been expected, that I grew up selfish or unaffectionate; but that, when affection did come, it came with violence utterly rampant and unmanageable, at least by me, who never before had anything to manage.

For (second of chief calamities) I had nothing to endure. Danger or pain of any kind I knew not: my strength was never exercised, my patience never tried, and my courage never fortified. Not that I was ever afraid of anything, – either ghosts, thunder or beasts; and one of the nearest approaches to insubordination which I was ever tempted into as a child, was in passionate effort to get leave to play with the lion's cubs in Wombwell's menagerie.

Thirdly. I was taught no precision nor etiquette of manners; it was enough if, in the little society we saw, I remained unobtrusive, and replied to a question without shyness: but the shyness came later, and increased as I grew conscious of the rudeness arising from the want of social discipline, and found it impossible to acquire, in advanced life, dexterity in any bodily exercise, skill in any pleasing accomplishment, or ease and tact in ordinary behaviour.

Lastly, and chief of evils. My judgement of right and wrong, and powers of independent action were left entirely undeveloped; because the bridle and blinkers were never taken off me. Children should have their times of being off duty, like soldiers; and when once the obedience, if required, is certain, the little creature should be very early put for periods of practice in complete command of itself; set on the barebacked horse of its own will, and left to break it by its own strength. But the ceaseless authority exercised over my youth left me, when cast out at last into the world, unable for some time to do more than drift with its vortices.

My present verdict, therefore, on the general tenor of my education at that time, must be, that it was at once too formal and too luxurious; leaving my character, at the most important moment for its construction, cramped indeed, but not disciplined; and only by protection innocent, instead of by practice virtuous. My mother saw this herself, and but too clearly, in later years; and whenever I did anything wrong, stupid, or hard-hearted, – (and I have done many things that were all three,) – always said, 'It is because you were too much indulged.'

From *Praeterita*, I, §§ 48–54

¶ 2
CHILDHOOD PERCEPTIONS

The first thing which I remember, as an event in life, was being taken by my nurse to the brow of Friar's Crag on Derwent Water; the intense joy, mingled with awe, that I had in looking through the hollows in the mossy roots, over the crag, into the dark lake, has associated itself more or less with all twining roots of trees ever since. Two other things I remember as, in a sort, beginnings of life; – crossing Shapfells (being let out of the chaise to run up the hills), and going through Glenfarg, near Kinross, in a winter's morning, when the rocks were hung with icicles; these being culminating points in an early life of more travelling than is usually indulged to a child. In such journeyings, whenever they brought me near hills, and in all mountain ground and scenery, I had a pleasure, as early as I can remember, and continuing till I was eighteen or twenty, infinitely greater than any which has been since possible to me in anything. . . .

From *Modern Painters*, Vol. III, ch. XVII, § 13

¶ 3
PEOPLE, BE GOOD

My mother had, as she afterwards told me, solemnly 'devoted me to God' before I was born; in imitation of Hannah. . . .

'Devoting me to God,' meant, as far as my mother knew herself what she meant, that she would try to send me to college, and make a clergyman of me: and I was accordingly bred for 'the Church.' My father, who – rest be to his soul – had the exceedingly bad habit of yielding to my mother in large things and taking his own way in little ones, allowed me, without saying a word, to be thus withdrawn from the sherry trade as an unclean thing; not without some pardonable participation in my mother's ultimate views for me. For, many and many a year afterwards, I remember, while he was speaking to one of our artist friends, who admired Raphael, and greatly regretted my endeavours to interfere with that popular taste, – while my father and he were condoling with each other on my having been impudent enough to think I could tell the public about Turner and Raphael, – instead of contenting myself, as I ought, with explaining the way of their souls' salvation to them – and what an amiable clergyman was lost in me, – 'Yes,' said my father, with tears in his eyes – (true and tender tears, as ever father shed,) 'he would have been a Bishop.'

Luckily for me, my mother, under these distinct impressions of her own duty, and with such latent hopes of my future eminence, took me very early to church; – where, in spite of my quiet habits, and my mother's golden vinaigrette, always indulged to me there, and there only, with its lid unclasped that I might see the wreathed open pattern above the sponge, I found the bottom of the pew so extremely dull a place to keep quiet in, (my best story-books being also taken away from me in the morning,) that . . . the horror of Sunday used even to cast its prescient gloom as far back in the week as Friday – and all the glory of Monday, with church seven days removed again, was no equivalent for it.

Notwithstanding, I arrived at some abstract in my own mind of the Rev. Mr Howell's sermons; and occasionally, in imitation of him, preached a sermon at home over the red sofa cushions; this performance being always called for by my mother's dearest friends, as the great accomplishment of my childhood. The sermon was, I believe, some eleven words long; very exemplary, it seems to me, in that respect – and I still think must have been the purest gospel, for I know it began with, 'People, be good.'

From *Praeterita*, I, §§ 19–22

¶ 4

A PURITAN CHILDHOOD

No toys of any kind were at first allowed; – and the pity of my Croydon aunt for my monastic poverty in this respect was boundless. On one of my birthdays, thinking to overcome my mother's resolution by splendour of temptation, she bought the most radiant Punch and Judy she could find in all the Soho bazaar – as big as a real Punch and Judy, all dressed in scarlet and gold, and that would dance, tied to the leg of a chair. I must have been greatly impressed, for I remember well the look of the two figures, as my aunt herself exhibited their virtues. My mother was obliged to accept them; but afterwards quietly told me it was not right that I should have them; and I never saw them again. . . .

I had a bunch of keys to play with, as long as I was capable only of pleasure in what glittered and jingled; as I grew older, I had a cart, and a ball; and when I was five or six years old, two boxes of well-cut wooden bricks. With these modest, but, I still think, entirely sufficient possessions, and being always summarily whipped if I cried, did not do as I was bid, or tumbled on the stairs, I soon attained serene and secure methods of life and motion; and could pass my days contentedly in tracing the squares and comparing the colours of my carpet; – examining the knots in the wood of the floor, or counting the bricks in the opposite houses; with rapturous intervals of excitement during the filling of the water-cart, through its leathern pipe, from the dripping iron post at the pavement edge; or the still more admirable proceedings of the turncock, when he turned and turned till a fountain sprang up in the middle of the street. But the carpet, and what patterns I could find in bed-covers, dresses, or wall-papers to be examined, were my chief resources, and my attention to the particulars in these was soon so accurate, that when at three and a half I was taken to have my portrait painted by Mr Northcote,[1] I had not been ten minutes alone with him before I asked him why there were holes in his carpet.

From *Praeterita*, I, §§ 13–14

¶ 5
NARROW HAPPINESS

A great part of my acute perception and deep feeling of the beauty of architecture and scenery abroad, was owing to the well-formed habit of narrowing myself to happiness within the four brick walls of our fifty by one hundred yards of garden; and accepting with resignation the aesthetic external surrounding of a London suburb, and, yet more, of a London chapel.

From *Praeterita*, I, § 152

¶ 6
MOUNTAINS AND SEA

The beginning of all my own right art work in life, (and it may not be unprofitable that I should tell you this,) depended not on my love of art, but of mountains and sea. All boys with any good in them are fond of boats, and of course I liked the mountains best when they had lakes at the bottom; and I used to walk always in the middle of the loosest gravel I could find in the roads of the midland counties, that I might hear, as I trod on it, something like the sound of the pebbles on sea-beach.

From *The Eagle's Nest*, Lecture III, § 41

1. James Northcote, R.A. (1746–1831), a pupil of Sir Joshua Reynolds, was a successful portrait painter for over fifty years, but is now chiefly remembered for his conversations with Hazlitt. His portrait of Ruskin as a child is illustrated in C. & W., Vol. XXXV, plate II.

¶ 7
HAPPY SOLITUDE

In the beginning of the Carlyle–Emerson correspondence, edited with too little comment by my dear friend Charles Norton, I find at page 18 this – to me entirely disputable, and to my thought, so far as undisputed, much blameable and pitiable, exclamation of my master's: 'Not till we can think that here and there one is thinking of us, one is loving us, does this waste earth become a peopled garden.' My training, as the reader has perhaps enough perceived, produced in me the precisely opposite sentiment. *My* times of happiness had always been when *nobody* was thinking of me; and the main discomfort and drawback to all proceedings and designs, the attention and interference of the public – represented by my mother and the gardener. The garden was no waste place to me, because I did not suppose myself an object of interest either to the ants or the butterflies; and the only qualification of the entire delight of my evening walk at Champagnole or St Laurent was the sense that my father and mother *were* thinking of me, and would be frightened if I was five minutes late for tea. . . .

My entire delight was in observing without being myself noticed, – if I could have been invisible, all the better. I was absolutely interested in men and their ways, as I was interested in marmots and chamois, in tomtits and trout. If only they would stay still and let me look at them, and not get into their holes and up their heights! The living inhabitation of the world – the grazing and nesting in it, – the spiritual power of the air, the rocks, the waters, to be in the midst of it, and rejoice and wonder at it, and help it if I could, – happier if it needed no help of mine, – this was the essential love *of Nature* in me, this the root of all that I have usefully become, and the light of all that I have rightly learned.

From *Praeterita*, I, § 192

¶ 8
LOVE OF NATURE

On the journey of 1837, when I was eighteen, I felt, for the last time, the pure childish love of nature which Wordsworth so idly takes for an intimation of immortality. We went down by the North Road, as usual; and on the fourth day arrived at Catterick Bridge, where there is a clear pebble-bedded stream, and both west and east some rising of hills, foretelling the moorlands and dells of upland Yorkshire; and there the feeling came back to me – as it could never return more.

It is a feeling only possible to youth, for all care, regret, or knowledge of evil destroys it; and it requires also the full sensibility of nerve and blood, the conscious strength of heart, and hope; not but that I suppose the purity of youth may feel what is best of it even through sickness and the waiting for death; but only in thinking death itself God's sending.

In myself, it has always been quite exclusively confined to *wild*, that is to say, wholly natural places, and especially to scenery animated by streams, or by the sea. The sense of the freedom, spontaneous, unpolluted power of nature was essential in it. I enjoyed a lawn, a garden, a daisied field, a quiet pond, as other children do; but by the side of Wandel, or on the downs of Sandgate, or by a Yorkshire stream under a cliff, I was different from other children, that ever I have noticed: but the feeling cannot be described by any of us that have it. Wordsworth's 'haunted me like a passion' is no description of it, for it is not *like*, but *is*, a passion; the point is to define how it *differs* from other passions, – what sort of human, pre-eminently human, feeling it is that loves a stone for a stone's sake, and a cloud for a cloud's. A monkey loves a monkey for a monkey's sake, and a nut for the kernel's, but not a stone for a stone's. I took stones for bread, but not certainly at the Devil's bidding.

I was different, be it once more said, from other children even of my own type, not so much in the actual nature of the feeling, but in the mixture of it. I had, in my little clay pitcher, vialfuls, as it were, of Wordsworth's reverence, Shelley's sensitiveness, Turner's accuracy, all in one. A snowdrop was to me, as to Wordsworth, part of the Sermon on the Mount; but I never should have written sonnets to the celandine, because it is of a coarse yellow, and imperfect form. With Shelley, I loved blue sky and blue eyes, but never in the least confused the heavens with my own poor little Psychidion. And the reverence and passion were alike kept in their places by the constructive Turnerian element; and I did not weary myself in wishing that a daisy could see the beauty of its shadow, but in trying to draw the shadow rightly, myself.

But so stubborn and chemically inalterable the laws of the prescription were, that now, looking back from 1886 to that brook shore of 1837, whence I could see the whole of my youth, I find myself in nothing whatsoever *changed*. Some of me is dead, more of me stronger; I have learned a few things, forgotten many; in the total of me, I am but the same youth, disappointed and rheumatic.

From *Praeterita*, I, §§ 244–6

¶ 9
HIS FOUR INSTINCTS AS A CHILD

The work to which, as partly above described, I set myself during the year 1834 under the excitement remaining from my foreign travels, was in four distinct directions, in any one of which my strength might at that time have been fixed by definite encouragement. There was first the effort to express sentiment in rhyme; the sentiment being really genuine, under all the superficial vanities of its display; and the rhymes rhythmic, only without any ideas in them. It was impossible to explain, either to myself or other people, why I liked staring at the sea, or scampering on a moor; but, one had pleasure in making some sort of melodious noise about it, like the waves themselves, or the peewits. Then, secondly, there was the real love of engraving, and of such characters of surface and shade as it could give. I have never seen drawing, by a youth, so entirely industrious in delicate line; and there was really the making of a fine landscape, or figure outline, engraver in me. But fate having ordered otherwise, I mourn the loss to engraving less than that before calculated, or rather incalculable, one, to geology. Then there was, thirdly, the violent instinct for architecture; but I never could have built or carved anything, because I was without power of design; and have perhaps done as much in that direction as it was worth doing with so limited faculty. And then, fourthly, there was the

23

unabated, never to be abated, geological instinct, now fastened on the Alps.

From *Praeterita*, I, § 139

¶ 10
THE RUSKIN FAMILY'S TASTE

The ... reader ... must have felt, long since, that, though very respectable people in our way, we were all of us definitely vulgar people; just as my aunt's dog Towzer was a vulgar dog, though a very good and dear dog. Said reader should have seen also that we had not set ourselves up to have a taste in anything. There was never any question about matching colours in furniture, or having the correct pattern in china. Everything for service in the house was bought plain, and of the best; our toys were what we happened to take a fancy to in pleasant places – a cow in stalactite from Matlock, fisher-wife doll from Calais, a Swiss farm from Berne, Bacchus and Ariadne from Carrara. But, among these toys, principal on the drawing-room chimney-piece, always put away by my mother at night, and 'put out' in the afternoon, were some pieces of Spanish clay, to which, without knowing it, I owed a quantity of strenuous teaching. Native baked clay figures, painted and gilded by untaught persons who had the gift; manufacture mainly practised along the Xeres coast, I believe, and of late much decayed, but then flourishing, and its work as good as the worker could make it. There was a Don Whiskerandos contrabandista, splendidly handsome and good-natured, on a magnificent horse at the trot, brightly caparisoned; everything finely finished, his gun loose in his hand. There was a lemonade seller, a pomegranate seller, a matador with his bull – animate all, and graceful, the colouring chiefly ruddy brown. Things of constant interest to me, and altogether wholesome; vestiges of living sculpture come down into the Herne Hill times from the days of Tanagra.

For loftier admiration, as before told, Chantrey in Lichfield, Roubilliac in Westminster, were set forth to me, and honestly felt; a scratched white outline or two from Greek vases on the black Derbyshire marble did not interfere with my first general feeling about sculpture, that it should be living, and emotional; that the flesh should be like flesh, and the drapery like clothes; and that, whether trotting contrabandista, dancing girl, or dying gladiator, the subject should have an interest of its own, and not consist merely of figures with torches or garlands standing alternately on their right and left legs. Of 'ideal' form and the like, I fortunately heard and thought nothing.

From *Praeterita*, II, § 113

¶ 11

FIRST SIGHT OF TURNER

Mr Telford had a singularly important influence in my education. By, I believe, his sisters' advice, he gave me, as soon as it was published, the illustrated edition of Rogers's *Italy*. This book was the first means I had of looking carefully at Turner's work: and I might, not without some appearance of reason, attribute to the gift the entire direction of my life's energies. But it is the great error of thoughtless biographers to attribute to the accident which introduces some new phase of character, all the circumstances of character which gave the accident importance. The essential point to be noted, and accounted for, was that I could understand Turner's work, when I saw it; – not by what chance, or in what year, it was first seen. Poor Mr Telford, nevertheless, was always held by papa and mamma primarily responsible for my Turner insanities.

From *Praeterita*, I, § 28

¶ 12

FIRST MEETING WITH TURNER

'Introduced to-day to the man who beyond all doubt is the greatest of the age; greatest in every faculty of the imagination, in every branch of scenic knowledge; at once *the* painter and poet of the day, J. M. W. Turner. Everybody had described him to me as coarse, boorish, unintellectual, vulgar. This I knew to be impossible. I found in him a somewhat eccentric, keen-mannered, matter-of-fact, English-minded – gentleman; good-natured evidently, bad-tempered evidently, hating humbug of all sorts, shrewd, perhaps a little selfish, highly intellectual, the powers of the mind not brought out with any delight in their manifestation, or intention of display, but flashing out occasionally in a word or a look.'[1]

From *Praeterita*, II, § 66

§ 13
FIRST LOVE

The entirely inscrutable thing to me, looking back on myself, is my total want of all reason, will, or design in the business: I had neither the resolution to win Adèle,[2] the courage to do without her, the sense to consider what was at last to come of it all, or the grace to think how disagreeable I was making myself at the time to everybody about me. There was really no more capacity nor intelligence in me than in a just fledged owlet, or just open-eyed puppy, disconsolate at the existence of the moon.

From *Praeterita*, I, § 210

§ 14
TRAVEL BY COACH

The poor modern slaves and simpletons who let themselves be dragged like cattle, or felled timber, through the countries they imagine themselves visiting, can have no conception whatever of the complex joys, and ingenious hopes, connected with the choice and arrangement of the travelling carriage in old times. The mechanical questions first, of strength – easy rolling – steady and safe poise of persons and luggage; the general stateliness of effect to be obtained for the abashing of plebeian beholders; the cunning

1. The actual words of Ruskin's Journal written on 22 June 1840.
2. Adèle was the eldest of the four daughters of Mr Domecq, old Mr Ruskin's partner, who came to stay at Herne Hill, and as Ruskin said 'reduced me to a mere heap of white ashes in four days'. Ruskin fell passionately in love with her, but could not propose to her, partly from timidity, partly because she was a Catholic. His passion brought on a mild attack of tuberculosis, on account of which he was removed from Oxford and taken on the journey to Italy mentioned in the next seven extracts. His poem entitled 'To Adèle' was published in *Friendship's Offering* for 1840.

design and distribution of store-cellars under the seats, secret drawers under front windows, invisible pockets under padded lining, safe from dust, and accessible only by insidious slits, or necromantic valves like Aladdin's trapdoor; the fitting of cushions where they would not slip, the rounding of corners for more delicate repose; the prudent attachments and springs of blinds; the perfect fitting of windows, on which one-half the comfort of a travelling carriage really depends; and the adaptation of all these concentrated luxuries to the probabilities of who would sit where, in the little apartment which was to be virtually one's home for five or six months; – all this was an imaginary journey in itself, with every pleasure, and none of the discomfort, of practical travelling. . . .

For a family carriage of this solid construction, with its luggage, and load of six or more persons, four horses were of course necessary to get any sufficient way on it; and half-a-dozen such teams were kept at every post-house. . . .

The French horses, and more or less those on all the great lines of European travelling, were properly stout trotting cart-horses, well up to their work and over it; untrimmed, long-tailed, good-humouredly licentious, whinneying and frolicking with each other when they had a chance; sagaciously steady to their work; obedient to the voice mostly, to the rein only for more explicitness; never touched by the whip, which was used merely to express the driver's exultation in himself and them, – signal obstructive vehicles in front out of the way, and advise all the inhabitants of the villages and towns traversed on the day's journey, that persons of distinction were honouring them by their transitory presence.

From *Praeterita*, I, §§ 123 and 125

§ 15
SCHAFFHAUSEN

And then, with Salvador was held council in the inn-parlour of Strasburg, whether – it was then the Friday afternoon – we should push on to-morrow for our Sunday's rest to Basle, or to Schaff-hausen.

How much depended – if ever anything 'depends' on anything else, – on the issue of that debate! Salvador inclined to the straight and level Rhine-side road, with the luxury of the 'Three Kings' attainable by sunset. But at Basle, it had to be admitted, there were no Alps in sight, no cataract within hearing, and Salvador honourably laid before us the splendid alternative possibility of reaching, by traverse of the hilly road of the Black Forest, the gates of Schaffhausen itself, before they closed for the night.

The Black Forest! The fall of Schaffhausen! The chain of the Alps! within one's grasp for Sunday! What a Sunday, instead of customary Walworth and the Dulwich fields! My impassioned petition at last carried it, and the earliest morning saw us trotting over the bridge of boats to Kehl, and in the eastern light I well remember watching the line of the Black Forest hills enlarge and rise, as we crossed the plain of the Rhine. 'Gates of the hills'; opening for me to a new life – to cease no more, except at the Gates of the Hills whence one returns not.

And so, we reached the base of the Schwarzwald, and entered an ascending dingle; and scarcely, I think, a quarter of an hour after entering, saw our first 'Swiss cottage.' How much it meant to all of us, – how much prophesied to me, no modern traveller could the least conceive, if I spent days in trying to tell him. A sort of triumphant shriek – like all the railway whistles going off at once at Clapham Junction – has gone up from the Fooldom of Europe at the destruction of the myth of William Tell. To us, every word of it was true – but mythically luminous with more than mortal truth; and here, under the black woods, glowed the visible, beautiful, tangible testimony to it in the purple larch timber, carved to exquisiteness by the joy of peasant life, continuous, motionless there in the pine shadow on its ancestral turf, – unassailed and unassailing, in the blessedness of righteous poverty, of religious peace.

The myth of William Tell is destroyed forsooth? and you have tunnelled Gothard, and filled, it may be, the Bay of Uri; – and it was all for you and your sake that the grapes dropped blood from the press of St Jacob, and the pine club struck down horse and helm in Morgarten Glen?

Difficult enough for you to imagine, that old travellers' time when Switzerland was yet the land of the Swiss, and the Alps had never been trod by foot of man. Steam, never heard of yet, but for short fair weather crossing at sea (were there paddle-packets across Atlantic? I forget). Any way, the roads by land were safe; and entered once into this mountain Paradise, we wound on through its balmy glens, past cottage after cottage on their lawns, still glistering in the dew.

The road got into more barren heights by the mid-day, the hills arduous; once or twice we had to wait for horses, and we were still twenty miles from Schaffhausen at sunset; it was past midnight when we reached her closed gates. The disturbed porter had the grace to open them – not quite wide enough; we carried away one of our lamps in collision with the slanting bar as we drove through the arch. How much happier the privilege of dreamily entering a mediæval city, though with the loss of a lamp, than the free ingress of being jammed between a dray and a tramcar at a railroad station.

It is strange that I but dimly recollect the following morning; I fancy we must have gone to some sort of church or other; and certainly, part of the day went in admiring the bow-windows projecting into the clean streets. None of us seem to have thought the Alps would be visible without profane exertion in climbing hills. We dined at four, as usual, and the evening being entirely fine, went out to walk, all of us, – my father and mother and Mary and I.

We must have still spent some time in town-seeing, for it was drawing towards sunset when we got up to some sort of garden promenade – west of the town, I believe; and high above the Rhine, so as to command the open country across it to the south and west. At which open country of low undulation, far into blue, – gazing as at one of our own distances from Malvern of Worcestershire, or Dorking of Kent, – suddenly – behold – beyond!

There was no thought in any of us for a moment of their being clouds. They were clear as crystal, sharp on the pure horizon sky, and already tinged with rose by the sinking sun. Infinitely beyond all that we had ever thought or dreamed, – the seen walls of lost

Eden could not have been more beautiful to us; not more awful, round heaven, the walls of sacred Death.

From *Praeterita*, I, §§ 129–34

¶ 16

ROME, AGED 21

St Peter's I expected to be *disappointed* in. I was *disgusted*. . . . In the city, if you take a carriage and drive to express points of lionization, I believe that most people of good taste would expect little and find less. The Capitol is a melancholy rubbishy square of average Palladian – modern; the Forum, a good group of smashed columns, just what, if it were got up, as it very easily might be, at Virginia Water, we should call a piece of humbug – the kind of thing that one is sick to death of in 'compositions'; the Coliseum I have always considered a public nuisance, like Jim Crow; and the rest of the ruins are mere mountains of shattered, shapeless brick, covering miles of ground with a Babylon-like weight of red tiles. But if, instead of driving, with excited expectation, to particular points, you saunter leisurely up one street and down another, yielding to every impulse, peeping into every corner, and keeping your observation active, the impression is exceedingly changed. There is not a fragment, a stone, or a chimney, ancient or modern, that is not in itself a study, not an inch of ground that can be passed over without its claim of admiration and offer of instruction, and you return home in hopeless conviction that were you to substitute years for the days of your appointed stay, they would not be enough for the estimation or examination of Rome.

Yet the impression of this perpetual beauty is more painful than pleasing, for there is a strange horror lying over the whole city, which I can neither describe nor account for; it is a shadow of death, possessing and penetrating all things. The sunlight is lurid and ghastly, though so intense that neither the eye nor the body can bear it long; the shadows are cold and sepulchral; you feel like an artist in a fever, haunted by every dream of beauty that his imagination ever dwelt upon, but all mixed with the fever fear. I am certain this is not imagination, for I am not given to such nonsense, and, even in illness, never remember feeling anything approaching to the horror with which some objects here can affect me. It is all like a vast churchyard, with a diseased and dying population living in the shade of its tombstones.

From a letter to the Rev. T. Dale,[1] 31 December 1840

¶ 17
LOSS OF FEELING

'I am gradually losing my zest for scenery, and stood at the window to-night, while the sunset was touching the sprinkled snow on the lovely forms of the Mt. Angelo, rather with the sense of discharging a duty in drinking the draught of beauty than because it gave me pleasure. The sea horizon was dark, sharp, and blue, and far beyond it, faint with trebled distance, came the red, vertical cliffs, with the infinite delicacy of multitudinous touches of light which one cannot see without remembering Turner – and yet all subdued into one soft grey tone, on which the snowy peaked forms were touched, bright and pure, but still faint; and one sail, square, and as much fed with sun as with wind – a blaze of bright light – moving fast along the azure horizon. Yet all this could not touch me. I felt as if my whole spirit had been turned into ice.'

From the Journal, 27 January 1841: *The Diaries of John Ruskin*, ed. Joan Evans, p. 146

¶ 18
NAPLES – VESUVIUS

The first sight of the Alps had been to me as a direct revelation of the benevolent will in creation. Long since, in the volcanic powers of destruction, I had been taught by Homer, and further forced by my own reason, to see, if not the personality of an Evil Spirit, at all events the permitted symbol of evil, unredeemed; wholly distinct from the conditions of storm, or heat, or frost, on which the healthy courses of organic life depended. In the same literal way in which

1. The Rev. Thomas Dale was head of the day school at Camberwell where Ruskin studied from 1833 to 1836.

the snows and Alpine roses of Lauterbrunnen were visible Paradise, here, in the valley of ashes and throat of Lava, were visible Hell. If thus in the natural, how else should it be in the spiritual world?

The common English traveller, if he can gather a black bunch of grapes with his own fingers, and have his bottle of Falernian brought him by a girl with black eyes, asks no more of this world, nor the next; and declares Naples a Paradise. But I knew, from the first moment when my foot furrowed volcanic ashes, that no mountain form or colour could exist in perfection when everything was made of scoria, and that blue sea was to be little boasted if it broke on black sand. And I saw also, with really wise anger, the horror of neglect in the governing power, which Mr Gladstone found, forsooth, in the Neapolitan prisons! but which neither he nor any other Englishman, so far as I know, except Byron and I, saw to have made the Apennines one prison wall, and all the modern life of Italy one captivity of shame and crime; alike against the honour of her ancestors, and the kindness of her God.[1]

From *Praeterita*, II, §§ 50–1

¶ 19
THE RIVIERA

I don't think the reader has yet been informed that I inherited to the full my mother's love of tidiness and cleanliness; so that quite one of the most poetical charms of Switzerland to me, next to her white snows, was her white sleeves. Also I had my father's love of solidity and soundness, – of unveneered, unroughed, and well-finished things; and here on the Riviera there were lemons and palms, yes, – but the lemons pale, and mostly skin; the palms not much larger than parasols; the sea – blue, yes, but its beach nasty; the buildings, pompous, luxurious, painted like Grimaldi, – usually broken down at the ends, and in the middle, having sham architraves daubed over

1. This refers to his visit to Naples in the winter of 1840–1. But in his Journal he wrote: 'I wish Vesuvius could love me like a living thing; I would rather make a friend of him than of any morsel of humanity.'

windows with no glass in them; the rocks shaly and ragged, the people filthy: and over everything, a coat of plaster dust.

From *Praeterita*, II, § 23

¶ 20
BACK IN THE ALPS

I woke from a sound tired sleep in a little one-windowed room at Lans-le-bourg, at six of the summer morning, June 2nd, 1841; the red aiguilles on the north relieved against pure blue – the great pyramid of snow down the valley in one sheet of eastern light. I dressed in three minutes, ran down the village street, across the stream, and climbed the grassy slope on the south side of the valley, up to the first pines.

I had found my life again; – all the best of it. What good of religion, love, admiration or hope, had ever been taught me, or felt by my best nature, rekindled at once; and my line of work, both by my own will and the aid granted to it by fate in the future, determined for me. I went down thankfully to my father and mother, and told them I was sure I should get well.

From *Praeterita*, II, § 57

¶ 21
GENEVA

A little canton, four miles square, and which did not wish to be six miles square! A little town, composed of a cluster of watermills, a street of penthouses, two wooden bridges, two dozen of stone houses on a little hill, and three or four perpendicular lanes up and down the hill. The four miles of acreage round, in grass, with modest gardens, and farm-dwelling houses; the people, pious, learned, and busy, to a man, to a woman – to a boy, to a girl, of them; progressing to and fro mostly on their feet, and only where they had business. And this bird's-nest of a place, to be the centre of religious and social thought, and of physical beauty, to all living Europe! That is to say, thinking and designing Europe, – France, Germany, and Italy. They, and their pieties, and their prides, their arts and their insanities, their wraths and slaughters, springing and flowering, building and fortifying, foaming and thundering round this inconceivable point of patience: and most lovely spot, and the most notable, without any possible dispute, of the European universe; yet the nations do not covet it, do not gravitate to it, – what is more wonderful, do not make a wilderness of it.[1]

From *Praeterita*, II, § 84

¶ 22
ART AND SCIENCE

The first thing I did[2] was to go to the library and choose a book to work at. After due examination, I bought Agassiz' *Poissons Fossiles*! and set myself to counting of scales and learning of hard names, – thinking, as some people do still, that in that manner I might best advance in geology. Also I supplied myself with some Captain Marryat; and some beautiful new cakes of colour wherewith to finish a drawing, in Turner's grandest manner, of the Château of Amboise at sunset, with the moon rising in the distance, and shining through a bridge.

The *Poissons Fossiles* turned out a most useful purchase, enabling me finally to perceive, after steady work on them, that Agassiz was a mere blockhead to have paid for all that good drawing of the nasty ugly things, and that it didn't matter a stale herring to any mortal whether they had any names or not.

For any positive or useful purpose, I could not more utterly have wasted my time; but it was no small gain to know that time spent in that sort of work *was* wasted; and that to have caught a chub in the Avon, and learned how to cook it spicily and herbaceously, so as to have pleased Izaak Walton, if the odour of it could reach him in the Anglers' Paradise, would have been a better result of six weeks' study than to be able to count and call by their right names every scale stuck in the mud of the universe.

Also I got a wholesome perception, from the book, of the true

1. The last sentence is an extreme example of Carlyle's influence on Ruskin's style.
2. Ruskin had been sent to Leamington Spa in August 1841 to rest under the supervision of Dr Jephson.

relation between artists and scientific gentlemen. For I saw that the real genius concerned in the *Poissons Fossiles* was the lithographer's, and not at all the scientific gentleman's; and that the book ought to have been called after the lithographer, *his* fishes, only with their scales counted and called bad names by subservient Mons. Agassiz.

From *Praeterita*, II, § 62

§ 23

READING THE ESSAY

It was an institution of the college[1] that every week the under-graduates should write an essay on a philosophical subject, ex-plicatory of some brief Latin text of Horace, Juvenal, or other accredited and pithy writer; and, I suppose, as a sort of guarantee to the men that what they wrote was really looked at, the essay pronounced the best was read aloud in hall on Saturday afternoon, with enforced attendance of the other undergraduates. Here, at least, was something in which I felt that my little faculties had some scope, and both conscientiously, and with real interest in the task, I wrote my weekly essay with all the sagacity and eloquence I possessed. And therefore, though much flattered, I was not surprised when a few weeks after coming up, my tutor announced to me, with a look of approval, that I was to read my essay in hall next Saturday.

Serenely, and on good grounds, confident in my powers of reading rightly, and with a decent gravity which I felt to be be-coming on this my first occasion of public distinction, I read my essay, I have reason to believe, not ungracefully; and descended from the rostrum to receive – as I doubted not – the thanks of the gentlemen-commoners for this creditable presentment of the wis-dom of the body. But poor Clara, after her first ball, receiving her cousin's compliments in the cloak-room, was less surprised than I by my welcome from my cousins of the long-table. Not in envy, truly, but in fiery disdain, varied in expression through every form and manner of English language, from the Olympian sarcasm of

1. Christ Church.

Charteris to the level-delivered volley of Grimston, they explained to me that I had committed grossest *lèse-majesté* against the order of gentlemen-commoners; that no gentleman-commoner's essay ought ever to contain more than twelve lines, with four words in each; and that even indulging to my folly, and conceit, and want of *savoir faire*, the impropriety of writing an essay with any meaning in it, like vulgar students, – the thoughtlessness and audacity of writing one that would take at least a quarter of an hour to read, and then reading it all, might for this once be forgiven to such a greenhorn, but that Coventry wasn't the word for the place I should be sent to if ever I did such a thing again. I am happy at least in remembering that I bore my fall from the clouds without much hurt, or even too ridiculous astonishment. I at once admitted the justice of these representations, yet I do not remember that I modified the style of my future essays materially in consequence, neither do I remember what line of conduct I had proposed to myself in the event of again obtaining the privilege of edifying the Saturday's congregation. Perhaps my essays really diminished in value, or perhaps even the tutors had enough of them. All I know is, I was never asked to.

From *Praeterita*, I, §§ 222-3

§ 24

THE DONS AT CHRIST CHURCH

I am amused, as I look back, in now perceiving what an æsthetic view I had of all my tutors and companions, – how consistently they took to me the aspect of pictures, and how I from the first declined giving any attention to those which were not well painted enough. My ideal of a tutor was founded on what Holbein or Dürer had represented in Erasmus or Melanchthon, or, even more solemnly, on Titian's Magnificoes or Bonifazio's Bishops. No presences of that kind appeared either in Tom or Peckwater; and even Doctor Pusey (who also never spoke to me) was not in the least a picturesque or tremendous figure, but only a sickly and rather ill put together English clerical gentleman, who never looked one in the face, or appeared aware of the state of the weather.

My own tutor was a dark-eyed, animated, pleasant, but not in the least impressive person, who walked with an unconscious air of assumption, noticeable by us juniors not to his advantage. Kynaston was ludicrously like a fat schoolboy. Hussey, grim and brown as I said, somewhat lank, incapable of jest, equally incapable of enthusiasm; for the rest doing his duty thoroughly, and a most estimable member of the college and university, – but to me, a resident calamity far greater than I knew, whose malefic influence I recognize in memory only.

Finally, the Dean himself, though venerable to me from the first, in his evident honesty, self-respect, and real power of a rough kind, was yet in his general aspect too much like the sign of the Red Pig which I afterwards saw set up in pudding raisins, with black currants for eyes, by an imaginative grocer in Chartres fair; and in the total bodily and ghostly presence of him was to me only a rotundly progressive terror, or sternly enthroned and niched Anathema.

There was one tutor, however, out of my sphere, who reached my ideal, but disappointed my hope, then, – as perhaps his own, since; – a man sorrowfully under the dominion of the Greek ἀνάγκη – the present Dean. He was, and is, one of the rarest types of nobly-presenced Englishmen, but I fancy it was his adverse star that made him an Englishman at all – the prosaic and practical element in him having prevailed over the sensitive one. He was the only man in Oxford among the masters of my day who knew anything of art; and his keen saying of Turner, that he 'had got hold of a false ideal,' would have been infinitely helpful to me at that time, had he explained and enforced it. But I suppose he did not see enough in me to make him take trouble with me, – and, what was much more serious, he saw not enough in himself to take trouble, in that field, with himself.

There was a more humane and more living spirit, however, inhabitant of the north-west angle of the Cardinal's Square: and a great many of the mischances which were only harmful to me through my own folly may be justly held, and to the full, counter-balanced by that one piece of good fortune, of which I had the wit to take advantage. Dr Buckland was a Canon of the Cathedral, and he, with his wife and family, were all sensible and good-natured, with originality enough in the sense of them to give sap and savour to the whole college.

Originality – passing slightly into grotesqueness, and a little diminishing their effective power. The Doctor had too much humour ever to follow far enough the dull side of a subject. Frank was too fond of his bear cub to give attention enough to the training of the cubbish element in himself; and a day scarcely passed without Mit's committing herself in some manner disapproved by the statelier college demoiselles. But all were frank, kind, and clever, vital in the highest degree; to me, medicinal and saving.

Dr Buckland was extremely like Sydney Smith in his staple of character; no rival with him in wit, but like him in humour, common sense, and benevolently cheerful doctrine of Divinity. At his breakfast-table I met the leading scientific men of the day, from Herschel downwards, and often intelligent and courteous foreigners, – with whom my stutter of French, refined by Adèle into some precision of accent, was sometimes useful. Every one was at ease and amused at that breakfast-table, – the menu and service of it usually in themselves interesting. I have always regretted a day of unlucky engagement on which I missed a delicate toast of mice; and remembered, with delight, being waited upon one hot summer morning by two graceful and polite little Carolina lizards, who kept off the flies.

From *Praeterita*, I, §§ 229-31

¶ 25

MISS WARDELL

It would have been an extremely delightful afternoon for any youth not a simpleton. Miss Wardell had often enough heard me spoken of by her father as a well-conducted youth, already of some literary reputation – author of *The Poetry of Architecture* – winner of the Newdigate, – First class man in expectation. She herself had been brought up in a way closely resembling my own, in severe seclusion by devoted parents, at a suburban villa with a pretty garden, to skip, and gather flowers, in. The chief difference was that, from the first, Miss Wardell had had excellent masters, and was now an extremely accomplished, intelligent, and faultless maid of seventeen; fragile and delicate to a degree enhancing her beauty with some solemnity of fear, yet in perfect health, as far as a fast-growing girl could be; a softly moulded slender brunette, with her father's dark curling hair transfigured into playful grace round the pretty modest, not unthoughtful, grey-eyed face. Of the afternoon at Hampstead, I remember only that it was a fine day, and that we walked in the garden; mamma, as her mere duty to me in politeness at a first visit, superintending, – it would have been wiser to have left us to get on how we could. I very heartily and reverently admired the pretty creature, and would fain have done, or said, anything I could to please her. Literally to *please* her, for that is, indeed, my hope with all girls, in spite of what I have above related of my mistaken ways of recommending myself. My primary thought is how to serve *them*, and make them happy, and if they could use me for a plank bridge over a stream, or set me up for a post to tie a swing to, or anything of the sort not requiring me to talk, I should be always quite happy in such promotion. This sincere devotion to them, with intense delight in whatever beauty or grace they chance to have, and in most cases, perceptive sympathy, heightened by faith in their right feelings, for the most part gives me considerable power with girls: but all this prevents me from ever being in the least at ease with them, – and I have no doubt that during the whole afternoon at Hampstead, I gave little pleasure to my companion. For the rest, though I extremely admired Miss Wardell, she was not my sort of beauty. I like oval faces, crystalline blonde, with straightish, at the utmost wavy (or, in length, wreathed) hair, and the form elastic, and foot firm. Miss Wardell's dark and tender grace had no power over me, except to make me extremely afraid of being tiresome to her. On the whole, I suppose I came off pretty well, for she afterwards allowed herself to be brought out to Herne Hill to see the pictures, and so on; and I recollect her looking a little frightenedly pleased at my kneeling down to hold a book for her, or some such matter.

After this second interview, however, my father and mother asking me seriously what I thought of her, and I explaining to them that though I saw all her beauty and merit, and niceness, she yet was not my sort of girl, – the negotiations went no farther at that time, and a little while after, were ended for all time; for at Hampstead they went on teaching the tender creature High German, and French of Paris, and Kant's *Metaphysics*, and Newton's *Principia*; and then they took her to Paris, and tired her out with seeing everything every day, all day long, besides the dazzle and excitement of such a first outing from Hampstead; and she at last getting too pale and weak, they brought her back to some English seaside place, I forget where: and there she fell into nervous fever and faded away, with the light of death flickering clearer and clearer in her soft eyes, and never skipped in Hampstead garden more.

How the parents, especially the father, lived on, I never could understand; but I suppose they were honestly religious without talking of it, and they had nothing to blame themselves in, except not having known better. The father, though with grave lines altering his face for ever, went steadily on with his business, and lived to be old.

From *Praeterita*, I, §§ 258-9

¶ 26

MR BAUTTE AND THE RHÔNE

Virtually there was no other jeweller in Geneva, in the great times. There were some respectable, uncompetitive shops, not dazzling, in the main street; and smaller ones, with an average supply of miniature watches, that would go well for ten years; and uncostly, but honest, trinketry. But one went to Mr Bautte's with awe, and of necessity, as one did to one's bankers. There was scarcely any external sign of Bautte whatever – a small brass plate at the side of a narrow arched door, into an alley – into a secluded alley – leading into a monastic courtyard, out of which – or rather out of the alley, where it opened to the court, you ascended a winding stair, wide enough for two only, and came to a green door, swinging, at the top of it; and there you paused to summon courage to enter.

A not large room, with a single counter at the further side. Nothing shown on the counter. Two confidential attendants behind it, and – it might possibly be Mr Bautte! – or his son – or his partner – or anyhow the Ruling power – at his desk beside the back window. You told what you wanted: it was necessary to know your mind, and to be sure you *did* want it; there was no showing of things for temptation at Bautte's. You wanted a bracelet, a brooch, a watch – plain or enamelled. Choice of what was wanted was quietly given. There were no big stones, nor blinding galaxies of wealth. Entirely sound workmanship in the purest gold that could be worked; fine enamel for the most part, for colour, rather than jewels; and a certain Bauttesque subtlety of linked and wreathed design, which the experienced eye recognized when worn in Paris or London. Absolutely just and moderate price; wear, – to the end of your days. You came away with a sense of duty fulfilled, of treasure possessed, and of a new foundation to the respectability of your family.

You returned into the light of the open street with a blissful sense of a parcel being made up to be sent after you, and in the consequently calm expiation of mind, went usually to watch the Rhône.

Bautte's was in the main street, out of which one caught glimpses down the short cross-ones, of the passing water; as at Sandgate, or the like fishing towns, one got peeps of the sea. With twenty steps you were beside it.

For all other rivers there is a surface, and an underneath, and a vaguely displeasing idea of the bottom. But the Rhone flows like one lambent jewel; its surface is nowhere, its ethereal self is everywhere, the iridescent rush and translucent strength of it blue to the shore, and radiant to the depth.

Fifteen feet thick, of not flowing, but flying water; not water, neither, – melted glacier, rather, one should call it; the force of the ice is with it, and the wreathing of the clouds, the gladness of the sky, and the continuance of Time.

Waves of clear sea are, indeed, lovely to watch, but they are always coming or gone, never in any taken shape to be seen for a second. But here was one mighty wave that was always itself, and every fluted swirl of it, constant as the wreathing of a shell. No wasting away of the fallen foam, no pause for gathering of power, no helpless ebb of discouraged recoil; but alike through bright day and lulling night, the never-pausing plunge, and never-fading flash, and never-hushing whisper, and, while the sun was up, the ever-answering glow of unearthly aquamarine, ultramarine, violet-blue, gentian-blue, peacock-blue, river-of-paradise blue, glass of a painted window melted in the sun, and the witch of the Alps flinging the spun tresses of it for ever from her snow.[1]

The innocent way, too, in which the river used to stop to look into every little corner. Great torrents always seem angry, and great rivers too often sullen; but there is no anger, no disdain, in the Rhône. It seemed as if the mountain stream was in mere bliss at recovering itself again out of the lake-sleep, and raced because it rejoiced in racing, fain yet to return and stay. There were pieces of wave that danced all day as if Perdita were looking on to learn; there were little streams that skipped like lambs and leaped like chamois; there were pools that shook the sunshine all through them, and were rippled in layers of overlaid ripples, like crystal sand; there were currents that twisted the light into golden braids, and inlaid the threads with turquoise enamel; there were strips of stream that had certainly above the lake been millstreams, and were looking busily for mills to turn again; there were shoots of stream that had once shot fearfully into the air, and now sprang up again laughing that they had only fallen a foot or two; – and in the midst of all the gay glittering and eddied lingering, the noble bearing by of the midmost depth, so mighty, yet so terrorless and harmless, with its swallows skimming instead of petrels, and the dear old decrepit town as safe in the embracing sweep of it as if it were set in a brooch of sapphire.

From *Praeterita*, II, §§ 89-91

§ 27

DRAWING THE IVY

Considering of these matters, one day on the road to Norwood, I noticed a bit of ivy round a thorn stem, which seemed, even to

1. This paragraph is a good example of how, in *Praeterita*, Ruskin re-used old material, for it was certainly written much earlier, perhaps in 1844.

my critical judgment, not ill 'composed'; and proceeded to make a light and shade pencil study of it in my grey paper pocket-book, carefully, as if it had been a bit of sculpture, liking it more and more as I drew. When it was done, I saw that I had virtually lost all my time since I was twelve years old, because no one had ever told me to draw what was really there! All my time, I mean, given to drawing as an art; of course I had the records of places, but had never seen the beauty of anything, not even of a stone – how much less of a leaf!

From *Praeterita*, II, § 73

§ 28
DRAWING THE ASPEN

The 'hideous rocks' of Fontainebleau were, I grieve to say, never hideous enough to please me. They always seemed to me no bigger than I could pack and send home for specimens, had they been worth carriage; and in my savage dislike of palaces and straight gravel walks, I never found out the spring which was the soul of the place. And to-day, I missed rocks, palace, and fountain all alike, and found myself lying on the bank of a cart-road in the sand, with no prospect whatever but that small aspen tree against the blue sky.

Languidly, but not idly, I began to draw it; and as I drew, the languor passed away: the beautiful lines insisted on being traced, – without weariness. More and more beautiful they became, as each rose out of the rest, and took its place in the air. With wonder increasing every instant, I saw that they 'composed' themselves, by finer laws than any known of men. At last, the tree was there, and everything that I had thought before about trees, nowhere.

The Norwood ivy had not abased me in that final manner, because one had always felt that ivy was an ornamental creature, and expected it to behave prettily, on occasion. But that all the trees of the wood (for I saw surely that my little aspen was only one of their millions) should be beautiful – more than Gothic tracery, more than Greek vase-imagery, more than the daintiest embroiderers of the East could embroider, or the artfullest painters of the West could limn, – this was indeed an end to all former thoughts with me, an insight into a new silvan world.

Not silvan only. The woods, which I had only looked on as wilderness, fulfilled I then saw, in their beauty, the same laws which guided the clouds, divided the light, and balanced the wave. 'He hath made everything beautiful, in his time,' became for me thenceforward the interpretation of the bond between the human mind and all visible things; and I returned along the wood-road feeling that it had led me far; – Farther than ever fancy had reached, or theodolite measured.

From *Praeterita*, II, § 77

¶ 29
DRAWING GRASSES

The admiration of tree-branches taught me at Fontainebleau, led me now into careful discernment of their species; and while my father, as was his custom, read to my mother and me for half-an-hour after breakfast, I always had a fresh-gathered outer spray of a tree before me, of which the mode of growth, with a single leaf full size, had to be done at that sitting in fine pen outline, filled with the simple colour of the leaf at one wash. On fine days, when the grass was dry, I used to lie down on it and draw the blades as they grew, with the ground herbage of buttercup or hawkweed mixed among them, until every square foot of meadow, or mossy bank, became an infinite picture and possession to me, and the grace and adjustment to each other of growing leaves, a subject of more curious interest to me than the composition of any painter's masterpiece. The love of complexity and quantity before noticed as influencing my preference of flamboyant to purer architecture, was here satisfied, without qualifying sense of wasted labour, by what I felt to be the constant working of Omnipotent kindness in the fabric of the food-giving tissues of the earth; nor less, morning after morning, did I rejoice in the traceries and the painted glass of the sky at sunrise.

From *Praeterita*, II, § 199

¶ 30
ILARIA[1]

The accurate study of tree branches, growing leaves, and foreground herbage, had more and more taught me the difference between violent and graceful lines; the beauty of Clotilde and Cécile,
essentially French–Gothic . . . had fixed in my mind and heart . . .
the purest standards of breathing womanhood; and here suddenly,
in the sleeping Ilaria, was the perfectness of these, expressed with
harmonies of line which I saw in an instant were under the same
laws as the river wave, and the aspen branch, and the stars' rising
and setting; but treated with a modesty and severity which read
the laws of nature by the light of virtue.

From *Praeterita*, II, § 114

¶ 31
DISCIPLINE IN PISA (1845)

In summer I have been always at work, or out walking, by six
o'clock, usually awake by half-past four; but I keep to Pisa for the
present, where my monkish discipline arranged itself thus. Out,
anyhow, by six, quick walk to the field, and as much done as I
could, and back to breakfast at half-past eight. Steady bit of Sismondi
over bread and butter, then back to Campo Santo, draw till twelve;
quick walk to look about me and stretch my legs, in shade if it might
be, before lunch, on anything I chanced to see nice in a fruit shop,
and a bit of bread. Back to lighter work, or merely looking and
thinking, for another hour and a half, and to hotel for dinner at
four. Three courses and a flask of Aleatico (a sweet, yet rather
astringent, red, rich for Italian, wine – provincial, and with lovely
basket-work round the bottle). Then out for saunter with Couttet;
he having leave to say anything he had a mind to, but not generally
communicative of his feelings; he carried my sketchbook, but in

1. The recumbent effigy of Ilaria di Caretto (*c.* 1406) by the Sienese sculptor
Jacopo della Quercia (1374-1438), in the Cathedral of Lucca, was first seen by Ruskin
in June 1845. He fell in love with her, as he was later to fall in love with Carpaccio's
St Ursula (cf. no. 296). This was the beginning of his study of fifteenth-century figure
art which was so greatly to alter the direction of his critical writings.

the evening there was too much always to be hunted out, of city; or watched, of hills, or sunset; and I rarely drew, – to my sorrow, now. I wish I knew less, and had drawn more.

Homewards, from wherever we had got to, the moment the sun was down, and the last clouds had lost their colour. I avoided marshy places, if I could, at all times of the day, because I didn't like them; but I feared neither sun nor moon, dawn nor twilight, malaria nor anything else malefic, in the course of work, except only draughts and ugly people.

From *Praeterita*, II, § 122

¶ 32

CAMPO SANTO: ST RANIERI

I cajoled the Abbé Rosini into letting me put up a scaffold level with the frescoes; set steadily to work with what faculty in outline I had; and being by this time practised in delicate curves, by having drawn trees and grass rightly, got far better results than I had hoped, and had an extremely happy fortnight of it! For as the triumph of Death was no new thought to me, the life of hermits was no temptation; but the stories of Abraham, Job, and St Ranieri, well told, were like three new – Scott's novels, I was going to say, and will say, for I don't see my way to anything nearer the fact, and the work on them was pure delight. I got an outline of Abraham's parting with the last of the three angels; of the sacrifice of Job; of the three beggars, and a fiend or two, out of the Triumph of Death; and of the conversion of St Ranieri, for which I greatly pitied him.

For he is playing, evidently with happiest skill, on a kind of zithern-harp, held upright as he stands, to the dance of four sweet Pisan maids, in a round, holding each other only by the bent little fingers of each hand. And one with graver face, and wearing a purple robe, approaches him, saying – I knew once what she said, but forget now; only it meant that his joyful life in that kind was to be ended. And he obeys her, and follows, into a nobler life.

From *Praeterita*, II, § 120

33

HIS WAY OF WRITING

In calling my authorship, drudgery, I do not mean that writing ever gave me the kind of pain of which Carlyle so wildly complains, – to my total amazement and boundless puzzlement, be it in passing said; for he talked just as vigorously as he wrote, and the book he makes bitterest moan over, *Friedrich*, bears the outer aspect of richly enjoyed gossip, and lovingly involuntary eloquence of description or praise. My own literary work, on the contrary, was always done as quietly and methodically as a piece of tapestry. I knew exactly what I had got to say, put the words firmly in their places like so many stitches, hemmed the edges of chapters round with what seemed to me graceful flourishes, touched them finally with my cunningest points of colour, and read the work to papa and mamma at breakfast next morning, as a girl shows her sampler.

'Drudgery' may be a hard word for this often complacent, and entirely painless occupation; still, the best that could be said for it, was that it gave me no serious trouble; and I should think the pleasure of driving, to a good coachman, of ploughing, to a good farmer, much more of dressmaking, to an inventive and benevolent modiste, must be greatly more piquant than the most proudly ardent hours of book-writing have ever been to me, or as far as my memory ranges, to any conscientious author of merely average power. How great work is done, under what burden of sorrow, or with what expense of life, has not been told hitherto, nor is likely to be; the best of late time has been done recklessly or contemptuously. Byron would burn a canto if a friend disliked it, and Scott spoil a story to please a bookseller.

From *Praeterita*, II, §§ 135–6

34

DOING THINGS

And (to get this needful bit of brag, and others connected with it, out of the way at once), I have to say that half my power of ascertaining facts of any kind connected with the arts, is in my stern habit of doing the thing with my own hands till I know its difficulty; and though I have no time nor wish to acquire showy skill in anything, I make myself clear as to what the skill means, and is. Thus, when I had to direct road-making at Oxford, I sate, myself, with an iron-masked stone-breaker, on his heap, to break stones beside the London road, just under Iffley Hill, till I knew how to advise my too impetuous pupils to effect their purposes in that matter, instead of breaking the heads of their hammers off, (a serious item in our daily expenses). I learned from an Irish street crossing-sweeper what he could teach me of sweeping; but found myself in that matter nearly his match, from my boy-gardening; and again and again I swept bits of St Giles' foot-pavements, showing my corps of subordinates how to finish into depths of gutter. I worked with a carpenter until I could take an even shaving six feet long off a board; and painted enough with properly and delightfully soppy green paint to feel the master's superiority in the use of a blunt brush. But among all these and other such studentships, the reader will be surprised, I think, to hear, seriously, that the instrument I finally decided to be the most difficult of management was the trowel. For accumulated months of my boy's life I watched bricklaying and paving; but when I took the trowel into my own hand, abandoned at once all hope of attaining the least real skill with it, unless I gave up all thoughts of any future literary or political career. But the quite happiest bit of manual work I ever did was for my mother in the old inn at Sixt, where she alleged the stone staircase to have become unpleasantly dirty, since last year. Nobody in the inn appearing to think it possible to wash it, I brought the necessary buckets of water from the yard myself, poured them into a beautiful image of Versailles waterworks down the fifteen or twenty steps of the great staircase, and with the strongest broom I could find, cleaned every step into its corners. It was quite lovely work to dash the water and drive the mud, from each, with accumulating splash down to the next one.

From *Praeterita*, II, § 197

¶ 35
HIS GENIUS

Miss Edgeworth may abuse the word 'genius', but there is such a thing, and it consists mainly in a man's doing things because he cannot help it, – intellectual things, I mean. I don't think myself a great genius, but I believe I have genius; something different from mere cleverness, for I am *not* clever in the sense that millions of people are – lawyers, physicians, and others. But there is the strong instinct in me which I cannot analyse to draw and describe the things I love – not for reputation, nor for the good of others, nor for my own advantage, but a sort of instinct like that for eating or drinking. I should like to draw all St Mark's, and all this Verona stone by stone, to eat it all up into my mind, touch by touch.

From a letter to his father, 2 June 1852

¶ 36
PICTURES ARE MY FRIENDS

Men are more evanescent than pictures, yet one sorrows for lost friends, and pictures *are* my friends. I have none others. I am never long enough with men to attach myself to them; and whatever feelings of attachment I have are to material things. If the great Tintoret here were to be destroyed, it would be precisely to me what the death of Hallam was to Tennyson – as far as *this* world is concerned – with an addition of bitterness and indignation, for my friend would perish murdered, *his* by a natural death. Hearing of plans for its restoration is just the same to me as to another man hearing talk behind an Irish hedge of shooting his brother.

From a letter to his father, 28 January 1852

¶ 37
FRIENDSHIP

The thoughtful reader must have noted with some displeasure that I have scarcely, whether at college or at home, used the word 'friendship' with respect to any of my companions. The fact is, I am a little puzzled by the specialty and singularity of poetical and classic friendship. I get, distinctively, attached to places, to pictures, to dogs, cats, and girls: but I have had, Heaven be thanked, many and true friends, young and old, who have been of boundless help and good to me, – nor I quite helpless to them; yet for none of whom have I ever obeyed George Herbert's mandate, 'Thy friend put in thy bosom; wear his eyes, Still in thy heart, that he may see what's there; If cause require, thou art his sacrifice,' etc. Without thinking myself particularly wicked, I found nothing in my heart that seemed to me worth anybody's seeing; nor had I any curiosity for insight into those of others; nor had I any notion of being a sacrifice for them, or the least wish that they should exercise for my good any but their most pleasurable accomplishments.

From *Praeterita*, II, § 195

¶ 38

AN IVORY FOOT-RULE

In blaming myself, as often I have done, and may have occasion to do again, for my want of affection to other people, I must also express continually, as I think back about it, more and more wonder that ever anybody had any affection for *me*. I thought they might as well have got fond of a camera-lucida, or an ivory foot-rule: all my faculty was merely in showing that such and such things were so; I was no orator, no actor, no painter but in a minute and generally invisible manner; and I couldn't bear being interrupted in anything I was about.

From *Praeterita*, II, § 225

¶ 39

ENTRY IN HIS DIARY A MONTH AFTER THE ANNULMENT OF HIS MARRIAGE
13th August, 1854

How little I thought God would bring me here again just now – and I am here, stronger in health, higher in hope, deeper in peace, than I have been for years. The green pastures and pine forests of

the Varens softly seen through the light of my window. I cannot be
thankful enough, nor happy enough. Psalm lxvi. 8–20.

From *The Diaries of John Ruskin*, ed. Joan Evans, Vol. II, p. 500

¶ 40

CONVERSION FROM EVANGELICISM

So I settled at Turin for the autumn [of 1858].

There, one Sunday morning, I made my way in the south suburb
to a little chapel which, by a dusty roadside, gathered to its un-
observed door the few sheep of the old Waldensian faith who had
wandered from their own pastures under Monte Viso into the
worldly capital of Piedmont.

The assembled congregation numbered in all some three or four
and twenty, of whom fifteen or sixteen were grey-haired women.
Their solitary and clerkless preacher, a somewhat stunted figure in
a plain black coat, with a cracked voice, after leading them through
the languid forms of prayer which are all that in truth are possible
to people whose present life is dull and its terrestrial future unchangeable, put his utmost zeal into a consolatory discourse on the
wickedness of the wide world, more especially of the plain of Piedmont and city of Turin, and on the exclusive favour with God,
enjoyed by the between nineteen and twenty-four elect members
of his congregation, in the streets of Admah and Zeboim.

Myself neither cheered nor greatly alarmed by this doctrine, I
walked back into the condemned city, and up into the gallery where
Paul Veronese's Solomon and the Queen of Sheba glowed in full
afternoon light. The gallery windows being open, there came in
with the warm air, floating swells and falls of military music, from
the courtyard before the palace, which seemed to me more devotional, in their perfect art, tune, and discipline, than anything I
remembered of evangelical hymns. And as the perfect colour and
sound gradually asserted their power on me, they seemed finally to
fasten me in the old article of Jewish faith, that things done delightfully and rightly were always done by the help and in the Spirit of
God.

From *Praeterita*, III, § 23

¶ 41

UN-LIBERAL CHRISTIANITY

The subject of lesson, Jael's slaying of Sisera. Concerning which, Maurice taking an enlightened modern view of what was fit and not, discoursed in passionate indignation; and warned his class, in the most positive and solemn manner, that such dreadful deeds could only have been done in cold blood in the Dark Biblical ages; and that no religious and patriotic Englishwoman ought ever to think of imitating Jael by nailing a Russian's or Prussian's skull to the ground, – especially after giving him butter in a lordly dish. At the close of the instruction, through which I sate silent, I ventured to enquire, why then had Deborah the prophetess declared of Jael, 'Blessed above women shall the wife of Heber the Kenite be'? On which Maurice, with startled and flashing eyes, burst into partly scornful, partly alarmed, denunciation of Deborah the prophetess, as a mere blazing Amazon; and of her Song as a merely rhythmic storm of battle-rage, no more to be listened to with edification or faith than the Norman's sword-song at the battle of Hastings.

Whereupon there remained nothing for *me*, – to whom the Song of Deborah was as sacred as the Magnificat, – but total collapse in sorrow and astonishment; the eyes of all the class being also bent on me in amazed reprobation of my benighted views, and unchristian sentiments. And I got away how I could, but never went back.

From *Praeterita*, III, § 14

¶ 42

THE PRODIGAL SON

Somewhat before the date of my farewell to Maurician free-thinking, I had come into still more definite collision with the Puritan dogmata which forbid thinking at all, in a séance to which I was invited, shyly, by my friend Macdonald, – fashionable séance of Evangelical doctrine, at the Earl of Ducie's; presided over by Mr Molyneux, then a divine of celebrity in that sect; who sate with one leg over his other knee in the attitude always given to Herod at the massacre of the Innocents in mediæval sculpture; and discoursed in

52

tones of consummate assurance and satisfaction, and to the entire comfort and consent of his Belgravian audience, on the beautiful parable of the Prodigal Son. Which, or how many, of his hearers he meant to describe as having personally lived on husks, and devoured their fathers' property, did not of course appear; but that something of the sort was necessary to the completeness of the joy in heaven over them, now in Belgrave Square, at the feet, – or one foot – of Mr Molyneux, could not be questioned.

Waiting my time, till the raptures of the converted company had begun to flag a little, I ventured, from a back seat, to enquire of Mr Molyneux what we were to learn from the example of the *other* son, not prodigal, who was, his father said of him, 'ever with me, and all that I have, thine'? A sudden horror, and unanimous feeling of the serpent having, somehow, got over the wall into their Garden of Eden, fell on the whole company; and some of them, I thought, looked at the candles, as if they expected them to burn blue. After a pause of a minute, gathering himself into an expression of pity and indulgence, withholding latent thunder, Mr Molyneux explained to me that the home-staying son was merely a picturesque figure introduced to fill the background of the parable agreeably, and contained no instruction or example for the well-disposed scriptural student, but, on the contrary, rather a snare for the unwary, and a temptation to self-righteousness, – which was, of all sins, the most offensive to God.

Under the fulmination of which answer I retired, as from Maurice's, from the séance in silence; nor ever attended another of the kind from that day to this.

From *Praeterita*, III, § 16

¶ 43

THE PROTESTANT APPROACH TO ST MARK'S

As I re-read the description I gave, thirty years since, of St Mark's Church; – much more as I remember, forty years since, and before, the first happy hour spent in trying to paint a piece of it, with my six-o'clock breakfast on the little café table beside me on the pavement in the morning shadow, I am struck, almost into silence, by wonder at my own pert little Protestant mind, which never thought for a moment of asking what the Church had been built for!

Tacitly and complacently assuming that I had had the entire truth of God preached to me in Beresford Chapel in the Walworth Road, – recognizing no possible Christian use or propriety in any other sort of chapel elsewhere; and perceiving, in this bright phenomenon before me, nothing of more noble function than might be in some new and radiant sea-shell, thrown up for me on the sand; – nay, never once so much as thinking, of the fair shell itself, 'Who built its domed whorls, then?' or 'What manner of creature lives in the inside?' Much less ever asking, 'Who is lying dead therein?'

A marvellous thing – the Protestant mind! Don't think I speak as a Roman Catholic, good reader: I am a mere wandering Arab, if that will less alarm you, seeking but my cup of cold water in the desert; and I speak only as an Arab, or an Indian, – with faint hope of ever seeing the ghost of Laughing Water.

From *St Mark's Rest*, § 88

¶ 44

TURNING-POINT AT FORTY

I have had cloud upon me this year, and don't quite know the meaning of it; only I've had no heart to write to anybody. I suppose the real gist of it is that next year I shall be forty, and begin to see what life and the world mean, seen from the middle of them – and the middle inclining to the dustward end. I believe there is something owing to the violent reaction often after the excitement of the arrangement of Turner's sketches; something to my ascertaining in the course of that work how the old man's soul had been gradually crushed within him, leaving him at the close of his life weak, sinful, desolate – nothing but his generosity and kindness of heart left; something to my having enjoyed too much of lovely things, till they almost cease to be lovely to me, and because I have no monotonous or disagreeable work by way of foil to them; – but, however it may be, I am not able to write as I used to do, nor to feel, and can only make up my mind to the state as one that has to be gone through, and from which I hope some day to come out on the other side.

From a letter to Elizabeth Barrett Browning, 14 October 1858

¶ 45
I WANT, I WANT

I rather want good wishes just now, for I am tormented by what I cannot get said, nor done. I want to get all the Titians, Tintorets, Paul Veroneses, Turners, and Sir Joshuas in the world into one great fireproof Gothic gallery of marble and serpentine. I want to get them all perfectly engraved. I want to go and draw all the subjects of Turner's 19,000 sketches in Switzerland and Italy, elaborated by myself. I want to get everybody a dinner who hasn't got one. I want to macadamize some new roads to Heaven with broken fools'-heads. I want to hang up some knaves out of the way, not that I've any dislike to them, but I think it would be wholesome for them, and for other people, and that they would make good crows' meat. I want to play all day long and arrange my cabinet of minerals with new white wool. I want somebody to amuse me when I'm tired. I want Turner's pictures not to fade. I want to be able to draw clouds, and to understand how they go, and I can't make them stand still, nor understand them – they all go sideways.

From a letter to Charles Eliot Norton,[1] 28 December 1858

¶ 46
THE AIM AND ORIGIN OF MODERN PAINTERS

These oscillations of temper, and progressions of discovery, extending over a period of seventeen years, ought not to diminish the

1. Charles Eliot Norton, later Professor of Fine Arts in the University of Harvard, first met Ruskin (introduced by J. J. Jarves) in the autumn of 1855. The following year they met again on a steam-boat on the lake of Geneva, and a lasting friendship developed. Ruskin wrote to him more freely than to any other man, and called him 'my second friend (after Dr Brown) and my first real tutor'. *The Letters of John Ruskin to C. E. Norton*, Boston, 1905, is, after *Praeterita*, the best source for the understanding of Ruskin's character.

reader's confidence in the book. Let him be assured of this, that unless important changes are occurring in his opinions continually, all his life long, not one of those opinions can be on any questionable subject true. All true opinions are living, and show their life by being capable of nourishment; therefore of change. But their change is that of a tree – not of a cloud.

In the main aim and principle of the book, there is no variation, from its first syllable to its last. It declares the perfectness and eternal beauty of the work of God; and tests all work of man by concurrence with, or subjection to that. And it differs from most books, and has a chance of being in some respects better for the difference, in that it has not been written either for fame, or for money, or for conscience-sake, but of necessity.

It has not been written for praise. Had I wished to gain present reputation, by a little flattery adroitly used in some places, a sharp word or two withheld in others, and the substitution of verbiage generally for investigation, I could have made the circulation of these volumes tenfold what it has been in modern society. Had I wished for future fame I should have written one volume, not five. Also, it has not been written for money. In this wealth-producing country, seventeen years' labour could hardly have been invested with less chance of equivalent return.

Also, it has not been written for conscience-sake. I had no definite hope in writing it; still less any sense of its being required of me as a duty. It seems to me, and seemed always, probable, that I might have done much more good in some other way. But it has been written of necessity. I saw an injustice done, and tried to remedy it. I heard falsehood taught, and was compelled to deny it. Nothing else was possible to me. I knew not how little or how much might come of the business, or whether I was fit for it; but here was the lie full set in front of me, and there was no way round it, but only over it. So that, as the work changed like a tree, it was also rooted like a tree – not where it would, but where need was; on which, if any fruit grow such as you can like, you are welcome to gather it without thanks; and so far as it is poor or bitter, it will be your justice to refuse it without reviling.

From *Modern Painters*, Vol. v, Preface, § 8

§ 47
THE LOCOMOTIVE

I cannot express the amazed awe, the crushed humility, with which I sometimes watch a locomotive take its breath at a railway station, and think what work there is in its bars and wheels, and what manner of men they must be who dig brown iron-stone out of the ground, and forge it into THAT! What assemblage of accurate and mighty faculties in them; more than fleshly power over melting crag and coiling fire, fettered, and finessed at last into the precision of watchmaking; Titanian hammer-strokes beating, out of lava, these glittering cylinders and timely-respondent valves, and fine ribbed rods, which touch each other as a serpent writhes, in noiseless gliding, and omnipotence of grasp; infinitely complex anatomy of active steel, compared with which the skeleton of a living creature would seem, to a careless observer, clumsy and vile – a mere morbid secretion and phosphatous prop of flesh! What would the men who thought out this – who beat it out, who touched it into its polished calm of power, who set it to its appointed task, and triumphantly saw it fulfil this task to the utmost of their will – feel or think about this weak hand of mine, timidly leading a little strain of water-colour, which I cannot manage, into an imperfect shadow of something else – mere failure in every motion, and endless disappointment; what, I repeat, would these Iron-dominant Genii think of me? and what ought I to think of them?

From *The Cestus of Aglaia*, § 9

§ 48
LETTER TO THE BROWNINGS

For the truth is that my own proper business is not that of writing; I am never happy as I write; never want to utter for my own delight, as you singers do (with all your pretences to benevolence and all that, you know you like singing just as well as the nightingales). But I'm truly benevolent, miserably benevolent. For my own pleasure I should be collecting stones and mosses, drying and ticketing them – reading scientific books – walking all day long in the summer

– going to plays, and what not, in winter – never writing nor saying a word – rejoicing tranquilly or intensely in pictures, in music, in pleasant faces, in kind friends. But now – about me there is this terrific absurdity and wrong going on. People kill my Turner with abuse of him – make rifle targets of my Paul Veroneses – make themselves, and me, unendurably wretched by all sorts of ridiculous doings – won't let me be quiet. I live the life of an old lady in a houseful of wicked children – can do nothing but cry out – they won't leave me to my knitting needles a moment.

From a letter to Mr and Mrs Robert Browning,[1] 15 January 1858

¶ 49

THE TASK OF POETRY

Treasures of wisdom there are in it,[2] and word-painting such as never was yet for concentration; nevertheless it seems to me that so great power ought not to be spent on visions of things past, but on the living present. For one hearer capable of feeling the depth of this poem I believe ten would feel a depth quite as great if the stream flowed through things nearer the hearer. And merely in the facts of modern life – not drawing-room, formal life, but the far-away and quite unknown growth of souls in and through any form of misery or servitude – there is an infinity of what men should be told, and what none but a poet can tell. I cannot but think that the intense, masterful, and unerring transcript of an actuality, and the relation of a story of any real human life as a poet would watch and analyse it, would make all men feel more or less what poetry was, as they felt what Life and Fate were in their instant workings.

This seems to me the true task of the modern poet. And I think I have seen faces, and heard voices, by road and street side, which claimed or conferred as much as ever the loveliest or saddest of Camelot. As I watch them, the feeling continually weighs upon me, day by day, more and more, that not the grief of the world but the

1. Ruskin first met the Brownings in 1852, when they came to look at his Turner drawings at Denmark Hill. They remained close friends till Mrs Browning's death in 1861. He did not greatly admire Browning's poetry, and protested at the injustice of *Mr Sludge*, '*the Medium*'; but he thought Mrs Browning's *Aurora Leigh* 'the greatest poem of the century'.   2. *Idylls of the King*.

loss of it is the wonder of it. I see creatures so full of all power and beauty, with none to understand or teach or save them. The making in them of miracles, and all cast away, for ever lost as far as we can trace. And no 'in memoriam.'

From a letter to Tennyson,[1] September 1859

¶ 50

A PUZZLED OLD GENTLEMAN

So there's a letter – about myself and nothing else. I wonder I have the face to send it, but you know you asked me once to write you a sort of account of the things that made me, as you were pleased to say, 'what I am,' which is at present an entirely puzzled, helpless, and disgusted old gentleman. As for things that have influenced me, I believe hard work, love of justice and of beauty, good nature, and great vanity, have done all of me that was worth doing. I've had my heart broken, ages ago, when I was a boy – then mended, cracked, beaten in, kicked about old corridors, and finally, I think, flattened fairly out. I've picked up what education I've got in an irregular way – and it's very little. I suppose that on the whole as little has been got into me and out of me as under any circumstances was probable; it is true, had my father made me his clerk I might have been in a fair way of becoming a respectable Political Economist in the manner of Ricardo or Mill – but granting liberty and power of travelling, and working as I chose, I suppose everything I've chosen to have been about as wrong as wrong could be. I ought not to have written a word; but should have merely waited on Turner as much as he would have let me, putting in writing every word that fell from him, and drawing hard. By this time, I might have been an accomplished draughtsman, a fair musician, and a thoroughly good scholar in art literature, and in good health besides. As it is, I've written a few second-rate books, which nobody minds; I can't draw, I can't play nor sing, I can't ride, I walk worse and worse, I can't digest. And I can't help it. – There!

From a letter to Charles Eliot Norton, 20 July 1862

1. Tennyson was an admirer of *Modern Painters*, Vol. 1, but he does not seem to have met Ruskin till 1854, and the two men never became friends.

¶ 51

HISTORY

There is no law of history any more than of a kaleidoscope. With certain bits of glass – shaken so, and so – you will get pretty figures, but what figures, heaven only knows. Add definite attractions and repulsions to the angles of the tube – your figures will have such and such modifications. But the history of the world will be for ever new.

The wards of a Chubb's lock are infinite in their chances. Is the Key of Destiny made on a less complex principle?

From a letter to J. A. Froude,[1] February 1864

¶ 52

PAMPERED AND THWARTED

I have always been so able until now to shake off regret and amuse myself with work of some sort, that now, when my mountains and cathedrals fail me, and I find myself feeling dull in a pine forest or a country town, I directly think I must be dying. . . . Men ought to be severely disciplined and exercised in the sternest way in daily life – they should learn to lie on stone beds and eat black soup, but they should never have their hearts broken – a noble heart, once broken, never mends – the best you can do is to rivet it with iron and plaster the cracks over – the blood never flows rightly again. The two terrific mistakes which Mama and you involuntarily fell into were the exact reverse *in both* ways – you fed me effeminately and luxuriously to that extent that I actually now could not travel in rough countries without taking a cook with me! – but you thwarted me in all the earnest fire of passion and life. About Turner you indeed never knew how much you thwarted me – for I thought it my duty to be thwarted – it was the religion that led me all wrong there; if I had had courage and knowledge enough to insist on having my own way resolutely, you would now have had me in happy

1. James Anthony Froude, 1818–94, historian and man of letters, was one of Ruskin's most devoted friends in his later life. They had in common a passionate admiration for Carlyle, and Ruskin strongly supported the controversial account of Carlyle's character in Froude's *Life*.

health, loving you twice as much (for, depend upon it, love taking much of its own way, a fair share, is in generous people all the brighter for it), and full of energy for the future – and of power of self-denial: now, my power of *duty* has been exhausted in vain, and I am forced for life's sake to indulge myself in all sorts of selfish ways, just when a man ought to be knit for the duties of middle life by the good success of his youthful life.

From a letter to his father,[1] 16 December 1863

¶ 53
DEATH OF HIS FATHER

You never have had – nor with all your medical experience have you ever, probably, seen – the loss of a father who would have sacrificed his life for his son, and yet forced his son to sacrifice his life to him, and sacrifice it in vain. It is an exquisite piece of tragedy altogether – very much like Lear, in a ludicrous commercial way – Cordelia remaining unchanged and her friends writing to her afterwards – wasn't she sorry for the pain she had given her father by not speaking when she should?

From a letter to H. W. Acland,[2] 9 March 1864

¶ 54
PRAYER ON SKIDDAW

I thought I should like a long, quiet day on Skiddaw by myself, so I gave Crawley some work at home, in packing stones, and took my hammer and compass, and sauntered up leisurely. It was threatening rain, in its very beauty of stillness, – no sunshine – only dead calm under grey sky. I sate down for a while on the highest shoulder of

1. This is Ruskin's last surviving letter to his devoted father, who died in the following March. The reference to Turner is hard to understand, as John Ruskin senior had spent thousands of pounds buying Turners for his son's collection.

2. Henry Wentworth Acland (1815–1900), later Sir Henry Acland, was two years senior to Ruskin at Christ Church, Oxford, and befriended him as a freshman. He became the owner of Millais's portrait of Ruskin painted during the break-up of his marriage, and continued to be one of Ruskin's wisest friends and counsellors. From 1858 to 1894 he was Regius Professor of Medicine in Oxford, and was instrumental in the appointment of Ruskin as Slade Professor of Fine Art in 1869.

the hill under the summit – in perfect calm of air – as if in a room! Then, suddenly – in a space of not more than ten minutes – vast volumes of white cloud formed in the west. When I first sate down, all the Cumberland mountains, from Scawfell to the Penrith Hills, lay round me like a clear model, cut in wood – I never saw anything so *ridiculously* clear – great masses 2000 feet high looking like little green bosses under one's hand. Then as I said, in ten minutes, the white clouds formed, and came foaming from the west towards Skiddaw; then answering white fleeces started into being on Scawfell and Helvellyn – and the moment they were formed, the unnatural clearness passed away, and the mountains, where still visible, resumed their proper distances. I rose and went on along the stately ridge towards the summit, hammering and poking about for fibrous quartz. . . . It was very beautiful, with the white cloud filling all the western valley – and the air still calm – and the desolate peak and moors, motionless for many a league, but for the spots of white – which were sheep, one knew – and were sometimes to be seen to move.

I always – even in my naughtiest times – had a way of praying on hill summits, when I could get quiet on them; so I knelt on a bit of rock to pray – and there came suddenly into my mind the clause of the Litany, 'for all that travel by land or water,' etc. So I prayed it, and you can't think what a strange, intense meaning it had up there – one felt so much more the feebleness of the feeble there, where all was wild and strong, and there 'Show thy pity on all prisoners and captives' came so wonderfully where I had the feeling of absolutely boundless liberty. I could rise from kneeling and dash away to any quarter of heaven – east or west or south or north – with leagues of moorland tossed one after another like sea waves.

From a letter to Miss Joan Agnew,[1] 15 August 1867

1. Joan Ruskin Agnew was Ruskin's Scottish cousin who, after the death of his father in 1864, came to live with his mother at Denmark Hill, and remained as her companion till 1871, when she married Arthur Severn, the son of Keats's friend. Later she and her husband settled in Ruskin's old house at Herne Hill, and devoted their lives to looking after him. She nursed him through his attacks of madness, although in one of them he turned against her and made her leave the house. The last thing Ruskin wrote is the unfinished chapter of *Praeterita* called 'Joanna's Care'. He gave her Brantwood and made her one of his literary executors. Ruskin died holding her hand, and it was she who insisted that he be buried in the churchyard at Coniston rather than in Westminster Abbey.

¶ 55
DICKENS

I knew you would deeply feel the death of Dickens. It is very frightful to me – among the blows struck by the fates at worthy men, while all mischievous ones have ceaseless strength. The literary loss is infinite – the political one I care less for than you do. Dickens was a pure modernist – a leader of the steam-whistle party *par excellence* – and he had no understanding of any power of antiquity except a sort of jackdaw sentiment for cathedral towers. He knew nothing of the nobler power of superstition – was essentially a stage manager, and used everything for effect on the pit. His Christmas meant mistletoe and pudding – neither resurrection from dead, nor rising of new stars, nor teaching of wise men, nor shepherds. His hero is essentially the ironmaster; in spite of *Hard Times*, he has advanced by his influence every principle that makes them harder – the love of excitement, in all classes, and the fury of business competition, and the distrust both of nobility and clergy which, wide enough and fatal enough, and too justly founded, needed no apostle to the mob, but a grave teacher of priests and nobles themselves, for whom Dickens had essentially no word.[1]

From a letter to Charles Eliot Norton, 17 June 1870

¶ 56
DON QUIXOTE

It was always *throughout*, *real* chivalry to me; and it is precisely because the most touching valour and tenderness are rendered vain by madness, and because, thus vain, they are made a subject of laughter to vulgar and shallow persons, and because *all* true chivalry is thus by implication accused of madness, and involved in shame, that I call the book so deadly.

From a letter to Charles Eliot Norton, 9 August 1870

1. In spite of the critical tone of this letter, Ruskin had the warmest admiration for Dickens, referred frequently to all his works, and considered *Hard Times* 'in many respects his greatest book'.

¶ 57
THE WANDERING MIND

The first quiet and pure light that has risen this many a day, was increasing through the tall stems of the trees of our garden, which is walled by the walls of old Oxford; and a bird (I am going to lecture on ornithology next term, but don't know *what* bird, and couldn't go to ask the gardener,) singing steady, sweet, momentary notes, in a way that would have been very pleasant to me, once. And as I was breathing out of the window, thrown up as high as I could (for my servant had made me an enormous fire, as servants always do on hot mornings), and looking at the bright sickle of a moon, fading as she rose, the verse came into my mind, – I don't in the least know why, – 'Lifting up holy hands, without wrath, and doubting'; – which chanced to express in the most precise terms, what I want you to feel, about Edward III's fighting (though St Paul is speaking of prayer, not of fighting, but it's all the same); as opposed to this modern British fighting, which is the lifting up of unholy hands, – feet, at least, – *in* wrath, and doubting.

From *Fors Clavigera*, II, Letter xxv, § 20, 26 December 1872

¶ 58
MUSING

You have, I hope, noticed that throughout these letters addressed to you as workmen and labourers, – though I have once or twice ventured to call myself your fellow-workman, I have oftener spoken as belonging to, and sharing main modes of thought with, those who are not labourers, but either live in various ways by their wits – as lawyers, authors, reviewers, clergymen, parliamentary orators, and the like – or absolutely in idleness on the labour of others, – as the representative Squire. And, broadly speaking, I address you as workers, and speak in the name of the rest as idlers, thus not estimating the mere wit-work as work at all: it is always play, when it is good.

Speaking to you, then, as workers, and of myself as an idler, tell me honestly whether you consider me as addressing my betters or my worses? Let us give ourselves no airs on either side. Which of us, do you seriously think, you or I, are leading the more honourable life? Would you like to lead my life rather than your own; or, if you couldn't help finding it pleasanter, would you be ashamed of yourselves for leading it? Is your place, or mine, considered as cure and sinecure, the better? And are either of us legitimately in it? I would fain know your own real opinion on these things.

But note further; there is another relation between us than of idler and labourer; the much more direct one of Master and Servant. I can set you to any kind of work I like, whether it be good for you or bad, pleasant to you or painful. Consider, for instance, what I am doing at this very instant – half-past seven, morning, 25th February, 1873. It is a bitter black frost, the ground deep in snow, and more falling. I am writing comfortable in a perfectly warm room; some of my servants were up in the cold at half-past five to get it ready for me; others, a few days ago, were digging my coals near Durham, at the risk of their lives; an old woman brought me my watercresses through the snow for breakfast yesterday; another old woman is going two miles through it to-day to fetch me my letters at ten o'clock. Half-a-dozen men are building a wall for me to keep the sheep out of my garden, and a railroad stoker is holding his own against the north wind, to fetch me some Brobdignag raspberry plants to put in it. Somebody in the east end of London is making boots for me, for I can't wear those I have much longer; a washerwoman is in suds, somewhere, to get me a clean shirt for to-morrow; a fisherman is in dangerous weather somewhere, catching me some fish for Lent; and my cook will soon be making me pancakes, for it is Shrove Tuesday. Having written this sentence, I go to the fire, warm my fingers, saunter a little, listlessly, about the room, and grumble because I can't see to the other side of the lake.

And all these people, my serfs or menials, who are undergoing any quantity or kind of hardship I choose to put on them, – all these people, nevertheless, are more contented than I am: I can't be happy, not I, – for one thing, because I haven't got the MS. Additional, (never mind what number) in the British Museum, which they bought in 1848, for two hundred pounds, and I never saw it! And have never been easy in my mind, since. . . .

But I used another terrible word just now – 'menial.' The modern English vulgar mind has a wonderful dread of doing anything of that sort!

I suppose there is scarcely another word in the language which people more dislike having applied to them, or of which they less understand the application. It comes from a beautiful old Chaucerian word, 'menie,' or many, signifying the attendant company of any one worth attending to; the disciples of a master, scholars of a teacher, soldiers of a leader, lords of a King. Chaucer says the God of Love came, in the garden of the Rose, with 'his many'; – in the court of the King of Persia spoke a Lord, one 'of his many.' Therefore there is nothing in itself dishonourable in being menial: the only question is – *whose* many you belong to, and whether he is a person worth belonging to, or even safe to be belonged to; also, there is somewhat in the cause of your following: if you follow for love, it is good to be menial – if for honour, good also; – if for ten per cent. – as a railroad company follows its Director, it is not good to be menial. Also there is somewhat in the manner of following: if you obey your Taskmaster's eye, it is well; – if only his whip, still, well; but not so well: – but, above all, or below all, if you have to obey the whip as a bad hound, because you have no nose, like the members of the present House of Commons, it is a very humble form of menial service indeed.

But even as to the quite literal form of it, in house or domestic service, are you sure it is so very disgraceful a state to live in?

Among the people whom one must miss out of one's life, dead, or worse than dead, by the time one is fifty-four, I can only say, for my own part, that the one I practically and truly miss most, next to father and mother (and putting losses of imaginary good out of the question), was a 'menial,' my father's nurse, and mine. She was one of our many – (our many being always but few), and from her girlhood to her old age, the entire ability of her life was given to serving us. She had a natural gift and specialty for doing disagreeable things; above all, the service of a sick room; so that she was never quite in her glory unless some of us were ill. She had also some parallel specialty for *saying* disagreeable things; and might be relied upon to give the extremely darkest view of any subject, before

proceeding to ameliorative action upon it. And she had a very creditable and republican aversion to doing immediately, or in set terms,
as she was bid; so that when my mother and she got old together,
and my mother became very imperative and particular about having
her teacup set on one side of her little round table, Anne would
observantly and punctiliously put it always on the other; which
caused my mother to state to me, every morning after breakfast,
gravely, that, if ever a woman in this world was possessed by the
Devil, Anne was that woman. But in spite of these momentary and
petulant aspirations to liberality and independence of character, poor
Anne remained verily servile in soul, all her days; and was altogether
occupied from the age of fifteen to seventy-two in doing other
people's wills instead of her own, and seeking other people's good
instead of her own: nor did I ever hear on any occasion of her doing
harm to a human being, except by saving two hundred and some
odd pounds for her relations; in consequence of which some of them,
after her funeral, did not speak to the rest for several months.

Two hundred and odd pounds; – it might have been more; but
I used to hear of little loans to the relations occasionally; and besides,
Anne would sometimes buy a quite unjustifiably expensive silk
gown. People in her station of life are always so improvident. Two
hundred odd pounds at all events she had laid by, in her fifty-seven
years of unselfish labour. Actually twenty ten-pound notes.

From *Fors Clavigera*, II, Letter xxviii, § 10, 20 February 1873

§ 59

THE COCKLE-SHELL

Here is a little grey cockle-shell, lying beside me, which I gathered,
the other evening, out of the dust of the Island of St Helena; and a
brightly-spotted snail-shell, from the thistly sands of Lido; and I
want to set myself to draw these, and describe them, in peace.

'Yes,' all my friends say, 'that is my business; why can't I mind
it, and be happy?'

Well, good friends, I would fain please you, and myself with you;
and live here in my Venetian palace, luxurious; scrutinant of dome,

cloud, and cockle-shell. I could even sell my books for not inconsiderable sums of money if I chose to bribe all the reviewers, pay half of all I got to the booksellers, stick bills on the lamp-posts, and say nothing but what would please the Bishop of Peterborough.

I could say a great deal that would please him, and yet be very good and useful; . . . And little enough mind have I for any work, in this seventy-seventh year that's coming of our glorious century, wider than I could find in the compass of my cockle-shell.

But alas! my prudent friends, little enough of all that I have a mind to may be permitted me. For this green tide that eddies by my threshold is full of floating corpses, and I must leave my dinner to bury them, since I cannot save; and put my cockle-shell in cap, and take my staff in hand, to seek an unencumbered shore.

From *Fors Clavigera*, VI, Letter LXXII, §§ 2 and 3, 9 November 1876

¶ 60
TRANSLATION

What translation of Aristophanes is that? I must get it. I've lost I can't tell you how much knowledge and power through false pride in refusing to read translations, though I couldn't read the original without more trouble and time than I could spare. Nevertheless, you must not think this English gives you a true idea of the original. The English is much more 'English' in its temper than its words. Aristophanes is far more dry, severe, and concentrated; his words are fewer, and have fuller flavour; this English is to him very nearly what currant jelly is to currants. But it's immensely useful to me.

From a letter to Miss Susan Beever,[1] 17 December 1873

1. Miss Susan Beever of Thwack, Coniston, and thus Ruskin's near neighbour, was sixty-eight when Ruskin first met her. She made the selection of passages from *Modern Painters*, published under the title of *Frondes Agrestes* in 1875, which did much to spread his fame as a master of prose. Ruskin wrote her more than nine hundred letters, a selection of which was published in 1887 with the title *Hortus Inclusus*. In them he always refers to her as if she were a little girl, and sometimes writes in baby language.

¶ 61
CARLYLE

His own first teacher in Latin, an old clergyman. He had indeed been sent first to a schoolmaster in his own village, 'the joyfullest little mortal, he believed, on earth,' learning his declensions out of an eighteen-penny book! giving his whole might and heart to understand. And the master could teach him nothing, merely involved him day by day in misery of non-understanding, the boy getting crushed and sick, till (his mother?) saw it, and then he was sent to this clergyman, 'a perfect sage, on the humblest scale.' Seventy pounds a year, his income at first entering into life; never more than a hundred. Six daughters and two sons; the eldest sister, Margaret, 'a little bit lassie,' – then in a lower voice, 'the flower of all the flock to *me*.' Returning from her little visitations to the poor, dressed in her sober prettiest, 'the most amiable of possible objects.' Not beautiful in any notable way afterwards, but 'comely in the highest degree.' With dutiful sweetness, 'the right hand of her father.' Lived to be seven-and-twenty. 'The last time that I wept aloud in the world, I think was at her death.'

From *Praeterita*, II, § 230

¶ 62
A PROJECTED IRRIGATION

Yesterday morning I was climbing among the ravines of marble to the south; and came on a cottage like a Highland one – for roughness of look – only the mountain path winding round beneath it, went under a roof of vines trellised from its eaves, and opened, before it entered the darkness of green leaves, into a golden threshing floor – the real 'area' of the Latins. That so few people passed that the people could make their threshing floor of the path, was the first deep prettiness of it. Then, they *had* been threshing and winnowing – the little level field was soft with chaff. The marble rocks, bright grey, came down steep into it, as at Loch Katrine the rocks into the water – below, on the other side, the hill went down steep to the blue plain of Lucca, itself (the hillside) one grove of olive, but, as I saw, without fruit, or nearly so.

I crossed the threshing floor, and met the peasant under his vines, looking pale and worn – the Lucchese 'Good even, Signoria,' given with more than usual gentleness. I said to him what I thought of his happy place, as well as I could. Yes, he said, but it was a 'very dry' country. 'The olives had no fruit this year – see – the berries had all fallen, withered for want of rain.' – For want of *water*, yes, I said – why don't you catch it on the hillside, before it runs to the Serchio and the sea? In short, I found him able to hear and think. He was actually building a cistern behind his house to catch the rain. 'From the *roof*!' (And the Roof from which he ought to receive it rose above him – 1500 feet of pure marble!) I had a long talk; I examined the place; and though I've to go to Florence to-day to hunt down St Dominic, if I don't come back to do a little bit of engineering beside that man's threshing floor, it will be – not my fault, God willing.

From a letter to Thomas Carlyle, 19 August 1874

¶ 63

THE GUILD OF ST GEORGE

For my own part, I entirely hate the whole business; I dislike having either power or responsibility; am ashamed to ask for money, and plagued in spending it. I don't want to talk, nor to write, nor to advise or direct anybody. I am far more provoked at being thought foolish by foolish people, than pleased at being thought sensible by sensible people; and the average proportion of the numbers of each is not to my advantage. If I could find anyone able to carry on the plan instead of me, I never should trouble myself about it more; and even now, it is only with extreme effort and chastisement of my indolence that I go on; but, unless I am struck with palsy, I do not seriously doubt my perseverance, until I find somebody able to take up the matter in the same mind, and with a better heart.

From *Fors Clavigera*, Letter xxxvii, § 10, 1 January 1874

¶ 64
DARWINISM

I got your happy letter to-day, but am a little provoked with you for talking nonsense about Darwinism, even in play. Of course you might just as well say that grass was green because the cows selected the flowers, or that moths were brown because sparrows catch the conspicuous ones. Nature shows and conceals exactly as she chooses. It is true that *we* have only sparrows because we shoot the kingfishers; but God makes gentians gay and lichens grave as it pleases Him, and by no other law, no other reason. Do you suppose a gnat escapes a trout because it is grey, and that dragon-flies are blue because salmon like red ones – if they do!

Also, I hope you will soon see that modern political economy is not a bore merely, but a lie, and one which it will be incumbent upon you to detect and proclaim.

From a letter to Dawtrey Drewitt,[1] 12 September 1874

¶ 65
ANTI-SCIENCE

Flowers, like everything else that is lovely in the visible world, are only to be seen rightly with the eyes which the God who made them gave us; and neither with microscopes nor spectacles. These have their uses for the curious and the aged; as stilts and crutches have for people who want to walk in mud, or cannot safely walk but on three legs anywhere. But in health of mind and body, men should see with their own eyes, hear and speak without trumpets, walk on their feet, not on wheels, and work and war with their arms, not with engine-beams, nor rifles warranted to kill twenty men at a shot before you can see them. The use of the great mechanical powers may indeed sometimes be compatible with the due exercise of our own; but the use of instruments for exaggerating the powers of sight necessarily deprives us of the best pleasures of sight. A flower is to be watched as it grows, in its association with

1. Dawtrey Drewitt, physician, was in his last year at Christ Church when Ruskin became Slade Professor. Ruskin was attracted by his love of natural history.

the earth, the air, and the dew; its leaves are to be seen as they expand in sunshine; its colours, as they embroider the field, or illumine the forest. Dissect or magnify them, and all you discover or learn at last will be that oaks, roses, and daisies, are all made of fibres and bubbles; and these again, of charcoal and water; but, for all their peeping and probing, nobody knows how.

From *Praeterita*, II, § 200

¶ 66
'THE OLD SHOWY STYLE'

I couldn't help touching up a bit in the old showy style this morning – it took me a while, too. 'Tide, that takes a year to rise; Cataract, that takes fifty to fall; River, that is ribbed like a dragon; and Rock, that is diffused like a lake!' Don't you tell anybody now!

From a letter to Mrs John Simon,[1] 14 October 1874

¶ 67
DEPRESSION

Instead of the drive with the poor over-laboured one horse through the long wet day, here, when I was a youth, my father and mother brought me, and let me sketch in the Abbey [at Bolton] and ramble in the woods as I chose, only demanding promise that I should not go near the Strid. Pleasant drives, with, on the whole, well paid and pleased drivers, never with over-burdened cattle; cheerful dinner or tea waiting for me always, on my return from solitary rambles. Everything right and good for me, except only that they never put me through any trials to harden me, or give me decision of character, or make me feel how much they did for me.

But that error was a fearful one, and cost them and me, Heaven only knows how much. And now, I walk to Strid, and Abbey, and everywhere, with the ghosts of the past days haunting me, and

---

1. Mrs John Simon, afterwards Lady Simon, first met Ruskin in Savoy in 1856 and became one of his most trusted friends. The 'bit' referred to is in a lecture on glaciers delivered at the Royal Institution in March 1875. (C. & W., Vol. XXVI, p. 163.)

other darker spirits of sorrow and remorse and wonder. Black spirits among the grey, all like a mist between me and the green woods. And I feel like a caterpillar, – stung *just enough*. Foul weather and mist enough, of quite a real kind besides. An hour's sunshine to-day, broken up speedily, and now veiled utterly.

From a letter to Miss Susan Beever, 24 January 1875

¶ 68

DISCIPLINE IN VENICE (1876)

It always seems to me that whenever I write a careful letter, people don't get it. I'm sure one or two long ones to you have been lost. However, I have yours, to-day, and sit down to tell you how my days pass. I wake as a matter of course, about half-past five, and get up and go out on my balcony in my nightgown to see if there's going to be a nice dawn.

That's the view I have from it – with the pretty traceried balcony of the Contarini Fasan next door. Generally there is a good dawn (nothing but sunshine and moonlight for the last month). At six I get up, and dress, with, occasionally, balcony interludes – but always get to my writing table at seven, where, by scolding and paying, I secure my punctual cup of coffee, and do a bit of the *Laws* of Plato to build the day on. I find Jowett's translation is good for nothing and shall do one myself, as I've intended these fifteen years.

At half-past seven the gondola is waiting and takes me to the bridge before St John and Paul, where I give an hour of my very best day's work to painting the school of Mark and vista of Canal to Murano. It's a great Canaletto view, and I'm painting it against him.

I am rowed back to breakfast at nine, and, till half-past ten, think over and write what little I can of my new fourth vol. of *Stones of Venice*. At half-past ten I go to the Academy, where I find Moore [1] at work; and we sit down to our picture together. They have been very good to me in the Academy, and have taken down St Ursula and given her to me all to myself in a locked room and perfect light. I'm painting a small carefully toned general copy of it for

1. C. H. Moore was a friend of Norton and succeeded him as Professor of Fine Arts in Harvard. He was introduced to Ruskin by Norton, and they spent much time together during the preparation of *St Mark's Rest*.

Oxford, and shall make a little note of it for you, and am drawing various parts larger.

I strike work at two or a little after – go home, read letters, and dine at three; lie on sofa and read any vicious book I can find to amuse me – to prevent St Ursula having it all her own way. Am greatly amused with the life of Casanova at present.

At half-past four, gondola again – I am floated, half asleep, to Murano – or the Armenians – or the San Giorgio in Alga – wake up, and make some little evening sketch, by way of diary. Then take oar myself, and row into the dark or moonlight.

Home at seven, well heated – quiet tea – after that, give audiences, if people want me; otherwise read Venetian history – if no imperative letters – and to bed at ten.

From a letter to Charles Eliot Norton, 5 October 1876

¶ 69

A DREAM

The second was of a preparation at Rome, in St Peter's (or a vast hall as large as St Peter's), for the exhibition of a religious drama. Part of the play was to be a scene in which demons were to appear in the sky; and the stage servants were arranging grey fictitious clouds, and painted fiends, for it, under the direction of the priests. There was a woman dressed in black, standing at the corner of the stage watching them, having a likeness in her face to one of my own dead friends; and I knew somehow that she was not that friend, but a spirit; and she made me understand, without speaking, that I was to watch, for the play would turn out other than the priests expected. And I waited; and when the scene came on, the clouds became real clouds, and the fiends real fiends, agitating them in slow quivering, wild and terrible, over the heads of the people and priests. I recollected distinctly, however, when I woke, only the figure of the black woman mocking the people, and of one priest in an agony of terror, with the sweat pouring from his brow, but violently scolding one of the stage servants for having failed in some ceremony, the omission of which, he thought, had given the devils their power.

From *Ariadne Fiorentina*, § 213

¶ 70
HIS MADNESS

It was utterly wonderful to me to find that I could go so heartily and headily mad; for you know I had been priding myself on my peculiar sanity! And it was more wonderful yet to find the madness made up into things so dreadful, out of things so trivial. One of the most provoking and disagreeable of the spectres was developed out of the firelight on my mahogany bed-post; and my fate, for all futurity, seemed continually to turn on the humour of dark personages who were materially nothing but the stains of damp on the ceiling. But the sorrowfullest part of the matter was, and is, that while my illness at Matlock encouraged me by all its dreams in after work, this one has done nothing but humiliate and terrify me; and leaves me nearly unable to speak any more except of the natures of stones and flowers.

From a letter to Thomas Carlyle, 23 June 1878

¶ 71
THE FAILURE OF DESIRE

I think one of my best mythological discoveries was that the Sirens were not pleasures, but *desires*, and part of the cheerfulness in which I now am able to live is in the accomplishment of that word upon me – 'Desire shall fail, because man goeth to his long home.' The taking away from me of all feverish hope, and the ceasing of all feverish effort, leaves me to enjoy, at least without grave drawback or disturbance, the Veronica blue, instead of the Forget-me-not, and above all, the investigation of any pretty natural problem, the ways of a wave, or the strength of a stem. With the persons whom I most loved, joy in the *beauty* of nature is virtually dead in me, but I can still interest myself in her doings.

From a letter to Dr John Brown,[1] 22 June 1879

1. Dr John Brown (1810–82), Edinburgh physician. Ruskin considered him the 'best and truest friend' of all his life. They first met in 1853 staying with Sir Walter and Lady Trevelyan at Wallington. Brown strongly disapproved of Ruskin's views on political economy, but their friendship survived.

¶ 72

LAST WORDS TO ROSE'S MOTHER

My dear Lacy,

What a beautifully written lava-flow of a letter! It's like a litho-graphed edition of the fleshly tables of the heart. Do you always growl and wowl as straight as that, or is it all written clear for me to read? When I have growling to do or to can't help, I write like that, [there follows a fierce scrawl] and get blacker and blacker all down the page, if it's a private letter. Public growling, one oils one's whiskers for, and stands upon one leg with the other disposed of in some stork or flamingo-like manner. By the way, Lacy – did you ever see the crested stork at the Zoo when anyone paid him a visit? I don't really mean to say anything nasty – but he did just now come into my head, and you should see him if you haven't – only let it be somebody else who's visiting him.

From a letter to Mrs La Touche,[1] 3 August 1881

¶ 73

IMPORTUNATE FRIENDS

I am better, but almost dead for want of sleep and fearful cough; and all my friends are throwing stones through my window, and dropping parcels down the chimney, and shrieking through the keyhole that they must and will see me instantly, and lying in wait for me if I want a breath of fresh air, to say their life depends on my instantly superintending the arrangements of their new Chapel, or Museum, or Model Lodging-house, or Gospel steam-engine. And I'm in such a fury at them all that I can scarcely eat.

From a letter to the Rev. J. P. Faunthorpe,[2] 3 March 1882

1. Mrs La Touche was, of course, the mother of Rose (see p. 8), who at first encouraged Ruskin, being herself in love with him, and afterwards prevented him from meeting or corresponding with her daughter. After the death of Rose (1875) he gradually resumed relations with her mother, although the letter suggests that they were not cordial.

2. The Rev. John Pincher Faunthorpe, principal of Whitelands Training College, had met Ruskin in connexion with St George's Guild. He later made himself useful to Ruskin by reading his proofs, compiling an index for Fors Clavigera, and revising an edition of The Queen of the Air.

¶ 74
THE MEISTERSINGERS

Of all the *bête*, clumsy, blundering, boggling, baboon-blooded stuff I ever saw on a human stage, that thing last night beat – as far as the story and acting went – and of all the affected, sapless, soulless, beginningless, endless, topless, bottomless, topsiturviest, tuneless, scrannelpipiest – tongs and boniest – doggrel of sounds I ever endured the deadliness of, that eternity of nothing was the deadliest, as far as its sound went. I never was so relieved, so far as I can remember, in my life, by the stopping of any sound – not excepting railroad whistles – as I was by the cessation of the cobbler's bellowing.

From a letter to Mrs Burne-Jones,[1] 30 June 1882

¶ 75
DR JOHNSON

I never for an instant compared Johnson to Scott, Pope, Byron, or any of the really great writers whom I loved. But I at once and for ever recognized in him a man entirely sincere, and infallibly wise in the view and estimate he gave of the common questions, business, and ways of the world. I valued his sentences not primarily because they were symmetrical, but because they were just, and clear; it is a method of judgement rarely used by the average public, who ask from an author always, in the first place, arguments in favour of their own opinions, in elegant terms; and are just as ready with their applause for a sentence of Macaulay's, which may have no more sense in it than a blot pinched between doubled paper, as to reject

1. Edward Burne-Jones, who was fourteen years younger than Ruskin, was first taken to see him by Rossetti in the autumn of 1856, and immediately became a devoted admirer. 'Oh! he is so good and kind – better than his books, which are the best books in the world.' He was further endeared to Ruskin when he married his enchanting young wife, Georgiana. They became very close friends and for a time Ruskin showed them great kindness, taking them with him to Italy as his guests in 1863. Later, when Burne-Jones became successful and independent, there was a coolness; but he maintained an uneasy friendship till the end. Ruskin had no ear for music, although he laid down the law on this, as on all other subjects.

one of Johnson's, telling against their own prejudice, – though its symmetry be as of thunder answering from two horizons.

From Praeterita, 1, § 251

¶ 76
RUSKIN'S STYLE

Although my readers say that I wrote then better than I write now, I cannot refer you to the passage [1] without asking you to pardon in it what I now hold to be the petulance and vulgarity of expression, disgracing the importance of the truth it contains. A little while ago, without displeasure, you permitted me to delay you by the account of a dispute on a matter of taste between my father and me, in which he was quietly and unavailingly right. It seems to me scarcely a day since, with boyish conceit, I resisted his wise entreaties that I would re-word this clause, and especially take out of it the description of a sea-wave as 'laying a great white table-cloth of foam' all the way to the shore. Now, after an interval of twenty years, I refer you to the passage, repentant and humble as far as regards its style, which people sometimes praised, but with absolute reassertion of the truth and value of its contents, which people always denied.

From Val d'Arno, Lecture VII, § 171

¶ 77
PROJECTS, (c. 1883)

The emotions of indignation, grief, controversial anxiety and vanity, or hopeless, and therefore uncontending, scorn, are all of them as deadly to the body as poisonous air or polluted water; and when I reflect how much of the active part of my past life has been spent in these states, – and that what may remain to me of life can never more be in any other, – I begin to ask myself, with somewhat pressing arithmetic, how much time is likely to be left me, at the age of fifty-six, to complete the various designs for which, until past fifty, I was merely collecting materials.

Of these materials, I have now enough by me for a most interest-

1. *The Stones of Venice*, Vol. 1, ch. xxx.

ing (in my own opinion) history of fifteenth-century Florentine art, in six octavo volumes; an analysis of the Attic art of the fifth century B.C., in three volumes; an exhaustive history of northern thirteenth-century art, in ten volumes; a life of Turner, with analysis of modern landscape art, in four volumes; a life of Walter Scott, with analysis of modern epic art, in seven volumes; a life of Xenophon, with analysis of the general principles of Education, in ten volumes; a commentary on Hesiod, with final analysis of the principles of Political Economy, in nine volumes; and a general description of the geology and botany of the Alps, in twenty-four volumes.

Of these works, though all carefully projected, and some already in progress, – yet, allowing for the duties of my Professorship, possibly continuing at Oxford, and for the increasing correspondence relating to *Fors Clavigera*, – it does not seem to me, even in my most sanguine moments, now probable that I shall live to effect such conclusion as would be satisfactory to me; and I think it will therefore be only prudent, however humiliating, to throw together at once, out of the heap of loose stones collected for this many-towered city which I am not able to finish, such fragments of good marble as may perchance be useful to future builders; and to clear away, out of sight, the lime and other rubbish which I meant for mortar.

From *Deucalion*, I, Introduction, §§ 1–3

¶ 78
GROWING OLD

Among the many discomforts of advancing age, which no one understands till he feels them, there is one which I seldom have heard complained of, and which, therefore, I find unexpectedly disagreeable. I knew, by report, that when I grew old I should most probably wish to be young again; and, very certainly, be ashamed of much that I had done, or omitted, in the active years of life. I was prepared for sorrow in the loss of friends by death; and for pain, in the loss of myself, by weakness or sickness. These, and many other minor calamities, I have been long accustomed to anticipate; and therefore to read, in preparation for them, the confessions of the weak, and the consolations of the wise.

But, as the time of rest, or of departure, approaches me, not only do many of the evils I had heard of, and prepared for, present themselves in more grievous shapes than I had expected; but one which I had scarcely ever heard of, torments me increasingly every hour.

I had understood it to be in the order of things that the aged should lament their vanishing life as an instrument they had never used, now to be taken away from them; but not as an instrument, only then perfectly tempered and sharpened, and snatched out of their hands at the instant they could have done some real service with it. Whereas, my own feeling, now, is that everything which has hitherto happened to me, or been done by me, whether well or ill, has been fitting me to take greater fortune more prudently, and do better work more thoroughly. And just when I seem to be coming out of school – very sorry to have been such a foolish boy, yet having taken a prize or two, and expecting to enter now upon some more serious business than cricket, – I am dismissed by the Master I hoped to serve, with a – 'That's all I want of you, sir.'

From *St Mark's Rest*, ch. XI, § 207

¶ 79
TO BE LEFT ALONE

With me, it is not grasping a thing, but letting it go, that does my brains mischief, and above all, I find it needful that henceforward I should decline endeavours to teach or advise, except through my books. The sense of responsibility involved in giving personal advice, and the time required to give it rightly, are entirely incompatible with any possibility for me of prolonged future work and life.

From *Notes by Mr Ruskin on His Own Handiwork Illustrative of Turner*, Part II (reference to example no. 20)

¶ 80
DISILLUSION

Morning breaks as I write, along those Coniston Fells, and the level mists, motionless, and grey beneath the rose of the moorlands, veil the lower woods, and the sleeping village, and the long lawns by the lake-shore.

Oh, that some one had but told me, in my youth, when all my heart seemed to be set on these colours and clouds, that appear for a little while and then vanish away, how little my love of them would serve me, when the silence of lawn and wood in the dews of morning should be completed; and all my thoughts should be of those whom, by neither, I was to meet more!

From *Notes by Mr Ruskin on His Drawings by the late J. M. W. Turner, R.A.*, Part I, Introduction

¶ 81

THE FIREFLIES OF FONTE BRANDA

Fonte Branda I last saw with Charles Norton, under the same arches where Dante saw it. We drank of it together, and walked together that evening on the hills above, where the fireflies among the scented thickets shone fitfully in the still undarkened air. *How* they shone! moving like fine-broken starlight through the purple leaves. How they shone! through the sunset that faded into thunderous night as I entered Siena three days before, the white edges of the mountainous clouds still lighted from the west, and the openly golden sky calm behind the Gate of Siena's heart, with its still golden words, 'Cor magis tibi Sena pandit,' and the fireflies everywhere in sky and cloud rising and falling, mixed with the lightning, and more intense than the stars.

From *Praeterita*, III, § 86

2

NATURE

A NOTE ON RUSKIN'S WRITINGS
ON NATURE

Ruskin approached art through nature. During the first half of his life he believed that nature – by which he meant the mountains, rocks, trees, plants, skies, and rivers of Western Europe – was a direct revelation of God's glory, designed for the edification of man; and that it should be interpreted as an expression of His Word. Nature could be read like a holy book, which it was his privilege to interpret. He often spoke of himself as nature's priest. In this he was to some extent the successor of Wordsworth, and a quotation from the *Excursion* was printed on the title page of each of the five volumes of *Modern Painters*.

> Accuse me not
> Of arrogance
> If, having walked with Nature,
> And offered, far as frailty would allow,
> My heart a daily sacrifice to Truth,
> I now affirm of Nature and of Truth,
> Whom I have served, that their Divinity
> Revolts, offended at the ways of men.

Wordsworth is not often as Ruskinian as this; and in fact Ruskin's admiration did not go very deep. As poets he preferred Scott and Byron, and even claimed that their descriptions of nature were more precise. His encyclopedic intelligence was not satisfied by Wordsworth's immediate delight, and his strict religious upbringing made it impossible for him to accept the pantheism of the Immortality ode, which he refers to as 'absurd'. As a child, however, he had responded to nature with almost Wordsworthian intensity. He says of his early journeys that 'whenever they brought me near hills, and in all mountain ground and scenery, I had a pleasure, as early as I can remember, and continuing till I was eighteen or twenty, infinitely greater than any which has been since possible to me in anything'. This is borne out by the extraordinarily vivid descriptions of nature in the diaries which he wrote at the age of sixteen, direct notations which were often the basis of famous passages in his later writings. The passage from *Deucalion* written in the 1870s, which I quote in no. 111, echoes almost exactly a note in the Journal of 1835, and shows how little Ruskin's fundamental sympathies changed. Both are concerned with mountain peaks, in mist, and throughout this selection it will be evident how greatly this experience affected him. Streams and flowers gave him pleasure, but clouds and mountains aroused in him an excitement bordering on delirium. Again and again they appear in his writings as the purest evidence of God's power; and he came to write on art largely because he felt that Turner, alone among painters, ancient or modern, was capable of seeing what he himself saw in these divine revelations.

The descriptions of nature, which he transferred from his notebooks to his final texts, show an amazing combination of accuracy and eloquence, and were the part of Ruskin's works most admired by his contemporaries. He himself did not greatly value them, perhaps because they came so easily. He wrote to his friend Miss Beever, who was compiling the selection from *Modern Painters* called *Frondes Agrestes*, 'It is the chief provocation of my life to be called a word painter instead of a thinker. I hope you haven't filled your book with descriptions.' He did, however, set much store by his disciplined observations of clouds, plants, and stones. He said that he bottled skies as carefully as his father bottled sherries, and it is true that his studies of clouds, both in drawings and words, show an almost incredible sharpness of detail. But in the end the clouds disappointed him, because, although he could bottle them, he could not use them as medicine. He could not explain them. When he returned to them in the fifth volume of *Modern Painters*, he says, most uncharacteristically, that the reader must work it out for himself, and some years later he consigned the inexplicable firmament to the hazards of mythology in a book called *The Queen of the Air*.

Plants were more rewarding, partly because they could be more easily classified, partly because their systems of growth seemed to illustrate certain laws. The descriptions of plant life in *Modern Painters* are not anthology pieces and have little interest out of their contexts, but they show his exceptionally keen powers of analysis, and the beautiful lucidity which often distinguishes his writings when he is not over-excited. Finally rocks, his first and last love, rocks large and small, varying from the Col de la Faucille to diamonds, opals, and amethysts. His travel diaries of 1835 are full of descriptions of quartz, gneiss, and jurassic limestone, and the fourth volume of *Modern Painters*, written at the height of his powers, is almost entirely taken up with the analysis of rock formations. Nowhere else in his works does Ruskin stick to the same subject for so long. He often said it was his chief regret that he had not written the Stones of Chamouni instead of *The Stones of Venice*, although *Modern Painters*, Vol. IV, probably contains all that he had to say on the subject, and his collection of papers on Geology, entitled *Deucalion*, is feeble and disorderly. He formed numerous collections of minerals, which he gave away to the people or institutions he loved. His greatest extravagance was the purchase of a perfect diamond which he later presented to the Natural History Museum. At the end of his life, when his mind had collapsed, the contemplation of his drawers full of minerals was his most certain source of comfort. What was it made him love them so much? Their permanence, their delicate veining, their magical colouring, an echo from the Book of Revelation; or simply the fact that they were inanimate? Whatever the reason, they excited him more than anything else, except little girls and moral laws – three obsessions which he managed to combine in the book called *The Ethics of the Dust*.

Ruskin's belief that nature was specially designed for the convenience of man is emphatically not for today. To us it is surprising that so clever a man could have believed anything as ridiculous. But we must remember that in his youth the doctrine of special creation was accepted without question. Scientists, no less than churchmen, wrote treatises on 'design in nature'. Darwin's *Origin of Species* did not appear till 1859, just after the last volume of *Modern Painters* had been completed. Ruskin rejected Darwinism, and criticized the theory of evolution, not without reason, on the same lines as Samuel Butler. But already in the fifties he had lost some of his confidence in his doctrine of convenient nature; and at the end of his great work he could write the beautiful invocation of humanism quoted in no. 310: 'Therefore it is that all the power of nature depends on subjection to the human soul. Man is the sun of the world; more than the real sun.'

This was probably written after 1858, the year in which Ruskin suffered an extraordinary change of heart. For the first time he was bored with mountains. 'To my great surprise I felt the top of St Gothard, snow, gentians, and all, neither more nor less than melancholy and dull.' [1] (The effect on his criticism of art is discussed on p. 130.) It was a sudden and violent conversion. The effect on his feeling for nature was more gradual. Of course, he returned to Switzerland again and again, and even thought of retiring there in 1861, after the attacks on *Unto this Last*. But, all the same, some vital link had snapped. Later, in the sixties, he began to complain that Switzerland had been 'defiled'. The light was 'umbered and faint', the water 'dimmed and foul' (no. 114). In the next few years this became an obsession to him, and in 1871 he wrote to Charles Eliot Norton: 'Of all the things that oppress me, this sense of the evil working of nature herself – my disgust at her barbarity – clumsiness – darkness – bitter mocking of herself – is the most desolating.' Just as it never occurred to him that the convenience of benevolent nature had been his personal interpretation, or, at least, a gloss on the gradual adaptation of man to his environment, so he firmly believed that in 1871 the weather really had changed. There was a lot of rain in France that year, resulting in floods, which delighted the eyes of

---

[1]. It is worth noting, however, that during his fits of depression Ruskin had often found himself unable to enjoy nature. Cf. entry in Journal of 27 January 1841, quoted in no. 17.

Monet, Sisley, and Pissarro. After that the weather seems to have been normal. But Ruskin was convinced that the change was fundamental, and in 1884 he gave, in the Royal Institution, two lectures called *The Storm Cloud of the Nineteenth Century*, illustrated with diagrams to prove his point.

This view of nature as a moral being, whether benevolent or evil, is illustrated in almost all his descriptions. Sometimes inanimate objects, clouds, or the pines are made to pronounce moral laws with a human voice (no. 84): absurd enough to us, who can hardly bring ourselves to treat the human biped as a moral being. But the laws which Ruskin deduced from his observation of nature, and applied by analogy to art and society, are by no means absurd. The socialized tree (no. 85) is a convincing symbol; the way in which an ounce of mud, by cooperation and quiet submission, is transformed into a sapphire, an opal, and a diamond (no. 103), is a parable more persuasive than many pages of economic argument. And it is from plants that Ruskin derives a doctrine which runs through all his thought, the Law of Help (no. 102). 'The power which causes the several portions of the plant to help each other, we call life . . . intensity of life is also intensity of helpfulness. . . . The ceasing of this help is what we call corruption.' I do not know how far modern science would confirm the evidence for this doctrine, which Ruskin discovered in nature: but I am certain that the law he deduced from it, when applied to art, society, and the life of the imagination, is of inestimable value.

We must remember that this marriage of natural science with morality was not peculiar to Ruskin. Before he was born, both Goethe and Coleridge made similar attempts. As an observer, Ruskin was probably superior to either. But he lacked Goethe's realism and Coleridge's grasp of philosophy; and in the end his encyclopedic urge produced something more like the *specula* of the Middle Ages than the dispassionate records on which nineteenth-century science was based. His later studies of birds and snakes in *Love's Mienie* and *Proserpina* are so packed with symbolism, and pass so mysteriously from observation to allegory, from etymology to free association, that we cease to know how much we are meant to believe, and how much is a kind of ritual play. Nowhere else are we more conscious of the medieval quality of Ruskin's mind.[1]

1. His medieval love of symbols, condensing different meanings and capable of varying interpretations, is responsible for the cryptic titles of his later books, which mystify and repel the modern reader.

THE WORLD PREPARED FOR MAN

We have seen that when the earth had to be prepared for the habitation of man, a veil, as it were, of intermediate being was spread between him and its darkness, in which were joined, in a subdued measure, the stability and insensibility of the earth, and the passion and perishing of mankind.

But the heavens, also, had to be prepared for his habitation.

Between their burning light, – their deep vacuity, and man, as between the earth's gloom of iron substance, and man, a veil had to be spread of intermediate being; – which should appease the unendurable glory to the level of human feebleness, and sign the changeless motion of the heavens with a semblance of human vicissitude.

Between the earth and man arose the leaf. Between the heaven and man came the cloud. His life being partly as the falling leaf, and partly as the flying vapour.

From *Modern Painters*, Vol. v, Part vii, ch. 1, § 1

¶ 83
THE PINE

Of the many marked adaptations of nature to the mind of man, it seems one of the most singular, that trees intended especially for the adornment of the wildest mountains should be in broad outline the most formal of trees. The vine, which is to be the companion of man, is waywardly docile in its growth, falling into festoons beside his cornfields, or roofing his garden-walks, or casting its shadow all summer upon his door. Associated always with the trimness of cultivation, it introduces all possible elements of sweet wildness. The pine, placed nearly always among scenes disordered and desolate, brings into them all possible elements of order and precision. Lowland trees may lean to this side and that, though it is but a meadow breeze that bends them, or a bank of cowslips from which their trunks lean aslope. But let storm and avalanche do their worst, and let the pine find only a ledge of vertical precipice to cling to, it will nevertheless grow straight. Thrust a rod from its last shoot down the stem; it shall point to the centre of the earth as long as the tree lives.

Also it may be well for lowland branches to reach hither and thither for what they need, and to take all kinds of irregular shape and extension. But the pine is trained to need nothing, and to endure everything. It is resolvedly whole, self-contained, desiring nothing but rightness, content with restricted completion. Tall or short, it will be straight. Small or large, it will be round. It may be permitted also to these soft lowland trees that they should make themselves gay with show of blossom, and glad with pretty charities of fruitfulness. We builders with the sword have harder work to do for man, and must do it in close-set troops. To stay the sliding of the mountain snows, which would bury him; to hold in divided drops, at our sword-points, the rain which would sweep away him and his treasure-fields; to nurse in shade among our brown fallen leaves the tricklings that feed the brooks in drought; to give massive shield against the winter wind, which shrieks through the bare branches of the plain: – such service must we do him stedfastly while we live. Our bodies, also, are at his service: softer than the bodies of other trees, though our toil is harder than theirs. Let him take them as pleases him, for his houses and ships. So also it may be well for these timid lowland trees to tremble with all their leaves, or turn their paleness to the sky, if but a rush of rain passes by them; or to let fall their leaves at last, sick and sere. But we pines must live carelessly amidst the wrath of clouds. We only wave our branches to and fro when the storm pleads with us, as men toss their arms in a dream.

From *Modern Painters*, Vol. v, Part vi, ch. ix, §§ 4–5

¶ 84

THE PINE AND NATIONAL CHARACTER

I have watched them in such scenes with the deeper interest, because of all trees they have hitherto had most influence on human character. The effect of other vegetation, however great, has been divided by mingled species; elm and oak in England, poplar in France, birch in Scotland, olive in Italy and Spain, share their power with inferior trees, and with all the changing charm of successive agriculture. But the tremendous unity of the pine absorbs and moulds the life of a race. The pine shadows rest upon a nation. The Northern peoples, century after century, lived under one or other of the two great powers of the Pine and the Sea, both infinite. They dwelt amidst the forests, as they wandered on the waves and saw no end, nor any other horizon; still the dark green trees, or the dark green waters, jagged the dawn with their fringe or their foam. And whatever elements of imagination, or of warrior strength, or of domestic justice, were brought down by the Norwegian and the Goth against the dissoluteness or degradation of the South of Europe, were taught them under the green roofs and wild penetralia of the pine.

From *Modern Painters*, Vol. v, Part vi, ch. ix, § 11

¶ 85
THE SOCIALIZED TREE

Liberty of each bough to seek its own livelihood and happiness according to its needs, by irregularities of action both in its play and its work, either stretching out to get its required nourishment from light and rain, by finding some sufficient breathing-place among the other branches, or knotting and gathering itself up to get strength for any load which its fruitful blossoms may lay upon it, and for any stress of its storm-tossed luxuriance of leaves; or playing hither and thither as the fitful sunshine may tempt its young shoots, in their undecided states of mind about their future life.

Imperative requirement of each bough to stop within certain limits, expressive of its kindly fellowship and fraternity with the boughs in its neighbourhood; and to work with them according to its power, magnitude, and state of health, to bring out the general perfectness of the great curve, and circumferent stateliness of the whole tree.

From *The Elements of Drawing*, Letter III, § 215

NOTE IN RUSKIN'S DIARY – 1846[1]

Champagnole, April 18— ... I have been walking in the woods beside the river on the ascent towards St Laurent, and I have never seen anything like the luxuriance of the wood anemone and oxalis; I think Shelley's 'pearled Arcturi of the earth' would apply better to the anemone than the daisy, for the star shape is seen more definitely at a little distance, and reminded me over and over again of constellations. The oxalis, is however, the more exquisite flower, two or three vertical and dark clefts in the limestone being filled with them as with snow, and touched with ivy besides, like the rock of Titian's St Jerome, ivy lighter and lovelier in leaf than ours, one wreath of it upon a pine trunk looking like vine; and the ground all blue with violets besides, and cowslips in sunny clusters, and wild strawberries, though these had only come into blossom on one high rock in the more open sunshine, and raspberries (these rarer) all on cushions of moss richer than I ever saw even among the Alps, with clusters of beech stem and ash – chiefly the latter, glittering among the solemn pine trunks; and in the more open ground the vetch and comfrey and mezereon, and a lovely four-petalled lilac flower in clusters on a long stalk, and the delicate blue flower that I found on the granite rocks of the Glacier des Bois, though this seemed not in a place of its liking. And when I got to the edge of the ravine, and an abrupt one it is enough (seen on the right in the dark sketch of yesterday in the little book), and commanded the steep and far ridges of the higher Jura, there was a hawk sailing slowly along the opposite cliff, just off the brow of it so as to get the deep river under him, and the solemn roar of the water came up from beneath, mixed with the singing of the thrushes among the pine branches. I felt it more than usual, but it struck me suddenly how utterly different the impression of such a scene would be, if it were in a strange land, and in one without history; how dear to the feeling is the pine of Switzerland compared to that of Canada. I have allowed too little weight to these deep sympathies, for I think if that pine forest had

1. This is the note or rough sketch from which the following entry (87) was composed.

been among the Alleghenys, or if the stream had been Niagara, I should only have looked at them with intense melancholy and desire for home.

From *The Seven Lamps of Architecture,* ch. VI, § I (note)

§ 87

NATURAL BEAUTY AND ASSOCIATION

Among the hours of his life to which the writer looks back with peculiar gratitude, as having been marked by more than ordinary fulness of joy or clearness of teaching, is one passed, now some years ago, near time of sunset, among the broken masses of pine forest which skirt the course of the Ain, above the village of Champagnole, in the Jura. It is a spot which has all the solemnity, with none of the savageness, of the Alps; where there is a sense of a great power beginning to be manifested in the earth, and of a deep and majestic concord in the rise of the long low lines of piny hills; the first utterance of those mighty mountain symphonies, soon to be more loudly lifted and wildly broken along the battlements of the Alps. But their strength is as yet restrained ; and the far reaching ridges of pastoral mountain succeed each other, like the long and sighing swell which moves over quiet water from some far off stormy sea. And there is a deep tenderness pervading that vast monotony. The destructive forces and the stern expression of the central ranges are alike withdrawn. No frost-ploughed, dust-encumbered paths of ancient glacier fret the soft Jura pastures; no splintered heaps of ruin break the fair ranks of her forest; no pale, defiled, or furious rivers send their rude and changeful ways among her rocks. Patiently, eddy by eddy, the clear green streams wind along their well-known beds; and under the dark quietness of the undisturbed pines, there spring up, year by year, such company of joyful flowers as I know not the like of among all the blessings of the earth. It was spring time, too; and all were coming forth in clusters crowded for very love; there was room enough for all, but they crushed their leaves into all manner of strange shapes only to be nearer each other. There was the wood anemone, star after star, closing every now and then into nebulae; and there was the oxalis, troop by troop, like virginal processions of the Mois de Marie, the dark vertical clefts in the limestone choked up with them as with heavy snow, and touched with ivy on the edges – ivy as light and lovely as the vine; and, ever and anon, a blue gush of violets, and cowslip bells in sunny places; and in the more open ground, the vetch, and comfrey, and mezereon, and the small sapphire buds of the Polygala Alpina, and the wild strawberry, just a blossom or two, all showered amidst the golden softness of deep, warm, amber-coloured moss. I came out presently on the edge of the ravine: the solemn murmur of its waters rose suddenly from beneath, mixed with the singing of the thrushes among the pine boughs; and, on the opposite side of the valley, walled all along as it was by grey cliffs of limestone, there was a hawk sailing slowly off their brow, touching them nearly with his wings, and with the shadows of the pines flickering upon his plumage from above; but with the fall of a hundred fathoms under his breast, and the curling pools of the green river gliding and glittering dizzily beneath him, their foam globes moving with him as he flew. It would be difficult to conceive a scene less dependent upon any other interest than that of its own secluded and serious beauty; but the writer well remembers the sudden blankness and chill which were cast upon it when he endeavoured, in order more strictly to arrive at the sources of its impressiveness, to imagine it, for a moment, a scene in some aboriginal forest of the New Continent. The flowers in an instant lost their light, the river its music; the hills became oppressively desolate; a heaviness in the boughs of the darkened forest showed how much of their former power had been dependent upon a life which was not theirs, how much of the glory of the imperishable, or continually renewed, creation is reflected from things more precious in their memories than it, in its renewing. Those ever springing flowers and ever flowing streams had been dyed by the deep colours of human endurance, valour and virtue; and the crests of the sable hills that rose against the evening sky received a deeper worship, because their far shadows fell eastward over the iron wall of Joux, and the four-square keep of Granson.

From *The Seven Lamps of Architecture*, ch. VI, § I

¶ 88
NATURE THE ARTIST

When a rock of any kind has lain for some time exposed to the weather, Nature finishes it in her own way; first, she takes wonderful pains about its forms, sculpturing it into exquisite variety of dint and dimple, and rounding or hollowing it into contours, which for fineness no human hand can follow; then she colours it; and every one of her touches of colour, instead of being a powder mixed with oil, is a minute forest of living trees, glorious in strength and beauty, and concealing wonders of structure.

From *Modern Painters*, Vol. III, Part IV, ch. IX, § 6

On the broken rocks of the foreground in the crystalline groups the mosses seem to set themselves consentfully and deliberately to the task of producing the most exquisite harmonies of colour in their power. They will not conceal the form of the rock, but will gather over it in little brown bosses, like small cushions of velvet made of mixed threads of dark ruby silk and gold, rounded over more subdued films of white and grey, with lightly crisped and curled edges like hoar frost on fallen leaves, and minute clusters of upright orange stalks with pointed caps, and fibres of deep green and gold, and faint purple passing into black, all woven together, and following with unimaginable fineness of gentle growth, the undulation of the stone they cherish, until it is charged with colour so that it can receive no more;[1] and instead of looking rugged, or cold, or stern, as anything that a rock is held to be at heart, it seems to be clothed with a soft, dark leopard skin, embroidered with arabesque of purple and silver.

From *Modern Painters*, Vol. IV, Part V, ch. XI, § 6

¶ 89
LIVE IN A CLOUD

Our whole happiness and power of energetic action depend upon our being able to breathe and live in the cloud; content to see it

1. Thus in all editions, although the sense would seem to demand 'or'.

opening here and closing there; rejoicing to catch, through the thinnest films of it, glimpses of stable and substantial things; but yet perceiving a nobleness even in the concealment, and rejoicing that the kindly veil is spread where the untempered light might have scorched us, or the infinite clearness wearied.

From *Modern Painters*, Vol. iv, Part v, ch. v, § 3

§ 90
CLOUD SHAPES

How is a cloud outlined? Granted whatever you choose to ask, concerning its material, or its aspect, its loftiness and luminousness, – how of its limitation? What hews it into a heap, or spins it into a web? Cold is usually shapeless, I suppose, extending over large spaces equally, or with gradual diminution. You cannot have, in the open air, angles, and wedges, and coils, and cliffs of cold. Yet the vapour stops suddenly, sharp and steep as a rock, or thrusts itself across the gates of heaven in likeness of a brazen bar; or braids itself in and out, and across and across, like a tissue of tapestry; or falls into ripples like sand; or into waving shreds and tongues, as fire. On what anvils and wheels is the vapour pointed, twisted, hammered, whirled, as the potter's clay? By what hands is the incense of the sea built up into domes of marble?

From *Modern Painters*, Vol. v, Part vii, ch. i, § 9

§ 91
RAIN IN THE MOSS-LANDS

Far away in the south the strong river Gods have all hasted, and gone down to the sea. Wasted and burning, white furnaces of blasting sand, their broad beds lie ghastly and bare; but here in the moss-lands, the soft wings of the Sea Angel droop still with dew, and the shadows of their plumes falter on the hills: strange laughings and glitterings of silver streamlets, born suddenly, and twined about the mossy heights in trickling tinsel, answering to them as they wave.

Nor are those wings colourless. We habitually think of the rain-cloud only as dark and grey; not knowing that we owe to it perhaps the fairest, though not the most dazzling of the hues of heaven. Often in our English mornings, the rain-clouds in the dawn form soft, level fields, which melt imperceptibly into the blue; or, when of less extent, gather into apparent bars, crossing the sheets of broader cloud above; and all these bathed throughout in an unspeakable light of pure rose-colour, and purple, and amber, and blue; not shining, but misty-soft; the barred masses, when seen nearer, composed of clusters or tresses of cloud, like floss silk looking as if each knot were a little swathe or sheaf of lighted rain. No clouds form such skies, none are so tender, various, inimitable. Turner himself never caught them. Correggio, putting out his whole strength, could have painted them, no other man. . . .

But the Angel of the Sea has also another message, – in the 'great rain of his strength,' rain of trial, sweeping away ill-set foundations. Then his robe is not spread softly over the whole heaven, as a veil, but sweeps back from his shoulders, ponderous, oblique, terrible – leaving his sword-arm free.

The approach of trial-storm, hurricane-storm, is indeed in its vast-ness as the clouds of the softer rain. But it is not slow nor horizontal, but swift and steep: swift with passion of ravenous winds; steep as slope of some dark hollowed hill. The fronting clouds come leaning forward, one thrusting the other aside, or on; impatient, ponderous, impendent, like globes of rock tossed of Titans – Ossa on Olympus – but hurled forward all, in one wave of cloud-lava – cloud whose throat is as a sepulchre. Fierce behind them rages the oblique wrath of the rain, white as ashes, dense as showers of driven steel; the pillars of it full of ghastly life; Rain-Furies, shrieking as they fly; – scourg-ing, as with whips of scorpions; – the earth ringing and trembling under them, heaven wailing wildly, the trees stooped blindly down, covering their faces, quivering in every leaf with horror, ruin of their branches flying by them like black stubble.

From *Modern Painters*, Vol. v, Part vii, ch. iv, §§ 5, 6, and 8

THE WEARY IMAGINATION

It [the imagination] is eminently a *weariable* faculty, eminently delicate, and incapable of bearing fatigue; so that if we give it too many objects at a time to employ itself upon, or very grand ones for a long time together, it fails under the effort, becomes jaded, exactly as the limbs do by bodily fatigue, and incapable of answering any farther appeal till it has had rest. . . .

I well recollect the walk on which I first found out this; it was on the winding road from Sallenches, sloping up the hills towards St Gervais, one cloudless Sunday afternoon. The road circles softly between bits of rocky bank and mounded pasture; little cottages and chapels gleaming out from among the trees at every turn. Behind me, some leagues in length, rose the jagged range of the mountains of the Réposoir; on the other side of the valley, the mass of the Aiguille de Varens, heaving its seven thousand feet of cliff into the air at a single effort, its gentle gift of waterfall, the Nant d'Arpenaz, like a pillar of cloud at its feet; Mont Blanc and all its aiguilles, one silver flame, in front of me; marvellous blocks of mossy granite and dark glades of pine around me; but I could enjoy nothing, and could not for a long while make out what was the matter with me, until at last I discovered that if I confined myself to one thing, – and that a little thing, – a tuft of moss, or a single crag at the top of the Varens, or a wreath or two of foam at the bottom of the Nant d'Arpenaz, I began to enjoy it directly, because then I had mind enough to put into the thing, and the enjoyment arose from the quantity of the imaginative energy I could bring to bear upon it; but when I looked at or thought of all together, moss, stones, Varens, Nant d'Arpenaz, and Mont Blanc, I had not mind enough to give to all, and none were of any value. The conclusion which would have been formed, upon this, by a German philosopher, would have been that the Mont Blanc *was* of no value; that he and his imagination only were of value; that the Mont Blanc, in fact, except so far as he was able to look at it, could not be considered as having any existence. But the only conclusion which occurred to me as reasonable under the circumstances (I have seen no ground for altering it since) was, that I was an exceedingly small creature, much tired, and, at the moment, not a little stupid, for whom a blade of grass, or a wreath of foam, was quite food enough and to spare, and that if I tried to take any more, I should make myself ill. Whereupon, associating myself fraternally with some ants, who were deeply interested in the conveyance of some small sticks over the road, and rather, as I think they generally are, in too great a hurry about it, I returned home in a little while with great contentment; thinking how well it was ordered that, as Mont Blanc and his pine forests could not be everywhere, nor all the world come to see them, the human mind, on the whole, should enjoy itself most surely, in an antlike manner, and be happy and busy with the bits of sticks and grains of crystal that fall in its way to be handled, in daily duty.

From *Modern Painters*, Vol. iii, Part iv, ch. x, §§ 14 and 15

¶ 93

THE SOUND OF SCOTTISH STREAMS

I know no other waters to be compared with them; – such streams can only exist under very subtle concurrence of rock and climate. There must be much soft rain, not (habitually) tearing the hills down with floods; and the rocks must break irregularly and jaggedly. Our English Yorkshire shales and limestones merely form – carpenter-like – tables and shelves for the rivers to drip and leap from; while the Cumberland and Welsh rocks break too boldly, and lose the multiplied chords of musical sound. Farther, the looselybreaking rock must contain hard pebbles, to give the level shore of white shingle, through which the brown water may stray wide, in rippling threads. The fords even of English rivers have given the names to half our prettiest towns and villages – (the difference between ford and bridge curiously – if one may let one's fancy loose for a moment – characterizing the difference between the baptism of literature, and the edification of mathematics, in our two great universities); but the pure crystal of the Scottish pebbles, giving the stream its gradations of amber to the edge, and the sound as of 'ravishing division to the lute,' make the Scottish fords the happiest pieces of all one's day walk.

From *Fors Clavigera*, Letter XXXII, August 1873, § 14

¶ 94
GRASS[1]

Consider a little what a depth there is in this great instinct of the human race. Gather a single blade of grass, and examine for a minute, quietly, its narrow sword-shaped strip of fluted green. Nothing, as it seems there, of notable goodness or beauty. A very little strength, and a very little tallness, and a few delicate long lines meeting in a point, – not a perfect point neither, but blunt and unfinished, by no means a creditable or apparently much cared-for example of Nature's workmanship; made, as it seems, only to be trodden on to-day, and to-morrow to be cast into the oven; and a little pale and hollow stalk, feeble and flaccid, leading down to the dull brown fibres of roots. And yet, think of it well, and judge whether of all the gorgeous flowers that beam in summer air, and of all strong and goodly trees, pleasant to the eyes or good for food, – stately palm and pine, strong ash and oak, scented citron, burdened vine, – there be any by man so deeply loved, by God so highly graced, as that narrow point of feeble green. . . . And well does it fulfil its mission. Consider what we owe merely to the meadow grass, to the covering of the dark ground by that glorious enamel, by the companies of these soft, and countless, and peaceful spears. The fields! Follow but forth for a little time the thoughts of all that we ought to recognize in those words. All spring and summer is in them, – the walks by silent, scented paths, – the rest in noonday heat, – the joy of herds and flocks, – the power of all shepherd life and meditation, – the life of sunlight upon the world, falling in emerald streaks, and failing in soft blue shadows, where else it would have struck upon the dark mould, or scorching dust, – pastures beside the pacing brooks, – soft banks and knolls of lowly

1. This was the passage quoted by Matthew Arnold as a good example of Ruskin's poetic prose. It is based on an entry in Ruskin's Journal made at Vevey, 3 June 1849 (quoted on p. xviii of Vol. V of *The Works of John Ruskin*, C. & W. ed.).

hills, – thymy slopes of down overlooked by the blue line of lifted sea, – crisp lawns all dim with early dew, or smooth in evening warmth of barred sunshine, dinted by happy feet, and softening in their fall the sound of loving voices: all these are summed in those simple words; and these are not all. We may not measure to the full the depth of this heavenly gift in our own land; though still, as we think of it longer, the infinite of that meadow sweetness, Shakspere's peculiar joy, would open on us more and more, yet we have it but in part. Go out, in the spring-time, among the meadows that slope from the shores of the Swiss lakes to the roots of their lower mountains. There, mingled with the taller gentians and the white narcissus, the grass grows deep and free; and as you follow the winding mountain paths, beneath arching boughs all veiled and dim with blossom, – paths that for ever droop and rise over the green banks and mounds sweeping down in scented undulation, steep to the blue water, studded here and there with new-mown heaps, filling all the air with fainter sweetness, – look up towards the higher hills, where the waves of everlasting green roll silently into their long inlets among the shadows of the pines; and we may, perhaps, at last know the meaning of those quiet words of the 147th Psalm, 'He maketh grass to grow upon the mountains.'

From *Modern Painters*, Vol. III, Part IV, ch. XIV, § 51

¶ 95

MOUNTAINS SUPERIOR TO PLAINS

Let the reader imagine, first, the appearance of the most varied plain of some richly cultivated country; let him imagine it dark with graceful woods, and soft with deepest pastures; let him fill the space of it, to the utmost horizon, with innumerable and changeful incidents of scenery and life; leading pleasant streamlets through its meadows, strewing clusters of cottages beside their banks, tracing sweet footpaths through its avenues, and animating its fields with happy flocks, and slow wandering spots of cattle; and when he has wearied himself with endless imagining, and left no space without some loveliness of its own, let him conceive all this great plain, with its infinite treasures of natural beauty and happy human life, gathered up in God's hands from one edge of the horizon to the other, like a woven garment; and shaken into deep falling folds, as the robes droop from a king's shoulders; all its bright rivers leaping into cataracts along the hollows of its fall, and all its forests rearing themselves aslant against its slopes, as a rider rears himself back when his horse plunges; and all its villages nestling themselves into the new windings of the glens; and all its pastures thrown into steep waves of greensward, dashed with dew along the edges of their folds, and sweeping down into endless slopes, with a cloud here and there lying quietly, half on the grass, half in the air; and he will have as yet, in all this lifted world, only the foundation of one of the great Alps. And whatever is lovely in the lowland scenery becomes lovelier in this change; the trees which grew heavily and stiffly from the level line of plain assume strange curves of strength and grace as they bend themselves against the mountain side; they breathe more freely, and toss their branches more carelessly as each climbs higher, looking to the clear light above the topmost leaves of its brother tree: the flowers which on the arable plain fell before the plough, now find out for themselves unapproachable places, where year by year they gather into happier fellowship, and fear no evil; and the streams which in the level land crept in dark eddies by unwholesome banks, now move in showers of silver, and are clothed with rainbows, and bring health and life wherever the glance of their waves can reach.

From *Modern Painters*, Vol. IV, Part V, ch. VII, § 4

¶ 96

MOUNTAINS

Mountains are to the rest of the body of the earth, what violent muscular action is to the body of man. The muscles and tendons of its anatomy are, in the mountain, brought out with force and convulsive energy, full of expression, passion, and strength; the plains and the lower hills are the repose and the effortless motion of the frame, when its muscles lie dormant and concealed beneath the lines of its beauty, yet ruling those lines in their every undulation. This, then, is the first grand principle of the truth of the earth. The spirit of the hills is action, that of the lowlands repose; and between these there is to be found every variety of motion and of rest, from the inactive plain, sleeping like the firmament, with cities for stars, to the fiery peaks, which, with heaving bosoms and exulting limbs, with the clouds drifting like hair from their bright foreheads, lift up their Titan hands to heaven, saying, 'I live for ever!'

From *Modern Painters*, Vol. I, Part II, Section IV, ch. I, § 3

¶ 97

USE OF MOUNTAINS IN CHANGING AIR

The second great use of mountains is to maintain a constant change in the currents and nature of the *air*. Such change would, of course, have been partly caused by differences in soils and vegetation, even if the earth had been level; but to a far less extent than it is now by the chains of hills, which, exposing on one side their masses of rock to the full heat of the sun (increased by the angle at which the rays strike on the slope), and on the other casting a soft shadow for leagues over the plains at their feet, divide the earth not only into districts, but into climates, and cause perpetual currents of air to traverse their passes, and ascend or descend their ravines, altering both the temperature and nature of the air as it passes, in a thousand different ways; moistening it with the spray of their waterfalls, sucking it down and beating it hither and thither in the pools of their torrents, closing it within clefts and caves, where the sunbeams never reach, till it is as cold as November mists, then sending it forth again to breathe softly across the slopes of velvet fields, or to be scorched among sunburnt shales and grassless crags; then drawing it back in moaning swirls through clefts of ice, and up into dewy wreaths above the snow-fields; then piercing it with strange electric darts and flashes of mountain fire, and tossing it high in fantastic storm-cloud, as the dried grass is tossed by the mower, only suffering it to depart at last, when chastened and pure, to refresh the faded air of the far-off plains.

From *Modern Painters*, Part v, ch. VII, § 8

THE PRECIPICE

Such precipices are among the most impressive as well as the most really dangerous of mountain ranges; in many spots inaccessible with safety either from below or from above; dark in colour, robed with everlasting mourning, for ever tottering like a great fortress shaken by war, fearful as much in their weakness as in their strength, and yet gathered after every fall into darker frowns and unhumiliated threatening; for ever incapable of comfort or of healing from herb or flower, nourishing no root in their crevices, touched by no hue of life on buttress or ledge, but, to the utmost, desolate; knowing no shaking of leaves in the wind, nor of grass beside the stream, – no motion but their own mortal shivering, the dreadful crumbling of atom from atom in their corrupting stones; knowing no sound of living voice or living tread, cheered neither by the kid's bleat nor the marmot's cry; haunted only by uninterrupted echoes from far off, wandering hither and thither, among their walls, unable to escape, and by the hiss of angry torrents, and sometimes the shriek of a bird that flits near the face of them, and sweeps frightened back from under their shadow into the gulph of air; and, sometimes, when the echo has fainted, and the wind has carried the sound of the torrent away, and the bird has vanished, and the mouldering stones are still for a little time, – a brown moth, opening and shutting its wings upon a grain of dust, may be the only thing that moves, or feels, in all the waste of weary precipice, darkening five thousand feet of the blue depth of heaven.

From *Modern Painters*, Vol. IV, Part V, ch. XVI, § 21

¶ 99

SLATY CRYSTALLINES

It is to be remembered that these are the rocks which, on the average, will be oftenest observed, and with the greatest interest, by the human race. The central granites are too far removed, the lower rocks too common, to be carefully studied; these slaty crystallines form the noblest hills that are easily accessible, and seem to be thus calculated especially to attract observation, and reward it. Well, we begin to examine them; and, first, we find a notable hardness in them, and a thorough boldness of general character, which make us regard them as very types of perfect rocks. They have nothing of the look of dried earth about them, nothing petty or limited in the display of their bulk. Where they are, they seem to form the world; no mere bank of a river here, or of a lane there, peeping out among the hedges or forests: but from the lowest valley to the highest clouds, all is theirs – one adamantine dominion and rigid authority of rock. We yield ourselves to the impression of their eternal, unconquerable stubbornness of strength, their mass seems the least yielding, least to be softened, or in anywise dealt with by external force, of all earthly substance. And, behold, as we look farther into it, it is all touched and troubled, like waves by a summer breeze; rippled, far more delicately than seas or lakes are rippled: they only undulate along their surfaces – this rock trembles through its every fibre, like the chords of an Eolian harp – like the stillest air of spring with the echoes of a child's voice. Into the heart of all those great mountains, through every tossing of their boundless crests, and deep beneath all their unfathomable defiles, flows that strange quivering of their substance. Other and weaker things seem to express their subjection to an Infinite power only by momentary terrors: as the weeds bow down before the feverish wind, and the sound of the going in the tops of the taller trees passes on before the clouds, and the fitful opening of pale spaces on the dark water, as if some invisible hand were casting dust abroad upon it, gives warning of the anger that is to come, we may well imagine that there is indeed a fear passing upon the grass, and leaves, and waters, at the presence of some great spirit commissioned to let the tempest loose; but the terror passes, and their sweet rest is perpetually restored to the pastures and the waves. Not so to the mountains. They, which at first seemed strengthened beyond the dread of any violence or change, are yet also ordained to bear upon them the symbol of a perpetual Fear: the tremor which fades from the soft lake and gliding river is sealed, to all eternity, upon the rock; and while things that pass visibly from birth to death may sometimes forget their feebleness, the mountains are made to possess a perpetual memorial of their infancy, – that infancy which the prophet saw in his vision: 'I beheld the earth, and lo, it was without form and void, and the heavens and they had no light. I beheld the mountains, and lo, they *trembled*; and all the hills *moved lightly*.'

From *Modern Painters*, Vol. IV, Part V, ch. IX, § 6

¶ 100
THE MAKING OF ROCKS

By what furnaces of fire the adamant was melted, and by what wheels of earthquake it was torn, and by what teeth of glacier and weight of sea-waves it was engraven and finished into its perfect form, we may perhaps hereafter endeavour to conjecture.

From *Modern Painters*, Vol. IV, Part V, ch. VII, § 2

¶ 101
ROCK CHANGES

It would occupy the time of a whole lecture if I entered into the confused relations of the words derived from lectus, liquidus, delinquo, diliquo, and deliquesco; and of the still more confused, but beautifully confused, (and enriched by confusion,) forms of idea, whether respecting morality or marble, arising out of the meanings of these words: the notions of a bed gathered or strewn for the rest, whether of rocks or men; of the various states of solidity and liquidity connected with strength, or with repose; and of the duty of staying quiet in a place, or under a law, and the mischief of leaving in, being all fastened in the minds of early builders, and of the genera- tions of men for whom they built, by the unescapable bearing of geological laws on their life; by the ease or difficulty of splitting rocks, by the variable consistency of the fragments split, by the innumerable questions occurring practically as to bedding and cleavage in every kind of stone, from tufo to granite, and by the unseemly or beautiful, destructive or protective, effects of decompo- sition. The same processes of time which cause your Oxford oolite to flake away like the leaves of a mouldering book only warm with a glow of perpetually deepening gold the marbles of Athens and

Verona; and the same laws of chemical change which reduce the granites of Dartmoor to porcelain clay bind the sand of Coventry into stone which can be built half-way to the sky.

From *Val d'Arno*, Lecture VI, § 152

¶ 102
THE LAW OF HELP

In substance which we call 'inanimate,' as of clouds, or stones, their atoms may cohere to each other, or consist with each other, but they do not help each other. The removal of one part does not injure the rest.

But in a plant, the taking away of any one part does injure the rest. Hurt or remove any portion of the sap, bark, or pith, the rest is injured. If any part enters into a state in which it no more assists the rest, and has thus become 'helpless,' we call it also 'dead.'

The power which causes the several portions of the plant to help each other, we call life. Much more is this so in an animal. We may take away the branch of a tree without much harm to it; but not the animal's limb. Thus, intensity of life is also intensity of helpfulness – completeness of depending of each part on all the rest. The ceasing of this help is what we call corruption; and in proportion to the perfectness of the help, is the dreadfulness of the loss. The more intense the life has been, the more terrible is its corruption.

From *Modern Painters*, Vol. V, Part VIII, ch. I, § 4

¶ 103
THE FORMATION OF GEMS

Let us suppose that this ounce of mud is left in perfect rest, and that its elements gather together, like to like, so that their atoms may get into the closest relations possible.

Let the clay begin. Ridding itself of all foreign substance, it gradually becomes a white earth, already very beautiful; and fit, with help of congealing fire, to be made into finest porcelain, and painted on, and be kept in kings' palaces. But such artificial consistence is not its best. Leave it still quiet to follow its own instinct of unity, and it becomes not only white, but clear; not only clear, but hard; nor only clear and hard, but so set that it can deal with light in a wonderful way, and gather out of it the loveliest blue rays only, refusing the rest. We call it then a sapphire.

Such being the consummation of the clay, we give similar permission of quiet to the sand. It also becomes, first, a white earth, then proceeds to grow clear and hard, and at last arranges itself in mysterious, infinitely fine parallel lines, which have the power of reflecting not merely the blue rays, but the blue, green, purple, and red rays in the greatest beauty in which they can be seen through any hard material whatsoever. We call it then an opal.

In next order the soot sets to work; it cannot make itself white at first, but instead of being discouraged, tries harder and harder, and comes out clear at last, and the hardest thing in the world; and for the blackness that it had, obtains in exchange the power of reflecting all the rays of the sun at once in the vividest blaze that any solid thing can shoot. We call it then a diamond.

Last of all the water purifies or unites itself, contented enough if it only reach the form of a dew-drop; but if we insist on its proceeding to a more perfect consistence, it crystallizes into the shape of a star.

And for the ounce of slime which we had by political economy of competition, we have by political economy of co-operation, a sapphire, an opal, and a diamond, set in the midst of a star of snow.

From *Modern Painters*, Vol. v, Part viii, ch. i, §§ 8–9

¶ 104
THE SERPENT

The dead hieroglyph may have meant this or that – the living hieroglyph means always the same; but remember, it is just as much a hieroglyph as the other; nay, more, – a 'sacred or reserved sculpture,' a thing with an inner language. The serpent crest of the king's crown, or of the god's, on the pillars of Egypt, is a mystery; but the serpent itself, gliding past the pillar's foot, is it less a mystery? Is there, indeed, no tongue, except the mute forked flash from its lips, in that running brook of horror on the ground?

Why that horror? We all feel it, yet how imaginative it is, how disproportioned to the real strength of the creature! There is more poison in an ill-kept drain, – in a pool of dish-washings at a cottage door, – than in the deadliest asp of Nile. Every back-yard which you look down into from the railway, as it carries you out by Vauxhall or Deptford, holds its coiled serpent: all the walls of those ghastly suburbs are enclosures of tank temples for serpent worship; yet you feel no horror in looking down into them, as you would if you saw the livid scales and lifted head. There is more venom, mortal, inevitable, in a single word sometimes, or in the gliding entrance of a wordless thought, than ever 'vanti Libia con sua rena.' But that horror is of the myth, not of the creature. There are myriads lower than this, and more loathsome, in the scale of being; the links between dead matter and animation drift everywhere unseen. But it is the strength of the base element that is so dreadful in the serpent; it is the very omnipotence of the earth. That rivulet of smooth silver – how does it flow, think you? It literally rows on the earth, with every scale for an oar; it bites the dust with the ridges of its body. Watch it, when it moves slowly: – A wave, but without wind! a current, but with no fall! all the body moving at the same instant, yet some of it to one side, some to another, or some forward, and the rest of the coil backwards; but all with the same calm will and equal way – no contraction, no extension; one soundless, causeless march of sequent rings, and spectral procession of spotted dust, with dissolution in its fangs, dislocation in its coils. Startle it; – the winding stream will become a twisted arrow; – the wave of poisoned life will lash through the grass like a cast lance. It scarcely breathes with its one lung (the other shrivelled and abortive); it is passive to the sun and shade, and is cold or hot like a stone; yet, 'it can outclimb the monkey, outswim the fish, outleap the jerboa, outwrestle the athlete, and crush the tiger.' It is a divine hierogylph of the demoniac power of the earth, – of the entire earthly nature. As the bird is the clothed power of the air, so this is the clothed power of the dust; as the bird the symbol of the spirit of life, so this of the grasp and sting of death.

From *The Queen of the Air*, Lecture II, §§ 67, 68, and 69

THE BULLFINCH'S NEST

The other day, as I was calling on the ornithologist whose collection of birds is, I suppose, altogether unrivalled in Europe, – (at once a monument of unwearied love of science, and an example, in its treatment, of the most delicate and patient art) – Mr Gould – he showed me the nest of a common English bird; a nest which, notwithstanding his knowledge of the dexterous building of birds in all the world, was not without interest even to him, and was altogether amazing and delightful to me. It was a bullfinch's nest, which had been set in the fork of a sapling tree, where it needed an extended foundation. And the bird had built this first story of her nest with withered stalks of clematis blossom; and with nothing else. These twigs it had interwoven lightly, leaving the branched heads all at the outside, producing an intricate Gothic boss of extreme grace and quaintness, apparently arranged both with triumphant pleasure in the art of basket-making, and with definite purpose of obtaining ornamental form.

I fear there is no occasion to tell you that the bird had no purpose of the kind. I say that I *fear* this, because I would much rather have to undeceive you in attributing too much intellect to the lower animals, than too little. But I suppose the only error which, in the present condition of natural history, you are likely to fall into, is that of supposing that a bullfinch is merely a mechanical arrangement of nervous fibre, covered with feathers by a chronic cutaneous eruption; and impelled by a galvanic stimulus to the collection of clematis.

You would be in much greater, as well as in a more shameful, error, in supposing this, than if you attributed to the bullfinch the most deliberate rivalship with Mr Street's prettiest Gothic designs. The bird has exactly the degree of emotion, the extent of science, and the command of art, which are necessary for its happiness; it had felt the clematis twigs to be lighter and tougher than any others within its reach, and probably found the forked branches of them convenient for reticulation. It had naturally placed these outside, because it wanted a smooth surface for the bottom of its nest; and the beauty of the result was more dependent on the blossoms than the bird.

Nevertheless, I am sure that if you had seen the nest, – much more, if you had stood beside the architect at work upon it, – you would have greatly desired to express your admiration to her; and that if Wordsworth, or any other simple and kindly person, could even wish, for a little flower's sake,

> 'That to this mountain daisy's self were known
> The Beauty of its star-shaped shadow, thrown
> On the smooth surface of this naked stone,'

much more you would have yearned to inform the bright little nest-builder of your sympathy; and to explain to her, on art principles, what a pretty thing she was making.

Does it never occur to you, then, that to some of the best and wisest artists among ourselves, it may not be always possible to explain what pretty things they are making; and that, perhaps, the very perfection of their art is in their knowing so little about it?

Whether it has occurred to you or not, I assure you that it is so. The greatest artists, indeed, will condescend, occasionally, to be scientific; – will labour, somewhat systematically, about what they are doing, as vulgar persons do; and are privileged, also, to enjoy what they have made more than birds do; yet seldom, observe you, as being beautiful, but very much in the sort of feeling which we may fancy the bullfinch had also, – that the thing, whether pretty or ugly, could not have been better done; that they could not have made it otherwise, and are thankful it is no worse.

From *The Eagle's Nest*, Lecture III, §§ 48–52

§ 106
BIRDS

But indeed, primarily, you have to consider whether the bird altogether may not be little more than a fat, cheerful little stomach, in a spotted waistcoat, and with legs to it. That is the main definition of a great many birds – meant to eat all day, chiefly, grubs, or grain – not at all, unless under wintry and calamitous conditions, meant to fast painfully, or be in concern about their food. Faultless in digestion – dinner lasting all day long, with the delight of social intercourse – various chirp and chatter. Flying or fluttering in a practical, not stately, manner: hopping and creeping intelligently. Sociable to man extremely, building and nestling and rustling about him, – prying and speculating, curiously watchful of him at his work, if likely to be profitable to themselves, or even sometimes in mere pitying sympathy, and wonder how such a wingless and beak-less creature can do *any*thing.

Love's Meinie, Lecture III, § 83

¶ 107
THE SWALLOW

It is an owl that has been trained by the Graces. It is a bat that loves the morning light. It is the aërial reflection of a dolphin. It is the tender domestication of a trout.

From *Love's Meinie*, Lecture II, § 62

¶ 108
THE WHARFE IN FLOOD

The black rain, much as I growled at it, has let me see Wharfe in flood; and I would have borne many days of prison to see that.

No one need go to the Alps to see wild water. Seldom, unless in the Rhine or Rhone themselves at their rapids, have I seen anything much grander. An Alpine stream, besides, nearly always has its bed full of loose stones, and becomes a series of humps and dumps of water wherever it is shallow; while the Wharfe swept round its curves of shore like a black Damascus sabre, coiled into eddies of steel. At the Strid, it had risen eight feet, vertical, since yesterday, sheeting the flat rocks with foam from side to side, while the treacherous mid-channel was filled with a succession of boiling domes of water, charged through and through with churning white, and rolling out into the broader stream, each like a vast sea wave bursting on a beach. There is something in the soft and comparatively unbroken slopes of these Yorkshire shales which must give the water a peculiar *sweeping* power, for I have seen Tay and Tummel and Ness, and many a big stream besides, savage enough, but I don't remember anything so grim as this.

From a letter to Miss Susan Beever, 24 January 1875

¶ 109

CYCLAMENS AT LUCCA

It will be quite worth while, if those policemen will let you, to come to Lucca next year to see those cyclamens. They are the common mountain flower which grows in autumn everywhere in nooks of limestone, but at Lucca it has fine marble for the nooks, and these terraces of turf as I said for recreation: and truly it is a new vision in flower-life to see it clustering and scattering along them in that purity of lilac light. The colchicum is very like it in distant effect on fields, but has a way of dog's-earing itself, and dropping its petals in a tired way, while the cyclamen will fade white without looking tired; and then its tidyness and trimness and toiletteness and shyness are so precious, when it's all itself. Then it's worth while to see the olives in full fruit. There is the same romance and marvel in them as in the vine, and besides a Puritan severity with their Quaker-dim leaf and dark berry which nobody gets drunk with, nor takes sixteen cups of, like coffee (all the same I couldn't get along myself without my coffee). And I'm simply *never* tired of looking at its shoots of leaf against the sky, and the turning of trunk that is the only thing in all the world that can be eccentric and graceful in the same instant, and fantastically serene.

From a letter to Mrs La Touche, 2 November 1882

¶ 110

CONTRASTED LANDSCAPE[1]

In the climates of Greece and Italy, the monotonous sunshine, burning away the deep colours of everything into white and grey, and

1. One of the latest (1883) examples of Ruskin's 'fine writing'.

wasting the strongest mountain-streams into threads among their shingle, alternates with the blue-fiery thunder-cloud, with sheets of flooding rain, and volleying musquetry of hail. But throughout all the wild uplands of the former Saxon kingdom of Northumbria, from Edwin's crag to Hilda's cliff, the wreaths of softly resting mist, and wandering to and fro of capricious shadows of clouds, and drooping swathes, or flying fringes, of the benignant western rain, cherish, on every moorland summit, the deep-fibred moss, – embalm the myrtle, – gild the asphodel, – enchant along the valleys the wild grace of their woods, and the green elf land of their meadows; and passing away, or melting into the translucent calm of mountain air, leave to the open sunshine a world with every creature ready to rejoice in its comfort, and every rock and flower reflecting new loveliness to its light.

From *The Art of England*, Lecture VI, § 167

¶ III
ARONA FROM THE SIMPLON[1]

The whole valley was full of absolutely impenetrable wreathed cloud, nearly all pure white, only the palest grey rounding the changeful domes of it; and beyond these domes of heavenly marble, the great Alps stood up against the blue, – not wholly clear, but clasped by, and intertwined with, translucent folds of mist, traceable, but no more traceable, than the thinnest veil drawn over St Catherine's or the Virgin's hair by Lippi or Luini; and rising as they were withdrawn from such investiture, into faint oriflammes, as if borne by an angel host far distant; the peaks themselves strewn with strange light, by snow fallen but that moment, – the glory shed upon them as the veil fled; – the intermittent waves of still gaining seas of light increasing upon them, as if on the first day of creation.

From *Deucalion*, Vol. I, ch. X, § 10

1. The lectures collected in *Deucalion* were written in the 1870s, and this is therefore one of the last examples of Ruskin's love of mountain peaks wreathed in cloud.

ALMOND BLOSSOM

The first joy of the year being in its snowdrops, the second, and cardinal one, was in the almond blossom, – every other garden and woodland gladness following from that in an unbroken order of kindling flower and shadowy leaf; and for many and many a year to come, – until, indeed, the whole of life became autumn to me, – my chief prayer for the kindness of heaven, in its flowerful seasons, was that the frost might not touch the almond blossom.

From *Praeterita*, Vol. I, ch. II, § 59

¶ 113
EVIL NATURE

There are many spots among the inferior ridges of the Alps, such as the Col de Ferret, the Col d'Anterne, and the associated ranges of the Buet, which, though commanding prospects of great nobleness, are themselves very nearly types of all that is most painful to the human mind. Vast wastes of mountain ground, covered here and there with dull grey grass or moss, but breaking continually into black banks of shattered slate, all glistening and sodden with slow tricklings of clogged, incapable streams; the snow water oozing through them in a cold sweat, and spreading itself in creeping stains among their dust; ever and anon a shaking here and there, and a handful or two of their particles or flakes trembling down, one sees not why, into more total dissolution; leaving a few jagged teeth, like the edges of knives eaten away by vinegar, projecting through the half-dislodged mass from the inner rock, keen enough to cut the hand or foot that rests on them, yet crumbling as they wound, and soon sinking again into the smooth, slippery, glutinous heap, looking like a beach of black scales of dead fish, cast ashore from a poisonous sea; and sloping away into foul ravines, branched down immeasurable slopes of barrenness, where the winds howl and wander continually, and the snow lies in wasted and sorrowful fields, covered with sooty dust, that collects in streaks and stains at the bottom of all its thawing ripples.

From *Modern Painters*, Part v, ch. x, § 4

¶ 114
SWITZERLAND DEFILED[1]

This first day of May, 1869, I am writing where my work was begun thirty-five years ago, within sight of the snows of the higher Alps. In that half of the permitted life of man, I have seen strange evil brought upon every scene that I best loved, or tried to make beloved by others. The light which once flushed those pale summits with its rose at dawn, and purple at sunset, is now umbered and faint; the air which once inlaid the clefts of all their golden crags with azure is now defiled with languid coils of smoke, belched from worse than volcanic fires; their very glacier waves are ebbing, and their snows fading, as if Hell had breathed on them; the waters that once sank at their feet into crystalline rest are now dimmed and foul, from deep to deep, and shore to shore. These are no careless words – they are accurately – horribly – true. I know what the Swiss lakes were; no pool of Alpine fountain at its source was clearer. This morning, on the Lake of Geneva, at half a mile from the beach, I could scarcely see my oar-blade a fathom deep.

From *The Queen of the Air*, Preface

¶ 115
LOSS OF FAITH IN NATURE

Of all the things that oppress me, this sense of the evil working of nature herself – my disgust at her barbarity – clumsiness – darkness – bitter mockery of herself – is the most desolating. I am very sorry for my old nurse, but her death is ten times more horrible to me because the sky and blossoms are Dead also.

From a letter to Charles Eliot Norton, 3 April 1871

1. This is almost the first appearance in print of Ruskin's obsession that nature had 'gone bad'.

Do you know, Susie, everything that has happened to me is *little* in comparison to the crushing and depressing effect on me, of what I learn day by day as I work on, of the cruelty and ghastliness of the *Nature* I used to think so divine?

From a letter to Miss Susan Beever, 21 January 1875

The deadliest of all things to me is my loss of faith in nature. No spring – no summer. Fog always, and the snow faded from the Alps.

From a letter to Charles Eliot Norton, 13 February 1875

¶ 116

ATHENA, MYTH OF THE AIR

The deep of air that surrounds the earth enters into union with the earth at its surface, and with its waters; so as to be the apparent cause of their ascending into life. First, it warms them, and shades, at once, staying the heat of the sun's rays in its own body, but warding their force with its clouds. It warms and cools at once, with traffic of balm and frost; so that the white wreaths are withdrawn from the field of the Swiss peasant by the glow of Libyan rock. It gives its own strength to the sea; forms and fills every cell of its foam; sustains the precipices, and designs the valleys of its waves; gives the gleam to their moving under the night, and the white fire to their plains under sunrise; lifts their voices along the rocks, bears above them the spray of birds, pencils through them the dimpling of unfooted sands. It gathers out of them a portion in the hollow of its hand: dyes, with that, the hills into dark blue, and their glaciers with dying rose; inlays with that, for sapphire, the dome in which it has to set the cloud; shapes out of that the heavenly flocks; divides them, numbers, cherishes, bears them on its bosom, calls them to their journeys, waits by their rest; feeds from them the brooks that cease not, and strews with them the dews that cease. It spins and weaves their fleece into wild tapestry, rends it, and renews; and flits and flames, and whispers, among the golden threads, thrilling them with a plectrum of strange fire that traverses them to and fro, and is enclosed in them like life.

It enters into the surface of the earth, subdues it, and falls together with it into fruitful dust, from which can be moulded flesh; it joins itself, in dew, to the substance of adamant; and becomes the green leaf out of the dry ground; it enters into the separated shapes of the earth it has tempered, commands the ebb and flow of the current of their life, fills their limbs with its own lightness, measures their existence by its indwelling pulse, moulds upon their lips the words by which one soul can be known to another; is to them the hearing of the ear, and the beating of the heart; and, passing away, leaves them to the peace that hears and moves no more.[1]

From *The Queen of the Air*, Lecture II, § 98

1. This extract shows a remarkable, and not altogether accidental, resemblance to certain notes by Leonardo da Vinci.

3
ART

A NOTE ON RUSKIN'S WRITINGS
ON ART AND ARCHITECTURE

Ruskin's first writing on art remained unpublished during his lifetime. It was a letter he wrote to *Blackwood's Magazine* at the age of sixteen attacking a reviewer who had written disrespectfully of Turner's extraordinary picture, *Juliet and Her Nurse*. Ruskin's father sent it to Turner, who asked that it should not be printed, and the manuscript was lost; but a copy has been found, and I have included an extract (no. 211), which not only anticipates many passages in *Modern Painters*, but has a touching resemblance to the last words Ruskin ever published, the closing sentences of *Praeterita*. In the following year he wrote five articles on the Poetry of Architecture, which appeared, significantly, in the *Magazine of Natural History*. Here, too, there are anticipations of *The Seven Lamps*, and we have the impression that, at the age of seventeen, Ruskin's mind was already at full strength. There followed one of his periods of depression, spent in travelling and sketching; and then in 1842 a further attack on Turner in the *Literary Gazette* revived his creative faculties. He described his state of mind as a 'black rage'; 'I saw injustice done and tried to remedy it. I heard falsehood taught, and was compelled to deny it. . . . I knew not how little or how much might come of the business, or whether I was fit for it.'[1] Ruskin at first intended to call his book *Turner and the Ancients*, but his publisher had little difficulty in persuading him to rename it *Modern Painters*: 'Their Superiority in the Art of Landscape Painting to all the Ancient Masters, proved by examples of The True, The Beautiful and The Intellectual, from the Works of Modern Artists, especially from those of J. M. W. Turner, Esq., R.A.'

Ruskin was twenty-two when he set about this formidable task. Characteristically, it had been taken up as the result of a passionate

1. Preface to *Modern Painters*, Vol. v.

enthusiasm; and, characteristically, he had not paused to consider whether he was 'fit for it'. In fact his only equipment for dealing with those eternal enigmas, the True, the Beautiful, and the Intellectual, was a slight acquaintance with Aristotle's *Ethics* and Locke's *Essay on the Human Understanding*. Of Kant, Hegel, and the other founders of modern aesthetics he was, and remained, totally ignorant. What was more to the point, he had no knowledge of the 'ancient masters' whose inferiority he had set out to prove. In his youthful travels he had not been interested in pictures, and he had to make good his ignorance by hasty visits to the National Gallery (then quite a small collection) and the gallery at Dulwich. His qualifications were an imaginative grasp of first principles, an inspired self-confidence, and an eloquence which delighted his contemporaries and remains astonishing, even, although it is not to our taste.

The first volume of *Modern Painters* was received with enthusiasm. Reviewers gave it unstinted praise,[1] and we know that among his fellow authors Wordsworth, Tennyson, Charlotte Brontë, and George Eliot, to name only the greatest, were deeply impressed by it. But Ruskin realized that it was defective both in experience and philosophy. He therefore began to look more attentively at 'the ancient masters', and in 1845 succeeded in making a journey abroad without his parents. At Lucca, in front of Jacopo della Quercia's tomb of Ilaria di Carretto, he 'received the revelation of Christian art'. The great figure artists of the early Renaissance now, rather inconveniently, shared with Turner the summit of his enthusiasm. The definition of Truth in the first volume of *Modern Painters* could not be made to include them, and he determined to write a second volume which should deal more systematically with Ideas of Beauty.[2] The result is not a success. Ruskin was bothered by abstractions, and although the effort of concentration involved in *Modern Painters*,

1. Except for the *Athenæum* and *Blackwood's Magazine*. The *Athenæum* describes the author of *Modern Painters* as 'a whirling dervish who at the end of his well-sustained reel falls, with a higher jump and a shriller shriek, into a fit'.

2. The references to fifteenth-century artists in the ordinary editions of *Modern Painters*, Vol. I, were added in the second edition, and in fact rather weaken its effect by complicating the argument.

Vol. 11, is perhaps the greatest he ever made, it restricted the use of his particular gifts, imaginative insight and sensitive perception. Moreover, he chose to write it in a style based on that of Hooker, which deadened his natural eloquence; until towards the end, when these self-appointed limitations become intolerable to him, and he celebrated, with passionate energy, his recent discovery of Tintoretto (nos. 203 and 204).

After the spell of illness which, with Ruskin, inevitably followed the completion of any piece of work, he once more turned his attention to architecture. He had already written of it as the expression of national character, and he now determined 'to show that certain right states of temper and moral feeling were the magic process by which all good architecture has been produced'. The result was *The Seven Lamps of Architecture*. His thesis was provocative and, for the most part, original.[1] Painting had long been judged by moral principles, but architecture was generally supposed to follow its own laws of 'firmness, commodity and delight'.[2] Of Ruskin's *Seven Lamps*, only two, Power and Beauty, were attributes previously associated with building. The lamps of Sacrifice, Truth, and Obedience were unequivocally moral. Ruskin came to dislike *The Seven Lamps*. He called it 'a wretched rant of a book'. It is true that the opening paragraphs are in his worst vein of Low Church oratory; but as he progresses the moralizing becomes less oppressive, and Ruskin begins to reveal his powers of analysis, which are even more remarkable when applied to architecture than to painting, because they are concentrated on form and design. The book also contains many profound observations; for example, his anticipation of functionalism (no. 235), and his first criticism of conventional materialism (no. 263).

1. *The Seven Lamps* was written in the winter of 1848. Pugin's *Contrasts*, which anticipates it at many points, was published in 1836. Ruskin never acknowledged any indebtedness to Pugin, and spoke of him with contempt, but the possibility of influence cannot be ruled out.

2. 'Well building hath three conditions, commoditie, firmnesse, and delight' – Sir Henry Wotton, quoting from Leon Battista Alberti, who adapted it from Vitruvius.

While still in the same mood, he decided to test his principles by applying them to a single school of architecture, and in 1850 began to write *The Stones of Venice*. This time he took pains to acquaint himself with the subject. He studied Venetian history from the original documents, he drew and measured every Gothic building of importance, and he even drew the profiles of every characteristic moulding. He was determined that his readers should go through the same process, and his first volume consists of a detailed examination of the methods of construction in Venetian architecture. One would suppose this to be the prelude to well-founded deductions. But in Ruskin's mind the accumulation of evidence and the power of generalization were, so to say, in separate compartments; and the second volume draws little of its strength from the first. It opens with two of the finest pieces of architectural evocation and analysis he ever wrote, the chapters on Torcello and St Mark's. Then follows the noble, though somewhat confusing, chapter 'On the Nature of Gothic', which is in effect his first plea for social reform; and the volume ends with his eulogy of Venetian Gothic, which was to have such a pervasive and, as he thought, disastrous influence.[1] By the time he came to write the third volume he had lost interest in his subject.[2] The best passages in the book are not about Venice at all, but about the place of sensibility in art (e.g. no. 122).

Meanwhile he had returned to the criticism of painting. As before, he was moved to do so by an article in *The Times* (May 1851) attacking the group of young painters calling themselves Pre-Raphaelites. He was unfamiliar with their work, but when he saw it found that their aims coincided with his own. They too believed in a detailed truth to nature and sought inspiration in Italian art of the fifteenth century. He did not entirely approve of their practice, and was continually lecturing them on faulty execution; but they

1. 'I have had indirect influence on nearly every cheap villa-builder between this and Bromley; and there is scarcely a public house near the Crystal Palace but sells its gin and bitters under pseudo-Venetian capitals, copied from the Church of the Madonna of Health' (letter of March 1872, C. & W., Vol. x, p. 458).

2. Letter to Samuel Rogers, 23 June 1852 (C. & W., Vol. xi, p. xxvi).

came nearer to his ideals than any other living painters, and for this reason he gave his next piece of writing on art the title of *Pre-Raphaelitism*. As a matter of fact it is not about the Pre-Raphaelites (and here the reader should be warned once and for all that the titles of Ruskin's books and lectures seldom gave any indication of their contents), but about Turner, J. F. Lewis, and social conditions. But the defence of the Pre-Raphaelites brought him back to the criticism of contemporary painting. No doubt he hoped to influence taste, but it is not certain that he did so. The successful Academicians feared that this eloquent intruder would affect their sales,[1] his own protégés, Millais, Holman Hunt, and Rossetti disregarded his advice (Madox Brown always disliked him) and second-raters, like the wretched Brett, who followed his instructions, were rewarded by a rap on the knuckles. Meanwhile the public continued to buy what was put in front of it at the annual bazaar.

Ruskin's comments on contemporary exhibitions, published as *Academy Notes* (1855-9) are his least distinguished pieces of writing. Not only was he limited by the provincial pettiness of his theme, but he was strangely unperceptive of modern painting. It is perhaps understandable that he never mentions Ingres or Delacroix; but almost incredible that the prophet of naturalistic landscape seems to have been unaware of Rousseau or Corot, and that the author of *Fors Clavigera* ignored Jean-François Millet. Instead he continued for twenty years to praise the work of a painter named Édouard Frère, who, he said, had 'the depth of Wordsworth, the grace of Reynolds and the holiness of Angelico'.

However, his preoccupation with living painters did have one valuable result. It introduced him to the richest and most vitalizing

1. *Punch* printed a 'Poem by a perfectly furious Academician':

> I takes and paints,
> Hears no complaints,
> And sells before I'm dry
> Till savage Ruskin
> He sticks his tusk in,
> Then nobody will buy.

I doubt if Ruskin had as much influence as the Academician supposed.

of his contemporaries, Dante Gabriel Rossetti. With Rossetti he taught painting in the Working Men's College, and this, coinciding with his growing recognition of social injustice, freed him from the priggish isolation of his youth. As an immediate result, he began to write more directly. The book called *The Elements of Drawing* and the lectures collected under the title *The Two Paths*, are almost without the preaching tone of *Modern Painters*. The former, in particular, contains clear, incisive criticisms (e.g. nos. 158 and 161) which could still be valuable to a painter. It is almost incredible that this was written at the same time as the *Academy Notes*. But in its own day it was overshadowed by the publication of two more volumes of *Modern Painters*.

Ruskin took up his great work again, largely at the instigation of his father. He had little fresh to say, and the subtitle of Part IV, *Of Many Things*, suggests that his purpose was by no means clear to him. On the theoretical side he was still anxious to reconcile his doctrine of absolute truth to nature with the need for idealization, which his love of Christian art made continually more apparent to him. This dilemma is re-examined in the early chapters of Part IV on 'Greatness of Style', 'The True Ideal', 'The Pathetic Fallacy'. From these hard questions he escapes with relief to a detailed analysis of nature, in particular of mountains. This occupies practically the whole of Part V; and the titles of the chapters – 'Compact Crystallines', 'Slaty Coherents', 'Lateral Ranges', etc., show how far he had moved from the study of painting. It is the culmination of that geological enthusiasm which had occupied him since his earliest travels.

But if there is no marked change in his point of view, Ruskin's range of experience and powers of expression had developed enormously. These volumes were written at the same date as *The Stones of Venice* and they show an equal mastery of language. The argument is not followed for long, but there is no confusion within the actual paragraphs. In the final volume, written between 1856 and 1859, lack of concentration becomes embarrassingly evident.

After a beautiful, but inconclusive, examination of clouds, he turns from one subject to another, making liberal use of biblical texts, as he always did when he was unsure of himself, and finally breaking into prophetic incantations, of which I give an example in no. 216.

It is sometimes supposed that Ruskin lost his mental balance as a result of the tribulations which overcame him in the 1860s. The last chapters of *Modern Painters* show him already moving in a world of private symbols and incomprehensible associations. However, they achieve a certain unity through the reappearance of Turner, the *primum mobile* of the whole work. Ruskin had spent much of 1856 cataloguing the Turner bequest in the National Gallery, and as a result had learned a great deal more about his hero than he knew, or would have cared to know,[1] in 1842. So the last chapters of Vol. v (no. 212), cloudy and chaotic as they are, come nearer to conveying the quality of Turner's genius than the polished descriptions of Vol. I.

During the years in which he was writing this volume of *Modern Painters*, Ruskin's views on art and artists suffered another serious disturbance. In July 1858 he suddenly grew tired of Alpine austerity. At Turin he was glad to exchange his rustic inns for the best hotel, 'a Parisian dinner and a pint of Moet champagne'. Next day he visited the gallery and was bowled over by Paolo Veronese's picture of Solomon and the Queen of Sheba. The process was completed by attending a dismal service in a Waldensian Chapel. The immediate result was communicated to his father in a letter (no. 186).

Ruskin was not a man to do things by halves. Having come to the conclusion that 'a good, stout, self-commanding animality is the stuff for poets and artists', he went on to develop the theory that a painter must be of necessity irreligious. The passage in which he did so was intended as an addition to *Modern Painters*, Vol. II, but,

1. I have never been able to find the source of the story, frequently repeated, that in course of his labours, Ruskin destroyed a number of Turner drawings which he considered obscene. It may well be true, as he persuaded Mr Ellis, the bookseller, to burn a fine copy of Goya's *Caprichos*. At all events, after 1856 Ruskin writes about him in a very different tone. Cf. nos. 213, 214, and 215.

not surprisingly, was never included. I give a large part of it (no. 168) because, although it is not one of his most distinguished pieces of prose, it shows Ruskin's fundamental honesty of spirit. No doubt he had been prepared for this change of heart by his friendship with Rossetti and his fuller knowledge of Turner. But as with his conversion by Ilaria di Carretto, it was his complete absorption in a single work of art, which precipitated what he called his 'deconversion'. He was later able to reconcile this position with his belief in the morality of art, by transferring the concept of morality from the individual artist to the general climate of belief in which he worked. But the fact remained that for twenty-five years he had been telling his readers to treat sensuality with abhorrence, and his change of heart caused him embarrassment. It may be one reason why for the next ten years he hardly wrote about art at all; the other reason being, of course, his misery and indignation at the thought of capitalist society, which I discuss elsewhere. By 1865 he could say in a lecture on *The Study of Architecture*, 'I am weary of all writing and speaking about art, and most of all my own.'

Of course he could not keep away from the subject altogether. His books of the sixties, although nominally concerned with economics, geology, mythology, science, and war, are full of reference to art, and in these years, the incidental art-criticism in *The Queen of the Air* or *The Cestus of Aglaia* is sometimes as vivid as that of *Modern Painters*.

In 1859 Ruskin's friends persuaded him to accept the newly created post of Slade Professor at the University of Oxford. Unfortunately his first course of lectures was not about art at all, but about religion, patriotism, and other general topics, and is in his homiletic style. On the other hand, his second course, entitled *Aratra Pentelici*, is almost entirely concerned with sculpture, and contains some of his finest criticism. I have drawn on it largely in the following section because in spite of some confusion, especially towards the end, it is one of the few of Ruskin's books on art which can still be read in its entirety. Thenceforward the quality of his

Oxford lectures declined. More than any of his works they suffer from his inability, or rather his unwillingness, to concentrate. Before a devoted, captive audience of young people he allowed every fancy that came to his head, every prejudice, every false etymology or misinterpreted myth, to come tumbling out in no conceivable order. These fantasies sometimes rise to a kind of poetry; but in the aggregate they fill the reader with a sense of frustration. They must have been even stranger when first delivered, for we know that they were largely extemporized and accompanied by strange gestures, dances, and occasional song. Such was his fame that no one dared to suggest that he had gone mad. But in February 1878 his mind gave way altogether, and he resigned. He came back for a second spell in 1882, but the lectures he gave show a sad decline in intellectual power. It is pitiful to find the prophet of Turner, Giotto, and Tintoretto expounding, in a lecture called 'Fairyland', the virtues of Kate Greenaway and Mrs Allingham. He resigned the professorship in 1884, nominally in protest against vivisection, actually because he knew that his mind was no longer serviceable.

This short summary of Ruskin's writings on art suggests that his thoughts on the subject changed considerably with time. Is it possible to find anything that can be called a theory of art underlying these changes? Several critics have tried to do so and, since one can discover almost anything one likes in Ruskin, they have produced systems which reflect their own idiosyncrasies. But a dispassionate reading of his works reveals deep-rooted inconsistencies and contradictions which cannot be smoothed out into a single system. Take, for example, the first, basic doctrine of *Modern Painters* that art involves absolute truth to nature. 'Every alteration in the features of nature has its origin either in powerless indolence or blind audacity.'[1] This famous sentence, in its context, is part of a refutation of the worn-out theory of ideal form, and as such was worth writing. Constable and Courbet would have agreed. But it owes its value to an acceptance of sensuous perception; and this the youthful

1. *Modern Painters*, Vol. II, Preface to second edition, § 18.

Ruskin could not allow. 'I wholly deny', he said, 'that the impressions of beauty are in any way sensual; they are neither sensual nor intellectual, but moral.'[1] This position he completely reversed, not only in his praise of the sensual artists mentioned above, but in many of his finest passages of criticism written before his 'deconversion'; for example [2] in Vol. III of *The Stones of Venice*, which opens with a paean of praise of feeling and perception as opposed to knowledge and intellect. Later he wrote most intelligently of the abstract element in art (no. 137), but this too he never troubled to relate to 'truth to nature'.

The fact is that Ruskin continually, and increasingly, found his dogmatic statements falsified by his experiences, and not being a philosopher, but a poet, he changed the definitions of his terms to suit the flow of his thought. On a single page of *The Seven Lamps* [3] he says (a) 'That all most lovely forms and thoughts are taken from natural objects'; (b) 'All beauty is founded on the laws of natural forms'; and (c) 'forms are not beautiful because they are copies from nature; only it is out of the power of man to conceive beauty without her aid'. These are obviously three very different propositions. The first is what he would have liked to believe, and allowed himself to say in moments of dogmatic impatience; the second is the result of thought and experience, and is a valuable working hypothesis; by the time he comes to the third he is already tired of the subject, and his mind has lost its grip. If we can find such variations of meaning in a single paragraph of one of his most carefully thought-out books, we should be wasting our time to look for a coherent system of aesthetics (two words he hated) in his works as a whole.

Ruskin's thoughts on art are valuable each on their own account, and in the form in which they came to him most vividly; and the more he tries to give them aphoristic shape, the less valuable they become. His distinction, in *Modern Painters*, Vol. II, between Typical and Vital Beauty is not very satisfying. But his account of how he

---

1. *Modern Painters*, Vol. II, ch. II, § 1. 2. *The Stones of Venice*, Vol. III, ch. II, § 10.
3. Ch. IV, § 3.

came to *feel* that Typical Beauty is an attribute of God (no. 117) is moving and convincing, as are his numerous descriptions of Vital Beauty in rocks or trees. His attempts to argue the moral character of art leave us unpersuaded, until we come to the beautiful comparison of a Persian miniature and Turner's watercolour of Geneva (no. 119): then we see in a flash what he was driving at. He himself came to realize that he could convey his meaning more forcibly by vivid example than by exposition. In *Aratra Pentelici*, instead of giving reasons why sculpture is rooted in the instinct of mimesis, he tells the story of the little girl with the pastry (no. 148) and adds, 'You may read the works of the gravest critics of art from end to end; but you will find, at last, they can give you no other true account of the spirit of sculpture than that it is an irresistible human instinct for the making of cats and mice, and other imitable living creatures, in such permanent form that one may play with the images at leisure.'

But although Ruskin's moments of insight into the nature of art cannot be made to form a logical system, and perhaps owe to this fact a part of their value, I believe that a certain number of them should be recognized as representing his most cherished beliefs; and these could be so arranged as to support the view that 'Ruskin's thought is driving all one way'.[1] I will set down some examples of beliefs which, on balance, I do not think Ruskin would have disowned, and which have a certain coherence. He believed:

1. That art is not a matter of taste, but involves the whole man. Whether in making or perceiving a work of art, we bring to bear on it feeling, intellect, morals, knowledge, memory, and every other human capacity, all focused in a flash on a single point. Aesthetic man is a concept as false and dehumanizing as economic man.

2. That even the most superior mind and the most powerful imagination must found itself on facts, which must be recognized for what they are. The imagination will often reshape them in a

1. Laurence Binyon in *Ruskin the Prophet*, ed. by J. Howard Whitehouse.

way which the prosaic mind cannot understand; but this recreation will be based on facts, not on formulas or illusions.

3. That these facts must be perceived by the senses, or felt; not learnt.

4. That the greatest artists and schools of art have believed it their duty to impart important truths, not only about the facts of vision, but about religion and the conduct of life.

5. That beauty of form is revealed in organisms which have developed perfectly according to their laws of growth, and so give, in his own words, 'the appearance of felicitous fulfilment of function'.

6. That this fulfilment of function depends on all parts of an organism cohering and cooperating. This was what he called the 'Law of Help', one of Ruskin's fundamental beliefs, extending from nature and art to society.

7. That good art is done with enjoyment. The artist must feel that, within certain reasonable limits, he is free, that he is wanted by society, and that the ideas he is asked to express are true and important.

8. That great art is the expression of epochs where people are united by a common faith and a common purpose, accept their laws, believe in their leaders, and take a serious view of human destiny.

In choosing these examples I have tried to avoid the danger of taking from Ruskin's works only those beliefs which suit present-day opinions. Several of them, notably nos. 4 and 8, are fairly remote from contemporary trains of thought, and even further from contemporary practice. By selecting other opinions, notably those on the abstract nature of sculpture or the independence of colour, one could give Ruskin a more contemporary look; but it would be misleading, as these are only observations, unexpected truths which suddenly present themselves to his penetrating mind, and not part of a central body of belief. Nevertheless it is in such unconnected flashes of insight that the value of Ruskin's criticism largely consists.

Ruskin's view of art has serious defects arising out of the limitations of his personal tastes. His responsiveness to what he called 'Vital Beauty' in natural organisms was accompanied by an almost equal lack of interest in abstract proportions. He had made up his mind that geometrical form was evil and organic form was virtuous, and could not bring himself to believe that one could be a symbolic statement of the other. This accounts for his blindness to the merits of classical architecture, and for the least acceptable of all his opinions, that architecture was only a frame for sculpture.[1]

In painting, his lack of interest in proportion made him indifferent to harmonious disposition of forms and areas: for example he never mentioned the work of Piero della Francesca, although two of Piero's masterpieces were in the National Gallery.[2] In his own day he was criticized for lack of interest in 'composition', a charge which irritated him and which he tried to refute by elaborate analysis of Turner's compositions. But Turner himself had a very insecure sense of proportion, so that Ruskin's analysis never got to the root of the matter. His lack of feeling for large relationships was connected with a passion for detail. He confessed that he had 'an idiosyncrasy which extremely wise people do not share, my love of all kinds of filigree and embroidery, from hoar frost to high cloud'. This comes out strongly in his own drawings, and it also affected his judgement of, for example, fifteenth-century Florentine art, leading him to admire the goldsmith tradition of Fra Filippo and Botticelli, rather than the monumental tradition of Masaccio.

Here another personal characteristic intervened: his fear and hatred of all forms of ugliness or deformity, which led him to shrink away from roughness, even when that roughness had the moral grandeur of Masaccio and Donatello. That Ruskin in his perambulations of Florence should have found nothing to say in

1. I do not know how far he was aware of the geometric basis of Gothic architecture, although in his time it had already been examined by Viollet-le-Duc.

2. *The Baptism* was purchased in 1861, *The Nativity* in 1874.

praise of Donatello's prophets on his precious Campanile is one of his strangest surprises for the modern reader. The other is his wilful blindness to Rembrandt, whose name is seldom mentioned without the epithet 'foul'. This prejudice, which started as a result of excessive sensibility, ended as a symptom of feeble-mindedness. At the end of his life he was able to digest only the whey and cornflakes of art, and the word 'pretty' occurs in every other sentence. His own theory of the moral basis of art could not have been more ironically illustrated than by his praise of Kate Greenaway.

But granted these limitations, Ruskin's achievement as a writer on art is immense, and has certainly not lost its value to us today. Even his most unfashionable doctrines are less remote from us than they seem at first. In his youth the criticism of art was dominated by two concepts: the barren and arbitrary concept of taste and the academic concept of ideal form. Ruskin's much-derided moral theory of art was part of an attempt to show that this human activity, which we value so highly, engaged the whole of human personality. His insistence on the sanctity of nature was part of an attempt to develop Goethe's intuition that form cannot be put together in the mind by an additive process, but is to be deduced from the laws of growth in living organisms, and their resistance to the elements. These two theories can accommodate the sculpture of Henry Moore in a way that theories based on 'taste' and 'ideal form' cannot, even when disguised in modern dress. The value he placed on perception and sensibility, as opposed to knowledge and intellect, has become a commonplace of post-Crocean aesthetics. His concept of art as the expression of society has also become a commonplace, although Ruskin could not have foreseen the wooden and doctrinaire manner in which it was to be developed by Marxist historians. In freeing art from the rule of taste and specialized skills he also made it possible for modern man to look with sympathy on the art of all ages, even the most primitive and remote, and, as a result of his teaching, the moving passage in which he foresees a new brotherhood of art (no. 199) has been accurately fulfilled.

THE MEANING OF THE WORD BEAUTIFUL

I was lying by this fountain – on a dark evening of July, dark not with night, but with storm. The precipice above me lost itself in the air within fifty feet of my head – not in cloud – but in the dark, motionless atmosphere. The lower boughs of its pines shook like black plumes against the shade; their pointed tops faded into its body – faint as if woven of gossamer – spectral shadows of colossal strength. The valley lay for leagues on either side – roofed with the impenetrable gloom – walled with the steep bases of its hill – one boundless chamber – lighted only as it seemed, by the white foam of the forked Arve – cast like a stream of lightning along its floor. Through the veil of cloud, the presence of the great mountains was indicated only by the sound of their forests, by the sharp, sudden stroke – like a human cry, – the wail of the glacier upon its path of pain, and the gust – rising by fits and falling – of the wind, or the waves, the ear knew not which – among their chasms.

So it had been through the day – no rain – no motion – no light. One roof – one level veil, as of God's Holy Place, and the voices of the mountains from behind it and above.

I lay beside the fountain – watching the motion of its soundless domes, and the entangling within its depth of the green blades with their own shadows. From the rock above, a single oozy drop fell at intervals into the pool, with a sound like that of a passing bell far away. Among the thick herbage at its edge the grasshoppers, heavy and faint in the chill and darkness, climbed freely up the jointed stalks, staring about them with their black beaded eyes, and fell, rustling, – unable to lift their scarlet wings. It was as if the sun had been taken away from the world, and the life of the earth were ebbing away, groan by groan.

Suddenly, there came in the direction of Dome du Goûter a crash – of prolonged thunder; and when I looked up, I saw the cloud cloven, as it were by the avalanche itself, whose white stream came bounding down the eastern slope of the mountain, like slow lightning. The vapour parted before its fall, pierced by the whirlwind of its motion; the gap widened, the dark shade melted away on either side; and, like a risen spirit casting off its garment of corruption, and flushed with eternity of life, the Aiguilles of the south broke through the black foam of the storm clouds. One by one, pyramid above pyramid, the mighty range of its companions shot off their shrouds, and took to themselves their glory – all fire – no shade – no dimness. Spire of ice – dome of snow – wedge of rock – *all* fire in the light of the sunset, sank into the hollows of the crags – and pierced through the prisms of the glaciers, and dwelt within them – as it does in clouds. The ponderous storm writhed and moaned beneath them, the forests wailed and waved in the evening wind, the steep river flashed and leaped along the valley; but the mighty pyramids stood calmly – in the very heart of the high heaven – a celestial city with walls of amethyst and gates of gold – filled with the light and clothed with the Peace of God. And then I learned – what till then I had not known – the real meaning of the word Beautiful. With all that I had ever seen before – there had come mingled the associations of humanity – the exertion of human power – the action of human mind. The image of self had not been effaced in that of God. It was then only beneath those glorious hills that I learned how thought itself may become ignoble and energy itself become base – when compared with the absorption of soul and spirit – the prostration of all power – and the cessation of all will – before, and in the Presence of, the manifested Deity. It was then only that I understood that to become nothing might be to become more than Man; – how without desire – without memory – without sense even of existence – the very sense of its own lost perception of a mightier – the immortal soul might be held for ever – impotent as a leaf – yet greater than tongue can tell – wrapt in the one contemplation of the Infinite God.[1]

From *Modern Painters*, Vol. ii, Appendix i (C. & W., p. 363)

1. This is the draft of an introduction to *Modern Painters*, Vol. ii, which Ruskin never used owing to his unfortunate desire to make the volume more systematic. The original punctuation, or lack of it, has been retained. All Ruskin's early works were written in this way, and the punctuation was sorted out by his old friend W. H. Harrison.

ART IS NOT PLAY

The end of Art is as serious as that of all other beautiful things – of the blue sky and the green grass, and the clouds and the dew. They are either useless, or they are of much deeper function than giving amusement. Whatever delight we take in them, be it less or more, is not the delight we take in play, or receive from momentary surprise. It might be a matter of some metaphysical difficulty to define the two kinds of pleasure, but it is perfectly easy for any of us to feel that there *is* generic difference between the delight we have in seeing a comedy and in watching a sunrise. Not but that there is a kind of Divina Commedia, – a dramatic change and power, – in all beautiful things: the joy of surprise and incident mingles in music, painting, architecture, and natural beauty itself, in an ennobled and enduring manner, with the perfectness of eternal hue and form. But whenever the desire of change becomes principal; whenever we care only for new tunes, and new pictures, and new scenes, all power of enjoying Nature or Art is so far perished from us: and a child's love of toys has taken its place.

From *The Cestus of Aglaia*, ch. VIII, § 99

¶ 119

PERSIAN MANUSCRIPT AND TURNER DRAWING

At this moment there is open beside me as I write, a page of Persian manuscript, wrought with wreathed azure and gold, and soft green, and violet, and ruby and scarlet, into one field of pure resplendence. It is wrought to delight the eyes only; and it does delight them; and the man who did it assuredly had eyes in his head; but not much more. It is not didactic art, but its author was happy: and it will do the good, and the harm, that mere pleasure can do. But, opposite me, is an early Turner drawing of the lake of Geneva, taken about two miles from Geneva, on the Lausanne road, with Mont Blanc in the distance. The old city is seen lying beyond the waveless waters, veiled with a sweet misty veil of Athena's weaving:

a faint light of morning, peaceful exceedingly, and almost colour-less, shed from behind the Voirons, increases into soft amber along the slope of the Salève, and is just seen, and no more, on the fair warm fields of its summit, between the folds of a white cloud that rests upon the grass, but rises, high and towerlike, into the zenith of dawn above.

There is not as much colour in that low amber light upon the hill-side as there is in the palest dead leaf. The lake is not blue, but grey in mist, passing into deep shadow beneath the Voirons' pines; a few dark clusters of leaves, a single white flower – scarcely seen – are all the gladness given to the rocks of the shore. One of the ruby spots of the eastern manuscript would give colour enough for all the red that is in Turner's entire drawing. For the mere pleasure of the eye, there is not so much in all those lines of his, throughout the entire landscape, as in half an inch square of the Persian's page. What made him take pleasure in the low colour that is only like the brown of a dead leaf? in the cold grey of dawn – in the one white flower among the rocks – in these – and no more than these?

He took pleasure in them because he had been bred among English fields and hills; because the gentleness of a great race was in his heart, and its power of thought in his brain; because he knew the stories of the Alps, and of the cities at their feet; because he had read the Homeric legends of the clouds, and beheld the gods of dawn, and the givers of dew to the fields; because he knew the faces of the crags, and the imagery of the passionate mountains, as a man knows the face of his friend; because he had in him the wonder and sorrow concerning life and death which are the inheritance of the Gothic soul from the days of its first sea kings; and also the com-passion and the joy that are woven into the innermost fabric of every great imaginative spirit, born now in countries that have lived by the Christian faith with any courage or truth. And the picture contains also, for us, just this which its maker had in him to give; and can convey it to us, just so far as we are of the temper in which it must be received. It is didactic, if we are worthy to be taught, not otherwise. The pure heart, it will make more pure; the thoughtful, more thoughtful. It has in it no words for the reckless or the base.

As I myself look at it, there is no fault or folly of my life, – and both have been many and great, – that does not rise up against me, and take away my joy, and shorten my power of possession, of sight, of understanding. And every past effort of my life, every gleam of rightness or good in it, is with me now, to help me in my grasp of this art, and its vision. So far as I can rejoice in, or interpret either, my power is owing to what of right there is in me. I dare to say it, that, because throughout all my life I have desired good, and not evil; because I have been kind to many; have wished to be kind to all; have wilfully injured none; and because I have loved much, and not selfishly; – therefore, the morning light is yet visible to me on those hills, and you, who read, may trust my thought and word in such work as I have to do for you; and you will be glad afterwards that you have trusted them.

From *The Queen of the Air*, Lecture III, §§ 108–10

¶ 120
ART AND LIFE

There is nothing that I tell you with more eager desire that you should believe . . . than this, that you never will love art well, till you love what she mirrors better.

From *The Eagle's Nest*, Lecture III, § 41

¶ 121
THE ANALOGY OF ART AND MORALS

What grace of manner and refinement of habit are in society, grace of line and refinement of form are in the association of visible objects. What advantage or harm there may be in sharpness, ruggedness, or quaintness in the dealings or conversations of men; precisely that relative degree of advantage or harm there is in them as elements of pictorial composition. What power is in liberty or relaxation to strengthen or relieve human souls; that power, precisely in the same relative degree, play and laxity of line have to strengthen or refresh the expression of a picture. And what goodness or greatness we can conceive to arise in companies of men, from

141

chastity of thought, regularity of life, simplicity of custom, and balance of authority; precisely that kind of goodness and greatness may be given to a picture by the purity of its colour, the severity of its forms, and the symmetry of its masses.

You need not be in the least afraid of pushing these analogies too far. They cannot be pushed too far; they are so precise and complete, that the farther you pursue them, the clearer, the more certain, the more useful you will find them. They will not fail you in one particular, or in any direction of enquiry. There is no moral vice, no moral virtue, which has not its *precise* prototype in the art of painting; so that you may at your will illustrate the moral habit by the art, or the art by the moral habit. Affection and discord, fretfulness and quietness, feebleness and firmness, luxury and purity, pride and modesty, and all other such habits, and every conceivable modification and mingling of them, may be illustrated, with mathematical exactness, by conditions of line and colour; and not merely these definable vices and virtues, but also every conceivable shade of human character and passion, from the righteous or unrighteous majesty of the king to the innocent or faultful simplicity of the shepherd boy.

From *The Elements of Drawing*, §§ 134–5

¶ 122

A SEEING AND FEELING CREATURE

The whole function of the artist in the world is to be a seeing and feeling creature; to be an instrument of such tenderness and sensitiveness, that no shadow, no hue, no line, no instantaneous and evanescent expression of the visible things around him, nor any of the emotions which they are capable of conveying to the spirit which has been given him, shall either be left unrecorded, or fade from the book of record. It is not his business either to think, to judge, to argue, or to know. His place is neither in the closet, nor on the bench, nor at the bar, nor in the library. They are for other men, and other work. He may think, in a by-way; reason, now and then, when he has nothing better to do; know, such fragments of knowledge as he can gather without stooping, or reach without pains;

but none of these things are to be his care. The work of his life is to be two-fold only; to see, to feel.

From *The Stones of Venice*, Vol. III, ch. II, § 10

¶ 123

THE NATURE OF THE IMAGINATIVE MIND

Imagine all that any of these men had seen or heard in the whole course of their lives, laid up accurately in their memories as in vast storehouses, extending, with the poets, even to the slightest intonations of syllables heard in the beginning of their lives, and with the painters, down to minute folds of drapery, and shapes of leaves or stones; and over all this unindexed and immeasurable mass of treasure, the imagination brooding and wandering, but dream-gifted, so as to summon at any moment exactly such groups of ideas as shall justly fit each other: this I conceive to be the real nature of the imaginative mind, and this, I believe, it would be oftener explained to us as being, by the men themselves who possess it, but that they have no idea what the state of other persons' minds is in comparison; they suppose every one remembers all that he has seen in the same way, and do not understand how it happens that they alone can produce good drawings or great thoughts.

From *Modern Painters*, Vol. IV, Part V, ch. II, § 17

¶ 124

PERCEPTION

Whatever can be measured and handled, dissected and demonstrated, – in a word, whatever is of the body only, – that the schools of knowledge do resolutely and courageously possess themselves of, and portray. But whatever is immeasurable, intangible, indivisible, and of the spirit, that the schools of knowledge do as certainly lose, and blot out of their sight: that is to say, all that is worth art's possessing or recording at all; for whatever can be arrested, measured, and systematized, we can contemplate as much as we will in Nature herself. But what we want art to do for us is to stay what is fleeting, and to enlighten what is incomprehensible, to incorporate the things that have no measure, and immortalize the things that have no duration. The dimly seen, momentary glance, the flitting shadow of faint emotion, the imperfect lines of fading thought, and all that by and through such things as these is recorded on the features of man, and all that in man's person and actions, and in the great natural world, is infinite and wonderful; having in it that spirit and power which man may witness, but not weigh; conceive, but not comprehend; love, but not limit; and imagine, but not define; – this, the beginning and the end of the aim of all noble art, we have, in the ancient art, by perception; and we have *not*, in the newer art, by knowledge.

From *The Stones of Venice*, Vol. III, ch. II, § 23

¶ 125

THE ABSTRACT ELEMENT IN ART

We are to remember, in the first place, that the arrangement of colours and lines is an art analogous to the composition of music, and entirely independent of the representation of facts. Good colouring does not necessarily convey the image of anything but itself. It consists in certain proportions and arrangements of rays of light, but not in likenesses to anything. A few touches of certain greys and purples laid by a master's hand on white paper will be good colouring; as more touches are added beside them, we may find out that they were intended to represent a dove's neck, and we may praise, as the drawing advances, the perfect imitation of the dove's neck. But the good colouring does not consist in that imitation, but in the abstract qualities and relations of the grey and purple.

In like manner, as soon as a great sculptor begins to shape his work out of the block, we shall see that its lines are nobly arranged, and of noble character. We may not have the slightest idea for what the forms are intended, whether they are of man or beast, of vegetation or drapery. Their likeness to anything does not affect their nobleness. They are magnificent forms, and that is all we need care to know of them, in order to say whether the workman is a good or bad sculptor.

From *The Stones of Venice*, Vol. II, ch. VI, § 42

¶ 126

THE WHOLE CREATURE

We have just seen that all great art is the work of the whole living creature, body and soul, and chiefly of the soul. But it is not only *the work* of the whole creature, it likewise *addresses* the whole creature. That in which the perfect being speaks must also have the perfect being to listen. I am not to spend my utmost spirit, and give all my strength and life to my work, while you, spectator or hearer, will give me only the attention of half your soul. You must be all mine, as I am all yours; it is the only condition on which we can meet each other. All your faculties, all that is in you of greatest and best, must be awake in you, or I have no reward. The painter is not to cast the entire treasure of his human nature into his labour merely to please a part of the beholder: not merely to delight his senses, not merely to amuse his fancy, not merely to beguile him into emotion, not merely to lead him into thought; but to do *all* this. Senses, fancy, feeling, reason, the whole of the beholding spirit, must be stilled in attention or stirred with delight; else the labouring spirit has not done its work well.

From *The Stones of Venice*, Vol. III, ch. IV, § 21

¶ 127

DELIGHT AND PURPOSE

No Venetian painter ever worked with any aim beyond that of delighting the eye, or expressing fancies agreeable to himself or flattering to his nation. They could not be either, unless they were religious. But he did not desire the religion. He desired the delight.

The Assumption is a noble picture, because Titian believed in the Madonna. But he did not paint it to make any one else believe in her. He painted it, because he enjoyed rich masses of red and blue, and faces flushed with sunlight.

Tintoret's Paradise is a noble picture, because he believed in Paradise. But he did not paint it to make any one think of heaven; but to form a beautiful termination for the hall of the Greater Council.

Other men used their effete faiths and mean faculties with a high moral purpose. The Venetian gave the most earnest faith, and the lordliest faculty, to gild the shadows of an antechamber, or heighten the splendours of a holiday.

From *Modern Painters*, Vol. v, Part IX, ch. III, § 32

¶ 128

BEAUTY AND LAW

And I desire, especially, that the reader should note this, in now closing the work through which we have passed together in the investigation of the beauty of the visible world. For perhaps he expected more pleasure and freedom in that work; he thought that it would lead him at once into fields of fond imagination, and may have been surprised to find that the following of beauty brought him always under a sterner dominion of mysterious law; that brightness was continually based upon obedience, and all majesty only another form of submission. But this is indeed so. I have been perpetually hindered in this inquiry into the sources of beauty by fear of wearying the reader with their severities. It was always accuracy I had to ask of him, not sympathy; patience, not zeal; apprehension, not sensation. The thing to be shown him was not a pleasure to be snatched, but a law to be learned.

From *Modern Painters*, Vol. v, Part VII, ch. IV, § 23

¶ 129

AGAINST ART FOR ITS OWN SAKE

Wherever art is practised for its own sake, and the delight of the workman is in what he *does* and *produces*, instead of in what he *interprets* or *exhibits*, there art has an influence of the most fatal kind on brain and heart, and it issues, if long so pursued, in the *destruction both of intellectual power* and *moral principle*; whereas art, devoted humbly and self-forgetfully to the clear statement and record of the facts of the universe, is always helpful and beneficent to mankind, full of comfort, strength, and salvation.

From *The Two Paths*, Lecture I, § 15

THE TWO ERRORS

First [of the forms of dangerous error], when the men of facts despise design. This is the error of the common Dutch painters, of merely imitative painters of still life, flowers, etc., and other men who, having either the gift of accurate imitation or strong sympathies with nature, suppose that all is done when the imitation is perfected or sympathy expressed. A large body of English landscapists come into this class, including most clever sketchers from nature, who fancy that to get a sky of true tone, and a gleam of sunshine or sweep of shower faithfully expressed, is all that can be required of art. These men are generally themselves answerable for much of their deadness of feeling to the higher qualities of composition. They probably have not originally the high gifts of design, but they lose such powers as they originally possessed by despising, and refusing to study, the results of great power of design in others. Their knowledge, as far as it goes, being accurate, they are usually presumptuous and self-conceited, and gradually become incapable of admiring anything but what is like their own works. They see nothing in the works of great designers but the faults, and do harm almost incalculable in the European society of the present day by sneering at the compositions of the greatest men of the earlier ages, because they do not absolutely tally with their own ideas of 'Nature.'

The second form of error is when the men of design despise facts. All noble design must deal with facts to a certain extent, for there is no food for it but in nature. The best colourist invents best by taking hints from natural colours; from birds, skies, or groups of figures. And if, in the delight of inventing fantastic colour and form, the truths of nature are wilfully neglected, the intellect becomes comparatively decrepit, and that state of art results which we find among the Chinese. The Greek designers delighted in the facts of the human form, and became great in consequence; but the facts of lower nature were disregarded by them, and their inferior ornament became, therefore, dead and valueless.

From *The Stones of Venice*, Vol. II, ch. VI, § 46

¶ 131
UNEXPECTED BEAUTY

It is only by the habit of representing faithfully all things, that we can truly learn what is beautiful, and what is not. The ugliest objects contain some elements of beauty; and in all it is an element peculiar to themselves, which cannot be separated from their ugliness, but must either be enjoyed together with it or not at all. The more a painter accepts nature as he finds it, the more unexpected beauty he discovers in what he at first despised; but once let him arrogate the right of rejection, and he will gradually contract his circle of enjoyment, until what he supposed to be nobleness of selection ends in narrowness of perception. Dwelling perpetually upon one class of ideas, his art becomes at once monstrous and morbid; until at last he cannot faithfully represent even what he chooses to retain; his discrimination contracts into darkness, and his fastidiousness fades into fatuity.

From *Modern Painters*, Vol. III, Part IV, ch. III, § 15

¶ 132
THE POWER OF A GREAT ARTIST

The day's work of a man like Mantegna or Paul Veronese consists of an unfaltering, uninterrupted, succession of movements of the hand more precise than those of the finest fencer: the pencil leaving one point and arriving at another, not only with unerring precision at the extremity of the line, but with an unerring and yet varied course – sometimes over spaces a foot or more in extent – yet a course so determined everywhere, that either of these men could, and Veronese often does, draw a finished profile, or any other portion of the contour of the face, with one line, not afterwards changed. Try, first, to realize to yourselves the muscular precision of that action, and the intellectual strain of it; for the movement of a fencer is perfect in practised monotony; but the movement of the hand of a great painter is at every instant governed by a direct and new intention. Then imagine that muscular firmness and subtlety, and the instantaneously selective and ordinant energy of the brain, sustained all day long, not only without fatigue, but with a visible joy in the exertion, like that which an eagle seems to take in the wave of his wings; and this all life long, and through long life, not only without failure of power, but with visible increase of it, until the actually organic changes of old age. And then consider, so far as you know anything of physiology, what sort of an ethical state of body and mind that means! – ethic through ages past! what fineness of race there must be to get it, what exquisite balance and symmetry of the vital powers! And then, finally, determine for yourselves whether a manhood like that is consistent with any viciousness of soul, with any mean anxiety, any gnawing lust, any wretchedness of spite or remorse, any consciousness of rebellion against law of God or man, or any actual, though unconscious violation of even the least law to which obedience is essential for the glory of life and the pleasing of its Giver.

From *Lectures on Art*, Lecture III, § 71

¶ 133

THE IMPERATIVE DREAM

I say, he '*thinks*' this, and '*introduces*' that. But, strictly speaking, he does not think at all. If he thought, he would instantly go wrong; it is only the clumsy and uninventive artist who thinks. All these changes come into his head involuntarily; an entirely imperative dream, crying 'Thus is must be,' has taken possession of him; he can see, and do, no otherwise than as the dream directs.

From *Modern Painters*, Vol. IV, Part V, ch. II, § 15

¶ 134

TWO INGREDIENTS OF ART

You observe that I always say *interpretation*, never *imitation*. My reason for doing so is, first, that good art rarely imitates; it usually only describes or explains. But my second and chief reason is that good art always consists of two things: First, the observation of fact; secondly, the manifesting of human design and authority in the way that fact is told. Great and good art must unite the two; it cannot exist for a moment but in their unity.

From *The Two Paths*, Lecture I, § 19

¶ 135

PERCEPTION OF ROUNDED SURFACE

One of the most marked distinctions between one artist and another, in the point of skill, will be found in their relative delicacy of perception of rounded surface; the full power of expressing the perspective, fore-shortening, and various undulation of such surface is, perhaps, the last and most difficult attainment of the hand and eye. For instance: there is, perhaps, no tree which has baffled the landscape painter more than the common black spruce fir. It is rare that we see any representation of it other than caricature. It is conceived as if it grew in one plane, or as a section of a tree, with a set of boughs symmetrically dependent on opposite sides. It is thought formal, unmanageable, and ugly. It would be so, if it grew as it is drawn. But the Power of the tree is not in that chandelier-like section. It is in the dark, flat, solid tables of leafage, which it holds out on its strong arms, curved slightly over them like shields, and spreading towards the extremity like a hand. It is vain to endeavour to paint the sharp, grassy, intricate leafage, until this ruling form has been secured; and in the boughs that approach the spectator, the foreshortening of it is like that of a wide hill country, ridge just rising over ridge in successive distances; and the finger-like extremities, foreshortened to absolute bluntness, require a delicacy in the rendering of them like that of the drawing of the hand of the Magdalene upon the vase in Mr Rogers's Titian.[1] Get but the back of that foliage, and you have the tree; but I cannot name the artist who has thoroughly felt it. So, in all drawing and sculpture, it is the power of rounding, softly and perfectly, every inferior mass which preserves the serenity, as it follows the truth, of Nature, and which demands the highest knowledge and skill from the workman. A noble design may always be told by the back

1. '*Noli me tangere!*' bequeathed to the National Gallery by Samuel Rogers, the poet, in 1855.

of a single leaf, and it was the sacrifice of this breadth and refinement of surface for sharp edges and extravagant undercutting, which destroyed the Gothic mouldings, as the substitution of the line for the light destroyed the Gothic tracery.

From *The Seven Lamps of Architecture*, ch. III, § 17

¶ 136

THE SCIENCE OF SCULPTURE

The exact science of sculpture is that of the relations between outline and the solid form it limits; and it does not matter whether that relation be indicated by drawing or carving, so long as the expression of solid form is the mental purpose; it is the science always of the beauty of relation in three dimensions.

From *Aratra Pentelici*, Lecture I, § 15

¶ 137

FUNDAMENTAL LAWS OF SCULPTURE

Sculpture is essentially the production of a pleasant bossiness or roundness of surface.

If you look from some distance at these two engravings of Greek coins, you will find the relief on each of them simplifies itself into a pearl-like portion of a sphere, with exquisitely gradated light on its surface. When you look at them nearer, you will see that each smaller portion into which they are divided – cheek, or brow, or leaf, or tress of hair – resolves itself also into a rounded or undulated surface, pleasant by gradation of light. Every several surface is delightful in itself, as a shell, or a tuft of rounded moss, or the bossy masses of distant forest would be. That these intricately modulated masses present some resemblance to a girl's face, such as the Syracusans imagined that of the water-goddess Arethusa, is entirely a secondary matter; the primary condition is that the masses shall be beautifully rounded, and disposed with due discretion and order.

It is difficult for you, at first, to feel this order and beauty of surface, apart from the imitation. But you can see there is a pretty disposition of, and relation between, the projections of a fir-cone, though the studded spiral imitates nothing. Order exactly the same in kind, only much more complex; and an abstract beauty of surface rendered definite by increase and decline of light – (for every curve of surface has its own luminous law, and the light and shade on a parabolic solid differs, specifically, from that on an elliptical or spherical one) – it is the essential business of the sculptor to obtain; as it is the essential business of a painter to get good colour, whether he imitates anything or not. At a distance from the picture, or carving, where the things represented become absolutely unintelligible, we must yet be able to say, at a glance; 'That is good painting, or good carving.'

And you will be surprised to find, when you try the experiment, how much the eye must instinctively judge in this manner. Take the front of San Zenone, for instance. You will find it impossible without a lense, to distinguish in the bronze gates, and in great part of the wall, anything that their bosses represent. You cannot tell whether the sculpture is of men, animals, or trees; only you feel it to be composed of pleasant projecting masses; you acknowledge that both gates and wall are, somehow, delightfully roughened; and only afterwards, by slow degrees, can you make out what this roughness means; nay, though here I magnify one of the bronze plates of the gate to a scale, which gives you the same advantage as if you saw it quite close, in the reality, – you may still be obliged to me for the information, that this boss represents the Madonna asleep in her little bed, and this smaller boss, the Infant Christ in His; and this at the top, a cloud with an angel coming out of it, and these jagged bosses, two of the Three Kings, with their crowns on, looking up to the star, (which is intelligible enough, I admit); but what this straggling, three-legged boss beneath signifies, I suppose neither you nor I can tell, unless it be the shepherd's dog, who had come suddenly upon the Kings with their crowns on, and is greatly startled at them.

Farther, and much more definitely, the pleasantness of the surface decoration is independent of structure; that is to say, of any architectural requirement of stability. The greater part of the sculpture here is exclusively ornamentation of a flat wall, or of door-panelling; only a small portion of the church front is thus treated, and the sculpture has no more to do with the form of the building than a piece of lace veil would have, suspended beside its gates on a festal day; the proportions of shaft and arch might be altered in a hundred different ways, without diminishing their stability; and the pillars would stand more safely on the ground than on the backs of these carved animals.

I wish you especially to notice these points, because the false theory that ornamentation should be merely decorated structure is so pretty and plausible, that it is likely to take away your attention from the far more important abstract conditions of design. Structure should never be contradicted, and in the best buildings it is pleasantly exhibited and enforced: in this very porch the joints of every stone are visible, and you will find me in the Fifth Lecture insisting on this clearness of its anatomy as a merit; yet so independent is the mechanical structure of the true design, that when I begin my Lectures on Architecture, the first building I shall give you as a standard will be one in which the structure is wholly concealed. It will be the Baptistery of Florence, which is, in reality, as much a buttressed chapel with a vaulted roof, as the Chapter House of York; – but round it, in order to *conceal* that buttressed structure, (not to decorate, observe, but to conceal) a flat external wall is raised; simplifying the whole to a mere hexagonal box, like a wooden piece of Tunbridge ware on the surface of which the eye and intellect are to be interested by the relations of dimension and curve between pieces of encrusting marble of different colours, which have no more to do with the real make of the building than the diaper of a Harlequin's jacket has to do with his bones.

The sense of abstract proportion, on which the enjoyment of such a piece of art entirely depends, is one of the æsthetic faculties which nothing can develop but time and education. It belongs only to highly trained nations; and, among them, to their most strictly refined classes, though the germs of it are found, as part of their innate power, in every people capable of art. It has for the most part vanished at present from the English mind, in consequence of our eager desire for excitement, and for the kind of splendour that exhibits wealth, careless of dignity; so that, I suppose, there are very few now even of our best-trained Londoners who know the difference between the design of Whitehall and that of any modern club-house in Pall-mall. The order and harmony which, in his enthusiastic account of the Theatre of Epidaurus, Pausanias insists on before beauty, can only be recognized by stern order and harmony in our daily lives; and the perception of them is as little to be compelled, or taught suddenly, as the laws of still finer choice in the conception of dramatic incident which regulate poetic sculpture.

From *Aratra Pentelici*, Lecture 1, §§ 21–5

¶ 138

THE FUNCTION OF ENGRAVING

We are not talking of female beauty, so please you, just now, gentlemen, but of engraving. And the merit, the classical, indefeasible, immortal merit of this head of a Dutch girl with all the beauty left out,[1] is in the fact that every line of it, as engraving, is as good as can be; – good, not with the mechanical dexterity of a watchmaker, but with the intellectual effort and sensitiveness of an artist who knows precisely what can be done, and ought to be attempted, with his assigned materials. He works easily, fearlessly, flexibly; the dots are not all measured in distance; the lines not all mathematically parallel or divergent. He has even missed his mark at the mouth in one place, and leaves the mistake, frankly. But there are no petrified mistakes; nor is the eye so accustomed to the look of the mechanical furrow as to accept it for final excellence. The engraving is full of the painter's higher power and wider perception; it is classically perfect, because duly subordinate, and presenting for your applause only the virtues proper to its own sphere. Among these, I must now reiterate, the first of all is the *decorative* arrangement of *lines*.

You all know what a pretty thing a damask tablecloth is, and how a pattern is brought out by threads running one way in one space, and across in another. So, in lace, a certain delightfulness is given by the texture of meshed lines.

Similarly, on any surface of metal, the object of the engraver is,

1. The illustration was an engraving by Dürer of the Virgin and Child seated before a fence (1518).

or ought to be, to cover it with lovely *lines*, forming a lacework, and including a variety of spaces, delicious to the eye.

And this is his business, primarily; before any other matter can be thought of, his work must be ornamental. You know I told you a sculptor's business is first to cover a surface with pleasant *bosses*, whether they mean anything or not; so an engraver's is to cover it with pleasant *lines*, whether they mean anything or not. That they should mean something, and a good deal of something, is indeed desirable afterwards; but first we must be ornamental.

From *Ariadne Florentina*, Lecture 4, §§ 125–6

¶ 139

COMPOSITION

I have often been accused of slighting this quality in pictures; the fact being that I have avoided it only because I considered it too great and wonderful for me to deal with. The longer I thought, the more wonderful it always seemed; and it is, to myself personally, the quality, above all others, which gives me delight in pictures. Many others I admire, or respect; but this one I rejoice in. Expression, sentiment, truth to nature, are essential: but all these are not enough. I never care to look at a picture again, if it be ill composed; and if well composed I can hardly leave off looking at it.

'Well composed.' Does that mean according to rule?

No. Precisely the contrary. Composed as only the man who did it could have done it; composed as no other picture is, or was, or ever can be again. Every great work stands alone.

From *Modern Painters*, Vol. v, Part VIII, ch. 1, § 2

¶ 140

COLOUR

Colour is . . . the type of love. Hence it is especially connected with the blossoming of the earth; and again, with its fruits; also, with the spring and fall of the leaf, and with the morning and evening of the day, in order to show the waiting of love about the birth and death of man.

From *Modern Painters*, Vol. v, Part IX, ch. XI, § 9

¶ 141
THE SACREDNESS OF COLOUR

The fact is, we none of us enough appreciate the nobleness and sacredness of colour. Nothing is more common than to hear it spoken of as a subordinate beauty, – nay, even as the mere source of a sensual pleasure. . . . But it is not so. Such expressions are used for the most part in thoughtlessness; and if the speakers would only take the pains to imagine what the world and their own existence would become, if the blue were taken from the sky, and the gold from the sunshine, and the verdure from the leaves, and the crimson from the blood which is the life of man, the flush from the cheek, the darkness from the eye, the radiance from the hair, – if they could but see, for an instant, white human creatures living in a white world, – they would soon feel what they owe to colour. The fact is, that, of all God's gifts to the sight of man, colour is the holiest, the most divine, the most solemn. We speak rashly of gay colour and sad colour, for colour cannot at once be good and gay. All good colour is in some degree pensive, the loveliest is melancholy, and the purest and most thoughtful minds are those which love colour the most.

From *The Stones of Venice*, Vol. II, ch. v, § 30

¶ 142
DANCING RIGHTLY

And all these proportionate strengths and measured efforts of the bough produce its loveliness, and ought to be felt, in looking at it, not by any mathematical evidence, but by the same fine instinct which enables us to perceive, when a girl dances rightly, that she moves easily, and with delight to herself; that her limbs are strong enough, and her body tender enough, to move precisely as she wills them to move. You cannot say of any bend of arm or foot what precise relations of their curves to the whole figure manifest, in their changeful melodies, that ease of motion; yet you feel that they do so, and you feel it by a true instinct. And if you reason on the matter farther, you may know, though you cannot see, that an absolute mathematical necessity proportions every bend of the body to the rate and direction of its motion, and that the momentary fancy and fire of the will measure themselves, even in their gaily-fancied freedom, by stern laws of nervous life, and material attraction, which regulate eternally every pulse of the strength of man, and every sweep of the stars of heaven.

From *Modern Painters*, Vol. v, Part vi, ch. viii, § 3

¶ 143
FREEDOM

All freedom is error. Every line you lay down is either right or wrong: it may be timidly and awkwardly wrong, or fearlessly and impudently wrong: the aspect of the impudent wrongness is pleasurable to vulgar persons; and is what they commonly call 'free' execution: the timid, tottering, hesitating wrongness is rarely so attractive; yet sometimes, if accompanied with good qualities, and right aims in other directions, it becomes in a manner charming, like the inarticulateness of a child: but, whatever the charm or manner of the error there is but one question ultimately to be asked respecting every line you draw, Is it right or wrong? If right, it most assuredly is not a 'free' line, but an intensely continent, restrained, and considered line; and the action of the hand in laying it is just as decisive, and just as 'free' as the hand of a first-rate surgeon in a critical incision.

From *The Cestus of Aglaia*, ch. vi, § 72

¶ 144
LAW AND LIBERTY

I say, first, there must be observance of the ruling organic law. This is the first distinction between good artists and bad artists. Your common sketcher or bad painter puts his leaves on the trees as if they were moss tied to sticks; he cannot see the lines of action or growth; he scatters the shapeless clouds over his sky, not perceiving the sweeps of associated curves which the real clouds are following as they fly; and he breaks his mountain side into rugged fragments, wholly unconscious of the lines of force with which the real rocks have risen, or of the lines of couch in which they repose. On the contrary it is the main delight of the great draughtsman, to trace these laws of government; and his tendency to error is always in the exaggeration of their authority rather than in its denial.

Secondly, I say, we have to show the individual character and liberty of the separate leaves, clouds, or rocks. And herein the great masters separate themselves finally from the inferior ones; for if the men of inferior genius ever express law at all, it is by the sacrifice of individuality.... Now, although both these expressions of government and individuality are essential to masterly work, the individuality is the *more* essential, and the more difficult of attainment; and, therefore, that attainment separates the great masters *finally* from the inferior ones. It is the more essential, because, in these matters of beautiful arrangement in visible things, the same rules hold that hold in moral things. It is a lamentable and unnatural thing to see a number of men subject to no government, actuated by no ruling principle, and associated by no common affection: but it would be a more lamentable thing still, were it possible, to see a number of men so oppressed into assimilation as to have no more any individual hope or character, no differences in aim, no dissimilarities of passion, no irregularities of judgment; a society in which no man could help another, since none would be feebler than himself; no man admire another, since none would be stronger than himself; no man be grateful to another, since by none he could be relieved; no man reverence another, since by none he could be instructed; a society in which every soul would be as the syllable of a stammerer instead of the word of a speaker, in which every man would walk as in a frightful dream, seeing spectres of himself, in everlasting multiplication, gliding helplessly around him in a speechless darkness. Therefore it is that perpetual difference, play, and change in groups of form are more essential to them even than their being subdued by some great gathering law: the law is needful to them for their perfection and their power, but the difference is needful to them for their *life*.

From *The Elements of Drawing*, Letter II, §§ 132-3

¶ 145
FINISH

So the rule is simple: Always look for invention first, and after that, for such execution as will help the invention, and as the inventor is capable of without painful effort, and *no more*. Above all, demand no refinement of execution where there is no thought, for that is slaves' work, unredeemed. Rather choose rough work than smooth work, so only that the practical purpose be answered, and never imagine there is reason to be proud of anything that may be accomplished by patience and sand-paper.

From *The Stones of Venice*, Vol. II, ch. VI, § 19

¶ 146
DIFFICULT TRUTH

They think it easy, and therefore contemptible, to be truthful; they have been taught so all their lives. But it is not so, whoever taught it them. It is most difficult, and worthy of the greatest men's greatest effort, to render, as it should be rendered, the simplest of the natural features of the earth; but also be it remembered, no man is confined to the simplest; each may look out work for himself where he chooses, and it will be strange if he cannot find something hard enough for him. The excuse is, however, one of the lips only; for every painter knows, that when he draws back from the attempt to render nature as she is, it is oftener in cowardice than in disdain.

From *Reviews and Pamphlets on Art*, V, § 13

¶ 147
VITAL TRUTH

It is by seizing these leading lines, when we cannot seize all, that likeness and expression are given to a portrait, and grace and a kind of vital truth to the rendering of every natural form. I call it vital truth, because these chief lines are always expressive of the past history and present action of the thing. They show in a mountain, first, how it was built or heaped up; and secondly, how it is now being worn away, and from what quarter the wildest storms strike it. In a tree, they show what kind of fortune it has had to endure from its childhood: how troublesome trees have come in its way, and pushed it aside, and tried to strangle or starve it; where and when kind trees have sheltered it, and grown up lovingly together with it, bending as it bent; what winds torment it most; what boughs of it behave best, and bear most fruit; and so on. In a wave or cloud, these leading lines show the run of the tide and of the wind, and the sort of change which the water or vapour is at any moment enduring in its form, as it meets shore, or counter-wave, or melting sunshine. Now remember, nothing distinguishes great men from inferior men more than their always, whether in life or in art, *knowing the way things are going*. Your dunce thinks they are standing still, and draws them all fixed; your wise man sees the change or changing in them, and draws them so, – the animal in its motion, the tree in its growth, the cloud in its course, the mountain in its wearing away. Try always, whenever you look at a form, to see the lines in it which have had power over its past fate and will have power over its futurity.

From *The Elements of Drawing*, Letter II, § 104

¶ 148

THE INSTINCTS OF MIMICRY, IDOLATRY, AND DISCIPLINE

1. Mimicry

Beginning with the simple conception of sculpture as the art of fiction in solid substance, we are now to consider what its subject should be. What – having the gift of imagery – should we by preference endeavour to image? A question which is, indeed, subordinate to the deeper one – why we should wish to image anything at all.

Some years ago, having been always desirous that the education of women should begin in learning how to cook, I got leave, one day, for a little girl of eleven years old to exchange, much to her satisfaction, her schoolroom for the kitchen. But as ill fortune would have it, there was some pastry toward, and she was left unadvisedly in command of some delicately rolled paste; whereof she made no pies, but an unlimited quantity of cats and mice.

Now you may read the works of the gravest critics of art from end to end; but you will find, at last, they can give you no other true account of the spirit of sculpture than that it is an irresistible human instinct for the making of cats and mice, and other imitable living creatures, in such permanent form that one may play with the images at leisure.

Play with them, or love them, or fear them, or worship them. The cat may become the goddess Pasht, and the mouse, in the hand of a sculptured king, enforce his enduring words 'ἐς ἐμέ τις ὁρέων εὐδεβης ἔγτω;' but the great mimetic instinct underlies all such purpose; and is zooplastic, – life-shaping, – alike in the reverent and the impious....

2. Idolatry

They begin by scratching the reindeer, the most interesting object of sight. But presently, as the human creature rises in scale of intellect, it proceeds to scratch, not the most interesting object of sight only, but the most interesting object of imagination; not the reindeer, but the Maker and Giver of the reindeer. And the second great condition for the advance of the art of sculpture is that the race should possess, in addition to the mimetic instinct, the realistic or idolizing instinct; the desire to see as substantial the powers that are unseen, and bring near those that are far off, and to possess and cherish those that are strange. To make in some way tangible and visible the nature of the gods – to illustrate and explain it by symbols; to bring the immortals out of the recesses of the clouds, and make them Penates; to bring back the dead from darkness, and make them Lares....

3. Discipline

This, then, is the second instinct necessary to sculpture; the desire for the manifestation, description, and companionship of unknown powers; and for possession of a bodily substance – . . . instead of an abstract idea. But if you get nothing more in the depth of the national mind than these two feelings, the mimetic and idolizing instincts, there may be still no progress possible for the arts except in delicacy of manipulation and accumulative caprice of design. You must have not only the idolizing instinct, but an $\dot{\eta}\theta o\varsigma$ which chooses the right thing to idolize! Else, you will get states of art like those in China or India, non-progressive, and in great part diseased and frightful, being wrought under the influence of foolish terror, or foolish admiration. So that a third condition, completing and confirming both the others, must exist in order to the development of the creative power.

This third condition is that the heart of the nation shall be set on the discovery of just or equal law, and shall be from day to day developing that law more perfectly. The Greek school of sculpture is formed during, and in consequence of, the national effort to discover the nature of justice; the Tuscan, during, and in consequence of, the national effort to discover the nature of justification.

Now when a nation with mimetic instinct and imaginative longing is also thus occupied earnestly in the discovery of Ethic law, that effort gradually brings precision and truth into all its manual acts; and the physical progress of sculpture as in the Greek, so in the Tuscan, school, consists in gradually *limiting* what was before indefinite, in *verifying* what was inaccurate, and in *humanizing* what was monstrous.

From *Arata Pentelici*, Lecture II, §§ 28–9, 33, and 39–41 respectively

¶ 149
DRAPERY

All noble draperies, either in painting or sculpture (colour and texture being at present out of our consideration), have, so far as they are anything more than necessities, one of two great functions: they are the exponents of motion and of gravitation. They are the most valuable means of expressing past as well as present motion in the figure, and they are almost the only means of indicating to the eye the force of gravity which resists such motion. The Greeks used drapery in sculpture for the most part as an ugly necessity, but availed themselves of it gladly in all representation of action, exaggerating the arrangements of it which express lightness in the material, and follow gesture in the person. The Christian Sculptors, caring little for the body, or disliking it, and depending exclusively on the countenance, received drapery at first contentedly as a veil, but soon perceived a capacity of expression in it which the Greek had not seen or had despised. The principal element of this expression was the entire removal of agitation from what was so preeminently capable of being agitated. It fell from their human forms plumb down, sweeping the ground heavily, and concealing the feet; while the Greek drapery was often blown away from the thigh. The thick and coarse stuffs of the monkish dresses, so absolutely opposed to the thin and gauzy web of antique material, suggested simplicity of division as well as weight of fall. There was no crushing nor subdividing them. And thus the drapery gradually came to represent the spirit of repose as it before had of motion, repose saintly and severe. The wind had no power upon the garment, as the passion none upon the soul; and the motion of the figure only bent into a softer line the stillness of the falling veil,[1] followed by it like a slow cloud by drooping rain: only in links of lighter undulation it followed the dances of the angels.

From *The Seven Lamps of Architecture*, ch. IV, § 11

¶ 150
COLOUR SUPREME

For there is not any distinction between the artists of the inferior and the nobler schools more definite than this; that the first *colour for the sake of realization*, and the second *realize for the sake of colour*. I hope that . . . enough has been said to show the nobility of colour, though it is a subject on which I would fain enlarge whenever I approach it; for there is none that needs more to be insisted upon, chiefly on account of the opposition of the persons who have no

1. The MS. reads 'stillness of its fall'.

eye for colour, and who, being therefore unable to understand that is just as divine and distinct in its power as music (only infinitely more varied in its harmonies), talk of it as if it were inferior and servile with respect to the other powers of art: whereas it is so far from being this, that wherever it enters it must take the mastery, and whatever else is sacrificed for its sake, *it*, at least, must be right. This is partly the case even with music: it is at our choice whether we will accompany a poem with music or not; but, if we do, the music *must* be right, and neither discordant nor inexpressive. The goodness and sweetness of the poem cannot save it, if the music be harsh or false: but if the music be right, the poem may be insipid or inharmonious, and still saved by the notes to which it is wedded. But this is far more true of colour. If that be wrong, all is wrong.

No amount of expression or invention can redeem an ill-coloured picture; while, on the other hand, if the colour be right, there is nothing it will not raise or redeem; and, therefore, wherever colour enters at all, anything *may* be sacrificed to it, and, rather than it should be false or feeble, everything *must* be sacrificed to it: so that, when an artist touches colour, it is the same thing as when a poet takes up a musical instrument; he implies, in so doing, that he is a master, up to a certain point, of that instrument, and can produce sweet sound from it, and is able to fit the course and measure of his words to its tones, which, if he be not able to do, he had better not have touched it. In like manner, to add colour to a drawing is to undertake for the perfection of a visible music, which, if it be false, will utterly and assuredly mar the whole work; if true, proportion-ately elevate it, according to its power and sweetness. But, in no case ought the colour to be added in order to increase the realization. The drawing or engraving is all that the imagination needs. To 'paint' the subject merely to make it more real, is only to insult the imaginative power, and to vulgarize the whole. Hence the common, though little understood feeling, among men of ordinary cultivation, that an inferior sketch is always better than a bad painting; although, in the latter, there may verily be more skill than in the former. For the painter who has presumed to touch colour without perfectly understanding it, not for the colour's sake, nor because he loves it, but for the sake of completion merely, has committed two sins against us; he has dulled the imagination by not trusting it far enough, and then, in this languid state, he oppresses it with base and false colour; for all colour that is not lovely is discordant; there is no mediate condition. So, therefore, when it is permitted to enter at all, it must be with the predetermination that, cost what it will, the colour shall be right and lovely: and I only wish that, in general, it were better understood that a *painter's* business is to *paint*, primarily; and that all expression, and grouping, and conceiving, and what else goes to constitute design, *are of less importance than colour, in a coloured work.* and so they were always considered in the noble periods; and sometimes all resemblance to nature whatever (as in painted windows, illuminated manuscripts, and such other work) is sacrificed to the brilliancy of colour; sometimes distinctness of form to its richness, as by Titian, Turner, and Reynolds; and, which is the point on which we are at present insisting, sometimes, in the pursuit of its utmost refinements on the surfaces of objects, an amount of realization becomes consistent with noble art, which would otherwise be altogether inadmissible, that is to say, which no great mind could otherwise have either produced or enjoyed.

From *The Stones of Venice*, Vol. III, ch. IV, § 27

¶ 151
THE TWO BASES OF ART

I have here in my hand one of the simplest possible examples of the union of the graphic and constructive powers, – one of my breakfast plates. Since all the finely architectural arts, we said, began in the shaping of the cup and the platter, we will begin, ourselves, with the platter.

Why has it been made round? For two structural reasons: first, that the greatest holding surface may be gathered into the smallest space; and secondly, that in being pushed past other things on the table, it may come into least contact with them.

Next, why has it a rim? For two other structural reasons; first, that it is convenient to put salt or mustard upon; but secondly and chiefly, that the plate may be easily laid hold of. The rim is the simplest form of continuous handle.

Farther, to keep it from soiling the cloth, it will be wise to put this ridge beneath, round the bottom; for as the rim is the simplest possible form of continuous handle, so this is the simplest form of continuous leg. And we get the section given beneath the figure for the essential one of a rightly made platter.

Thus far our art has been strictly utilitarian, having respect to conditions of collision, of carriage, and of support. But now, on the surface of our piece of pottery, here are various bands and spots of colour which are presumably set there to make it pleasanter to the eye. Six of the spots, seen closely, you discover are intended to represent flowers. These then have as distinctly a graphic purpose as the other properties of the plate have an architectural one, and the first critical question we have to ask about them is, whether they are like roses or not. I will anticipate what I have to say in subsequent Lectures so far as to assure you that, if they are to be like roses at all, the liker they can be, the better. Do not suppose, as many people will tell you, that because this is a common manufactured article, your roses on it are the better for being ill-painted, or half-painted. If they had been painted by the same hand that did this peach, the plate would have been all the better for it; but, as it chanced, there was no hand such as William Hunt's to paint them, and their graphic power is not distinguished. In any case, however, that graphic power must have been subordinate to their effect as pink spots, while the band of green-blue round the plate's edge, and the spots of gold, pretend to no graphic power at all, but are meaningless spaces of colour or metal. Still less have they any mechanical office; they add nowise to the serviceableness of the plate; and their agreeableness, if they possess any, depends, therefore, neither on any imitative, nor any structural, character; but on some inherent pleasantness in themselves, either of mere colours to the eye, (as of taste to the tongue), or in the placing of those colours in relations which obey some mental principle of order, or physical principle of harmony.

These abstract relations and inherent pleasantnesses, whether in space, number, or time, and whether of colours or sounds, form what we may properly term the musical or harmonic element in every art; and the study of them is an entirely separate science. It is the branch of art-philosophy to which the word 'æsthetics' should be strictly limited, being the inquiry into the nature of things that in themselves are pleasant to the human senses or instincts, though they represent nothing, and serve for nothing, their only service *being* their pleasantness. Thus it is the province of æsthetics to tell you, (if you did not know it before,) that the taste and colour of a peach are pleasant, and to ascertain, if it be ascertainable, (and you have any curiosity to know,) why they are so.

The information would, I presume, to most of you, be gratuitous. If it were not, and you chanced to be in a sick state of body in which you disliked peaches, it would be, for the time, to you false information, and, so far as it was true of other people, to you useless. Nearly the whole study of æsthetics is in like manner either gratuitous or useless. Either you like the right things without being recommended to do so, or, if you dislike them, your mind cannot be changed by lectures on the laws of taste. . . . And the whole science of æsthetics is, in the depth of it, expressed by one passage of Goethe's in the end of the second part of *Faust*; – the notable one that follows the song of the Lemures, when the angels enter to dispute with the fiends for the soul of Faust. They enter singing – 'Pardon to sinners and life to the dust.' Mephistopheles hears them first, and exclaims to his troop, 'Discord I hear, and filthy jingling' – 'Mis-töne höre ich; garstiges Geklimper.' This, you see, is the extreme of bad taste in music. Presently the angelic host begin strewing roses, which discomfits the diabolic crowd altogether. Mephistopheles in vain calls to them – 'What do you duck and shrink for – is that proper hellish behaviour? Stand fast, and let them strew' – 'Was duckt and zuckt ihr; ist das Höllenbrauch? So haltet stand, und lasst sie streuen.' There you have, also, the extreme of bad taste in sight and smell. And in the whole passage is a brief embodiment for you of the ultimate fact that all æsthetics depend on the health of soul and body, and the proper exercise of both, not only through years, but generations. Only by harmony of both collateral and successive lives can the great doctrine of the Muses be received which enables men 'Χαίρειν ὀρῶθς,' – 'to have pleasure rightly;' and there is no other definition of the beautiful, nor of any subject of delight to the æsthetic faculty, than that it is what one noble spirit has created, seen and felt by another of similar or equal nobility. So much as there is in you of ox, or of swine, perceives no beauty, and creates none; what is human in you, in exact proportion to the perfectness of its humanity, can create it, and receive.

From *Aratra Pentelici*, Lecture I, §§ 9–12

¶ 152
GOOD MEN: GOOD ART

Great art is the expression of the mind of a great man, and mean art, that of the want of mind of a weak man. A foolish person builds foolishly, and a wise one, sensibly; a virtuous one, beautifully; and a vicious one, basely. If stone work is well put together, it means that a thoughtful man planned it, and a careful man cut it, and an honest man cemented it. If it has too much ornament, it means that its carver was too greedy of pleasure; if too little, that he was rude, or insensitive, or stupid, and the like. So that when once you have learned how to spell these most precious of all legends, – pictures and buildings, – you may read the characters of men, and of nations, in their art, as in a mirror; – nay, as in a microscope, and magnified a hundredfold; for the character becomes passionate in the art, and intensifies itself in all its noblest or meanest delights. Nay, not only as in a microscope, but as under a scalpel, and in dissection; for a man may hide himself from you, or misrepresent himself to you, every other way; but he cannot in his work: there, be sure, you have him to the inmost. All that he likes, all that he sees, – all that he can do, – his imagination, his affections, his perseverance, his impatience, his clumsiness, cleverness, everything is there.

From *The Queen of the Air*, Lecture III, § 102

¶ 153
THE AIM OF ART

Review for yourselves the history of art, and you will find this to be a manifest certainty, that *no great school ever yet existed which had not for primal aim the representation of some natural fact as truly as possible*. There have only yet appeared in the world three schools of perfect art – schools, that is to say, which did their work as well as it seems possible to do it. These are the Athenian, Florentine, and Venetian. The Athenian proposed to itself the perfect representation of the form of the human body. It strove to do that as well as it could; it did that as well as it can be done; and all its greatness was founded upon and involved in that single and honest effort. The Florentine school proposed to itself the perfect expression of human emotion – the showing of the effects of passion in the human face and gesture. I call this the Florentine school, because whether you take Raphael for the culminating master of expressional art in Italy, or Leonardo, or Michael Angelo, you will find that the whole energy of the national effort which produced those masters had its root in Florence; not at Urbino or Milan. I say, then, this Florentine or leading Italian school proposed to itself human expression for its aim in natural truth; it strove to do that as well as it could – did it as well as it can be done – and all its greatness is rooted in that single and honest effort. Thirdly, the Venetian school proposed to itself the representation of the effect of colour and shade on all things; chiefly on the human form. It tried to do that as well as it could – did it as well as it can be done – and all its greatness is founded on that single and honest effort.

From *The Two Paths*, Lecture 1, § 20

¶ 154
THE TWO PATHS

I will go back then first to the very beginnings of Gothic art, and before you, the students of Kensington, as an impannelled jury, I will bring two examples of the barbarism out of which Gothic art merges, approximately contemporary in date and parallel in executive skill; but, the one, a barbarism that did not get on, and could not get on; the other, a barbarism that could get on, and did get on; and you, the impannelled jury, shall judge what is the essential difference between the two barbarisms, and decide for yourselves what is the seed of life in the one, and the sign of death in the other.

The first, – that which has in it the sign of death, – furnishes us at the same time with an illustration far too interesting to be passed by, of certain principles much depended on by our common modern designers. Taking up one of our architectural publications the other day, and opening it at random, I chanced upon this piece of information, put in rather curious English; but you shall have it as it stands: –

'Aristotle asserts, that the greatest species of the beautiful are Order, Symmetry, and the Definite.' . . . .

As far as I can make it out, the lecture [in which this sentence occurs] appears to have been just one of those of which you will at present hear so many, the protests of architects who have no knowledge of sculpture – or of any other mode of expressing natural beauty – *against* natural beauty; and their endeavour to substitute mathematical proportions for the knowledge of life they do not possess, and the representation of life of which they are incapable. Now, this substitution of obedience to mathematical law for sympathy with observed life, is the first characteristic of the hopeless work of all ages; as such, you will find it eminently manifested in the specimen I have to give you of the hopeless Gothic barbarism; the barbarism from which nothing could emerge – for which no future was possible but extinction. The Aristotelian principles of the Beautiful are, you remember, Order, Symmetry, and the Definite. Here you have the three, in perfection, applied to the ideal of an angel, in a psalter of the eighth century, existing in the library of St John's College, Cambridge.

Now, you see the characteristics of this utterly dead school are, first, the wilful closing of its eyes to natural facts; – for, however ignorant a person may be, he need only look at a human being to see that it has a mouth as well as eyes; and secondly, the endeavour to adorn or idealize natural fact according to its own notions: it puts red spots in the middle of the hands, and sharpens the thumbs, thinking to improve them. Here you have the most pure type possible of the principles of idealism in all ages: whenever people don't look at Nature, they always think they can improve her. You will also admire, doubtless, the exquisite result of the application of our great modern architectural principle of beauty – symmetry, or equal balance of part by part; you see even the eyes are made symmetrical – entirely round, instead of irregularly oval; and the iris is set properly in the middle, instead of – as nature has absurdly put it – rather under the upper lid. You will also observe the 'principle of the pyramid' in the general arrangement of the figure, and the value of 'series' in the placing of the dots.

From this dead barbarism we pass to living barbarism – to work done by hands quite as rude, if not ruder, and by minds as uninformed; and yet work which in every line of it is prophetic of power, and has in it the sure dawn of day. You have often heard it said that Giotto was the founder of art in Italy. He was not: neither he, nor Giunta Pisano, nor Niccolo Pisano. They all laid strong hands to the work, and brought it first into aspect above ground; but the foundation had been laid for them by the builders of the Lombardic churches in the valleys of the Adda and the Arno. It is in the sculpture of the round arched churches of North Italy, bearing disputable dates, ranging from the eighth to the twelfth century, that you will find the lowest struck roots of the art of Titian and Raphael. I go therefore, to the church which is certainly the earliest of these, St Ambrogio, of Milan, said still to retain some portions of the actual structure from which St Ambrose excluded Theodosius, and at all events furnishing the most archaic examples of Lombardic sculpture in North Italy. I do not venture to guess their date; they are barbarous enough for any date.

We find the pulpit of this church covered with interlacing patterns, closely resembling those of the manuscript at Cambridge, but among them is figure sculpture of a very different kind. It is wrought with mere incisions in the stone, of which the effect may be tolerably given by single lines in a drawing. Remember, therefore, for a moment – as characteristic of culminating Italian art – Michael Angelo's fresco of the 'Temptation of Eve,' in the Sistine chapel, and you will be more interested in seeing the birth of Italian art, illustrated by the same subject, from St Ambrogio, of Milan, the 'Serpent beguiling Eve.'

Yet, in that sketch, rude and ludicrous as it is, you have the elements of life in their first form. The people who could do that were sure to get on. For, observe, the workman's whole aim is straight at the facts, as well as he can get them; and not merely at the facts, but at the very heart of the facts. A common workman might have looked at nature for his serpent, but he would have thought only of its scales. But this fellow does not want scales, nor coils; he can do without them; he wants the serpent's heart – malice and insinuation; – and he has actually got them to some extent. So also a common workman, even in this barbarous stage of art, might have carved Eve's arms and body a good deal better; but this man does not care about arms and body, if he can only get at Eve's mind – show that she is pleased at being flattered, and yet in a stage of uncomfortable hesitation. And some look of listening, of complacency, and of embarrassment he has verily got: – note the eyes slightly askance, the lips compressed, and the right hand nervously grasping the left arm: nothing can be declared impossible to the people who could begin thus – the world is open to them, and all that is in it; while, on the contrary, nothing is possible to the man who did the symmetrical angel – the world is keyless to him ; he has built a cell for himself in which he must abide, barred up for ever – there is no more hope for him than for a sponge or a madrepore.

From *The Two Paths*, Lecture I, §§ 25–32

¶ 155
SEEING CLEARLY

But not only is there a *partial* and variable mystery thus caused by clouds and vapours throughout great spaces of landscape; there is a continual mystery caused throughout *all* spaces, caused by the absolute infinity of things. WE NEVER SEE ANYTHING CLEARLY. I stated this fact partly in the chapter on Truth of Space, in the first volume, but not with sufficient illustration, so that the reader might by that chapter have been led to infer that the mystery spoken of belonged to some special distance of the landscape, whereas the fact is, that everything we look at, be it large or small, near or distant, has an equal quantity of mystery in it; and the only question is, not how much mystery there is, but at what part of the object mystification begins. We suppose we see the ground under our feet clearly, but if we try to number its grains of dust, we shall find that it is as full of confusion and doubtful form, as anything else; so that there is literally *no* point of clear sight, and there never can be. What we call seeing a thing clearly, is only seeing enough of it to *make out what it is*; this point of intelligibility varying in distance for different magnitudes and kinds of things, while the appointed quantity of mystery remains nearly the same for all. Thus: throwing an open book and an embroidered handkerchief on a lawn, at a distance of a quarter of a mile we cannot tell which is which; that is the point of mystery for the whole of those things. They are then merely white spots of indistinct shape. We approach them, and perceive that one is a book, the other a handkerchief, but cannot read the one, nor trace the embroidery of the other. The mystery has ceased to be in the whole things, and has gone into their details. We go nearer, and can now read the text and trace the embroidery, but cannot see the fibres of the paper, nor the threads of the stuff. The mystery has gone into a third place. We take both up and look closely at them; we see the watermark and the threads, but not the hills and dales in the paper's surface, nor the fine fibres which shoot off from every thread. The mystery has gone into a fourth place, where it must stay, till we take a microscope, which will send it into a fifth, sixth, hundredth, or thousandth place, according to the power we use. When, therefore, we say, we see the book *clearly*, we mean only that we know it is a book. When we say that we see the letters clearly, we mean that we know what letters they are; and artists feel that they are drawing objects at a convenient distance when they are so near them as to know, and to be able in painting to show that they know, what the objects are, in a tolerably complete manner: but this power does not depend on any definite distance of the object, but on its size, kind, and distance, together; so that a small thing in the foreground may be precisely in the same *phase* or place of mystery as a large thing far away.

The other day, as I was lying down to rest on the side of the hill round which the Rhone sweeps in its main angle, opposite Martigny, and looking carefully across the valley to the ridge of the hill which rises above Martigny itself, then distant about four miles, a plantain seed-vessel about an inch long, and a withered head of a scabious half an inch broad, happened to be seen rising up, out of the grass near me, across the outline of the distant hill, so as seemingly to set themselves closely beside the large pines and chestnuts which fringed that distant ridge. The plantain was eight yards from me, and the scabious seven; and to my sight, at these distances, the plantain and the far-away pines were equally clear (it being a clear day, and the sun stooping to the west). The pines, four miles off, showed their branches, but I could not count them: and two or three young and old Spanish chestnuts beside them showed their broken masses distinctly; but I could not count those masses, only I knew the trees to be chestnuts by their general look. The plantain and scabious in like manner I knew to be plantain and scabious by their general look. I saw the plantain seed-vessel to be, somehow, rough, and that there were two little projections at the bottom of the scabious head which I knew to mean the leaves of the calyx; but I could no more count distinctly the seeds of the plantain, or the group of leaves forming the calyx of the scabious, than I could count the branches of the far-away pines.

Under these circumstances, it is quite evident that neither the pine nor plantain could have been rightly represented by a single dot or stroke of colour. Still less could they be represented by a definite drawing, on a small scale, of a pine with all its branches clear, or of a plantain with all its seeds clear. The round dot or long stroke would represent nothing, and the clear delineation too much. They were not mere dots of colour which I saw on the hill, but something full of essence of pine; out of which I could gather which were young and which were old, and discern the distorted and crabbed pines from the symmetrical and healthy pines; and feel how the evening sun was sending its searching threads among their dark leaves; – assuredly they were more than dots of colour. And yet not one of their boughs or outlines could be distinctly made out, or distinctly drawn. Therefore, if I had drawn either a definite pine, or a dot, I should have been equally wrong, the right lying in an inexplicable, almost inimitable, confusion between the two.

From *Modern Painters*, Vol. IV, Part V, ch. IV, §§ 4–6

¶ 156

ECONOMY OF DESIGN

If you give one grain of weight too much, so as to increase fatigue without profit, or bulk without value – that added grain is hurtful:

if you put one spot or one syllable out of its proper place, that spot or syllable will be destructive – how far destructive it is almost impossible to tell: a misplaced touch may sometimes annihilate the labour of hours. Nor are any of us prepared to understand the work of any great master, till we feel this, and feel it as distinctly as we do the value of arrangement in the notes of music. Take any noble musical air, and you find, on examining it, that not one even of the faintest or shortest notes can be removed without destruction to the whole passage in which it occurs; and that every note in the passage is twenty times more beautifully so introduced, than it would have been if played singly on the instrument. Precisely this degree of arrangement and relation must exist between every touch and line in a great picture. You may consider the whole as a prolonged musical composition: its parts, as separate airs connected in the story; its little bits and fragments of colour and line, as separate passages or bars in melodies; and down to the minutest note of the whole – down to the minutest *touch*, – if there is one that can be spared – that one is doing mischief.

From *The Two Paths*, Lecture i, § 44

¶ 157

NOT TO IMITATE EXECUTION

In a great man's work, at its fastest, no line is thrown away, and it is not by the rapidity, but the *economy* of the execution that you know him to be great. Now to judge of this economy, you must know exactly what he meant to do, otherwise you cannot of course discern how far he has done it; that is, you must know the beauty and nature of the thing he was drawing. All judgement of art thus finally founds itself on knowledge of Nature.

But farther observe, that this scrawled, or economic, or impetuous execution is never affectedly impetuous. If a great man is not in a hurry, he never pretends to be; if he has no eagerness in his heart, he puts none into his hand; if he thinks his effect would be better got with *two* lines, he never, to show his dexterity, tries to do it with one. Be assured, therefore (and this is a matter of great importance), that you will never produce a great drawing by imitating the execution of a great master. Acquire his knowledge and share his feelings, and the easy execution will fall from your hand as it did from his; but if you merely scrawl because he scrawled, or blot because he blotted, you will not only never advance in power, but every able draughtsman, and every judge whose opinion is worth having, will know you for a cheat, and despise you accordingly.

From *The Elements of Drawing*, Letter I, §§ 94–5

¶ 158
HAND RESPONSIVE TO EYE

Resolve always, as you look at the thing, what you will take, and what miss of it, and never let your hand run away with you, or get into any habit or method of touch. If you want a continuous line, your hand should pass calmly from one end of it to the other without a tremor; if you want a shaking and broken line, your hand should shake, or break off, as easily as a musician's finger shakes or stops on a note: only remember this, that there is no general way of doing *any* thing; no recipe can be given you for so much as the drawing of a cluster of grass. The grass may be ragged and stiff, or tender and flowing; sunburnt and sheep-bitten, or rank and languid; fresh or dry; lustrous or dull: look at it and try to draw as it is, and don't think how somebody 'told you to *do* grass.' So a stone may be round or angular, polished or rough, cracked all over like an ill-glazed teacup, or as united and broad as the breast of Hercules. It may be as flaky as a wafer, as powdery as a field puff-ball; it may be knotted like a ship's hawser, or kneaded like hammered iron, or knit like a Damascus sabre, or fused like a glass bottle, or crystallized like hoar-frost, or veined like a forest leaf: look at it, and don't try to remember how anybody told you to 'do a stone.'

From *The Elements of Drawing*, Letter II, § 108

¶ 159
WATERCOLOUR

The extended practice of water-colour painting, as a separate skill, is in every way harmful to the arts: its pleasant slightness and plausible dexterity divert the genius of the painter from its proper aims, and withdraw the attention of the public from excellence of higher claim; nor ought any man, who has the consciousness of ability for good work, to be ignorant of, or indolent in employing, the methods of making its results permanent as long as the laws of Nature allow.

From *Lectures on Art*, Lecture v, § 128

¶ 160

HARMONY OF RADIATION

Now, there are two kinds of harmonies of lines. One in which, moving more or less side by side, they variously, but evidently with consent, retire from or approach each other, intersect or oppose each other: currents of melody in music, for different voices, thus approach and cross, fall and rise, in harmony; so the waves of the sea, as they approach the shore, flow into one another or cross, but with a great unity through all; and so various lines of composition often flow harmoniously through and across each other in a picture. But the most simple and perfect connexion of lines is by radiation; that is, by their all springing from one point, or closing towards it: and this harmony is often, in Nature almost always, united with the other; as the boughs of trees, though they intersect and play amongst each other irregularly, indicate by their general tendency their origin from one root. An essential part of the beauty of all vegetable form is in this radiation; it is seen most simply in a single flower or leaf, as in a convolvulus bell, or chestnut leaf; but more beautifully in the complicated arrangements of the large boughs and sprays. For a leaf is only a flat piece of radiation; but the tree throws its branches on all sides, and even in every profile view of it, which presents a radiation more or less correspondent to that of its leaves, it is more beautiful, because varied by the freedom of the separate branches.

From *The Elements of Drawing*, Letter iii, § 210

THE DIFFICULTY OF DRAWING LEAVES

All this difficulty, however, attaches to the rendering merely the dark form of the sprays as they come against the sky. Within those sprays, and in the heart of the tree, there is a complexity of a much more embarrassing kind; for nearly all leaves have some lustre, and all are more or less translucent (letting light through them); therefore, in any given leaf, besides the intricacies of its own proper shadows and foreshortenings, there are three series of circumstances which alter or hide its forms. First, shadows cast on it by other leaves, – often very forcibly. Secondly light reflected from its lustrous surface, sometimes the blue of the sky, sometimes the white of clouds, or the sun itself flashing like a star. Thirdly, forms and shadows of other leaves, seen as darknesses through the translucent parts of the leaf; a most important element of foliage effect, but wholly neglected by landscape artists in general.

The consequence of all this is, that except now and then by chance, the form of a complete leaf is never seen; but a marvellous and quaint confusion, very definite, indeed, in its evidence of direction of growth, and unity of action, but wholly indefinable and inextricable, part by part, by any amount of patience. You cannot possibly work it out in facsimile, though you took a twelvemonth's time to a tree; and you must therefore try to discover some mode of execution which will more or less imitate, by its own variety and mystery, the variety and mystery of Nature, without absolute delineation of detail.

From *The Elements of Drawing*, Letter I, §§ 83–4

COLOUR AND HEALTH

As to the choice and harmony of colours in general, if you cannot choose and harmonize them by instinct, you will never do it at all. If you need examples of utterly harsh and horrible colour, you may find plenty given in treatises upon colouring, to illustrate the laws of harmony; and if you want to colour beautifully, colour as best pleases yourself at *quiet times,* not so as to catch the eye, nor look as if it were clever or difficult to colour in that way, but so that the colour may be pleasant to you when you are happy or thoughtful. Look much at the morning and evening sky, and much at simple flowers – dog-roses, wood-hyacinths, violets, poppies, thistles, heather, and such like, – as Nature arranges them in the woods and fields. If ever any scientific person tells you that two colours are 'discordant,' make a note of the two colours, and put them together whenever you can. I have actually heard people say that blue and green were discordant; the two colours which Nature seems to intend never to be separated, and never to be felt, either of them, in its full beauty without the other! – a peacock's neck, or a blue sky through green leaves, or a blue wave with green lights through it, being precisely the loveliest things, next to clouds at sunrise, in this coloured world of ours. If you have a good eye for colours, you will soon find out how constantly Nature puts purple and green together, purple and scarlet, green and blue, yellow and neutral grey, and the like; and how she strikes these colour-concords for general tones, and then works into them with innumerable subordinate ones; and you will gradually come to like what she does, and find out new and beautiful chords of colour in her work every day. If you enjoy them, depend upon it you will paint them to a certain point right; or, at least, if you do not enjoy them, you are certain to paint them wrong. If colour does not give you intense pleasure, let it alone; depend upon it, you are only tormenting the eyes and senses of people who feel colour, whenever you touch it; and that is unkind and improper.

You will find, also, your power of colouring depend much on your state of health and right balance of mind; when you are fatigued or ill you will not see colours well, and when you are ill-tempered you will not choose them well: thus, though not infallibly a test of character in individuals, colour power is a great sign of mental health in nations; when they are in a state of intellectual decline, their colouring always gets dull. You must also take great care not to be misled by affected talk about colours from people who have not the gift of it; numbers are eager and voluble about it who probably never in all their lives received one genuine colour-sensation. The modern religionists of the school of Overbeck are just like people who eat slate-pencil and chalk, and assure people that they are nicer and purer than strawberries and plums.

From *The Elements of Drawing*, Letter III, §§ 181-2

¶ 163
COLOUR: NATURE'S ECONOMY

Nature is just as economical of *her* fine colours as I have told you to be of yours. You would think by the way she paints, that her colours cost her something enormous; she will only give you a single pure touch, just where the petal turns into light; but down in the bell all is subdued, and under the petal all is subdued, even in the showiest flower. What you thought was bright blue is, when you look close, only dusty grey, or green, or purple, or every colour in the world at once, only a single gleam or streak of pure blue in the centre of it.

From *The Elements of Drawing*, Letter III, § 175

¶ 164
COLOUR BY GRADATION

Give me some mud off a city crossing, some ochre out of a gravel pit, and little whitening, and some coal-dust, and I will paint you a luminous picture, if you give me time to gradate my mud, and subdue my dust: but though you had the red of the ruby, the blue of the gentian, snow for the light, and amber for the gold, you cannot paint a luminous picture, if you keep the masses of those colours unbroken in purity, and unvarying in depth.

From *The Elements of Drawing*, Letter III, § 169

¶ 165
COSTLY WHITE

I say, first, the white precious. I do not mean merely glittering or brilliant: it is easy to scratch white sea-gulls out of black clouds, and

dot clumsy foliage with chalky dew; but when white is well
managed, it ought to be strangely delicious, – tender as well as
bright, like inlaid mother of pearl, or white roses washed in milk.
The eye ought to seek it for rest, brilliant though it may be; and
to feel it as a space of strange, heavenly paleness in the midst of the
flushing of the colours. This effect you can only reach by general
depth of middle tint, by absolutely refusing to allow any white to
exist except where you need it, and by keeping the white itself subdued by grey, except at a few points of chief lustre.

From *The Elements of Drawing*, Letter III, § 177

¶ 166

SYMBOLIC COLOUR

Both music and colour are naturally influences of peace; but in the
war trumpet, and the war shield, in the battle song and battle
standard, they have concentrated by beautiful imagination the cruel
passions of men; and there is nothing in all the Divina Commedia
of history more grotesque, yet more frightful, than the fact that,
from the almost fabulous period when the insanity and impiety of
war wrote themselves in the symbols of the shields of the Seven
against Thebes, colours have been the sign and stimulus of the most
furious and fatal passions that have rent the nations: blue against
green, in the decline of the Roman Empire; black against white, in
that of Florence; red against white, in the wars of the Royal houses
in England; and at this moment, red against white, in the contest of
anarchy and loyalty, in all the world.

From *Aratra Pentelici*, Lecture I, § 13

¶ 167

ROSES AND LANCES

There is a beautiful type of this neglect of the perfectness of the
Earth's beauty, by reason of the passions of men, in that picture of
Paul Uccello's of the battle of Sant' Egidio, in which the armies
meet on a country road beside a hedge of wild roses; the tender red
flowers tossing above the helmets, and glowing between the lowered

lances. For in like manner the whole of Nature only shone hitherto for man between the tossing of helmet-crests.

From *Modern Painters*, Vol. v, Part vi, ch. i, § 6

¶ 168

THE CHARACTERISTICS OF A GREAT PAINTER

Observe first that a great painter must necessarily be a man of strong and perfect physical constitution. He must be intensely sensitive, active, and vigorous in all powers whatever; gifted especially with a redundant nervous energy, able to sustain his eye and hand in unbroken continuousness of perception and effort. I do not stay to prove this. It will be found a fact by those who care to enquire into the matter. And this being so, your great painter can only under the most extraordinary circumstances be liable to fits of physical exhaustion or depression, and assuredly he is never liable to any morbid conditions of either; he may be healthily tired when he has worked hard, and will be all right again after he has rationally rested; he may be profoundly vexed, or thrown into fierce passion, but he will never mistake his own vexation for a gloomy state of the universe, nor expect to find consolation or calm by any supernatural help; he will set himself to forget his vexation, and conquer his passion, as small irksome pieces of entirely his own business, precisely in the way he would set himself to mend a hole in his canvass, or cool a pan of dangerously hot varnish. Farther, he is gifted by his exquisite sensibility with continual power of pleasure in eye, ear, and fancy; and his business consists, one half of it, in the pursuit of that pleasure, and the other half in the pursuit of facts, which pursuit is another kind of pleasure, as great, and besides sharp and refreshing when the other is at all deadened by repetition.

Farther, it not only is his business to seek this pleasure, but he has no trouble in seeking it, it is everywhere ready to his hand, as ever fruit was in Paradise. Nothing exists in the world about him that is not beautiful in his eyes, in one degree or another; so far as not beautiful it is serviceable to set off beauty; nothing can possibly present itself to him that is not either lovely, or tractable, and shapeable into loveliness; there is no Evil in his eyes; – only Good, and that which displays good. Light is lovely to him; but not a whit more precious than shadow – white is pleasant to him, as it is to you and me; but he differs from you and me in having no less delight in black, when black is where black should be. Graceful and soft forms are indeed a luxury to him; but he would not thank you for them unless you allowed him also rugged ones. Feasting is consolatory to his system, as to yours and mine, but he differs from us in feeling also an exquisite complacency in Fasting, and taking infinite satisfaction in Emptiness. You can excite his intense gratitude by the gift of Anything, and if you have Nothing to give him, you will find that Nothing is exactly the thing he most wants, and that he will immediately proceed to make half a picture out of it. How can you make such a man as this Discontented with the world? There are Three colours in it – he wants no fourth – finds three quite as much as he can manage. There's good firm ground to set easels on in it – he is not sure that they would stand so firm upon clouds, or that he could paint flying. But the world is a passing, dreamy, visionary state of things! Do you then want them to be always the same – how could one vary one's picture if that were so? But people lose their beauty and get old in the world! Then they have long beards, nothing can be more picturesque. But people die out of the world! How else would there be room for the Children in it, and how could one paint without children? But how unhappy people are in the world. It must be their own fault surely, I'm not. But how thin and ugly their grief makes them – don't you mourn for the departure of the bloom of youth? Not at all – I like painting thin people as well as fat ones – one can see their skulls better. But how wicked people are in the world! is it not dreadful to see such wickedness? Not at all – it varies the expression of their faces; there would be no pleasure in painting if they all looked alike. . . .

What can be done with such a man? How are you to make him care about future things? Even if misfortunes fall upon him, such as would make other people religious, he will not seek for consolation in Heaven. He will seek it in his painting-room. So long as he can paint, nothing will crush him. Nothing short of blindness –

nothing, that is, but his ceasing to be a painter, will enable him to contemplate futurity.

Nay; – it may be replied – may he not be led, without suffering, but in his own work and his own way to that happy religion which you have admitted to be possible, in which this world may be enjoyed without forgetting the next? No; by no manner of means – at least of means hitherto brought to bear in this world's history. As far as we have seen, hitherto, all happy religious life has consisted in the fulfilment of direct social duty – in pure and calm domestic relations – in active charity, or in simply useful occupations, trades, husbandry, such as leave the mind free to dwell on matters connected with the spiritual life. You may have religious shepherds, labourers, farmers, merchants, shopmen, manufacturers – and Religious painters, so far as they make themselves manufacturers – so far as they remain painters – no.

For consider the first business of a painter; half, as I said, of his business in this world must consist in simply seeking his own pleasure, and that, in the main, a sensual pleasure. I don't mean a degrading one, but a bodily not a spiritual pleasure. Seeing a fine red, or a beautiful line is a bodily and selfish pleasure, at least as compared with Gratitude or Love – or the other feelings called into play by social action. And moreover, this bodily pleasure must be sought for Itself and Himself. Not for anybody else's sake. Unless a painter works wholly to please himself, he will please nobody; – he must not be thinking while he is at work of any human creature's likings, but his own. He must not benevolently desire to please any more than ambitiously – neither in kindness, nor in pride, may he defer to other people's sensations. 'I alone here, on my inch of earth, paint this thing for my own sole joy, and according to my own sole mind. So I should paint it, if no other human being existed but myself. Let who will get good or ill from this – I am not concerned therewith. Thus I must do it, for thus I see it, and thus I like it, woe be to me if I paint as other people see or like.' This is the first law of the painter's being; ruthless and selfish – cutting him entirely away from all love of his fellow-creatures, till the work is done. When done he may open the door to them, saying calmly 'If you like this – well, I am glad. If you like it not, away with you, I've nothing for you.' No great exertion of benevolence, even in this. But farther. In order to the pursuit of this beauty rightly, our great painter must not shrink in a timid way from any form of vice or ugliness. He must know them to the full, or he cannot understand the relations of beauty and virtue to them. . . .

And this being so, as the great painter is not allowed to be indignant or exclusive, it is not possible for him to nourish his (so called) spiritual desires, as it is to an ordinarily virtuous person. Your ordinarily good man absolutely avoids, either for fear of getting harm, or because he has no pleasure in such places or people, all scenes that foster vice, and all companies that delight in it. He spends his summer evenings on his own quiet lawn, listening to the blackbirds or singing hymns with his children. But you can't learn to paint of blackbirds, nor by singing hymns. You must be in the wildness of the midnight masque – in the misery of the dark street at dawn – in the crowd when it rages fiercest against law – in the council-chamber when it devises worst [   ]¹ against the people – on the moor with the wanderer, or the robber – in the boudoir with the delicate recklessness of female guilt – and all this, without being angry at any of these things – without ever losing your temper so much as to make your hand shake, or getting so much of the mist of sorrow in your eyes, as will at all interfere with your matching of colours; never even allowing yourself to disapprove of anything that anybody enjoys, so far as not to enter into their enjoyment. Does a man get drunk, you must be ready to pledge him. Is he preparing to cut purses – you must go to Gadshill with him – nothing doubting – no wise thinking yourself bound to play the Justice, yet always cool yourself as you either look on, or take any necessary part in the play. Cool, and strong-willed – moveless in observant soul. Does a man die at your feet – your business is not to help him, but to note the colour of his lips; does a woman embrace her destruction before you, your business is not to save her, but to watch how she bends her arms. Not a specially religious or spiritual business this, it might appear.

And then, lastly. Not only is your painter thus concerned wholly and indiscriminately with the affairs of this world, but the mechanism

1. A word is left blank in the MS. here.

of his own business is one which must occupy nearly all the thoughts of his leisure or seclusion. Whatever time others give to meditation, or other beneficial mental exercise, he must give to mere practice of touch, and study of hue. Painting cannot be learned in any other way. So many hours a day of steady practice – all your mind and nervous energy put into it – or no good painting. No genius will exempt you from this law of toil; a painter's genius especially signifies the love of beauty which will never let him rest in the effort to realize it. A man of science may, if he choose, rest content at any moment with the knowledge he has attained, for however much more he learns, he will be as far from knowing All, as ever he was; but to a painter, absolute perfectness of skill is an approachable, though not an attainable goal: every hour that he gives to his work, brings him nearer a conceivable faculty of laying on the exact colour he wants in the exact shape he wants; he feels himself every day able to do more and more as he would; and though he knows he can never be absolutely perfect, any more than a continually enlarging circle can become an infinite straight line, still, the straight line is before his eyes, and forces him for ever to strive to reach it more and more nearly. This continual mechanical toil, this fixed physical aim, occupies his intellect and energy at every spare moment – blunts his sorrows, restrains his enthusiasms, limits his speculations, takes away all common chances of his being affected by the feelings or imaginations which lead other men to religion.[1]

From *Modern Painters*, Vol. II, Appendix II (C. & W., pp. 386–9), §§ 7–13

¶ 169

ORIGINALITY

In all base schools of art, the craftsman is dependent for his bread on originality; that is to say, on finding in himself some fragment of isolated faculty, by which his work may be recognized as distinct

1. This passage, so much at variance with Ruskin's earlier teaching, must have been written after his 'de-conversion' of 1858 (cf. pp. 7 and 129). He apparently intended to include it in a new edition of *Modern Painters*, Vol. II, but it would have been completely out of place and was rightly left in MS. It cannot therefore have been known to Walter Pater or Oscar Wilde, whose doctrine of the amoral artist it so surprisingly anticipates.

from that of other men. We are ready enough to take delight in our little doings, without any such stimulus; – what must be the effect of the popular applause which continually suggests that the little thing we can separately do is as excellent as it is singular! and what the effect of the bribe, held out to us through the whole of life, to produce – it being also at our peril *not* to produce – something different from the work of our neighbours? In all great schools of art these conditions are exactly reversed. An artist is praised in these not for what is different in him from others, nor for solitary performance of singular work; but only for doing most strongly what all are endeavouring; and for contributing, in the measure of his strength, to some great achievement, to be completed by the unity of multitudes, and the sequence of ages.

From *The Eagle's Nest*, Lecture II, § 32

¶ 170
THE YOUNG ARTIST

No man can pursue his own track in peace, nor obtain consistent guidance, if doubtful of his track. All places are full of inconsistent example, all mouths of contradictory advice, all prospects of opposite temptations. The young artist sees myriads of things he would like to do, but cannot learn from their authors how they were done, nor choose decisively any method which he may follow with the accuracy and confidence necessary to success. He is not even sure if his thoughts are his own; for the whole atmosphere around him is full of floating suggestion: those which are his own he cannot keep pure, for he breathes a dust of decayed ideas, wreck of the souls of dead nations, driven by contrary winds. . . . Even were the style chosen true to his own nature, and persisted in, there is harm in the very eminence of the models set before him at the beginning of his career. If he feels their power, they make him restless and impatient, it may be despondent, it may be madly and fruitlessly ambitious. If he does not feel it, he is sure to be struck by what is weakest or slightest of their peculiar qualities; fancies that *this* is what they are praised for; tries to catch the trick of it; and whatever easy vice or mechanical habit the master may have been betrayed or warped into, the unhappy pupil watches and adopts, triumphant in its ease.

From *The Cestus of Aglaia*, Prefatory, § 4

¶ 171

TRAINING THE POET AND THE PAINTER

But is there to be no place left, it will be indignantly asked, for imagination and invention, for poetical power or love of ideal beauty? Yes; the highest, the noblest place – that which these only can attain when they are all used in the cause, and with the aid of truth. Wherever imagination and sentiment are, they will either show themselves without forcing, or, if capable of artificial development, the kind of training which such a school of art would give them would be the best they could receive. The infinite absurdity and failure of our present training consists mainly in this, that we do not rank imagination and invention high enough, and suppose that they *can* be taught. Throughout every sentence that I have ever written, the reader will find the same rank attributed to these powers – the rank of purely divine gift, not to be attained, increased, or in anywise modified by teaching, only in various ways capable of being concealed or quenched. Understand this thoroughly; know once for all, that a poet on canvas is exactly the same species of creature as a poet in song, and nearly every error in our methods of teaching will be done away with. For who among us now thinks of bringing men up to be poets? – of producing poets by any kind of general recipe or method of cultivation? Suppose even that we see in a youth that which we hope may, in its development, become a power of this kind, should we instantly, supposing that we wanted to make a poet of him, and nothing else, forbid him all quiet, steady, rational labour? Should we force him to perpetual spinning of new crudities out of his boyish brain, and set before him, as the only objects of his study, the laws of versification which criticism has supposed itself to discover in the works of previous writers? Whatever gifts the boy had, would much be likely to come of them so treated? unless, indeed, they were so great as to break through all such snares of falsehood and vanity, and build their own foundation in spite of us; whereas if, as in cases numbering millions against units, the natural gifts were too weak to do this, could anything come of such training but utter inanity and spuriousness of the whole man? But if we had sense, should we not rather restrain and bridle the first flame of invention in early youth, heaping material on it as one would on the first sparks and tongues of a fire which we desired to feed into greatness? Should we not educate the whole intellect into general strength, and all the affections into warmth and honesty, and look to heaven for the rest? This, I say, we should have sense enough to do, in order to produce a poet in words: but, it being required to produce a poet on canvas, what is our way of setting to work? We begin, in all probability, by telling the youth of fifteen or sixteen, that Nature is full of faults, and that he is to improve her; but that Raphael is perfection, and that the more he copies Raphael the better; that after much copying of Raphael, he is to try what he can do himself in a Raphaelesque, but yet original manner: that is to say, he is to try to do something very clever, all out of his own head, but yet this clever something is to be properly subjected to Raphaelesque rules, is to have a principal light occupying one seventh of its space, and a principal shadow occupying one third of the same; that no two people's heads in the picture are to be turned the same way, and that all the personages represented are to possess ideal beauty of the highest order, which ideal beauty consists partly in a Greek outline of nose, partly in proportions expressible in decimal fractions between the lips and chin; but mostly in that degree of improvement which the youth of sixteen is to bestow upon God's work in general. This I say is the kind of teaching which through various channels, Royal Academy lecturings, press criticisms, public enthusiasm, and not least by solid weight of gold, we give to our young men. And we wonder we have no painters!

From *Pre-Raphaelitism*, § 16

¶ 172

ART MUST RESEMBLE

All second-rate artists – (and remember, the second-rate ones are a loquacious multitude, while the great come only one or two in a century; and then, silently) – all second-rate artists will tell you that the object of fine art is not resemblance, but some kind of abstraction more refined than reality. Put that out of your heads at once. The object of the great Resemblant Arts is, and always has been, to resemble; and to resemble as closely as possible. It is the function of a good portrait to set the man before you in habit as he lived, and I would we had a few more that did so. It is the function of a good landscape to set the scene before you in its reality; to make you, if it may be, think the clouds are flying, and the streams foaming. It is the function of the best sculptor – the true Dædalus – to make stillness look like breathing, and marble look like flesh.

And in all great times of art, this purpose is as naïvely expressed as it is steadily held. All the talk about abstraction belongs to periods of decadence. In living times, people see something living that pleases them; and they try to make it live for ever, or to make something as like it as possible, that will last for ever. They paint their statues, and inlay the eyes with jewels, and set real crowns on the heads; they finish, in their pictures, every thread of embroidery, and would fain, if they could, draw every leaf upon the trees. And their only verbal expression of conscious success is, that they have made their work 'look real.'

You think all that very wrong. So did I, once; but it was I that was wrong. A long time ago, before ever I had seen Oxford, I painted a picture of the Lake of Como, for my father. It was not at all like the Lake of Como; but I thought it rather the better for that. My father differed with me; and objected particularly to a boat with a red and yellow awning, which I had put into the most conspicuous corner of my drawing. I declared this boat to be 'necessary to the composition.' My father not the less objected, that he had never seen such a boat, either at Como or elsewhere; and suggested that if I would make the lake look a little more like water, I should be under no necessity of explaining its nature by the presence of floating objects. I thought him at the time a very simple person for his pains; but have since learned, and it is the very gist of all practical matters, which, as Professor of Fine Art, I have now to tell you, that the great point in painting a lake is – to get it to look like water.

From *Aratra Pentelici*, Lecture IV, §§ 122–4

REWARDS TOO LATE

Even on the present system, the boys who have really intense art capacity, generally make painters of themselves; but then, the best half of their early energy is lost in the battle of life. Before a good painter can get employment, his mind has always been embittered, and his genius distorted. A common mind usually stoops, in plastic chill, to whatever is asked of it, and scrapes or daubs its way complacently into public favour. But your great men quarrel with you, and you revenge yourselves by starving them for the first half of their lives. Precisely in the degree in which any painter possesses original genius, is at present the increase of moral certainty that during his early years he will have a hard battle to fight; and that just at the time when his conceptions ought to be full and happy, his temper gentle, and his hopes enthusiastic – just at that most critical period, his heart is full of anxieties and household cares; he is chilled by disappointments, and vexed by injustice; he becomes obstinate in his errors, no less than in his virtues, and the arrows of his aims are blunted, as the reeds of his trust are broken. . . .

For it is only the young who can receive much reward from men's praise; the old, when they are great, get too far beyond and above you to care what you think of them. You may urge them then with sympathy, and surround them then with acclamation; but they will doubt your pleasure, and despise your praise. . . .

Every noble youth looks back, as to the chiefest joy which this world's honour ever gave him, to the moment when first he saw his father's eyes flash with pride, and his mother turn away her head, lest he should take her tears for tears of sorrow. Even the lover's joy, when some worthiness of his is acknowledged before his mistress, is not so great as that, for it is not so pure – the desire to exalt himself in her eyes mixes with that of giving her delight; but he does not need to exalt himself in his parents' eyes: it is with the pure hope of giving them pleasure that he comes to tell them what he has done, or what has been said of him; and therefore he has a purer pleasure of his own. And this purest and best of rewards you keep from him if you can; you feed him in his tender youth with ashes and dishonour; and then you come to him obsequious, but too late, with your sharp laurel crown, the dew all dried off its leaves; and you thrust it into his languid hand, and he looks at you wistfully. What shall he do with it? What can he do, but go and lay it on his mother's grave?

From *A Joy for Ever*, Lecture I, §§ 23 and 26–7

¶ 174

EXECUTION IN PAINTING

You will continually hear artists disputing about grounds, glazings, vehicles, varnishes, transparencies, opacities, oleaginousnesses. All that talk is as idle as the east wind. Get a flat surface that won't crack, – some coloured substance that will stick upon it, and remain always of the colour it was when you put it on, – and a pig's bristle or two, wedged in a stick; and if you can't paint, you are no painter; and had better not talk about the art.

The one thing you have to learn – the one power truly called that of 'painting' – is to lay on any coloured substance, whatever its consistence may be, (from mortar to ether,) *at once*, of the exact tint you want, in the exact form you want, and in the exact quantity you want. *That* is painting.

Now you are well aware that to play on the violin well, requires some practice. Painting is playing on a colour-violin, seventy-times-seven stringed, and inventing your tune as you play it! That is the easy, simple, straightforward business you have to learn. . . .

Perfectly, you never can, but by birth-gift. The entirely first-rate musicians and painters are born, like Mercury; – their words are music, and their touch is gold: sound and colour wait on them from their youth; and no practice will ever enable other human creatures to do anything like them. The most favourable conditions, the most docile and apt temper, and the unwearied practice of life, will never enable any painter of merely average human capacity to lay a single touch like Gainsborough, Velasquez, Tintoret, or Luini.

From *The Laws of Fésole*, ch. VII, §§ 5–7

¶ 175

SCIENCE AND THE ARTIST

With increasingly evil results to all of us, the separation is every day widening between the man of science and the artist – in that, whether painter, sculptor, or musician, the latter is pre-eminently a person who sees with his Eyes, hears with his Ears, and labours with his Body, as God constructed them; and who, in using instruments, limits himself to those which convey or communicate his human power, while he rejects all that increase it. Titian would refuse to quicken his touch by electricity; and Michael Angelo to substitute a steam-hammer for his mallet. Such men not only do not desire, they imperatively and scornfully refuse, either the force, or the information, which are beyond the scope of the flesh and the senses of humanity.

From *Deucalion*, Vol. I, ch. II, § 4

¶ 176

SOCIETY AND THE ARTIST

Society always has a destructive influence upon an artist: first, by its sympathy with his meanest powers; secondly, by its chilling want of understanding of his greatest; and, thirdly, by its vain occupation of his time and thoughts. Of course a painter of men must be *among* men; but it ought to be as a watcher, not as a companion.

From *The Stones of Venice*, Vol. III, ch. II, n. to § 13

¶ 177

FOR ART EDUCATION

Now I assure you solemnly that these squalid spaces of filth and disorder, and these frescoes of the bill-sticker – one more monstrous than the other – and these shops in your main public thoroughfares filled with base photographs and the woodcuts of murder and burglary, which render your penny literature chiefly saleable, these are your true elements of popular education – these, as opposed to the frescoed cloister of the Campo Santo of Pisa and frescoed streets of Padua and Verona – and against this popular education your art schools cannot stand.

From *Modern Art*, § 17

¶ 178

RESTORED PICTURES

The greater number of persons or societies throughout Europe, whom wealth, or chance, or inheritance has put in possession of valuable pictures, do not know a good picture from a bad one, and have no idea in what the value of a picture really consists. The reputation of certain works is raised, partly by accident, partly by the just testimony of artists, partly by the various and generally bad taste of the public (no picture, that I know of, has ever, in modern times, attained popularity, in the full sense of the term, without having some exceedingly bad qualities mingled with its good ones), and when this reputation has once been completely established, it little matters to what state the picture may be reduced: few minds are so completely devoid of imagination as to be unable to invest it with the beauties which they have heard attributed to it.

This being so, the pictures that are most valued are for the most part those by masters of established renown, which are highly or neatly finished, and of a size small enough to admit of their being placed in galleries or saloons, so as to be made subjects of ostentation, and to be easily seen by a crowd. For the support of the fame and value of such pictures, little more is necessary than that they should be kept bright, partly by cleaning, which is incipient destruction, and partly by what is called 'restoring,' that is, painting over, which is of course total destruction. Nearly all the gallery pictures in modern Europe have been more or less destroyed by one or other of these operations, generally exactly in proportion to the estimation in which they are held; and as, originally, the smaller and more highly finished works of any great master are usually his worst, the contents of many of our most celebrated galleries are by this time, in reality, of very small value indeed.

On the other hand, the most precious works of any noble painter are usually those which have been done quickly, and in the heat of the first thought, on a large scale, for places where there was little likelihood of their being well seen, or for patrons from whom there was little prospect of rich remuneration. In general, the best things are done in this way, or else in the enthusiasm and pride of accomplishing some great purpose, such as painting a cathedral or a campo-santo from one end to the other, especially when the time has been short and circumstances disadvantageous.

Works thus executed are of course, despised, on account of their quantity, as well as their frequent slightness, in the places where they exist; and they are too large to be portable, and too vast and comprehensive to be read on the spot, in the hasty temper of the present age. They are, therefore, almost universally neglected, whitewashed by custodes, shot at by soldiers, suffered to drop from the walls piecemeal in powder and rags by society in general; but, which is an advantage more than counterbalancing all this evil, they are not often 'restored.' What is left of them, however fragmentary, however ruinous, however obscured and defiled, is almost always *the real thing*; there are no fresh readings: and therefore the greatest treasures of art which Europe at this moment possesses are pieces of old plaster on ruinous brick walls, where the lizards burrow and bask, and which few other living creatures ever approach: and torn sheets of dim canvas, in waste corners of churches; and mildewed stains, in the shape of human figures, on the walls of dark chambers, which now and then an exploring traveller causes to be unlocked by their tottering custode, looks hastily around, and retreats from in a weary satisfaction at his accomplished duty.

From *The Stones of Venice*, Vol. II, ch. VIII, §§ 135–8

¶ 179
COPYING

But how difficult it is, to tell any man not to 'improve' his copy! All one's little character and life goes into the minute preferences which are shown in the copy. In one's own feeble sort, it must be prettier than the original, or it is dead.

From a letter to Charles Eliot Norton, 11 April 1874

ART AND HISTORY

Great nations write their autobiographies in three manuscripts; – the book of their deeds, the book of their words, and the book of their art. Not one of these books can be understood unless we read the two others; but of the three, the only quite trustworthy one is the last. The acts of a nation may be triumphant by its good fortune; and its words mighty by the genius of a few of its children: but its art, only by the general gifts and common sympathies of the race.

Again, the policy of a nation may be compelled, and, therefore, not indicative of its true character. Its words may be false, while yet the race remain unconscious of their falsehood; and no historian can assuredly detect the hypocrisy. But art is always instinctive; and the honesty or pretence of it is therefore open to the day. The Delphic oracle may or may not have been spoken by an honest priestess, – we cannot tell by the words of it; a liar may rationally believe them a lie, such as he would himself have spoken; and a true man, with equal reason, may believe them spoken in truth. But there is no question possible in art: at a glance (when we have learned to read) we know the religion of Angelico to be sincere, and of Titian, assumed.

The evidence, therefore, of the third book is the most vital to our knowledge of any nation's life; and the history of Venice is chiefly written in such manuscript. It once lay open on the waves, miraculous, like St Cuthbert's book, – a golden legend on countless leaves: now, like Baruch's scroll, it is being cut with the penknife, leaf by leaf, and consumed in the fire of the most brutish of the fiends. What fragments of it may yet be saved in blackened scroll, like those withered Cottonian relics in our National library, of which so much has been redeemed by love and skill, this book will help you, partly, to read.

From the Preface to *St Mark's Rest*

¶ 181

BYZANTINE ART

Every man of real genius took up his function of illustrating the scheme of human morality and salvation, as naturally, and faithfully, as an English mother of today giving her children their first lessons in the Bible. In this endeavour to teach they almost unawares taught themselves; the question 'How shall I represent this most clearly?' became to themselves, presently, 'How was this most likely to have happened?' and habits of fresh and accurate thought thus quickly enlivened the formalities of the Greek pictorial theology; formalities themselves beneficient, because restraining by their severity and mystery the wantonness of the newer life. Foolish modern critics have seen nothing in the Byzantine school but a barbarism to be conquered and forgotten. But that school brought to the art scholars of the thirteenth century, laws which had been serviceable to Phidias, and symbols which had been beautiful to Homer: and methods and habits of pictorial scholarship which gave a refinement of manner to the work of the simplest craftsman, and became an education to the higher artists which no discipline of literature can now bestow, developed themselves in the effort to decipher, and the impulse to re-interpret, the Eleusinian divinity of Byzantine tradition.

From *Val d'Arno*, Lecture III, § 87

¶ 182

NORTHERN AND SOUTHERN ART

Now therefore, when you hear me so often say that the Northern races – Norman and Lombard, – are active, or dramatic, in their art; and that the Southern races – Greek and Arabian – are contemplative, you ought instantly to ask farther, Active in what? Contemplative of what? And the answer is, The active art – Lombardic, – rejoices in hunting and fighting; the contemplative art – Byzantine, – contemplates the mysteries of the Christian faith.

And at first, on such answer, one would be apt at once to conclude – All grossness must be in the Lombard; all good in the Byzantine.

But again we should be wrong, – and extremely wrong. For the hunting and fighting did practically produce strong, and often virtuous men; while the perpetual and inactive contemplation of what it was impossible to understand, did not on the whole render the contemplative persons stronger, wiser, or even more amiable. So that, in the twelfth century, while the Northern art was only in need of direction, the Southern was in need of life. The North was indeed spending its valour and virtue on ignoble objects; but the South disgracing the noblest objects by its want of valour and virtue.

From *Mornings in Florence*, 'The Second Morning', § 32

¶ 183

ART AND WARLIKE NATIONS

Young soldiers, I do not doubt but that many of you came unwillingly to-night, and many in merely contemptuous curiosity, to hear what a writer on painting could possibly say, or would venture to say, respecting your great art of war. You may well think within yourselves that a painter might, perhaps without immodesty, lecture younger painters upon painting, but not young lawyers upon law, nor young physicians upon medicine – least of all, it may seem to you, young warriors, upon war. . . .

But being asked, not once nor twice, I have not ventured persistently to refuse; and I will try, in very few words, to lay before you some reason why you should accept my excuse, and hear me patiently. You may imagine that your work is wholly foreign to, and separate from, mine. So far from that, all the pure and noble arts of peace are founded on war; no great art ever yet rose on earth, but among a nation of soldiers. There is no art among a shepherd people, if it remains at peace. There is no art among an agricultural people, if it remains at peace. Commerce is barely consistent with fine art; but cannot produce it. Manufacture not only is unable to produce it, but invariably destroys whatever seeds of it exist. There is no great art possible to a nation but that which is based on battle.

From *The Crown of Wild Olive*, Lecture III, §§ 85–6

ART AND WARLIKE IMPLEMENTS

A nation which lives a pastoral and innocent life never decorates the shepherd's staff or the plough-handle; but races who live by depredation and slaughter nearly always bestow exquisite ornaments on the quiver, the helmet, and the spear.

From *The Two Paths*, Lecture I, § 7

¶ 185

FOILS TO BEAUTY

Beauty deprived of its proper foils and adjuncts ceases to be enjoyed as beauty, just as light deprived of all shadow ceases to be enjoyed as light. A white canvas cannot produce an effect of sunshine; the painter must darken it in some places before he can make it look luminous in others; nor can an uninterrupted succession of beauty produce the true effect of beauty; it must be foiled by inferiority before its own power can be developed. Nature has for the most part mingled her inferior and noble elements as she mingles sunshine with shade, giving due use and influence to both, and the painter who chooses to remove the shadow, perishes in the burning desert he has created. The truly high and beautiful art of Angelico is continually refreshed and strengthened by his frank portraiture of the most ordinary features of his brother monks and of the recorded peculiarities of ungainly sanctity; but the modern German and Raphaelesque schools lose all honour and nobleness in barber-like admiration of handsome faces, and have, in fact, no real faith except in straight noses, and curled hair. Paul Veronese opposes the dwarf to the soldier, and the negress to the queen; Shakspeare places Caliban beside Miranda, and Autolycus beside Perdita; but the vulgar idealist withdraws his beauty to the safety of the saloon, and his innocence to the seclusion of the cloister; he pretends that he does this in delicacy of choice and purity of sentiment, while in truth he has neither courage to front the monster, nor wit enough to furnish the knave.

From *Modern Painters*, Vol. III, Part IV, ch. III, § 14

MAGNIFICENT ANIMALITY

Certainly it seems intended that strong and frank animality, rejecting all tendency to asceticism, monachism, pietism, and so on, should be connected with the strongest intellects. Dante, indeed, is severe, at least, of all nameable great men; he is the severest I know. But Homer, Shakespeare, Tintoret, Veronese, Titian, Michael Angelo, Sir Joshua, Rubens, Velasquez, Correggio, Turner, are all of them boldly Animal. Francia and Angelico and all the purists, however beautiful, are poor weak creatures in comparison. I don't understand it; one would have thought purity gave strength, but it doesn't. A good, stout, self-commanding, magnificent Animality is the make for poets and artists, it seems to me. . . .

Has God made faces beautiful and limbs strong, and created these strange, fiery, fantastic energies, and created the splendour of substance and the love of it; created gold, and pearls, and crystal, and the sun that makes them gorgeous; and filled human fancy with all splendid thoughts; and given to the human touch its power of placing and brightening and perfecting, only that all these things may lead His creatures away from Him? And is this mighty Paul Veronese, in whose soul there is a strength as of the snowy mountains, and within whose brain all the pomp and majesty of humanity floats in a marshalled glory, capacious and serene like clouds at sunset – this man whose finger is as fire, and whose eye is like the morning – is he a servant of the devil; and is the poor little wretch in a tidy black tie, to whom I have been listening this Sunday morning expounding Nothing with a twang – is he a servant of God?

It is a great mystery. I begin to suspect we are all wrong together – Paul Veronese in letting his power waste into wantonness, and the religious people in mistaking their weakness and dulness for seriousness and piety. It is all very well for people to fast, who can't eat; and to preach, who cannot talk nor sing; and to walk barefoot, who cannot ride, and then think themselves good. Let them learn to master the world before they abuse it.

From *Modern Painters*, Vol. v, Introduction, notes on the Turin Gallery sent in letter or note form to his father (C. & W., pp. xl–xli)

¶ 187
THE TASTE OF THE PURE IN HEART

I cannot answer for the experience of others, but I never yet met with a Christian whose heart was thoroughly set upon the world to come, and, so far as human judgment could pronounce, perfect and right before God, who cared about art at all. I have known several very noble Christian men who loved it intensely, but in them there was always traceable some entanglement of the thoughts with the matters of this world, causing them to fall into strange distresses and doubts, and often leading them into what they themselves would confess to be errors in understanding, or even failures in duty. I do not say that these men may not, many of them, be in very deed nobler than those whose conduct is more consistent; they may be more tender in the tone of all their feelings, and farther-sighted in soul, and for that very reason exposed to greater trials and fears, than those whose hardier frame and naturally narrower vision enable them with less effort to give their hands to God and walk with Him. But still, the general fact is indeed so, that I have never known a man who seemed altogether right and calm in faith, who seriously cared about art; and when casually moved by it, it is quite impossible to say beforehand by what class of art this impression will on such men be made. Very often it is by a theatrical commonplace, more frequently still by false sentiment.

From *The Stones of Venice*, Vol. II, ch. IV, § 58

¶ 188
THE TWO DOGS

Ignorance, which is contented and clumsy, will produce what is imperfect, but not offensive. But ignorance *dis*contented and dexterous, learning what it cannot understand, and imitating what it cannot enjoy, produces the most loathsome forms of manufacture that can disgrace or mislead humanity. Some years since, as I was looking through the modern gallery at the quite provincial German School of Düsseldorf, I was fain to leave all their epic and religious designs, that I might stay long before a little painting of a shepherd boy carving his dog out of a bit of deal. The dog was sitting by, with the satisfied and dignified air of a personage about for the first time in his life to be worthily represented in sculpture; and his master was evidently succeeding to his mind in expressing the features of his friend. The little scene was one which, as you know, must take place continually among the cottage artists who supply the toys of Nuremberg and Berne. Happy, these! so long as, undisturbed by ambition, they spend their leisure time in work pretending only to amuse, yet capable, in its own way, of showing accomplished dexterity, and vivid perception of nature. We, in the hope of doing great things, have surrounded our workmen with Italian models, and tempted them with prizes into competitive mimicry of all that is best, or that we imagine to be best, in the work of every people under the sun. And the result of our instruction is only that we are able to produce, – I am now quoting the statement I made last May, 'the most perfectly and roundly ill-done things' that ever came from human hands. I should thankfully put upon my chimney-piece the wooden dog cut by the shepherd boy; but I should be willing to forfeit a large sum rather than keep in my room the number 1 of the Kensington Museum – thus described in its catalogue – 'Statue in black and white marble, of a Newfoundland dog standing on a serpent, which rests on a marble cushion; – the pedestal ornamented with Pietra Dura fruits in relief.'

From *The Eagle's Nest*, ch. v, § 88

¶ 189

VULGAR PURISTS

The world is full of vulgar Purists, who bring discredit on all selection by the silliness of their choice; and this the more, because the very becoming a Purist is commonly indicative of some slight degree of weakness, readiness to be offended, or narrowness of understanding of the ends of things.[1]

From *The Stones of Venice*, Vol. II, ch. VI, § 62

1. Ruskin is evidently thinking of the group of German painters known as the Nazarener, founded by Overbeck in 1809, which had a considerable influence on English painters such as Dyce.

¶ 190
GOOD ART MUST BE A SETTLED HABIT

No nation ever had, or will have, the power of suddenly developing, under the pressure of necessity, faculties it had neglected when it was at ease; nor of teaching itself, in poverty, the skill to produce what it has never, in opulence, had the sense to admire.

From *Lectures on Art*, Lecture 1, § 6

¶ 191
FOR TELEVISION

This fury for the sight of new things, with which we are now infected and afflicted, though partly the result of everything being made a matter of trade, is yet more the consequence of our thirst for dramatic instead of classic work. For when we are interested by the beauty of a thing, the oftener we can see it the better; but when we are interested only by the story of a thing, we get tired of hearing the same tale told over and over again, and stopping always at the same point – we want a new story presently, a new and better one – and the picture of the day, and novel of the day, become as ephemeral as the coiffure or the bonnet of the day. Now this spirit is wholly adverse to the existence of any lovely art. If you mean to throw it aside to-morrow, you never can have it to-day.

From *Modern Art*, § 16

¶ 192
PRESERVING LOCAL ARTS

Be assured that you can no more drag or compress men into perfection than you can drag or compress plants. If ever you find yourselves set in a position of authority, and are entrusted to determine modes of education, ascertain first what the people you would teach have been in the habit of doing, and encourage them to do *that* better. Set no other excellence before their eyes; disturb none of their reverence for the past; do not think yourselves bound to dispel their ignorance, or to contradict their superstitions; teach them only gentleness and truth; redeem them by example from habits which you know to be unhealthy or degrading; but cherish, above all things, *local associations*, and *hereditary skill*.

From *The Eagle's Nest*, ch. v, § 94

¶ 193
GRAMMAR

They [the men of the Renaissance] discovered suddenly that the world for ten centuries had been living in an ungrammatical manner, and they made it forthwith the end of human existence to be grammatical. And it mattered thenceforth nothing what was said, or what was done, so only that it was said with scholarship, and done with system. Falsehood in a Ciceronian dialect had no opposers; truth in patois no listeners. A Roman phrase was thought worth any number of Gothic facts. The sciences ceased at once to be anything more than different kinds of grammars, – grammar of language, grammar of logic, grammar of ethics, grammar of art; and the tongue, wit, and invention of the human race were supposed to have found their utmost and most divine mission in syntax and syllogism, perspective and five orders.

From *The Stones of Venice*, Vol. III, ch. II, § 32

¶ 194
NINETEENTH-CENTURY ART

There has not before appeared a race like that of civilized Europe at this day, thoughtfully unproductive of all art – ambitious – industrious – investigative – reflective, and incapable. Disdained by the savage, or scattered by the soldier, dishonoured by the voluptuary, or forbidden by the fanatic, the arts have not, till now, been extinguished by analysis and paralyzed by protection. Our lecturers, learned in history, exhibit the descents of excellence from school to school, and clear from doubt the pedigrees of powers which they cannot re-establish, and of virtues no more to be revived; the scholar is early acquainted with every department of the Impossible, and expresses in proper terms his sense of the deficiencies of Titian and the errors of Michael Angelo; the metaphysician weaves from field to field his analogies of gossamer, which shake and glitter fairly in the sun, but must be torn asunder by the first plough that passes: geometry measures out, by line and rule, the light which is to illustrate heroism, and the shadow which should veil distress; and anatomy counts muscles, and systematizes motion, in the wrestling of Genius with its angel. Nor is ingenuity wanting – nor patience; apprehension was never more ready, nor execution more exact – yet nothing is of us, or in us, accomplished; – the treasures of our wealth and will are spent in vain – our cares are as clouds without water – our creations fruitless and perishable; the succeeding Age will trample 'sopra lor vanita che par persona,' and point wonderingly back to the strange colourless tessera in the mosaic of human mind.

> From § 2 of a review of Lord Lindsay's 'Sketches of the
> History of Christian Art' in the *Quarterly Review*, June 1847
> (C. & W., Vol. XII, p. 169)

¶ 195

STATUS OF THE MEDIEVAL ARTIST

The necessary consequence of this enthusiasm in useful building, was the formation of a vast body of craftsmen and architects; corresponding in importance to that which the railway, with its associated industry, has developed in modern times, but entirely different in personal character, and relation to the body politic.

Their personal character was founded on the accurate knowledge of their business in all respects; the ease and pleasure of unaffected invention; and the true sense of power to do everything better than it had ever been yet done, coupled with general contentment in life, and in its vigour and skill.

It is impossible to overrate the difference between such a condition of mind, and that of the modern artist, who either does not know his business at all, or knows it only to recognize his own inferiority to every former workman of distinction.

Again the political relation of these artificers to the State was that of a caste entirely separate from the noblesse; paid for their daily work what was just, and competing with each other to supply the best article they could for the money. And it is, again, impossible to overrate the difference between such a social condition and that of the artists of to-day, struggling to occupy a position of equality in wealth with the noblesse, – paid irregular and monstrous prices by an entirely ignorant and selfish public; and competing with each other to supply the worst article they can for the money.

I never saw anything so impudent on the walls of any exhibition, in any country, as last year in London. It was a daub professing to be a 'harmony in pink and white' (or some such nonsense); absolute rubbish, and which had taken about a quarter of an hour to scrawl or daub – it had no pretence to be called painting. The price asked for it was two hundred and fifty guineas.[1]

From *Val d'Arno*, Lecture III, §§ 78–9

¶ 196

VENETIAN MOSAICS

Those were the kind of images and shadows they lived on: you may think of them what you please, but the historic fact is, beyond all possible debate, that these thin dry bones of art were nourishing meat to the Venetian race: that they grew and throve on that diet, every day spiritually fatter for it, and more comfortably round in human soul: – no illustrated papers to be had, no Academy Exhibition to be seen. If their eyes were to be entertained at all, such must be their lugubrious delectation; pleasure difficult enough to imagine, but real and pure, I doubt not; even passionate. In as quite singularly incomprehensible fidelity of sentiment, my cousin's least baby has fallen in love with a wooden spoon; Paul not more devoted to Virginia. The two are inseparable all about the house, vainly the un-imaginative bystanders endeavouring to perceive, for their part, any

1. This is the first of Ruskin's offensive references to Whistler, whose *Symphony in Grey and Green* was exhibited at the Dudley Gallery in 1872. Four years later Ruskin returned to the attack in *Fors Clavigera*, No. 79, July 1877. 'I never expected', he says, 'to hear a coxcomb ask two hundred guineas for flinging a pot of paint in the public's face.' In consequence Whistler took an action for libel against Ruskin which ended by Whistler being awarded a farthing's damages. It is a sad irony that the attack on Turner in the *Literary Gazette* of May 1842, which provoked Ruskin into writing *Modern Painters*, had said that his pictures were produced 'as if by throwing handfuls of white, blue, and red at the canvas, and letting what would stick, stick'.

amiableness in the spoon. But baby thrives in his pacific attachment, – nay, is under the most perfect moral control, pliant as a reed, under the slightest threat of being parted from his spoon. And I am assured that the crescent Venetian imagination did indeed find pleasantness in these figures; more especially, – which is notable – in the extreme emaciation of them, – a type of beauty kept in their hearts down to the Vivarini days; afterwards rapidly changing to a very opposite ideal indeed.

From *St Mark's Rest*, ch. VIII, § 110

¶ 197

VENETIAN COLOUR

The perception of colour is a gift just as definitely granted to one person, and denied to another, as an ear for music; and the very first requisite for true judgment of St Mark's, is the perfection of that colour-faculty which few people ever set themselves seriously to find out whether they possess or not. For it is on its value as a piece of perfect and unchangeable colouring, that the claims of this edifice to our respect are finally rested; and a deaf man might as well pretend to pronounce judgment on the merits of a full orchestra, as an architect trained in the composition of form only, to discern the beauty of St Mark's. It possesses the charm of colour in common with the greater part of the architecture, as well as of the manu-factures, of the East; but the Venetians deserve especial note as the only European people who appear to have sympathized to the full with the great instinct of the Eastern races. They indeed were com-pelled to bring artists from Constantinople to design the mosaics of the vaults of St Mark's, and to group the colour of its porches; but they rapidly took up and developed, under more masculine condi-tions, the system of which the Greeks had shown them the example : while the burghers and barons of the North were building their dark streets and grisly castles of oak and sandstone, the merchants of Venice were covering their palaces with porphyry and gold; and at last, when her mighty painters had created for her a colour more priceless than gold or porphyry, even this, the richest of her treasures, she lavished upon walls whose foundations were beaten by the sea :

and the strong tide, as it runs beneath the Rialto, is reddened to this day by the reflection of the frescoes of Giorgione.

From *The Stones of Venice*, Vol. II, ch. IV, § 28

¶ 198
STUDY OF ICONOGRAPHY

And thus, as we follow our proposed examination of the arts of the Christian centuries, our understanding of their work will be absolutely limited by the degree of our sympathy with the religion which our fathers have bequeathed to us. You cannot interpret classic marbles without knowing and loving your Pindar and Æschylus, neither can you interpret Christian pictures without knowing and loving your Isaiah and Matthew. And I shall have continually to examine texts of the one as I would verses of the other; nor must you retract yourselves from the labour in suspicion that I desire to betray your scepticism, or undermine your positivism, because I recommend to you the accurate study of books which have hitherto been the light of the world.

From *Val d'Arno*, Lecture x, § 257

¶ 199
THE BROTHERHOOD OF ART

Those small and dexterous creatures whom once we worshipped, those fur-capped divinities with sceptres of camel's hair, peering and poring in their one-windowed chambers over the minute preciousness of the laboured canvas; how are they swept away and crushed into unnoticeable darkness! And in their stead, as the walls of the dismal rooms that enclosed them, and us, are struck by the four winds of Heaven, and rent away, and as the world opens to our sight, lo! far back into all the depths of time, and forth from all the fields that have been sown with human life, how the harvest of the dragon's teeth is springing! how the companies of the gods are ascending out of the earth! The dark stones that have so long been the sepulchres of the thoughts of nations, and the forgotten ruins wherein their faith lay charnelled, give up the dead that were in them; and beneath the Egyptian ranks of sultry and silent rock, and amidst the dim golden lights of the Byzantine dome, and out of the confused and cold shadows of the Northern cloister, behold, the multitudinous souls come forth with singing, gazing on us with the soft eyes of newly comprehended sympathy, and stretching their white arms to us across the grave, in the solemn gladness of ever-lasting brotherhood.

From *The Stones of Venice*, Vol. III, ch. IV, § 28

¶ 200

A CHARACTERISTIC OF GREAT PAINTERS

It is a characteristic – (as far as I know, quite a universal one) – of the greatest masters, that they never expect you to look at them; – seem always rather surprised if you want to; and not overpleased. Tell them you are going to hang their picture at the upper end of the table at the next great City dinner, and that Mr So-and-so will make a speech about it; you produce no impression upon them whatever, or an unfavourable one. The chances are ten to one they send you the most rubbishy thing they can find in their lumber-room. But send for one of them in a hurry, and tell him the rats have gnawed a nasty hole behind the parlour door, and you want it plastered and painted over; – and he does you a masterpiece which the world will peep behind your door to look at for ever.

From *Mornings in Florence*, 'The Third Morning', § 45

¶ 201

GIOTTO

For he defines, explains, and exalts every sweet incident of human nature; and makes dear to daily life every mystic imagination of natures greater than our own. He reconciles, while he intensifies, every virtue of domestic and monastic thought. He makes the simplest household duties sacred; and the highest religious passions, serviceable, and just.

From *Mornings in Florence*, 'The Second Morning', § 37

¶ 202

TITLE

TITIAN

Vandyke is popular, and Rembrandt is popular, but nobody cares much at heart about Titian; only there is a strange undercurrent of everlasting murmur about his name, which means the deep consent of all great men that he is greater than they – the consent of those who, having sat long enough at his feet, have found in that re-strained harmony of his strength there are indeed depths of each balanced power more wonderful than all those separate manifesta-tions in inferior painters.

From *The Two Paths*, Lecture II, § 57

¶ 203

TINTORETTO'S 'MASSACRE OF THE INNOCENTS'

Knowing or feeling, that the expression of the human face was, in such circumstances, not to be rendered, and that the effort could only end in an ugly falsehood, he denies himself all aid from the features, he feels that if he is to place himself or us in the midst of that mad-dened multitude, there can be no time allowed for watching ex-pression. Still less does he depend on details of murder or ghastliness of death; there is no blood, no stabbing or cutting, but there is an awful substitute for these in the chiaroscuro. The scene is the outer vestibule of a palace, the slippery marble floor is fearfully barred across by sanguine shadows, so that our eyes seem to become bloodshot and strained with strange horror and deadly vision; a lake of life before them, like the burning seen of the doomed Moabite on the water that came by the way of Edom; a huge flight of stairs, without parapet, descends on the left; down this rush a crowd of women mixed with the murderers; the child in the arms of one has been seized by the limbs, she hurls herself over the edge, and falls head downmost, dragging the child out of the grasp by her weight; – she will be dashed dead in a second; two others are farther in flight, they reach the edge of a deep river, – the water is beat into a hollow by the force of their plunge; – close to us is the great struggle; a heap of the mothers entangled in one mortal writhe with each other and the swords, one of the murderers dashed down and crushed beneath them, the sword of another caught by the blade and dragged at by a woman's naked hand; the youngest and fairest of the women, her child just torn away from a death grasp, and clasped to her breast with the grip of a steel vice, falls backwards, helplessly over the heap, right on the sword points; all knit together and hurled down in one hopeless, frenzied, furious abandonment of body and soul in the effort to save. Their shrieks ring in our ears till the marble seems rending around us, but far back, at the bottom of the stairs, there is something in the shadow like a heap of clothes. It is a woman, sitting quiet, – quite quiet, – still as any stone; she looks down steadfastly on her dead child, laid along on the floor before her, and her hand is pressed softly upon her brow.

From *Modern Painters*, Vol. II, Part III, Sec. II, ch. III, § 21

¶ 204

TINTORETTO IN SAN ROCCO

I should exhaust the patience of the reader, if I were to dwell at length on the various stupendous developments of the imagination of Tintoret in the Scuola di San Rocco alone. I would fain join awhile in that solemn pause of the journey into Egypt, where the silver boughs of the shadowy trees lace with their tremulous lines the alternate folds of fair cloud, flushed by faint crimson light, and lie across the streams of blue between those rosy islands, like the white wakes of wandering ships; or watch beside the sleep of the disciples, among those massy leaves that lie so heavily on the dead of the night beneath the descent of the angel of the agony, and toss fearfully above the motion of the torches as the troop of the betrayer emerges out of the hollows of the olives; or wait through the hour of accusing beside the judgment seat of Pilate, where all is unseen, unfelt, except the one figure that stands with its head bowed down, pale, like a pillar of moonlight, half bathed in the glory of the Godhead, half wrapt in the whiteness of the shroud.

From *Modern Painters*, Vol. II, Part III, Sec. II, ch. III, § 22

VERONESE'S CUCCINE FAMILY

In front of the mother kneel her two eldest children, a girl of about sixteen, and a boy a year or two younger. They are both rapt in adoration – the boy's being the deepest. Nearer us, at their left side, is a younger boy, about nine years old – a black-eyed fellow, full of life – and evidently his father's darling (for Veronese has put him full in the light in the front; and given him a beautiful white silken jacket, barred with black, that nobody may ever miss seeing him to the end of time). He is a little shy about being presented to the Madonna, and for the present has got behind the pillar, blushing, but opening his black eyes wide; he is just summoning courage to peep round and see if she looks kind. A still younger child, about six years old, is really frightened, and has run back to his mother, catching hold of her dress at the waist. She throws her right arm round him and over him, with exquisite instinctive action, not moving her eyes from the Madonna's face. Last of all, the youngest child, perhaps about three years old, is neither frightened nor interested, but finds the ceremony tedious, and is trying to coax the dog to play with him; but the dog, which is one of the little curly, short-nosed, fringy-pawed things, which all Venetian ladies petted, will not now be coaxed. For the dog is the last link in the chain of lowering feeling, and takes his doggish views of the matter. He cannot understand, first, how the Madonna got into the house; nor, secondly, why she is allowed to stay, disturbing the family, and taking all their attention from his dogship. And he is walking away, much offended.

From *Modern Painters*, Vol. v, Part ix, ch. iii, § 21

ENGLISH ART

But we shall never excel in decorative design. Such design is usually produced by people of great natural powers of mind, who have no variety of subjects to employ themselves on, no oppressive anxieties, and are in circumstances either of natural scenery or of daily life, which cause pleasurable excitement. *We* cannot design, because we have too much to think of, and we think of it too anxiously. It has long been observed how little real anxiety exists in the minds of the partly savage races which excel in decorative art; and we must not suppose that the temper of the Middle Ages was a troubled one, because every day brought its danger or its change. The very eventfulness of the life rendered it careless, as generally is still the case with soldiers and sailors. Now, when there are great powers of thought, and little to think of, all the waste energy and fancy are thrown into the manual work, and you have so much intellect as would direct the affairs of a large mercantile concern for a day, spent all at once, quite unconsciously, in drawing an ingenious spiral.

Also, powers of doing fine ornamental work are only to be reached by a perpetual discipline of the hand as well as of the fancy; discipline as attentive and painful as that which a juggler has to put himself through, to overcome the more palpable difficulties of his profession. The execution of the best artists is always a splendid tour-de-force; and much that in painting is supposed to be dependent on material is indeed only a lovely and quite inimitable legerdemain. Now, when powers of fancy, stimulated by this triumphant precision of manual dexterity, descend uninterruptedly from generation to generation, you have at last, what is not so much a trained artist, as a new species of animal, with whose instinctive gifts you have no chance of contending. And thus all our imitations of other people's work are futile. We must learn first to make honest English wares, and afterwards to decorate them as may please the then approving Graces.

Secondly – and this is an incapacity of a graver kind, yet having its own good in it also – we shall never be successful in the highest fields of ideal or theological art.

For there is one strange, but quite essential, character in us – ever since the Conquest, if not earlier – a delight in the forms of burlesque which are connected in some degree with the foulness of evil. I think the most perfect type of a true English mind in its best possible temper, is that of Chaucer; and you will find that, while it is for the most part full of thoughts of beauty, pure and wild like that of an April morning, there are, even in the midst of this, sometimes momentarily jesting passages which stoop to play with evil – while the power of listening to and enjoying the jesting of entirely gross persons, whatever the feeling may be which permits it, afterwards degenerates into forms of humour which render some of quite the greatest, wisest, and most moral of English writers now almost useless for our youth. And yet you will find that whenever Englishmen are wholly without this instinct, their genius is comparatively weak and restricted.

Now, the first necessity for the doing of any great work in ideal art, is the looking upon all foulness with horror, as a contemptible though dreadful enemy. You may easily understand what I mean, by comparing the feelings with which Dante regards any form of obscenity or of base jest, with the temper in which the same things are regarded by Shakespeare. And this strange earthly instinct of ours, coupled as it is, in our good men, with great simplicity and common sense, renders them shrewd and perfect observers and delineators of actual nature, low or high; but precludes them from that speciality of art which is properly called sublime.

From *Lectures on Art*, Lecture I, §§ 13–15

¶ 207

THE MINOR ENGLISH LANDSCAPE PAINTERS

They were, themselves, a kind of contemplative cattle, and flock of the field, who merely liked being out of doors, and brought as much painted fresh air as they could back into the house with them.

From *The Art of England*, Lecture VI, § 170

¶ 208

THE SNOBBISHNESS OF ENGLISH PAINTERS

Why did not Sir Joshua – or could not – or would not Sir Joshua – paint Madonnas? neither he, nor his great rival-friend Gainsborough? Both of them painters of women, such as since Giorgione and Correggio had not been; both painters of men, such as had not been since Titian. How is it that these English friends can so brightly paint that particular order of humanity which we call 'gentlemen and ladies,' but neither heroes, nor saints, nor angels? Can it be because they were both country-bred boys, and for ever after strangely sensitive to courtliness? Why, Giotto also was a country-bred boy. Allegri's native Correggio, Titian's Cadore, were but hill villages; yet these men painted not the court, nor the drawing-room, but the Earth: and not a little of Heaven besides: while our good Sir Joshua never trusts himself outside the park palings. He could not even have drawn the strawberry girl, unless she had got through a gap in them – or rather, I think, she must have been let in at the porter's lodge, for her strawberries are in a pottle, ready for the ladies at the Hall. Giorgione would have set them, wild and fragrant, among their leaves, in her hand. Between his fairness, and Sir Joshua's May-fairness, there is a strange impassable limit – as of the white reef that in Pacific isles encircles their inner lakelets, and shuts them from the surf and sound of sea. Clear and calm they rest, reflecting fringed shadows of the palm-trees, and the passing of fretted clouds across their own sweet circle of blue sky. But beyond, and round and round their coral bar, lies the blue of sea and heaven together – blue of eternal deep.

You will find it a pregnant question, if you follow it forth, and leading to many others, not trivial. Why it is, that in Sir Joshua's girl, or Gainsborough's, we always think first of the Ladyhood; but in Giotto's, of the Womanhood? Why, in Sir Joshua's hero, or Vandyck's, it is always the Prince or the Sir whom we see first; but in Titian's, the man?

Not that Titian's gentlemen are less finished than Sir Joshua's; but their gentlemanliness is not the principal thing about them; their manhood absorbs, conquers, wears it as a despised thing. Nor – and this is another stern ground of separation – will Titian make a gentleman of every one he paints. He will make him so if he is so, not otherwise; and this not merely in general servitude to truth, but because, in his sympathy with deeper humanity, the courtier is not more interesting to him than anyone else. 'You have learned to dance and fence; you can speak with clearness, and think with precision; your hands are small, your senses acute, and your features well-shaped. Yes: I see all this in you, and will do it justice. You shall stand as none but a well-bred man could stand; and your fingers shall fall on the sword-hilt as no fingers could but those that knew the grasp of it. But for the rest, this grisly fisherman, with rusty cheek and rope-frayed hand, is a man as well as you, and might possibly make several of you, if souls were divisible. His bronze colour is quite as interesting to me, Titian, as your paleness, and his hoary sprays of stormy hair takes the light as well as your waving curls. Him also I will paint, with such picturesqueness as he may have; yet not putting the picturesqueness first in him, as in you I have not put the gentlemanliness first. In him I see a strong human creature, contending with all hardship: in you also a human creature, uncontending, and possibly not strong. Contention or strength, weakness or picturesqueness, and all other such accidents in either, shall have due place. But the immortality and miracle of you – this clay that burns, this colour that changes – are in truth the awful things in both; these shall be first painted – and last.'

From 'Sir Joshua and Holbein', §§ 5–6, *Cornhill Magazine*, March 1860

¶ 209

THE ENGLISHMAN'S PORTRAIT

An English gentleman, desiring his portrait, gives probably to the painter a choice of several actions, in any of which he is willing to be represented. As for instance, riding his best horse, shooting with his favourite pointer, manifesting himself in his robes of state on some great public occasion, meditating in his study, playing with his children, or visiting his tenants; in any of these or other such circumstances, he will give the artist free leave to paint him. But in one important action he would shrink even from the suggestion of being drawn. He will assuredly not let himself be painted praying.

From *Modern Painters*, Vol. v, Part IX, ch. III, § 15

CONTRASTED FACULTIES: MILLAIS AND TURNER

Suppose, for instance, two men, equally honest, equally industrious, equally impressed with a humble desire to render some part of what they saw in nature faithfully; and, otherwise, trained in convictions such as I have above endeavoured to induce. But one of them is quiet in temperament, has a feeble memory, no invention and excessively keen sight. The other is impatient in temperament, has a memory which nothing escapes, an invention which never rests, and is comparatively near-sighted.

Set them both free in the same field in a mountain valley. One sees everything, small and large, with almost the same clearness; mountains and grasshoppers alike; the leaves on the branches, the veins in the pebbles, the bubbles in the stream; but he can remember nothing and invent nothing. Patiently he sets himself to his mighty task; abandoning at once all thoughts of seizing transient effects, or giving general impressions of that which his eyes present to him in microscopical dissection, he chooses some small portion out of the infinite scene, and calculates with courage the number of weeks which must elapse before he can do justice to the intensity of his perceptions, or the fulness of matter in his subject.

Meantime, the other has been watching the change of the clouds, and the march of the light along the mountain sides; he beholds the entire scene in broad, soft masses of true gradation, and the very feebleness of his sight is in some sort an advantage to him, in making him more sensible of the aerial mystery of distance, and hiding from him the multitudes of circumstances which it would have been impossible for him to represent. But there is not one change in the casting of the jagged shadows along the hollows of the hills, but it is fixed on his mind for ever; not a flake of spray has broken from the sea of cloud about their bases, but he has watched it as it melts away, and could recall it to its lost place in heaven by the slightest effort of his thoughts. Not only so, but thousands and thousands of such images, of older scenes, remain congregated in his mind, each mingling in new associations with those now visibly passing before him, and these again confused with other images of his own cease-less, sleepless imagination, flashing by in sudden troops. Fancy how his paper will be covered with stray symbols and blots, and un-decipherable shorthand: – as for his sitting down to 'draw from Nature', there was not one of the things which he wished to repre-sent, that stayed for so much as five seconds together: but none of them escaped for all that: they are sealed up in that strange storehouse of his; he may take one of them out perhaps, this day twenty years, and paint it in his dark room, far away. Now observe, you may tell both of these men, when they are young, that they are to be honest, that they have an important function, and that they are not to care what Raphael did. This you may wholesomely impress on them both. But fancy the exquisite absurdity of expecting either of them to possess any of the qualities of the other.

I have supposed the feebleness of sight in the last, and of invention in the first painter, that the contrast between them might be more striking; but, with very slight modification, both the characters are real. Grant to the first considerable inventive power, with exquisite sense of colour; and give to the second, in addition to all his other faculties, the eye of an eagle; and the first is John Everett Millais, the second Joseph Mallord William Turner.

From *Pre-Raphaelitism*, §§ 21–4

¶ 211

TURNER'S 'JULIET AND HER NURSE'[1]

Had the scene of 'Juliet and her Nurse' risen up before the mind of a poet, and had been described in 'words that burn', it had been the admiration of the world. . . . Many-coloured mists are floating above the distant city, but such mists as you might imagine to be

---

1. This is an extract from Ruskin's first defence of Turner, written when he was seventeen. It was intended for publication in *Blackwood's Magazine*, where the attack on Turner had been printed, but his father first of all sent it to Turner for his approval. Turner said he would rather not reply to attacks, and sent the manuscript to Munro of Novar, who had bought the picture; and the manuscript was lost. This extract is from a copy found later and printed in C. & W., Vol. III. There is a touching similarity between the central metaphor of lights moving and mingling with the stars, and the concluding paragraph of *Praeterita* (No. 81), the last words Ruskin ever published.

ethereal spirits, souls of the mighty dead breathed out of the tombs of Italy into the blue of her bright heaven, and wandering in vague and infinite glory around the earth that they have loved. Instinct with the beauty of uncertain light, they move and mingle among the pale stars, and rise up into the brightness of the illimitable heaven, whose soft, sad blue eye gazes down into the deep waters of the sea for ever. . . . And the spires of the glorious city rise indistinctly bright into those living mists, like pyramids of pale fire from some vast altar; and amidst the glory of the dream, there is as it were the voice of a multitude entering by the eye, – arising from the stillness of the city like the summer wind passing over the leaves of the forest, when a murmur is heard amidst their multitudes.

From *Modern Painters*, Vol. 1, Appendix 1, § 5

¶ 212
TURNER'S COLOUR

Thus, then, for the last time, rises the question, what is the true dignity of colour? We left that doubt a little while ago among the clouds, wondering what they had been made so scarlet for. Now Turner brings the doubt back to us, unescapable any more. No man, hitherto, had painted the clouds scarlet. Hesperid Æglé, and Erytheia, throned there in the west, fade into the twilights of four thousand years, unconfessed. Here is at last one who confesses them, but is it well? Men say these Hesperides are sensual goddesses, – traitresses, – that the Graiæ are the only true ones. Nature made the western and the eastern clouds splendid in fallacy. Crimson is impure and vile; let us paint in black if we would be virtuous.

Note, with respect to this matter, that the peculiar innovation of Turner was the perfection of the colour chord by means of *scarlet*. Other painters had rendered the golden tones, and the blue tones, of sky; Titian especially the last, in perfectness. But none had dared to paint, none seem to have seen, the scarlet and purple.

Nor was it only in seeing this colour in vividness when it occurred in full light, that Turner differed from preceding painters. His most distinctive innovation as a colourist was his discovery of the scarlet *shadow*. 'True, there is a sunshine whose light is golden, and its shadow gray; but there is another sunshine, and that the purest, whose light is white, and its shadow scarlet.' This was the essentially offensive, inconceivable thing, which he could not be believed in. There was some ground for the incredulity, because no colour is vivid enough to express the pitch of light of pure white sunshine, so that the colour given without the true intensity of light *looks* false. Nevertheless, Turner could not but report of the colour truly. 'I must indeed be lower in the key, but that is no reason why I should be false in the note. Here is sunshine which glows even when sub-dued; it has not cool shade, but fiery shade.' This is the glory of sunshine.

From *Modern Painters*, Vol. v, Part IX, ch. XI, §§ 5–6

¶ 213

TURNER'S MANNERISM

But as for Turner – I can positively tell you, there was no possi-bility of his drawing flowers or trees, rightly, after he had once left Yorkshire for Rome. Michael Angelo's sprawling prophets, and Bernini's labyrinthine arcades wholly bewildered him, and dragged him into their false and fantastic world; out of which he broke at last, only in the strength of sympathy with human suffering; not again capable of understanding human simplicity and peace.

From *Notes by Mr Ruskin on His Own Handiwork Illustrative of Turner*, Part II (reference to example no. 33)

¶ 214

TURNER'S VULGARITY

He saw, and more clearly than he knew himself, the especial forte of England in 'vulgarity.' I cannot better explain the word than by pointing to those groups of Turner's figures exaggerating this special quality as it manifested itself to him, either in Richmond picnics, barrack domestic life, jockey commerce, or here, finally, in the general relationships of Jack ashore. With all this, nevertheless, he had in himself no small sympathy; he liked it at once and was disgusted by it; and while he lived, in imagination, in ancient

Carthage, lived, practically, in modern Margate. I cannot understand these ways of his; only be assured that what offends us in these figures was also, in a high degree, offensive to him, though he chose to paint it as a peculiarly English phenomenon, and though he took in the midst of it, ignobly, an animal English enjoyment, acknowledging it all the while to be ugly and wrong.

From *Notes by Mr Ruskin on His Drawings by the late*
J. M. W. Turner, R.A., Part I (drawing no. 36)

¶ 215

TURNER'S MELANCHOLY

How this sadness came to be persistent over Turner, and to conquer him, we shall see in a little while. It is enough for us to know at present that our most wise and Christian England, with all her appurtenances of school-porch and church-spire, had so disposed her teaching as to leave this somewhat notable child of hers without even cruel Pandora's gift. . . .

He was without hope.

What, for us, his work yet may be, I know not. But let not the real nature of it be misunderstood any more.

He is distinctively, as he rises into his own peculiar strength, separating himself from all men who had painted forms of the physical world before, – the painter of the loveliness of nature, with the worm at its root: Rose and cankerworm, – both with his utmost strength; the one *never* separate from the other.

In which his work was the true image of his own mind.

I would fain have looked last at the rose; but that is not the way Atropos will have it, and there is no pleading with her.

So, therefore, first of the rose.

That is to say, of this vision of the loveliness and kindness of Nature, as distinguished from all visions of her ever received by other men. By the Greek she had been distrusted. She was to him Calypso, the Concealer, Circe, the Sorceress. By the Venetian, she had been dreaded. Her wildernesses were desolate; her shadows stern. By the Fleming, she had been despised; what mattered the heavenly colours to him? But at last, the time comes for her loveliness

221

and kindness to be declared to men. Had they helped Turner, listened to him, believed in him, he had done it wholly for them. But they cried out for Python, and Python came; came literally as well as spiritually; all the perfectest beauty and conquest which Turner wrought is already withered. The cankerworm stood at his right hand, and of all his richest, most precious work, there remains only the shadow. Yet that shadow is more than other men's sunlight; it is the scarlet shade, shade of the Rose. Wrecked, and faded, and defiled, his work still, in what remains of it, or may remain, is the loveliest ever yet done by man, in imagery of the physical world. Whatsoever is there of fairest, you will find recorded by Turner, and by him alone.

I say *you* will find, not knowing to how few I speak; for in order to find what is fairest, you must delight in what is fair; and I know not how few or how many there may be who take such delight. Once I could speak joyfully about beautiful things, thinking to be understood; – now I cannot any more; for it seems to me that no one regards them. Wherever I look or travel in England or abroad, I see that men, wherever they can reach, destroy all beauty. They seem to have no other desire or hope but to have large houses and to be able to move fast. Every perfect and lovely spot which they can touch, they defile.

From *Modern Painters*, Vol. v, Part ix, ch. xi, §§ 12–15

§ 216

THE END OF MODERN PAINTERS

The fact is verily so. The greatest man of our England, in the first half of the nineteenth century, in the strength and hope of his youth, perceives this to be the thing he has to tell us of utmost moment, connected with the spiritual world. In each city and country of past time, the master-minds had to declare the chief worship which lay at the nation's heart; to define it; adorn it; show the range and authority of it. Thus in Athens, we have the triumph of Pallas, and in Venice the Assumption of the Virgin; here, in England, is our great spiritual fact for ever interpreted to us – the Assumption of the Dragon. No St George any more to be heard of; no more dragon-slaying possible: this child, born on St George's Day, can only make manifest the dragon, not slay him, sea-serpent as he is; whom the English Andromeda, not fearing, takes for her lord. The fairy English Queen once thought to command the waves, but it is the sea-dragon now who commands her valleys; of old the Angel of the Sea ministered to them, but now the Serpent of the Sea; where once flowed their clear springs now spreads the black Cocytus pool; and the fair blooming of the Hesperid meadows fades into ashes beneath the Nereid's Guard.

Yes, Albert of Nuremberg; the time has at last come. Another nation has arised in the strength of its Black anger; and another hand has pourtrayed the spirit of its toil. Crowned with fire, and with the wings of the bat.[1]

From *Modern Painters*, Vol. v, Part ix, ch. x, § 25

1. These are the last words of *Modern Painters* and show what a strange world of private symbolism Ruskin had come to inhabit before the age of forty.

4

ARCHITECTURE

ARCHITECTURE AND ORNAMENT

Architecture consists distinctively in the adaptation of form to resist force; – that, practically, it may be always thought of as doing this by the ingenious adjustment of various pieces of solid material; that the perception of this ingenious adjustment, or structure, is to be always joined with our admiration of the super-added ornament; and that all delightful ornament is the honouring of such useful structures; but that the beauty of the ornament itself is independent of the structure, and arrived at by powers of mind of a very different class from those which are necessary to give skill in architecture proper.

From *Val d'Arno*, ch. VI, § 141

¶ 218

ARCHITECTURE THE FRAME OF SCULPTURE AND PAINTING

I found, after carefully investigating the character of the emotions which were generally felt by well-educated people respecting various forms of good architecture, that these emotions might be separated into four general heads:

1. Sentimental Admiration. – The kind of feeling which most travellers experience on first entering a cathedral by torchlight, and hearing a chant from concealed choristers; or in visiting a ruined abbey by moonlight, or any building with which interesting associations are connected, at any time when they can hardly see it.

2. Proud Admiration. – The delight which most worldly people take in showy, large or complete buildings, for the sake of the importance which such buildings confer on themselves, as their possessors, or admirers.

3. Workmanly Admiration. – The delight of seeing good and neat masonry, together with that belonging to incipient developments of taste; as, for instance, a perception of proportion in lines, masses, and mouldings.

4. Artistical and rational Admiration. – The delight taken in reading the sculpture or painting on walls, capitals, friezes, etc. . . .

I found, finally, that this, the only admiration worth having, attached itself *wholly* to the meaning of the sculpture and colour on the building. That it was very regardless of general form and size; but intensely observant of the statuary, floral mouldings, mosaics, and other decorations. Upon which, little by little, it gradually became manifest to me that the sculpture and painting were, in fact, the all in all of the thing to be done; that these, which I had long been in the careless habit of thinking subordinate to the architecture, were in fact the entire masters of the architecture; and that the architect who was not a sculptor or a painter, was nothing better than a frame-maker on a large scale. Having once got this clue to the truth, every question about architecture immediately settled itself without further difficulty. I saw that the idea of an independent architectural profession was a mere modern fallacy, the thought of which had never so much as entered the heads of the great nations of earlier times; but that it had always, till lately, been understood, that in order to have a Parthenon, one had to get a preliminary Phidias; and to have a Cathedral of Florence, a preliminary Giotto; and to have even a Saint Peter's at Rome, a preliminary Michael Angelo. And as, with this new light, I examined the nobler examples of our Gothic cathedrals, it became apparent to me that the master workman must have been the person who carved the bas-reliefs in the porches; that to him all others must have been subordinate, and by him all the rest of the cathedral essentially arranged; but that in fact the whole company of builders, always large, were more or less divided into two great flocks of stone-layers, and sculptors; and that the number of sculptors was so great, and their average talent so considerable, that it would no more have been thought necessary to state respecting the master builder that he could carve a statue, than that he could measure an angle, or strike a curve.

If the reader will think over this statement carefully he will find that it is indeed true, and a key to many things. The fact is, there are only two fine arts possible to the human race, sculpture and painting. What we call architecture is only the association of these in noble masses, or the placing of them in fit places. All architecture other than this is, in fact, mere building; and though it may sometimes be graceful, as in the groinings of an abbey roof; or sublime, as in the battlement of a border tower; there is, in such examples of it, no more exertion of the powers of high art, than in the gracefulness of a well-ordered chamber, or the nobleness of a well-built ship of war.

All high art consists in the carving or painting natural objects, chiefly figures: it has always subject and meaning, never consisting solely in arrangement of lines, or even of colours. It always paints or carves something that it sees or believes in; nothing ideal or un-credited. For the most part, it paints and carves the men and things that are visible around it. And as soon as we possess a body of sculptors able, and willing, and having leave from the English public, to carve on the façades of our cathedrals portraits of the living bishops, deans, canons, and choristers, who are to minister in the said cathedrals; and on the façades of our public buildings, portraits of the men chiefly moving or acting in the same; and on our build-ings, generally, the birds and flowers which are singing and budding in the fields around them, we shall have a school of English archi-tecture. Not till then.

From *The Seven Lamps of Architecture*, Preface to 2nd ed., §§ 2 and 6–7

¶ 219

THE NATURE OF ARCHITECTURAL ORNAMENT

The question is first to be clearly determined whether the architec-ture is a frame for the sculpture, or the sculpture an ornament of the architecture. If the latter, then the first office of that sculpture is not to represent the things it imitates, but to gather out of them those arrangements of form which shall be pleasing to the eye in their intended places. So soon as agreeable lines and points of shade have been added to the mouldings which were meagre, or to the lights which were unrelieved, the architectural work of the imitation is accomplished; and how far it shall be wrought towards complete-ness or not will depend upon its place, and upon other various cir-cumstances. If, in its particular use or position, it is symmetrically arranged, there is, of course, an instant indication of architectural subjection. But symmetry is not abstraction. Leaves may be carved in the most regular order, and yet be meanly imitative; or, on the other hand, they may be thrown wild and loose, and yet be highly architectural in their separate treatment *. . . .

Under these limitations, then, I think that perfect sculpture may be † made a part of the severest architecture; but this perfection was said in the outset to be dangerous. It is so in the highest degree; for the moment the architect allows himself to dwell on the imitated portions, there is a chance of his losing sight of the duty of his ornament, of its business as a part of the composition, and sacrificing its points of shade and effect to the delight of delicate carving. And then he is lost. His architecture has become a mere framework for the setting of delicate sculpture, which had better be all taken down and put into cabinets. It is well, therefore, that the young architect should be taught to think of imitative ornament as of the extreme of grace in language; not to be regarded at first, nor to be obtained at the cost of purpose, meaning, force or conciseness, yet, indeed a perfection – the least of all perfections, and yet the crowning one of all – one which by itself, and regarded in itself, is an architectural coxcombry ‡, but is yet the sign of the most highly-trained mind and power when it is associated with others.

From *The Seven Lamps of Architecture*, ch. IV, §§ 31 and 34

¶ 220

STYLE AND ORIGINALITY

The Architecture of a nation is great only when it is as universal and as established as its language; and when provincial differences of style are nothing more than so many dialects. Other necessities are matters of doubt: nations have been alike successful in their architecture in times of poverty and of wealth; in times of war and peace; in times of barbarism and of refinement; under governments the

---

* This short Aphorism is one of the most important in the book.

† I have written, it will be observed, '*should* be,' in the marginal definition of the Aphorism, and I ought to have written it in the text. See the next note.

‡ By no means. I much understated the truth in this matter, and should now say that sculpture should precede and govern all else. The pediment of Ægina determines the right – and ends controversy. [All footnotes Ruskin's notes of 1880.]

most liberal or the most arbitrary; but this one condition has been constant, this one requirement clear in all places and at all times, that the work shall be that of a *school*, that no individual caprice shall dispense with, or materially vary, accepted types and customary decorations; and that from the cottage to the palace, and from the chapel to the basilica, and from the garden fence to the fortress wall, every member and feature of the architecture of the nation shall be as commonly current, as frankly accepted, as its language or its coin. . . .

We want no new style of architecture. Who wants a new style of painting or sculpture? but we want *some* style. It is of marvellously little importance, if we have a code of laws and they be good laws, whether they be new or old, foreign or native, Roman or Saxon, or Norman, or English laws. But it is of considerable importance that we should have a code of laws of one kind or another, and that code accepted and enforced from one side of the island to another, and not one law made ground of judgement at York and another in Exeter. And in like manner it does not matter one marble splinter whether we have an old or new architecture, but it matters everything whether we have an architecture truly so called or not; that is, whether an architecture whose laws might be taught at our schools from Cornwall to Northumberland, as we teach English spelling and English grammar, or an architecture which is to be invented fresh every time we build a workhouse or a parish school. . . . Originality in expression does not depend on invention of new words; nor originality in poetry on invention of new measures; nor, in painting, on invention of new colours, or new modes of using them. . . . Originality depends on nothing of the kind. A man who has the gift, will take up any style that is going, the style of his day, and will work in that, and be great in that, and make everything that he does in it look as fresh as if every thought of it had just come down from heaven. I do not say that he will not take liberties with his materials, or with his rules: I do not say that strange changes will not sometimes be wrought by his efforts, or his fancies, in both. But those changes will be instructive, natural, facile, though sometimes marvellous; they will never be sought after as things necessary to his dignity or to his independence; and those liberties will be like the liberties that a great speaker takes with the language, not a defiance of its rules for the sake of singularity; but inevitable, uncalculated, and brilliant consequences of an effort to express what the language, without such infraction, could not.

From *The Seven Lamps of Architecture*, ch. VII, §§ 3–4

¶ 221

THE AIM OF HIS ARCHITECTURAL TEACHING

The law which it has been my effort chiefly to illustrate is the dependence of all noble design, in any kind, on the sculpture or painting of Organic Form.

This is the vital law; lying at the root of all that I have ever tried to teach respecting architecture or any other art. It is also the law most generally disallowed.

I believe this must be so in every subject. We are all of us willing enough to accept dead truths or blunt ones; which can be fitted harmlessly into spare niches, or shrouded and coffined at once out of the way, we holding complacently the cemetery keys, and supposing we have learned something. But a sapling truth, with earth at its root and blossom on its branches; or a trenchant truth, that can cut its way through bars and sods; most men, it seems to me, dislike the sight or entertainment of, if by any means such guest or vision may be avoided. And, indeed, this is no wonder; for one such truth, thoroughly accepted, connects itself strangely with others, and there is no saying what it may lead us to.

And thus the gist of what I have tried to teach about architecture has been throughout denied by my architect readers, even when they thought what I said suggestive in other particulars. 'Anything but that. Study Italian Gothic? – perhaps it would be as well: build with pointed arches? – there is no objection; use solid stone and well-burnt brick? – by all means: but – learn to carve or paint organic form ourselves! How can such a thing be asked? We are above all that. The carvers and painters are our servants – quite subordinate people. They ought to be glad if we leave room for them.'

Well, on that it all turns. For those who will not learn to carve or paint, and think themselves greater men because they cannot, it is wholly wasted time to read any words of mine; in the truest and sternest sense they *can* read no words of mine; for the most familiar I can use – 'form,' 'proportion,' 'beauty,' 'curvature,' 'colour,' – are used in a sense which by no effort I can communicate to such readers; and in no building that I praise is the thing that I praise it for, visible to them.

And it is the more necessary for me to state this fully, because so-called Gothic or Romanesque buildings are now rising every day around us, which might be supposed by the public more or less to embody the principles of those styles, but which embody not one of them, nor any shadow or fragment of them; but merely serve to caricature the noble buildings of past ages, and to bring their form into dishonour by leaving out their soul.

From *The Two Paths*, Preface

¶ 222

NINETEENTH-CENTURY STREET ARCHITECTURE

I am not aware of any town of wealth and importance in the Middle Ages, in which some proof does not exist that, at its period of greatest energy and prosperity, its streets were inwrought with rich sculpture, and even . . . glowing with colour and with gold. Now, therefore, let the reader, – forming for himself as vivid and real a conception as he is able, either of a group of Venetian palaces in the fourteenth century, or, if he likes better, of one of the more fantastic but even richer street scenes of Rouen, Antwerp, Cologne, or Nuremberg, and keeping this gorgeous image before him, – go out into any thoroughfare representative, in a general and characteristic way, of the feeling for domestic architecture in modern times: let him, for instance, if in London, walk once up and down Harley Street, or Baker Street, or Gower Street; and then, looking upon this picture and on this, set himself to consider . . . what have been the causes which have induced so vast a change in the European mind.

Renaissance architecture is the school which has conducted men's inventive and constructive faculties from the Grand Canal to

Gower Street; from the marble shaft, and the lancet arch, and the wreathed leafage, and the glowing and melting harmony of gold and azure, to the square cavity in the brick wall.

From *The Stones of Venice*, Vol. III, ch. I, §§ 1–2

¶ 223
TWO POWERS OF ARCHITECTURE

Now, the difference between these two orders of building is not merely that which there is in nature between things beautiful and sublime. It is, also, the difference between what is derivative and original in man's work; for whatever is in architecture fair or beautiful, is imitated from natural forms; and what is not so derived, but depends for its dignity upon arrangement and government received from human mind, becomes the expression of the power of that mind, and receives a sublimity high in proportion to the power expressed. All building, therefore, shows man either as gathering or governing; and the secrets of his success are his knowing what to gather and how to rule.

From *The Seven Lamps of Architecture*, ch. III, § 2

¶ 224
THE CONCEALING OF STRUCTURE

The architect is not *bound* to exhibit structure; nor are we to complain of him for concealing it, any more than we should regret that the outer surfaces of the human frame conceal much of its anatomy; nevertheless, that building will generally be the noblest, which to an intelligent eye discovers the great secrets of its structure, as an animal form does, although from a careless observer they may be concealed. In the vaulting of a Gothic roof it is no deceit to throw the strength into the ribs of it, and make the intermediate vault a mere shell. Such a structure would be presumed by an intelligent observer, the first time he saw such a roof; and the beauties of its traceries would be enhanced to him if they confessed and followed the lines of its main strength.

From *The Seven Lamps of Architecture*, ch. II, § 7

¶ 225
# THE LIE OF MACHINE-MADE ORNAMENT

Ornament . . . has two entirely distinct sources of agreeableness: one, that of the abstract beauty of its forms, which, for the present, we will suppose to be the same whether they come from the hand or the machine; the other, the sense of human labour and care spent upon it. How great this latter influence we may perhaps judge, by considering that there is not a cluster of weeds growing in any cranny of ruin which has not a beauty in all respects *nearly* equal, and, in some, immeasurably superior, to that of the most elaborate sculpture of its stones: and that all our interest in the carved work, our sense of its richness, though it is tenfold less rich than the knots of grass beside it; of its delicacy, though it is a thousandfold less delicate; of its admirableness, though a millionfold less admirable; results from our consciousness of its being the work of poor, clumsy, toilsome man. Its true delightfulness depends on our discovering in it the record of thoughts, and intents, and trials, and heartbreakings – of recoveries and joyfulnesses of success: all this *can* be traced by a practised eye; but, granting it even obscure, it is presumed or understood; and in that is the worth of the thing, just as much as the worth of any thing else we call precious.

From *The Seven Lamps of Architecture*, ch. II, § 19

¶ 226
# GOOD ORNAMENT DONE WITH ENJOYMENT

I believe the right question to ask, respecting all ornament, is simply this: Was it done with enjoyment – was the carver happy while he was about it? It may be the hardest work possible, and the harder because so much pleasure was taken in it; but it must have been happy too, or it will not be living. How much of the stone mason's toil this condition would exclude I hardly venture to consider, but the condition is absolute. There is a Gothic church lately built near Rouen, vile enough, indeed, in its general composition, but excessively rich in detail; many of the details are designed with taste, and all evidently by a man who has studied old work closely. But it is all as dead as leaves in December; there is not one tender touch, not one warm stroke on the whole façade. The men who did it hated it, and were thankful when it was done. And so long as they do so they are merely loading your walls with shapes of clay: the garlands of everlastings in Pere la Chaise are more cheerful ornaments. You cannot get the feeling by paying for it – money will not buy life. I am not sure even that you can get it by watching or waiting for it. It is true that here and there a workman may be found who has it in him, but he does not rest contented in the inferior work – he struggles forward into an Academician; and from the mass of available handicraftsmen the power is gone – how recoverable I know not; this only I know, that all expense devoted to sculptural ornament, in the present condition of that power, comes literally under the head of Sacrifice for the sacrifice's sake, or worse. I believe the only manner of rich ornament that is open to us is the geometrical colour-mosaic, and that much might result from our strenuously taking up this mode of design. But, at all events, one thing we have in our power – the doing without machine ornament and cast-iron work. All the stamped metals, and artificial stones, and imitation woods and bronzes, over the invention of which we hear daily exultation – all the short, and cheap, and easy ways of doing that whose difficulty is its honour – are just so many new obstacles in our already encumbered road. They will not make one of us happier or wiser – they will extend neither the pride of judgement nor the privilege of enjoyment. They will only make us shallower in our understandings, colder in our hearts, and feebler in our wits.

From *The Seven Lamps of Architecture*, ch. v, § 24

§ 227

ANALYSIS OF GOTHIC TRACERY

The change of which I speak, is expressible in few words; but one more important, more radically influential, could not be. It was the substitution of the *line* for the *mass*, as the element of decoration.

We have seen the mode in which the openings or penetration of the window expanded, until what were, at first, awkward forms of intermediate stone, became delicate lines of tracery; and I have been careful in pointing out the peculiar attention bestowed on the proportion and decoration of the mouldings of the window at Rouen, . . . as compared with earlier mouldings, because that beauty and care are singularly significant. They mark that the traceries had *caught the eye* of the architect. Up to that time, up to the very last instant in which the reduction and thinning of the intervening stone was consummated, his eye had been on the openings only, on the stars of light. He did not care about the stone; a rude border of moulding was all he needed, it was the penetrating shape which he was watching. But when that shape had received its last possible expansion, and when the stone-work became an arrangement of graceful and parallel lines, that arrangement, like some form in a picture, unseen and accidentally developed, struck suddenly, inevitably, on the sight. It had literally not been seen before. It flashed out in an instant, as an independent form. It became a feature of the work. The architect took it under his care, thought over it, and distributed its members as we see.

Now, the great pause was at the moment when the space and the dividing stone-work were both equally considered. It did not last fifty years. The forms of the tracery were seized with a childish delight in the novel source of beauty; and the intervening space was cast aside, as an element of decoration, for ever. . . .

The reader will observe that, up to the last expansion of the penetrations, the stone-work was necessarily considered, as it actually is, *stiff*, and unyielding. It was so, also, during the pause of which I have spoken, when the forms of the tracery were still severe and pure; delicate indeed, but perfectly firm.

At the close of the period of pause, the first sign of serious change was like a low breeze, passing through the emaciated tracery, and making it tremble. It began to undulate like the threads of a cobweb lifted by the wind. It lost its essence as a structure of stone. Reduced to the slenderness of threads, it began to be considered as possessing also their flexibility. The architect was pleased with this his new fancy, and set himself to carry it out; and in a little time, the bars of tracery were caused to appear to the eye as if they had been woven together like a net. This was a change which sacrificed a great principle of truth; it sacrificed the expression of the qualities of the material; and however delightful its results in their first developments, it was ultimately ruinous.

For, observe the difference between the supposition of ductility, and that of elastic structure noticed above in the resemblance to tree form. That resemblance was not sought, but necessary; it resulted from the natural conditions of strength in the pier or trunk, and slenderness in the ribs or branches, while many of the other suggested conditions of resemblance were perfectly true. A tree branch, though in a certain sense flexible, is not ductile; it is as firm in its own form as the rib of stone; both of them will yield up to certain limits, both of them breaking when those limits are exceeded; while the tree trunk will bend no more than the stone pillar. But when the tracery is assumed to be as yielding as a silken cord; when the whole fragility, elasticity, and weight of the material are to the eye, if not in terms, denied; when all the art of the architect is applied to disprove the first conditions of his working, and the first attributes of his materials; *this* is a deliberate treachery, only redeemed from the charge of direct falsehood by the visibility of the stone surface, and degrading all the traceries it affects exactly in the degree of its presence.

But the declining and morbid taste of the later architects was not satisfied with thus much deception. They were delighted with the subtle charm they had created, and thought only of increasing its power. The next step was to consider and represent the tracery, as not only ductile, but penetrable; and when two mouldings met each other, to manage their intersection, so that one should appear to pass through the other, retaining its independence; or when two ran parallel to each other, to represent the one as partly contained within the other, and partly apparent above it. This form of falsity was that which crushed the art. The flexible traceries were often beautiful, though they were ignoble; but the penetrated traceries, rendered, as they finally were, merely the means of exhibiting the dexterity of the stone-cutter, annihilated both the beauty and dignity of the Gothic types.

From *The Seven Lamps of Architecture*, ch. II, §§ 23-5

THE WALL

In the Greek temple the wall is as nothing; the entire interest is in the detached columns and the frieze they bear; in French Flamboyant, and in our detestable Perpendicular, the object is to get rid of the wall surface, and keep the eye altogether on tracery of line: in Romanesque work and Egyptian, the wall is a confessed and honoured member, and the light is often allowed to fall on large areas of it, variously decorated. Now, both these principles are admitted by Nature, the one in her woods and thickets, the other in her plains, and cliffs, and waters; but the latter is pre-eminently the principle of power, and, in some sense, of beauty also. For, whatever infinity of fair form there may be in the maze of the forest, there is a fairer, as I think, in the surface of the quiet lake; and I hardly know that association of shaft or tracery, for which I would exchange the warm sleep of sunshine on some smooth, broad, human-like front of marble. Nevertheless, if breadth is to be beautiful, its substance must in some sort be beautiful; and we must not hastily condemn the exclusive resting of the northern architects in divided lines, until at least we have remembered the difference between a blank surface of Caen stone, and one mixed from Genoa and Carrara, of serpentine with snow: but as regards abstract power and awfulness, there is no question; without breadth of surface it is in vain to seek them, and it matters little, so that the surface be wide, bold, and unbroken, whether it be of brick or of jasper; the light of heaven upon it, and the weight of earth in it, are all we need: for it is singular how forgetful the mind may become both of material and workmanship, if only it have space enough over which to range, and to remind it, however feebly, of the joy that it has in contemplating the flatness and sweep of great plains and broad seas. And it is a noble thing for men to do this with their cut stone or moulded clay, and to make the face of a wall look infinite, and its edge against the sky like an horizon: or even if less than this be reached, it is still delightful to mark the play of passing light on its broad surface, and to see by how many artifices and gradations of tinting and shadow, time and storm will set their wild signatures upon it; and how in the rising or declining of the day the unbroken twilight rests long and luridly on its high lineless forehead, and fades away untraceably down its tiers of confused and countless stone.

From *The Seven Lamps of Architecture*, ch. III, § 8

§ 229

THE CAPITAL IN LIGHT AND SHADOW

The rolling heap of the thunder-cloud, divided by rents, and multiplied by wreaths, yet gathering them all into its broad, torrid, and towering zone, and its midnight darkness opposite; the scarcely less majestic heave of the mountain side, all torn and traversed by depth of defile and ridge of rock, yet never losing the unity of its illumined swell and shadowy decline; and the head of every mighty tree, rich with tracery of leaf and bough, yet terminated against the sky by a true line, and rounded by a green horizon, which, multiplied in the distant forest, makes it look bossy from above; all these mark, for a great and honoured law, that diffusion of light for which the Byzantine ornaments were designed, and show us that those builders had truer sympathy with what God made majestic, than the self-contemplating and self-contented Greek *. . . .

I have endeavoured to give some idea of one of the hollow balls of stone which, surrounded by flowing leafage, occur in varied succession on the architrave of the central gate of St Mark's at Venice. . . . It seems to me singularly beautiful in its unity of lightness, and delicacy of detail, with breadth of light. It looks as if its leaves had been sensitive, and had risen and shut themselves into a bud at some sudden touch, and would presently fall back again into their wild flow. The cornices of San Michele of Lucca, seen above and below the arch, . . . show the effect of heavy leafage and thick stems arranged on a surface whose curve is a simple quadrant, the light dying from off them as it turns. It would be difficult, as I think, to invent any thing more noble: and I insist on the broad character of their arrangement the more earnestly, because, afterwards modified

* In this sentence of mine, the bit about self-contented Greeks must be omitted. A noble Greek was as little content without God, as George Herbert, or St Francis, and a Byzantine *was* nothing else than a Greek, – recognizing Christ for Zeus. [Ruskin's note of 1880.]

by greater skill in its management, it became characteristic of the richest pieces of Gothic design. The capital, . . . is of the noblest period of the Venetian Gothic; and it is interesting to see the play of leafage so luxuriant, absolutely subordinated to the breadth of two masses of light and shade. What is done by the Venetian architect, with a power as irresistible as that of the waves of his surrounding sea, is done by the masters of the Cis-Alpine Gothic, more timidly, and with a manner somewhat cramped and cold, but not less expressing their assent to the same great law. The ice spiculæ of the North, and its broken sunshine, seem to have image in, and influence on, the work; and the leaves which, under the Italian's hand, roll, and flow, and bow down over their black shadows, as in the weariness of noon-day heat, are, in the North, crisped and frostbitten, wrinkled on the edges, and sparkling as if with dew. But the rounding of the ruling form is not less sought and felt.

From *The Seven Lamps of Architecture*, ch. III, §§ 15–16

¶ 230

EXHAUSTING ORNAMENT

I do not know anything more painful or pitiful than the kind of ivory carving with which the Certosa of Pavia, and part of the Colleone sepulchral chapel at Bergamo, and other such buildings are incrusted, of which it is not possible so much as to think without exhaustion; and a heavy sense of the misery it would be, to be forced to look at it all. And this is not from the quantity of it, nor because it is bad work – much of it is inventive and able; but because it looks as if it were only fit to be put in inlaid cabinets and velveted caskets, and as if it could not bear one drifting shower or gnawing frost. We are afraid for it, anxious about it, and tormented by it; and we feel that a massy shaft and a bold shadow would be worth it all. Nevertheless, even in cases like these, much depends on the accomplishment of the great ends of decoration. If the ornament does its duty – if it *is* ornament, and its points of shade and light tell in the general effect, we shall not be offended by finding that the sculptor in his fulness of fancy has chosen to give much more than these mere points of light, and has composed them of groups of figures. But if the ornament does not answer its purpose, if it have no distant, no truly decorative power; if, generally seen, it be a mere incrustation and meaningless roughness, we shall only be chagrined by finding when we look close, that the incrustation has cost years of labour, and has millions of figures and histories in it; and would be the better for being seen through a Stanhope lens. Hence the greatness of the northern Gothic as contrasted with the latest Italian. It reaches nearly the same extreme of detail; but it never loses sight of its architectural purpose, never fails in its decorative power; not a leaflet in it but speaks, and speaks far off too; and so long as this be the case, there is no limit to the luxuriance in which such work may legitimately and nobly be bestowed.

From *The Seven Lamps of Architecture*, ch. I, § 14

§ 231

HOW ARCHITECTURE MAKES AN IMPRESSION

For there is a crust about the impressible part of men's minds, which must be pierced through before they can be touched to the quick; and though we may prick at it and scratch it in a thousand separate places, we might as well have let it alone if we do not come through somewhere with a deep thrust: and if we can give such a thrust anywhere, there is no need of another; it need not be even so 'wide as a church door,' so that it be *enough*. And mere weight will do this; it is a clumsy way of doing it, but an effectual one, too; and the apathy which cannot be pierced through by a small steeple, nor shone through by a small window, can be broken through in a moment by the mere weight of a great wall.

From *The Seven Lamps of Architecture*, ch. III, § 5

§ 232

LIGHT AND SHADE IN ARCHITECTURE

So that, after size and weight, the Power of architecture may be said to depend on the quantity . . . of its shadow; and it seems to me, that the reality of its works, and the use and influence they have in the daily life of men, ... require of it that it should express a kind of human sympathy, by a measure of darkness as great as there is in human life: and that as the great poem and great fiction generally affect us most by the majesty of their masses of shade, and cannot take hold upon us if they affect a continuance of lyric sprightliness, but must be often serious, and sometimes melancholy, else they do not express the truth of this wild world of ours; so there must be, in this magnificently human art of architecture, some equivalent expression for the trouble and wrath of life, for its sorrow and its mystery; and this it can only give by depth or diffusion of gloom, by the frown upon its front, and the shadow of its recess. So that Rembrandtism is a noble manner in architecture, though a false one in painting; and I do not believe that ever any building was truly great, unless it had mighty masses, vigorous and deep, of shadow mingled with its surface. And among the first habits that a young architect should learn, is that of thinking in shadow, not looking at a design in its miserable liny skeleton; but conceiving it as it will be when the dawn lights it, and the dusk leaves it; when its stones will be hot, and its crannies cool; when the lizards will bask on the one, and the birds build in the other. Let him design* with the sense of cold and heat upon him; let him cut out the shadows, as men dig wells in unwatered plains; and lead along the lights, as a founder does his hot metal; let him keep the full command of both, and see that he knows how they fall, and where they fade. His paper lines and proportions are of no value: all that he has to do must be done by spaces of light and darkness; and his business is to see that the one is broad and bold enough not to be swallowed up by twilight, and the other deep enough not to be dried like a shallow pool by a noon-day sun.

From *The Seven Lamps of Architecture*, ch. III, § 24

---

* 'let him – let him.' All very fine; but all the while, there wasn't one of the architects for whom this was written – nor is there one alive now – who could, or can, so much as shade an egg, or a tallow candle; how much less an egg-moulding or a shaft! [Ruskin's note of 1880.]

THE SMALLNESS OF ENGLISH ARCHITECTURE

But I know not how it is, unless that our English hearts have more oak than stone in them, and have more filial sympathy with acorns than Alps; but all that we do is small and mean, if not worse – thin, and wasted, and unsubstantial. It is not modern work only; we have built like frogs and mice since the thirteenth century (except only in our castles). What a contrast between the pitiful little pigeon-holes which stand for doors in the east front of Salisbury, looking like the entrances to a beehive or a wasp's nest, and the soaring arches and kingly crowning of the gates of Abbeville, Rouen, and Rheims, or the rock-hewn piers of Chartres, or the dark and vaulted porches and writhed pillars of Verona! Of domestic architecture what need is there to speak? How small, how cramped, how poor, how miserable in its petty neatness is our best! how beneath the mark of attack, and the level of contempt, that which is common with us! What a strange sense of formalized deformity, of shrivelled precision, of starved accuracy, of minute misanthropy have we, as we leave even the rude streets of Picardy for the market towns of Kent! Until that street architecture of ours is bettered, until we give it some size and boldness, until we give our windows recess, and our walls thickness, I know not how we can blame our architects for their feebleness in more important work; their eyes are inured to narrowness and slightness: can we expect them at a word to conceive and deal with breadth and solidity? They ought not to live in our cities; there is that in their miserable walls which bricks up to death men's imaginations, as surely as ever perished forsworn nun. An architect should live as little in cities as a painter. Send him to our hills, and let him study there what nature understands by a buttress, and what by a dome.   From *The Seven Lamps of Architecture*, ch. III, § 24

A PURITAN VIEW OF DECORATION

Hence then a general law, of singular importance in the present day, a law of simple common sense, – not to decorate things belonging to purposes of active and occupied life. Wherever you can rest, there decorate; where rest is forbidden, so is beauty. You must not mix ornament with business any more than you may mix play. Work first, and then rest. Work first, and then gaze, but do not use golden ploughshares, nor bind ledgers in enamel. Do not thrash with sculptured flails:* nor put bas-reliefs on millstones. What! it will be asked, are we in the habit of doing so? Even so; always and everywhere. The most familiar position of Greek mouldings is in these days on shop fronts. There is not a tradesman's sign nor shelf nor counter in all the streets of all our cities, which has not upon it ornaments which were invented to adorn temples and beautify kings' palaces. There is not the smallest advantage in them where they are. Absolutely valueless – utterly without the power of giving pleasure, they only satiate the eye, and vulgarize their own forms. Many of these are in themselves thoroughly good copies of fine things, which things themselves we shall never, in consequence, enjoy any more. Many a pretty beading and graceful bracket there is in wood, or stucco above our grocers' and cheesemongers' and hosiers' shops: how is it that the tradesmen cannot understand that custom is to be had only by selling good tea and cheese and cloth, and the people come to them for their honesty, and their readiness, and their right wares, and not because they have Greek cornices over their windows, or their names in large gilt letters on their house fronts? How pleasurable it would be to have the power of going through the streets of London, pulling down those brackets and friezes and large names, restoring to the tradesmen the capital they had spent in architecture, and putting them on honest and equal terms, each with his name in black letters over his door, not shouted down the street from the upper storeys, and each with a plain wooden shop casement, with small panes in it that people would not think of breaking in order to be sent to prison! How much better for them would it be – how much happier, how much wiser, to put their trust upon their own truth and industry, and not on the idiocy

* 'Nor fight with jewelled swords' should have been added. The principle is partial and doubtful however. One of the most beautiful bits of ironwork I ever saw was an apothecary's pestle and mortar (of the fourteenth century) at Messina: and a day may come when we shall wisely decorate the stilt of the plough. The error, however, – observe, – is again on the side of common sense! ... [Ruskin's note of 1880.]

of their customers. It is curious, and it says little for our national probity on the one hand, or prudence on the other, to see the whole system of our street decoration based on the idea that people must be baited to a shop as moths are to a candle.

From *The Seven Lamps of Architecture*, ch. IV, § 19

¶ 235

RAILWAY ARCHITECTURE

Another of the strange and evil tendencies of the present day is to the decoration of the railroad station.* Now, if there be any place in the world in which people are deprived of that portion of temper and discretion which is necessary to the contemplation of beauty, it is there. It is the very temple of discomfort, and the only charity that the builder can extend to us is to show us, plainly as may be, how soonest to escape from it. The whole system of railroad travelling is addressed to people who, being in a hurry, are therefore, for the time being, miserable. No one would travel in that manner who could help it – who had time to go leisurely over hills and between hedges, instead of through tunnels and between banks: at least, those who would, have no sense of beauty so acute as that we need consult it at the station. The railroad is in all its relations a matter of earnest business, to be got through as soon as possible. It transmutes a man from a traveller into a living parcel. For the time he has parted with the nobler characteristics of his humanity for the sake of a planetary power of locomotion. Do not ask him to admire anything. You might as well ask the wind. Carry him safely, dismiss him soon: he will thank you for nothing else. All attempts to please him in any other way are mere mockery, and insults to the things by which you endeavour to do so. There never was more flagrant nor impertinent folly than the smallest portion of ornament in anything concerned with railroads or near them. Keep them out of the way, take them through the ugliest country you can find, confess them but the miserable things they are, and spend nothing upon

---

* Common sense still! – and, this time, indisputable. Well had it been, for many a company, and many a traveller, had this 121st page of the Seven Lamps been taken for a railway signal. [Ruskin's note of 1880.]

them but for safety and speed. Give large salaries to efficient servants, large prices to good manufacturers, large wages to able workmen; let the iron be tough, and the brickwork solid, and the carriages strong. The time is perhaps not distant when these first necessities may not be easily met: and to increase expense in any other direction is madness. Better bury gold in the embankments than put it in ornaments on the stations. Will a single traveller be willing to pay an increased fare on the South Western, because the columns of the terminus are covered with patterns from Nineveh? – he will only care less for the Ninevite ivories in the British Museum: or on the North Western, because there are old English-looking spandrels to the roof of the station at Crewe? he will only have less pleasure in their prototypes at Crewe House. Railroad architecture has, or would have, a dignity of its own if it were only left to its work. You would not put rings on the fingers of a smith at his anvil.

From *The Seven Lamps of Architecture*, ch. IV, §§ 21 and 23

§ 236

ARCHITECTURAL COLOUR

I hold this, then, for the first great principle of architectural colour. Let it be visibly independent of form. Never paint a column with vertical lines, but always cross it. Never give separate mouldings separate colours (I know this is heresy, but I never shrink from any conclusions, however contrary to human authority, to which I am led by observance of natural principles); and in sculptured ornaments do not paint the leaves or figures (I cannot help the Elgin frieze) of one colour and their ground of another, but vary both the ground and the figures with the same harmony. Notice how Nature does it in a variegated flower; not one leaf red and another white, but a point of red and a zone of white, or whatever it may be, to each. In certain places you may run your two systems closer, and here and there let them be parallel for a note or two, but see that the colours and the forms coincide only as two orders of mouldings do; the same for an instant, but each holding its own course. So single members may sometimes have single colours; as a bird's head is sometimes of one colour and its shoulders another, you may

247

make your capital one colour and your shaft another; but in general the best place for colour is on broad surfaces, not on the points of interest in form. An animal is mottled on its breast and back, rarely on its paws or about its eyes; so put your variegation boldly on the flat wall and broad shaft, but be shy of it in the capital and moulding; in all cases it is a safe rule to simplify colour when form is rich, and *vice versa*; and I think it would be well in general to carve all capitals and graceful ornaments in white marble, and so leave them.

From *The Seven Lamps of Architecture*, ch. IV, § 36

§ 237

THE CAMPANILE OF GIOTTO

In its first appeal to the stranger's eye there is something unpleasing; a mingling, as it seems to him, of over severity with over minuteness. But let him give it time, as he should to all other consummate art. I remember well how, when a boy, I used to despise that Campanile, and think it meanly smooth and finished. But I have since lived beside it many a day, and looked out upon it from my windows by sunlight and moonlight, and I shall not soon forget how profound and gloomy appeared to me the savageness of the Northern Gothic, when I afterwards stood, for the first time, beneath the front of Salisbury. The contrast is indeed strange, if it could be quickly felt, between the rising of those grey walls out of their quiet swarded space, like dark and barren rocks out of a green lake, with their rude, mouldering, rough-grained shafts, and triple lights, without tracery or other ornament than the martins' nests in the height of them, and that bright, smooth, sunny surface of glowing jasper, those spiral shafts and fairy traceries, so white, so faint, so crystalline, that their slight shapes are hardly traced in darkness on the pallor of the Eastern sky, that serene height of mountain alabaster, coloured like a morning cloud, and chased like a sea shell.

From *The Seven Lamps of Architecture*, ch. IV, § 43

RESTORATION

Neither by the public, nor by those who have the care of public monuments, is the true meaning of the word *restoration* understood. It means the most total destruction which a building can suffer: a destruction out of which no remnants can be gathered: a destruction accompanied with false description of the thing destroyed.* Do not let us deceive ourselves in this important matter: it is *impossible*, as impossible as to raise the dead, to restore anything that has ever been great or beautiful in architecture. That which I have above insisted upon as the life of the whole, that spirit which is given only by the hand and eye of the workman, can never be recalled. Another spirit may be given by another time, and it is then a new building; but the spirit of the dead workman cannot be summoned up, and commanded to direct other hands, and other thoughts. And as for direct and simple copying, it is palpably impossible. What copying can there be of surfaces that have been worn half an inch down? The whole finish of the work was in the half inch that is gone; if you attempt to restore that finish, you do it conjecturally; if you copy what is left, granting fidelity to be possible, (and what care, or watchfulness, or cost can secure it,) how is the new work better than the old? There was yet in the old *some* life, some mysterious suggestion of what it had been, and of what it had lost; some sweetness in the gentle lines which rain and sun had wrought. There can be none in the brute hardness of the new carving.

From *The Seven Lamps of Architecture*, ch. VI, § 18

THE IMPORTANCE OF ARCHITECTURE IN MODERN LIFE

The very quietness of nature is gradually withdrawn from us; thousands who once in their necessarily prolonged travel were subjected to an influence, from the silent sky and slumbering fields,

* False, also, in the manner of parody, – the most loathesome manner of falsehood. [Ruskin's note of 1880.]

more effectual than known or confessed, now bear with them even there the ceaseless fever of their life; and along the iron veins that traverse the frame of our country, beat and flow the fiery pulses of its exertion, hotter and faster every hour. All vitality is concentrated through those throbbing arteries into the central cities; the country is passed over like a green sea by narrow bridges, and we are thrown back in continually closer crowds upon the city gates. The only influence which can in any wise *there* take the place of that of the woods and fields, is the power of ancient Architecture. Do not part with it for the sake of the formal square, or of the fenced and planted walk, nor of the goodly street nor opened quay. The pride of a city is not in these. Leave them to the crowd; but remember that there will surely be some within the circuit of the disquieted walls who would ask for some other spots than these wherein to walk; for some other forms to meet their sight familiarly.

From *The Seven Lamps of Architecture*, ch. VI, § 20

¶ 240

ARCHITECTURE SHOULD BE ENTERTAINING

It requires a strong effort of common sense to shake ourselves quit of all that we have been taught for the last two centuries, and wake to the perception of a truth just as simple and certain as it is new: that great art, whether expressing itself in words, colours, or stones, does *not* say the same thing over and over again; that the merit of architectural, as of every other art, consists in its saying new and different things; that to repeat itself is no more a characteristic of genius in marble than it is of genius in print; and that we may, without offending any laws of good taste, require of an architect, as we do of a novelist, that he should be not only correct, but entertaining. . . .

Let us then understand at once that change or variety is as much a necessity to the human heart and brain in buildings as in books; that there is no merit, though there is some occasional use, in monotony; and that we must no more expect to derive either pleasure or profit from an architecture whose ornaments are of one pattern, and whose pillars are of one proportion, than we should out of a universe in which the clouds were all of one shape, and the trees all of one size.

From *The Stones of Venice*, Vol. II, ch. VI, §§ 28–9

¶ 241

THE NATURE OF GOTHIC TO BE RICH

Commonly it is said of all Gothic, that it rose in simplicity, that it declined by becoming too florid and too rich.

Put that error at once out of your minds. All beautiful and perfect art, literature or nature, is rich. Titian is rich, Beethoven is rich, Shakespeare is rich, and the forests, and the fields, and the clouds are richest of all. And the two most beautiful Gothic pieces of work in the world, – the South door of the Cathedral of Florence, and the North transept door of the Cathedral of Rouen, – were both in the thirteenth century covered with sculpture as closely as a fretted morning sky with sands of cloud.

From *The Flamboyant Architecture of the Valley of the Somme*, § 26

¶ 242

MERE SIZE

Mere size has, indeed, under all disadvantage, some definite value; and so has mere splendour. Disappointed as you may be, or at least ought to be, at first, by St Peter's, in the end you will feel its size, – and its brightness. These are all you *can* feel in it – it is nothing more than the pump-room at Leamington built bigger; – but the bigness tells at last: and Corinthian pillars whose capitals alone are ten feet high, and their acanthus leaves three feet six long, give you a serious conviction of the infallibility of the Pope, and the fallibility of the wretched Corinthians, who invented the style indeed, but built with capitals no bigger than hand-baskets.

From *Mornings in Florence*, 'The Fourth Morning', § 72

ARCHITECTURAL TRAINING

My wish would be to see the profession of the architect united, not with that of the engineer, but of the sculptor. I think there should be a separate school and university course for engineers, in which the principal branches of study connected with that of practical building should be the physical and exact sciences, and honours should be taken in mathematics; but I think there should be another school and university course for the sculptor and architect, in which literature and philosophy should be the associated branches of study, and honours should be taken *in literis humanioribus*; and I think a young architect's examination for his degree (for mere pass) should be much stricter than that of youths intending to enter other professions. The quantity of scholarship necessary for the efficiency of a country clergyman is not great. So that he be modest and kindly, the main truths he has to teach may be learned better in his heart than in books, and taught in very simple English. The best physicians I have known spent very little time in their libraries; and though my lawyer sometimes chats with me over a Greek coin, I think he regards the time so spent in the light rather of concession to my idleness than as helpful to his professional labours.

But there is no task undertaken by a true architect of which the honourable fulfilment will not require a range of knowledge and habitual feeling only attainable by advanced scholarship.

From *The Study of Architecture in Our Schools*, § 16

¶ 244

THE TRAINING OF AN ARCHITECTURAL STUDENT

He should first be taught to draw largely and simply; then he should make quick and firm sketches of flowers, animals, drapery, and figures, from nature, in the simplest terms of line, and light and shade; always being taught to look at the organic, actions and masses, not at the textures or accidental effects of shade; meantime his sentiment respecting all these things should be cultivated by close and constant inquiry into their mythological significance and associated traditions; then, knowing the things and creatures thoroughly, and regarding them through an atmosphere of enchanted memory, he should be shown how the facts he has taken so long to learn are summed by a great sculptor in a few touches; how those touches are invariably arranged in musical and decorative relations; how every detail unnecessary for his purpose is refused; how those necessary for his purpose are insisted upon, or even exaggerated, or represented by singular artifice, when literal representation is impossible; and how all this is done under the instinct and passion of an inner commanding spirit which it is indeed impossible to imitate, but possible, perhaps, to share.

From *The Study of Architecture in Our Schools*, § 17

¶ 245

THE UNITY OF SACRED AND PROFANE ARCHITECTURE

Wherever Christian church architecture has been good and lovely, it has been merely the perfect development of the common dwelling-house architecture of the period; that when the pointed arch was used in the street, it was used in the church; when the round arch was used in the street, it was used in the church: when the pinnacle was set over the garret window, it was set over the belfry tower; when the flat roof was used for the drawing-room, it was used for the nave. There is no sacredness in round arches, nor in pointed; none in pinnacles, nor in buttresses; none in pillars, nor in traceries. Churches were larger than most other buildings, because they had to hold more people; they were more adorned than most other buildings, because they were safer from violence, and were the fitting subjects of devotional offering: but they were never built in any separate, mystical, and religious style; they were built in the manner that was common and familiar to everybody at the time. The flamboyant traceries that adorn the façade of Rouen Cathedral had once their fellows in every window of every house in the market-place; the sculptures that adorn the porches of St Mark's had once their match on the walls of every palace on the Grand

Canal; and the only difference between the church and the dwelling-house was, that there existed a symbolical meaning in the distribution of the parts of all buildings meant for worship, and that the painting or sculpture was, in the one case, less frequently of profane subject than in the other. A more severe distinction cannot be drawn: for secular history was constantly introduced into church architecture; and sacred history or allusion generally formed at least one half of the ornament of the dwelling-house.

From *The Stones of Venice*, ch. IV, § 53

¶ 246

THE BRADFORD EXCHANGE

My good Yorkshire friends, you asked me down here among your hills that I might talk to you about this Exchange you are going to build: but, earnestly and seriously asking you to pardon me, I am going to do nothing of the kind. . . . I cannot speak, to purpose, of anything about which I do not care; and most simply and sorrowfully I have to tell you, in the outset, that I do *not* care about this Exchange of yours.

If, however, when you sent me your invitation, I had answered, 'I won't come, I don't care about the Exchange of Bradford,' you would have been justly offended with me, not knowing the reasons of so blunt a carelessness. So I have come down, hoping that you will patiently let me tell you why, on this, and many other such occasions, I now remain silent, when formerly I should have caught at the opportunity of speaking to a gracious audience.

In a word, then, I do not care about this Exchange – because *you* don't; and because you know perfectly well I cannot make you. Look at the essential conditions of the case, which you, as business men, know perfectly well, though perhaps you think I forget them. You are going to spend £30,000, which to you, collectively, is nothing; the buying of a new coat, is, as to the cost of it, a much more important matter of consideration, to me, than building a new Exchange is to you. But you think you may as well have the right thing for your money. You know there are a great many odd styles of architecture about; you don't want to do anything ridiculous;

you hear of me, among others, as a respectable architectural man-milliner; and you send for me, that I may tell you the leading fashion; and what is, in our shops, for the moment, the newest and sweetest thing in pinnacles.

Now, pardon me for telling you frankly, you cannot have good architecture merely by asking people's advice on occasion. All good architecture is the expression of national life and character; and it is produced by a prevalent and eager national taste, or desire for beauty.

From *The Crown of Wild Olive*, Lecture II, §§ 52–4

¶ 247

THE SEPARATION OF LIFE AND RELIGION

I notice that among all the new buildings which cover your once wild hills, churches and schools are mixed in due, that is to say, in large proportion, with your mills and mansions; and I notice also that the churches and schools are almost always Gothic, and the mansions and mills are never Gothic. May I ask the meaning of this; for, remember, it is peculiarly a modern phenomenon? When Gothic was invented, houses were Gothic as well as churches; and when the Italian style superseded the Gothic, churches were Italian as well as houses. If there is a Gothic spire to the cathedral of Antwerp, there is a Gothic belfry to the Hôtel de Ville at Brussels; if Inigo Jones builds an Italian Whitehall, Sir Christopher Wren builds an Italian St Paul's. But now you live under one school of architecture, and worship under another. What do you mean by doing this? Am I to understand that you are thinking of changing your architecture back to Gothic; and that you treat your churches experimentally because it does not matter what mistakes you make in a church? Or am I to understand that you consider Gothic a pre-eminently sacred and beautiful mode of building, which you think, like the fine frankincense, should be mixed for the tabernacle only, and reserved for your religious services? For if this be the feeling, though it may seem at first as if it were graceful and reverent, at the root of the matter, it signifies neither more nor less than that you have separated your religion from your life.

From *The Crown of Wild Olive*, Lecture II, § 61

CONTRASTED DWELLINGS

The road from the village of Shirley, near Addington, where my father and mother are buried, to the house they lived in when I was four years old, lay, at that time, through a quite secluded district of field and wood, traversed here and there by winding lanes, and by one or two smooth mail-coach roads, beside which, at intervals of a mile or two, stood some gentleman's house, with its lawn, gardens, offices, and attached fields, indicating a country life of long continuance and quiet respectability. Except such an one here and there, one saw no dwellings above the size of cottages or small farmsteads; these, wood-built usually, and thatched, their porches embroidered with honeysuckle, and their gardens with daisies, their doors mostly ajar, or with one half shut to keep in the children, and a bricked or tiled footway from it to the wicket gate, – all neatly kept, and vivid with a sense of the quiet energies of their contented tenants, – made the lane-turnings cheerful, and gleamed in half-hidden clusters beneath the slopes of the wood-lands at Sydenham and Penge. There were no signs of distress, of effort, or of change; many of enjoyment, and not a few of wealth beyond the daily needs of life.

That same district is now covered by, literally, many thousands of houses built within the last ten years, of rotten brick, with various iron devices to hold it together. They, every one, have a drawing-room and dining-room, transparent from back to front, so that from the road one sees the people's heads inside, clear against the light. They have a second story of bedrooms, and an underground one of kitchen. They are fastened in a Siamese twin manner together by their sides, and each couple has a Greek or Gothic portico shared between them, with magnificent steps, and highly ornamented capitals. Attached to every double block are exactly similar double parallelograms of garden, laid out in new gravel and scanty turf, on the model of the pleasure grounds in the Crystal Palace, and enclosed by high, thin, and pale brick walls. The gardens in front are fenced from the road with an immense weight of cast iron, and entered between two square gate-posts, with projecting stucco cornices, bearing the information that the eligible residence within is Mortimer House or Montague Villa.

From *Fors Clavigera*, II, Letter XXIX, § 3, 2 April 1873

§ 249

MODERN CITIES

All lovely architecture was designed for cities in cloudless air; for cities in which piazzas and gardens opened in bright populousness and peace; cities built that men might live happily in them, and take delight daily in each other's presence and powers. But our cities, built in black air which, by its accumulated foulness, first renders all ornament invisible in distance, and then chokes its interstices with soot; cities which are mere crowded masses of store, and warehouse, and counter, and are therefore to the rest of the world what the larder and cellar are to a private house; cities in which the object of men is not life, but labour; and in which all chief magnitude of edifice is to enclose machinery; cities in which the streets are not the avenues for the passing and procession of a happy people, but the drains for the discharge of a tormented mob, in which the only object in reaching any spot is to be transferred to another; in which existence becomes mere transition, and every creature is only one atom in a drift of human dust, and current of interchanging particles, circulating here by tunnels underground, and there by tubes in the air; for a city, or cities, such as this no architecture is possible – nay, no desire of it is possible to their inhabitants.

From *The Study of Architecture in Our Schools*, § 4

§ 250

ORNAMENT AND FUNCTION

A good spire or porch retains the first idea of a roof usefully covering a space, as a Norman high cap or elongated Quaker's bonnet retains the original idea of a simple covering for the head; and any extravagance of subsequent fancy may be permitted, so long as the notion of use is not altogether lost. A girl begins by wearing a plain round hat to shade her from the sun; she ties it down over her ears on a windy day; presently she decorates the edge of it, so bent, with flowers in front, or the riband that ties it with a bouquet at the side, and it becomes a bonnet. This decorated construction may be discreetly changed, by endless fashion, so long as it does not become a clearly useless riband round the middle of the head, or a clearly useless saucer on the top of it.

From *Val d'Arno*, ch. VI, § 146

¶ 251
SPIRALS

Now all thirteenth-century ornament of every nation runs much into spirals, and Irish and Scandinavian earlier decoration into little else. But these spirals are different from theirs. The Northern spiral is always elastic – like that of a watch-spring. The Greek spiral, drifted like that of a whirlpool, or whirlwind. It is always an eddy or vortex – not a living rod, like the point of a young fern.

At least, not living its own life – but under another life. It is under the power of the Queen of the Air; the power also that is over the Sea, and over the human mind. The first leaves I ever drew from St Mark's were those drifted under the breathing of it; these on its uppermost cornice, far lovelier, are the final perfection of the Ionic spiral, and of the thought in the temple of the Winds.

From *St Mark's Rest*, ch. VIII, § 101

¶ 252
WINDOWS

Thus you probably have a distinct idea – those of you, at least, who are interested in architecture – of the shape of the windows in Westminster Abbey, in the Cathedral of Chartres, or in the Duomo of Milan. Can any of you, I should like to know, make a guess at the shape of the windows in the Sistine Chapel, the Stanza of the Vatican, the Scuola di San Rocco, or the lower church of Assisi? The soul or anima of the first three buildings is in their windows; but of the last three, in their walls.

From *Val d'Arno*, Lecture VI, § 158

CONTEMPORARY ARCHITECTURE

Nice sensible discussions you're having in England there about Gothic and Italian, aren't you? And the best of the jest is that besides nobody knowing which is which, there is not a man living who can build either. What a goose poor Scott (who will get his liver fit for *pâté de Strasburg* with vexation) must be, not to say at once he'll build anything. If I were he, I'd build Lord P[almerston] an office with all the capitals upside down; and tell him it was in the Greek style, inverted, to express typically Government by Party: Up to-day, down to-morrow.

From a letter to E. S. Dallas, 18 August 1859

5

SOCIETY AND ECONOMICS

A NOTE ON RUSKIN'S WRITINGS ON
SOCIETY AND ECONOMICS

Ruskin's elderly, devoted parents had sheltered him from any contact with the rough and squalid world of early Victorian England, and he tells us (no. 254) that his consciousness of economic injustice was first awakened in the 1830s by the way in which the wives of his father's Spanish partners, 'women of gentle and amiable disposition', spoke about their peasants. In the next years he was too much absorbed in Swiss scenery and Turner's paintings to give much thought to society, but when he began to write about architecture as a reflection of social conditions, his feelings of justice and compassion were aroused, and his clear, analytical eye, passing from Byzantine capitals to the theory of rent, showed him fundamental inconsistencies of design. The result can be seen in several passages in *The Seven Lamps*, which passed unnoticed among the many provocative opinions in that extraordinary book. In *The Stones of Venice*, however, his views on the place of labour in a social and economic system were concentrated in one chapter of the second volume, to which he gave the title 'The Nature of Gothic'. In 1854, the year after it was published, the founders of the first Working Men's College printed this chapter separately, as their introductory pamphlet, with the subtitle 'And herein of the True Functions of the Workman in Art'. In the same year Ruskin became a lecturer at the College. The practical application of his ideas to Society had begun.

His readers still believed that these ideas were no more than the harmless by-product of his idealistic theory of art. In 1857 he was invited to lecture at Manchester in connexion with the famous Art Treasures Exhibition, and no doubt his sponsors expected a speech of congratulation on the prosperity and enlightenment of their city. Instead they got an attack on false values in Ruskin's best Socratic style (no. 272) and an outline of paternal socialism which was of all things most hateful to the Manchester school of economic thought. These lectures, afterwards printed with the title *A Joy Forever*, in ironic reference to the motto of the Exhibition, contain not only the germ of Ruskin's social philosophy, but certain key phrases like 'soldiers of the ploughshare as well as soldiers of the sword'. But they did not attract much attention, and the final volume of *Modern Painters*, appearing three years later, confirmed in the public mind the image of Ruskin as an eloquent visionary, innocently occupied with Alpine scenery and Gothic architecture. In fact this volume contains (repeated in *Unto this Last*, cf. no. 258) the aphorism which was to become the foundation stone of his whole system: 'Government and co-operation are in all things and eternally the laws of life. Anarchy and competition eternally and in all things, the laws of death.' But this was thought to refer only to sapphires and snowflakes, and nobody supposed for a moment that it could be intended for application to ordinary human life.

Then, in the same year, he sent to the *Cornhill Magazine* the first of three essays, which were quite clearly and unmistakably concerned with political economy; and suddenly readers and reviewers saw what he was up to. The result was an outburst of hysteria, compared to which the reception of Post-Impressionist painting was relatively mild. 'Utter imbecility', 'Intolerable twaddle', the 'world was not going to be preached to death by a mad governess'. What did Thackeray (then editor of the *Cornhill*) mean by committing himself to such nonsense? Thackeray was a man of the world, and informed Ruskin that he could print no more of these dangerous papers. Two years later they were published with the title *Unto this Last*.

To understand the horror and repugnance with which this little book, with its simple truths and touching humanity, was greeted by every single reader except Thomas Carlyle, we must realize that in 1860, orthodox political economy was the theology of the only effective nineteenth-century religion. Its complex, abstract, and at times impenetrable arguments, gave to the middle-class heirs of the Industrial Revolution the feeling of certainty and mystic protection which scholastic philosophy had provided in the Middle Ages. It disguised, or justified, the fact that a few people were making more money than they required by exploiting the poor. To question this theology was a threat to the peace of mind of all property owners, and when reviewers spoke of Ruskin's papers as heresy, they were using the word as earnestly as a member of the Holy Office. 'If we do not crush him,' said one of them, 'his wild words will touch the springs of action in some hearts, and before we are aware, a moral floodgate may fly open and drown us all.' [1]

Ruskin considered *Unto this Last* his best book, 'the one that will stand (if anything stand) surest and longest of all works of mine'; and, on the whole, posterity has agreed. *Unto this Last* is one of the great prophetic books of the nineteenth century. It pierces through the smoke-screen of classical economics, and reveals true human realities. It does so in language of apparent simplicity, but an attentive reader will recognize the style of a great virtuoso holding his passion and eloquence under control and concealing his skill with a show of innocence.

Ruskin bore the attacks on his articles with great courage, but no sane human being can fail to be oppressed by the weight of universal reprobation, and no doubt Ruskin was more deeply wounded than he knew. He retired to the village of Mornex near Geneva, and seriously thought of making it his home. On his solitary walks he continued to think about political economy, and planned to write a long book on the subject. This, however, never went further than the introductory chapters of definition, which was subsequently printed with the obscure title of *Munera Pulveris*. As with the second volume of *Modern Painters*, Ruskin's attempt to concentrate on a systematic expression of his philosophy deprived him of his natural poetry and even weakened his powers of perception, and *Munera Pulveris* is one of his most disappointing books.

At the same time (1871) he discovered a way of writing about social problems which suited him better: the series of letters 'To the

1. Leading article in the *Manchester Examiner and Times*, 2 October 1860.

Workmen and Labourers of Great Britain' which he called *Fors Clavigera*. He wrote this regularly every month till his mind collapsed, in 1878, then irregularly from 1880 to 1884, and they form one of the most extraordinary communications from one human being to his fellows ever to appear in print. In English perhaps only Swift's *Journal to Stella* is equally exacerbated and equally lacking in reserve. Both these strange documents were written by men ot genius on the brink of madness; but whereas Swift's outpourings are dominated by private obsessions, Ruskin's are dominated by his horror of a social system which condemned four-fifths of the population to poverty and squalid ugliness. This was not a private obsession, but the simple truth; and Ruskin was almost the only man in England to tell it.

The tone of *Fors Clavigera* is exceedingly bitter. Ruskin's first essays in political economy, the Manchester Lectures of 1857, beneath their irony, had been hopeful. But after fifteen years of total incomprehension and obloquy he became savage, and often reckless, in his attacks – 'like a man in the pillory', said Leslie Stephen, 'pelted by a thick-skinned mob and urged, by a sense of his helplessness, to utter the bitterest taunts he can invent'. His fury progressed from *laissez faire* economics to the whole capitalist system. He thought that all investment was a form of usury, and so contrary to Christian and the best pagan teaching. I quote (in no. 289), an attack on capitalism from one of his Oxford Lectures, the *Val d'Arno*; dozens more could be found in *Fors Clavigera*. But besides these destructive lamentations, he also included a number of positive plans for regenerating society. They are first outlined in *Fors*, Letter xx, and Ruskin followed it up by founding an organization called the Guild of St George, with himself as Master, which would put the theories into practice. It was an act of almost incredible naïvety, and it was accompanied by various rather pathetic attempts at action – the sweeping of the streets, the making of a road at Hinksey, and the establishment of a tea room in Marylebone. These naturally gave his opponents the opportunity of saying that he was a mere *idealogue* whose theories need not be taken seriously. In fact the greater part of them are now the truisms of the Welfare State.

Ruskin's economic doctrines are summed up in his great saying, 'There is no wealth but life.' What is usually taken for wealth is in fact no more than a 'kind of Byzantine harness or trappings with which we bridle creatures'. Capital is only of value when it avails towards life. Even a ploughshare – the best type of capital – is only of value when it glows bright in the furrow, and the true question of every capitalist is not 'How many ploughs have you?' but 'Where are your furrows?' 'What substance will it furnish good for life?' Economic man is a revolting abstraction. Men are not moved by desire for gain, but by 'admiration, hope and love'. A rich country is one in which the men and women are healthy and content; a rich man is one who has power over healthy and contented human beings, and they, not his dividends, must be his first thought and responsibility.

So far Ruskin's position is unexceptionable: his next step is less certain. He believed that ultimately there was no way of making money except by taking it away from someone else. 'The only way to abolish the east-end is to abolish the west-end.' He did not foresee, any more than Marx, an economy of full production based on technical invention, which (perhaps only temporarily) has raised the standard of life without diminishing superfluous wealth. In politics he made an equally questionable step. He saw that the state must take control of the means of production and distribution, and organize them for the good of the community as a whole; but he was prepared to place the control of the state in the hands of a single man. 'My continual aim has been to show the eternal superiority of some men to others, sometimes even of one man to all others.' He had a very low opinion of democracy, and what he thought of freedom may be found in the passage which I quote (no. 293) on the common house-fly. These views are not at present accepted in the English-speaking world; and it must be admitted that the experiences of the last thirty years have done little to recommend them. No doubt Ruskin underrated the corruptibility of man and the coarseness inherent in all forms of government. He would have been horrified by the exploits of Hitler and Stalin. But I doubt if he would have shrunk from the results of his doctrine as much as one would suppose. In spite of its materialist philosophy, he would, I think, have approved of Communism: the peasant communes of China, in particular, are exactly on his model. He would not have thought the cure worse than the disease because he could not imagine a worse disease than the capitalist society of the nineteenth century. At least Communism gives men a common faith; at least it recognizes the dignity of labour and the brotherhood of man, and even gives those worn-out catchwords some reality; at least it encourages men to succeed by skill and hard work rather than by gambling, deception, and theft. And if it covers up injustices with canting ideology, how much more did capitalist greed cover up injustices with every species of elaborate hypocrisy, from economic science to organized religion. Such, at least, would be my reading of Ruskin's beliefs as they flash, and crackle, and vanish into the smoke of *Fors Clavigera*.

For better or worse Ruskin was entirely unaffected by the socialist and communist thinkers of his own time who were following a similar train of thought; the names of Marx, Engels, Proudhon, and Saint-Simon do not occur in his works.[1] The only contemporary who influenced him was Thomas Carlyle, whose first protests against *laissez faire* capitalism appeared when Ruskin was a youth. Ruskin revered him as his master; Carlyle, in his turn, was the solitary supporter of Ruskin's economic writings (though he broke down over the later *Fors*) and even admired such chaotic productions as the *Val d'Arno*. His influence on Ruskin's style (which I discuss elsewhere) seems to me to have been salutary. But I cannot say the same for his influence on Ruskin's thought. Carlyle's mind was

1. Yet he was not altogether unaware of what was going on, as he says in *Fors* of October 1872 that his definitions may sound 'very radical and International', in reference to the International Association of Working Men (the First International), which was holding a meeting in the Hague at the time.

tough and could accommodate the toughness, not to say the brutality, of heroes. Ruskin's mind was tender, and the ruthlessness of leadership did not really suit him. However, it may be argued that the authoritarian element in Ruskin's ideal policy was not due to Carlyle, but was derived directly from the source book of all dictatorships, Plato's *Republic*. He read Plato almost every day, and noted in his diary, when he failed to do so, 'never well without him'. I suppose that all systems of Communism, even Benedictine Monasticism, go back to Plato's admiration of Sparta. Intellectuals tend to have a girlish passion for soldiers (or would have if soldiers didn't write memoirs), and Ruskin spoke with enthusiasm of the art of war in one of his most famous lectures (no. 183). Later he wrote a description of capitalist war which a century of leftist propaganda has not bettered (no. 279), and a prophetic vision of England's position in a modern arms race (no. 280) which is all too topical.

The influence of Ruskin's ideas on social reform has been immense. Most of the changes which he advocated – free schools, free libraries, town planning, smokeless zones, green belts – are now taken for granted. Not only the direction but the whole style of attack of the early English socialists is unmistakably Ruskinian. William Morris was, of course, an immediate disciple, but one does not associate Ruskin with George Bernard Shaw. Yet I believe I could have printed many passages from Shaw's prefaces in this anthology and no one would have spotted that they did not come from *Fors*. Gandhi often said that Ruskin was one of the principal influences on his life, and I have been told by Chinese acquaintances (though I cannot check the statement) that Mao was thinking of Ruskin when he organized Chinese Communism. Sixty years ago Ruskin's attempt to put his beliefs into practice through the Guild of St George seemed to have ended in derisory failure. Today his thoughts influence the lives of millions. It is one of the queerest ironies in history.

Nevertheless I think that Ruskin's social and economic teaching suffers from two serious defects. By one of the many strokes of irony which accompanied his life, he was the dupe of the very materialism which he had been the first to denounce. When society rather than beauty came to occupy his mind he was so shocked by poverty that he misinterpreted its relation to the spiritual life, and came to believe that if we could 'keep the living creatures round us clean and in humble comfort' a new art would spring from better social conditions. In this he has proved pitifully wrong; and although we cannot blame him for failing to foresee the spiritual bankruptcy of a prosperous democracy, we may reckon this error as part of a more general weakness, the hasty and wilful manner in which he related social and economic life to periods of creative activity. Because he admired fifteenth-century Florentine painting, and Venetian Gothic architecture, he would not admit to himself the sordid meanness of Florentine economy and the sheer gangsterism of the Venetian.

Given this attitude to the past, it is not surprising that he showed a similar disinclination to face the economic problems of the modern world in all their complexity and fatal interdependence. The authors whom he read when writing *Munera Pulveris* were Homer, Xenophon, Horace, and Dante, and although we may concede that the wisdom of the greatest minds is eternally valuable, we may question how far these were effective guides through the labyrinth of industrial civilization. Ruskin hated blue books, and spoke slightingly of those who referred to them; but without Karl Marx's colossal power of digesting reports and statistics the Communist revolution could never have taken place. And yet changes in the structure of society are not brought about solely by massive engines of doctrine. The first flash of insight which persuades human beings to change their basic assumptions is usually contained in a few phrases. Poets may not be 'the unacknowledged legislators of the world'; but Ruskin, like Rousseau, changed the world by a vision which has the intensity and innocence of poetry.

¶ 254
THE DOMECQ GIRLS[1]

Mr Domecq's own habits of life were luxurious, but never extravagant. He had a house in Paris, chiefly for the sake of his daughters' education and establishment; the profits of the estate, though not to be named in any comparison with those of modern mercantile dynasty, were enough to secure annual income to each of his five girls large enough to secure their marriages in the best French circles: they became, each in her turn, baronne or comtesse; their father choosing their baron or count for them with as much discretion as he had shown in the choice of his own partner; and all the marriages turned out well. Elise, Comtesse des Roys and Caroline, Princess Bethune, once or twice came with their husbands to stay with us; partly to see London, partly to discuss with my father his management of the English market: and the way in which these lords, virtually, of lands both in France and Spain, though men of sense and honour, and their wives, though women of gentle and amiable disposition, (Elise, indeed, one of the kindest I ever have known,) spoke of their Spanish labourers and French tenantry, with no idea whatever respecting them but that, except as producers by their labour of money to be spent in Paris, they were cumberers of the ground, gave me the first clue to the real sources of wrong in the social laws of modern Europe; and led me necessarily into the political work which has been the most earnest of my life. But these visits and warnings were not till seven or eight years after the time at present rendered account of, in which, nevertheless, it was already beginning to be, if not a question, at least a marvel with me, that these graceful and gay Andalusians, who played guitars, danced boleros, and fought bulls, should virtually get no good of their own beautiful country but the bunch of grapes or stalk of garlic they frugally dined on; that its precious wine was not for them, still less the money it was sold for; but the one came to crown our Vandalic feasts, and the other furnished our Danish walls with pictures, our Danish gardens with milk and honey, and five noble

1. Mr Domecq was old Mr Ruskin's partner, and the girls came to stay with the Ruskins when John was a boy. One of them, Adèle, was his first love.

271

houses in Paris with the means of beautiful dominance in its Elysian fields.

From Praeterita, Vol. ii, ch. ix, § 178

¶ 255

BLESSINGS WITHHELD

I went into my garden at half-past six on the morning of April 21, 1870, to think over the final order of these examples for you.

The air was perfectly calm, the sunlight pure, and falling on the grass through thickets of the standard peach (which had bloomed that year perfectly), and of plum and pear trees, in their first showers of fresh silver, looking more like much-broken and far-tossed spray of fountains than trees; and just at the end of my hawthorn walk, one happy nightingale was singing as much as he could in every moment. Meantime, in the still air, the roar of the railroads from Clapham Junction, New Cross, and the Crystal Palace (I am between the three), sounded constantly and heavily, like the surf of a strong sea three or four miles distant; and the whistles of the trains passing nearer mixed with the nightingale's notes. That I could hear her at all, or see the blossoms, or the grass, in the best time of spring, depended on my having been long able to spend a large sum annually in self-indulgence, and in keeping my fellow-creatures out of my way. Of those who were causing all that murmur, like the sea, round me, and of the myriads imprisoned by the English Minotaur of lust for wealth, and condemned to live, if it is to be called life, in the labyrinth of black walls, and loathsome passages between them, which now fills the valley of the Thames, and is called London, not one could hear, that day, any happy bird sing, or look upon any quiet space of the pure grass that is good for seed.

But they might have the blessing of these things for all and each of them, if they chose, and that vast space of London might be full of gardens, and terraced round with Hawthorn walks, with children at play in them, as fair as their blossoms. And now, gentlemen, I beg you once for all to understand that unless you are minded to bring yourselves, and all whom you can help, out of this curse of darkness that has fallen on our hearts and thoughts, you need not try to do any art-work, – it is the vainest of affectations to try to put beauty into shadows, while all the real things that cast them are left in deformity and pain.

From *Notes on Educational Series*, Preface (C. & W., Vol. XXI, p. 103)

¶ 256

FROM ART TO SOCIETY

One day last November, at Oxford, as I was going in at the private door of the University galleries, to give a lecture on the Fine Arts in Florence, I was hindered for a moment by a nice little girl, whipping a top on the pavement. She was a *very* nice little girl; and rejoiced wholly in her whip, and top; but could not inflict the reviving chastisement with all the activity that was in her, because she had on a large and dilapidated pair of woman's shoes, which projected the full length of her own little foot behind it and before; and being securely fastened to her ankles in the manner of mocassins, admitted, indeed, of dextrous glissades, and other modes of progress quite sufficient for ordinary purposes; but not conveniently of all the evolutions proper to the pursuit of a whipping-top.

There were some worthy people at my lecture, and I think the lecture was one of my best. It gave some really trustworthy information about art in Florence six hundred years ago. But all the time I was speaking, I knew that nothing spoken about art, either by myself or other people, could be of the least use to anybody there. For their primary business, and mine, was with art in Oxford, now; not with art in Florence, then; and art in Oxford now was absolutely dependent on our power of solving the question – which I know that my audience would not even allow to be proposed for solution – 'Why have our little girls large shoes?'

From *Fors Clavigera*, Letter XXXVII, § 1, 1 July 1874

¶ 257

TRUE WEALTH

I desire, in closing the series of introductory papers, to leave this one great fact clearly stated. THERE IS NO WEALTH BUT LIFE. Life, including all its powers of love, of joy, and of admiration. That country is the richest which nourishes the greatest number of noble and happy human beings; that man is richest, who, having perfected the functions of his own life to the utmost, has also the widest helpful influence, both personal, and by means of his possessions, over the lives of others.

From *Unto this Last*, Essay IV, § 77

¶ 258

SOLDIERS OF THE PLOUGHSHARE

My continual aim has been to show the eternal superiority of some men to others, sometimes even of one man to all others; and to show also the advisability of appointing such persons or person to guide, to lead, or on occasion even to compel and subdue, their inferiors according to their own better knowledge and wiser will. My principles of Political Economy were all involved in a single phrase spoken three years ago at Manchester: 'Soldiers of the Ploughshare as well as Soldiers of the Sword': and they were all summed in a single sentence in the last volume of *Modern Painters* – 'Government and co-operation are in all things the Laws of Life; Anarchy and competition the Laws of Death.'

From *Unto this Last*, Essay III, § 54

¶ 259

PROPERTY

And with respect to the mode in which these general principles affect the secure possession of property, so far am I from invalidating such security, that the whole gist of these papers will be found ultimately to aim at an extension in its range; and whereas it has long been known and declared that the poor have no right to the property of the rich, I wish it also to be known and declared that the rich have no right to the property of the poor.

From *Unto this Last*, Essay III, § 54

¶ 260
THE LAW OF HELP

A pure or holy state of anything, therefore, is that in which all its parts are helpful or consistent. They may or may not be homogeneous. The highest or organic purities are composed of many elements in an entirely helpful state. The highest and first law of the universe – and the other name of life is, therefore, 'help.' The other name of death is 'separation'. Government and co-operation are in all things and eternally the laws of life. Anarchy and competition, eternally, and in all things, the laws of death.

From *Modern Painters*, Vol. v, Part VIII, ch. I, § 6

¶ 261
POLITICAL ECONOMY

Political economy (the economy of a State, or of its citizens) consists simply in the production, preservation, and distribution, at fittest time and place, of useful or pleasurable things. The farmer who cuts his hay at the right time; the shipwright who drives his bolts well home in sound wood; the builder who lays good bricks in well-tempered mortar; the housewife who takes care of her furniture in the parlour, and guards against all waste in her kitchen; and the singer who rightly disciplines, and never overstrains her voice, are all political economists in the true and final sense: adding continually to the riches and well-being of the nation to which they belong.

But mercantile economy, the economy of 'merces' or of 'pay,' signifies the accumulation, in the hands of individuals, of legal or moral claim upon, or power over, the labour of others; every such claim implying precisely as much poverty and debt on one side, as it implies riches or right on the other.

From *Unto this Last*, Essay II, § 28

¶ 262

LIES

That indignation which we profess to feel at deceit absolute, is indeed only at deceit malicious. We resent calumny, hypocrisy, and treachery, because they harm us, not because they are untrue. Take the detraction and the mischief from the untruth, and we are little offended by it; turn it into praise, and we may be pleased with it. And yet it is not calumny nor treachery that do the largest sum of mischief in the world; they are continually crushed, and are felt only in being conquered. But it is the glistening and softly spoken lie; the amiable fallacy; the patriotic lie of the historian, the provident lie of the politician, the zealous lie of the partizan, the merciful lie of the friend, and the careless lie of each man to himself, that cast that black mystery over humanity, through which we thank any man who pierces, as we would thank one who dug a well in a desert.

From *The Seven Lamps of Architecture*, ch. II, § 1

¶ 263

TRUE AND FALSE LIFE

[Man's] true life is like that of lower organic beings, the independent force by which he moulds and governs external things; it is a force of assimilation which converts everything around him into food, or into instruments; and which, however humbly or obediently it may listen to or follow the guidance of superior intelligence, never forfeits its own authority as a judging principle, as a will capable either of obeying or rebelling. His false life is, indeed, but one of the conditions of death or stupor, but it acts, even when it cannot be said to animate, and is not always easily known from the true. It is that life of custom and accident in which many of us pass much of our time in the world; that life in which we do what we have not proposed, and speak what we do not mean, and assent to what we do not understand; that life which is overlaid by the weight of things external to it, and is moulded by them, instead of assimilating them. . . .[1]

From *The Seven Lamps of Architecture*, ch. v, § 3

1. This is one of the first (1849) published expressions of Ruskin's social convictions.

ABBEVILLE: THE PICTURESQUE AND THE GOOD LIFE

You stopped at the brow of the hill to put the drag on, and looked up to see where you were: – and there lay beneath you, far as the eye could reach on either side, this wonderful valley of the Somme, – with line on line of tufted aspen and tall poplar, making the blue distances more exquisite in bloom by the gleam of their leaves; and in the midst of it, by the glittering of the divided streams of its river, lay the clustered mossy roofs of Abbeville, like a purple flake of cloud, with the precipitous mass of the Cathedral towers rising mountainous through them, and here and there, in the midst of them, spaces of garden close set with pure green trees, bossy and perfect. So you trotted down the hill between bright chalk banks, with a cottage or two nestled into their recesses, and little round children rolling about like apples before the doors, and at the bottom you came into a space of open park ground, divided by stately avenues of chestnut and acacia, – with long banks of outwork and massive walls of bastion seen beyond – then came the hollow thunder of the drawbridge and shadow of the gate – and in an instant, you were in the gay street of a populous yet peaceful city – a fellowship of ancient houses set beside each other, with all the active companionship of business and sociableness of old friends, and yet each with the staid and self-possessed look of country houses surrounded by hereditary fields – or country cottages nested in forgotten glens, – each with its own character and fearlessly independent ways – its own steep gable, narrow or wide – its special little peaked windows set this way and that as the fancy took them, – its most particular odd corners, and outs and ins of wall to make the most of the ground and sunshine, – its own turret staircase, in the inner angle of the courtyard, – its own designs and fancies in carving of bracket and beam – its own only bridge over the clear branchlet of the Somme that rippled at its garden gate.

From *The Flamboyant Architecture of the Valley of the Somme*, § 1

THE PRICE OF THE PICTURESQUE

I extract from my private diary a passage bearing somewhat on the matter in hand:–

'AMIENS, 11th May 18–. I had a happy walk here this afternoon down among the branching currents of the Somme; it divides into five or six, – shallow, green, and not overwholesome; some quite narrow and foul, running beneath clusters of fearful houses, reeling masses of rotten timber; and a few mere stumps of pollard willow sticking out of the banks of soft mud, only retained in shape of bank by being shored up by timbers; and boats like paper boats, nearly as thin at least, for the costermongers to paddle about in among the weeds, the water soaking through the lath bottoms, and floating the dead leaves from the vegetable-baskets with which they were loaded. Miserable little back yards, opening to the water, with steep stone steps down to it, and little platforms for the ducks; and separate duck staircases, composed of a sloping board with cross bits of wood leading to the ducks' doors; and sometimes a flower-pot or two on them, or even a flower, – one group, of wallflowers and geraniums, curiously vivid, being seen against the darkness of a dyer's back yard, who had been dyeing black all day, and all was black in his yard but the flowers, and they fiery and pure; the water by no means so, but still working its way steadily over the weeds, until it narrowed into a current strong enough to turn two or three mill-wheels, one working against the side of an old flamboyant Gothic church, whose richly traceried buttresses sloped into the filthy stream; – all exquisitely picturesque, and no less miserable. We delight in seeing the figures in these boats pushing them about the bits of blue water, in Prout's drawings; but as I looked to-day at the unhealthy face and melancholy mien of the man in the boat pushing his load of peats along the ditch, and of the people, men as well as women, who sat spinning gloomily at the cottage doors, I could not help feeling how many suffering persons must pay for my picturesque subject and happy walk.'

From *Modern Painters*, Vol. IV, Part V, ch. I, n. to § 12

THE HIGHLAND VALLEY

I was reading but the other day, in a book by a zealous, useful, and able Scotch clergyman, one of these rhapsodies, in which he described a scene in the Highlands to show (he said) the goodness of God. In this Highland scene there was nothing but sunshine, and fresh breezes, and bleating lambs, and clean tartans, and all manner of pleasantness. Now a Highland scene is, beyond dispute, pleasant enough in its own way; but, looked close at, has its shadows. Here, for instance, is the very fact of one, as pretty as I can remember – having seen many. It is a little valley of soft turf, enclosed in its narrow oval by jutting rocks and broad flakes of nodding fern. From one side of it to the other winds, serpentine, a clear brown stream, drooping into quicker ripple as it reaches the end of the oval field, and then, first islanding a purple and white rock with an amber pool, it dashes away into a narrow fall of foam under a thicket of mountain-ash and alder. The autumn sun, low but clear, shines on the scarlet ash-berries and on the golden birch-leaves, which, fallen here and there, when the breeze has not caught them, rest quiet in the crannies of the purple rock. Beside the rock, in the hollow under the thicket, the carcase of a ewe, drowned in the last flood, lies nearly bare to the bone, its white ribs protruding through the skin, raven-torn; and the rags of its wool still flickering from the branches that first stayed it as the stream swept it down. A little lower, the current plunges, roaring, into a circular chasm like a well, surrounded on three sides by a chimney-like hollowness of polished rock, down which the foam slips in detached snow-flakes. Round the edges of the pool beneath, the water circles slowly, like black oil; a little butterfly lies on its back, its wings glued to one of the eddies, its limbs feebly quivering; a fish rises, and it is gone. Lower down the stream, I can just see over a knoll, the green and damp turf roofs of four or five hovels, built at the edge of a morass, which is trodden by the cattle into a black Slough of Despond at their doors, and traversed by a few ill-set stepping-stones, with here and there a flat slab on the tops, where they have sunk out of sight, and at the turn of the brook I see a man fishing, with a boy and a dog –

a picturesque and pretty group enough certainly, if they had not been there all day starving. I know them, and I know the dog's ribs also, which are nearly as bare as the dead ewe's; and the child's wasted shoulders, cutting his old tartan jacket through, so sharp are they.

From *Modern Painters*, Vol. v, Part IX, ch. 2, § 11

¶ 267

WORK

It may be proved, with much certainty, that God intends no man to live in this world without working: but it seems to me no less evident that He intends every man to be happy in his work. It is written, 'in the sweat of thy brow,' but it was never written, 'in the breaking of thine heart,' thou shalt eat bread: and I find that, as on the one hand, infinite misery is caused by idle people, who both fail in doing what was appointed for them to do, and set in motion various springs of mischief in matters in which they should have had no concern, so on the other hand, no small misery is caused by over-worked and unhappy people, in the dark views which they necessarily take up themselves, and force upon others, of work itself. Were it not so, I believe the fact of their being unhappy is in itself a violation of divine law, and a sign of some kind of folly or sin in their way of life. Now in order that people may be happy in their work, these three things are needed: They must be fit for it: They must not do too much of it: and they must have a sense of success in it – not a doubtful sense, such as needs some testimony of other people for its confirmation, but a sure sense, or rather knowledge, that so much work has been done well, and fruitfully done, whatever the world may say or think about it. So that in order that a man may be happy, it is necessary that he should not only be capable of his work, but a good judge of his work.

From *Pre-Raphaelitism*, § 1

A TOOL OR A MAN

For the finer the nature, the more flaws it will show through the clearness of it; and it is a law of this universe, that the best things shall be seldomest seen in their best form. The wild grass grows well and strongly, one year with another; but the wheat is, according to the greater nobleness of its nature, liable to the bitterer blight. And therefore, while in all things that we see or do, we are to desire perfection, and strive for it, we are nevertheless not to set the meaner thing, in its narrow accomplishment, above the nobler thing, in its mighty progress; not to esteem smooth minuteness above shattered majesty; not to prefer mean victory to honourable defeat; not to lower the level of our aim, that we may the more surely enjoy the complacency of success. But, above all, in our dealings with the souls of other men, we are to take care how we check, by severe requirement or narrow caution, efforts which might otherwise lead to a noble issue; and, still more, how we withhold our admiration from great excellences, because they are mingled with rough faults. Now, in the make and nature of every man, however rude or simple, whom we employ in manual labour, there are some powers for better things; some tardy imagination, torpid capacity of emotion, tottering steps of thought, there are, even at the worst; and in most cases it is all our own fault that they *are* tardy or torpid. But they cannot be strengthened, unless we are content to take them in their feebleness, and unless we prize and honour them in their imperfection above the best and most perfect manual skill. And this is what we have to do with all our labourers; to look for the *thoughtful* part of them, and get that out of them, whatever we lose for it, whatever faults and errors we are obliged to take with it. For the best that is in them cannot manifest itself, but in company with much error. Understand this clearly: You can teach a man to draw a straight line, and to cut one; to strike a curved line, and to carve it; and to copy and carve any number of given lines or forms, with admirable speed and perfect precision; and you find his work perfect of its kind: but if you ask him to think about any of those forms, to consider if he cannot find any better in his own head, he stops; his execution becomes hesitating; he thinks, and ten to one he thinks wrong; ten to one he makes a mistake in the first touch he gives to his work as a thinking being. But you have made a man of him for all that. He was only a machine before, an animated tool.

From *The Stones of Venice*, Vol. II, ch. VI, § 11

¶ 269

THE DEGRADATION OF LABOUR

It is verily this degradation of the operative into a machine, which, more than any other evil of the times, is leading the mass of the nations everywhere into vain, incoherent, destructive struggling for a freedom of which they cannot explain the nature to themselves. Their universal outcry against wealth, and against nobility, is not forced from them either by the pressure of famine, or the sting of mortified pride. These do much, and have done much in all ages; but the foundations of society were never yet shaken as they are at this day. It is not that men are ill fed, but that they have no pleasure in the work by which they make their bread, and therefore look to wealth as the only means of pleasure. It is not that men are pained by the scorn of the upper classes, but they cannot endure their own; for they feel that the kind of labour to which they are condemned is verily a degrading one, and makes them less than men. Never had the upper classes so much sympathy with the lower, or charity for them, as they have at this day, and yet never were they so much hated by them: for, of old, the separation between the noble and the poor was merely a wall built by law; now it is a veritable difference in level of standing, a precipice between upper and lower grounds in the field of humanity, and there is pestilential air at the bottom of it.

From *The Stones of Venice*, Vol. II, ch. VI, § 15

¶ 270

THE 'DIVISION OF LABOUR'

We have much studied and much perfected, of late, the great civilized invention of the division of labour; only we give it a false name. It is not, truly speaking, the labour that is divided; but the men: – Divided into mere segments of men – broken into small fragments and crumbs of life; so that all the little piece of intelligence that is left in a man is not enough to make a pin, or a nail, but exhausts itself in making the point of a pin or the head of a nail. Now it is a good and desirable thing, truly, to make many pins in a day; but if we could only see with what crystal sand their points were polished, – sand of human soul, much to be magnified before it can be discerned for what it is – we should think there might be some loss in it also. And the great cry that rises from all our manufacturing cities, louder than their furnace blast, is all in very deed for this, – that we manufacture everything there except men; we blanch cotton, and strengthen steel, and refine sugar, and shape pottery; but to brighten, to strengthen, to refine, or to form a single living spirit, never enters into our estimate of advantages. And all the evil to which that cry is urging our myriads can be met only in one way: not by teaching nor preaching, for to teach them is but to show them their misery, and to preach to them, if we do nothing more than preach, is to mock at it. It can be met only by a right understanding, on the part of all classes, of what kinds of labour are good for men, raising them, and making them happy; by a determined sacrifice of such convenience or beauty, or cheapness as is to be got only by the degradation of the workman; and by equally determined demand for the products and results of healthy and ennobling labour.

From *The Stones of Venice*, Vol. II, ch. VI, § 16

¶ 271
RURAL INDUSTRY

As we drove down the hill a little farther towards Bewdley my host asked me if I would like to see 'nailing.' 'Yes, truly.' So he took me into a little cottage, where were two women at work, – one about seventeen or eighteen, the other perhaps four or five and thirty; this last intelligent of feature as well could be; and both, gentle and kind, – each with hammer in right hand, pincers in left (heavier hammer poised over her anvil, and let fall at need by the touch of her foot on a treadle like that of a common grindstone). Between them, a small forge, fed to constant brightness by the draught through the cottage, above whose roof its chimney rose: – in front of it, on a little ledge, the glowing lengths of cut iron rod, to be dealt with at speed. Within easy reach of this, looking up at us in quietly silent question, – stood, each in my sight an ominous Fors, the two Claviгeræ.

At a word, they laboured, with ancient Vulcanian skill. Foot and hand in perfect time: no dance of Muses on Parnassian mead in truer measure; – no sea fairies upon yellow sands more featly footed. Four strokes with the hammer in the hand: one ponderous and momentary blow ordered of the balanced mass by the touch of the foot; and the forged nail fell aside, finished, on its proper heap; – level-headed, wedge-pointed, a thousand lives soon to depend daily on its driven grip of the iron way.

So wrought they, – the English Matron and Maid; – so was it their darg to labour from morning to evening, – seven to seven, – by the furnace side, – the winds of summer fanning the blast of it. The wages of the Matron Fors, I found, were eight shillings a week; her husband, otherwise and variously employed, could make sixteen. Three shillings a week for rent and taxes, left, as I count, for the guerdon of their united labour, if constant, and its product providently saved, fifty-five pounds a year, on which they had to feed and clothe themselves and their six children; eight souls in their little Worcestershire ark. . . .

Yet it was not chiefly their labour in which I pitied them, but rather in that their forge-dress did not well set off their English beauty; nay, that the beauty itself was marred by the labour; so that to most persons, who could not have looked through such veil and shadow, they were as their Master, and had no form nor comeliness. And all the while, as I watched them, I was thinking of two other Englishwomen, of about the same relative ages, with whom, in planning last *Fors*, I had been standing a little while before Edward Burne-Jones's picture of Venus's Mirror, and mourning in my heart for its dulness, that it, with all its Forget-me-nots, would not forget the images it bore, and take the fairer and nobler reflection of their instant life. Were these then, here, – their sisters; who had only, for

Venus's mirror, a heap of ashes; compassed about with no Forget-me-nots, but with the Forgetfulness of all the world?[1]

From *Fors Clavigera*, Letter LXXX, §§ 4–6, 16 July 1877

¶ 272

POVERTY

Among the various characteristics of the age in which we live, as compared with other ages of this not yet *very* experienced world, one of the most notable appears to me to be the just and wholesome contempt in which we hold poverty. I repeat, the *just* and *wholesome* contempt; though I see that some of my hearers look surprised at the expression. I assure them, I use it in sincerity; and I should not have ventured to ask you to listen to me this evening, unless I had entertained a profound respect for wealth – true wealth, that is to say; for, of course, we ought to respect neither wealth nor anything else that is false of its kind: and the distinction between real and false wealth is one of the points on which I shall have a few words presently to say to you. But true wealth I hold, as I said, in great honour; and sympathize, for the most part, with that extraordinary feeling of the present age which publicly pays this honour to riches.

I cannot, however, help noticing how extraordinary it is, and how this epoch of ours differs from all bygone epochs in having no philosophical nor religious worshippers of the ragged godship of poverty. In the classical ages, not only were there people who voluntarily lived in tubs, and who used gravely to maintain the superiority of tub-life to town-life, but the Greeks and Latins seem to have looked on these eccentric, and I do not scruple to say absurd people, with as much respect as we do upon large capitalists and landed proprietors; so that really, in those days, no one could be described as purse proud, but only as empty-purse proud. And no less distinct than the honour which those curious Greek people pay to their conceited poor, is the disrespectful manner in which they speak of the rich; so that one cannot listen long either to them, or to the Roman writers who imitated them, without finding one-

1. Cf. his letter to Tennyson about the *Idylls of the King* (no. 49).

self entangled in all sorts of plausible absurdities; hard upon being convinced of the uselessness of collecting that heavy yellow substance which we call gold, and led generally to doubt all the most established maxims of political economy. . . .

But these Pagan views of the matter were indulgent, compared with those which were held in the Middle Ages, when wealth seems to have been looked upon by the best men not only as contemptible, but as criminal. The purse round the neck is, then, one of the principal signs of condemnation in the pictured Inferno; and the Spirit of Poverty is reverenced with subjection of heart, and faithfulness of affection, like that of a loyal knight for his lady, or a loyal subject for his queen. And truly, it requires some boldness to quit ourselves of these feelings, and to confess their partiality or their error, which, nevertheless, we are certainly bound to do. For wealth is simply one of the greatest powers which can be entrusted to human hands: a power, not indeed to be envied, because it seldom makes us happy; but still less to be abdicated or despised; while, in these days, and in this country, it has become a power all the more noteable, in that the possessions of a rich man are not represented, as they used to be, by wedges of gold or coffers of jewels, but by masses of men variously employed, over whose bodies and minds the wealth, according to its direction, exercises harmful or helpful influence, and becomes, in that alternative, Mammon either of Unrighteousness or of Righteousness.[1]

From *A Joy for Ever*, Lecture I, § I

§ 273

THE RICH AND THE POOR

It must be our work, in the issue, to examine what evidence there is of the effect of wealth on the minds of its possessors; also, what kind of person it is who usually sets himself to obtain wealth, and succeeds in doing so; and whether the world owes more gratitude

1. These are the opening words of two lectures which Ruskin delivered at Manchester in 1857 under the title *The Political Economy of Art*. Ruskin afterwards gave them the title *A Joy for Ever* because Keats's line had been used as a motto for the famous Manchester Art Treasures exhibition of that year.

to rich or to poor men, either for their moral influence upon it, or for chief goods, discoveries, and practical advancements. I may, however, anticipate future conclusions, so far as to state that in a community regulated only by laws of demand and supply, but protected from open violence, the persons who become rich are, generally speaking, industrious, resolute, proud, covetous, prompt, methodical, sensible, unimaginative, insensitive and ignorant. The persons who remain poor are the entirely foolish, the entirely wise, the idle, the reckless, the humble, the thoughtful, the dull, the imaginative, the sensitive, the well-informed, the improvident, the irregularly and impulsively wicked, the clumsy knave, the open thief, and the entirely merciful, just, and godly person.

From *Unto this Last*, Essay IV, § 65

¶ 274

WEALTH

Since the essence of wealth consists in power over men, will it not follow that the nobler and the more in number the persons are over whom it has power, the greater the wealth? Perhaps it may even appear, after some consideration, that the persons themselves *are* the wealth – that these pieces of gold with which we are in the habit of guiding them, are, in fact, nothing more than a kind of Byzantine harness or trappings, very glittering and beautiful in barbaric sight, wherewith we bridle the creatures; but that if these same living creatures could be guided without the fretting and jingling of the Byzants in their mouths and ears, they might themselves be more valuable than their bridles. In fact, it may be discovered that the true veins of wealth are purple – and not in Rock, but in Flesh – perhaps even that the final outcome and consummation of all wealth is in the producing as many as possible full-breathed, bright-eyed, and happy-hearted human creatures. Our modern wealth, I think, has rather a tendency the other way; – most political economists appearing to consider multitudes of human creatures not conducive to wealth, or at best conducive to it only by remaining in a dim-eyed and narrow-chested state of being.

From *Unto this Last*, Essay II, § 40

THE POOR

In all the ranges of human thought I know none so melancholy as the speculations of political economists on the population question. It is proposed to better the condition of the labourer by giving him higher wages. 'Nay,' says the economist, – 'if you raise his wages, he will either [drag]¹ people down to the same point of misery at which you found him, or drink your wages away.' He will. I know it. Who gave him this will? Suppose it were your own son of whom you spoke, declaring to me that you dared not take him into your firm, nor even give him his just labourer's wages, because if you did he would die of drunkenness, and leave half a score of children to the parish. 'Who gave your son these dispositions?' – I should inquire. Has he them by inheritance or by education? By one or other they *must* come; and as in him, so also in the poor. Either these poor are of a race essentially different from ours, and unredeemable (which, however often implied, I have heard none yet openly say), or else by such care as we have ourselves received, we may make them continent and sober as ourselves – wise and dispassionate as we are – models arduous of imitation. 'But,' it is answered, 'they cannot receive education.' Why not? That is precisely the point at issue. Charitable persons suppose the worst fault of the rich is to refuse the people meat; and the people cry for their meat, kept back by fraud, to the Lord of Multitudes. Alas! it is not meat of which the refusal is cruelest, or to which the claim is validest. The life is more than the meat. The rich not only refuse food to the poor; they refuse wisdom; they refuse virtue; they refuse salvation. Ye sheep without shepherd, it is not the pasture that has been shut from you, but the Presence. Meat! perhaps your right to that may be pleadable; but other rights have to be pleaded first. Claim your crumbs from the table if you will; but claim them as children, not as dogs; claim your right to be fed, but claim more loudly your right to be holy, perfect, and pure.

Strange words to be used of working people! 'What! holy; without any long robes or anointing oils; these rough-jacketed, rough-

1. A word has been omitted here in the first edition and all subsequent editions.

worded persons; set to nameless, dishonoured service? Perfect! – these, with dim eyes and cramped limbs, and slowly wakening minds? Pure! – these, with sensual desire and grovelling thought; foul of body and coarse of soul?' It may be so; nevertheless, such as they are, they are the holiest, perfectest, purest persons the earth can at present show. They may be what you have said; but if so, they yet are holier than we who have left them thus.

From *Unto this Last*, Essay IV, § 79

¶ 276
PLUS AND MINUS

If, in the exchange, one man is able to give what cost him little labour for what has cost the other much, he 'acquires' a certain quantity of the produce of the other's labour. And precisely what he acquires, the other loses. In mercantile language, the person who thus acquires is commonly said to have 'made a profit'; and I believe that many of our merchants are seriously under the impression that it is possible for everybody, somehow, to make a profit in this manner. Whereas, by the unfortunate constitution of the world we live in, the laws both of matter and motion have quite rigorously forbidden universal acquisition of this kind. Profit, or material gain, is attainable only by construction or by discovery; not by exchange. Whenever material gain follows exchange, for every *plus* there is precisely equal *minus*.

Unhappily for the progress of the science of Political Economy, the plus quantities, or – if I may be allowed to coin an awkward plural – the pluses, make a very positive and venerable appearance in the world, so that every one is eager to learn the science which produces results so magnificent; whereas the minuses have, on the other hand, a tendency to retire into back streets, and other places of shade, – or even to get themselves wholly and finally put out of sight in graves: which renders the algebra of this science peculiar, and difficultly legible; a large number of its negative signs being written by the account-keeper in a kind of red ink, which starvation thins, and makes strangely pale, or even quite invisible ink, for the present.

From *Unto this Last*, Essay IV, § 66

¶ 277

WHO KEEPS THE BANK?

Men of business do indeed know how they themselves made their money, or how, on occasion, they lost it. Playing a long-practised game, they are familiar with the chances of its cards, and can rightly explain their losses and gains. But they neither know who keeps the bank of the gambling-house, nor what other games may be played with the same cards, nor what other losses and gains, far away among the dark streets, are essentially, though invisibly, dependent on theirs in the lighted rooms. They have learned a few, and only a few, of the laws of mercantile economy; but not one of those of political economy.

From *Unto this Last*, Essay II, § 26

¶ 278

POSSESSIONS

Suppose any person to be put in possession of a large estate of fruitful land, with rich beds of gold in its gravel; countless herds of cattle in its pastures; houses, and gardens, and storehouses full of useful stores; but suppose, after all, that he could get no servants? In order that he may be able to have servants, some one in his neighbourhood must be poor, and in want of his gold – or his corn. Assume that no one is in want of either, and that no servants are to be had. He must, therefore, bake his own bread, make his own clothes, plough his own ground, and shepherd his own flocks. His gold will be as useful to him as any other yellow pebbles on his estate. His stores must rot, for he cannot consume them. He can eat no more than another man could eat, and wear no more than another man could wear. He must lead a life of severe and common labour to procure even ordinary comforts; he will be ultimately unable to keep either houses in repair, or fields in cultivation; and forced to content himself with a poor man's portion of cottage and garden, in the midst of a desert of waste land, trampled by wild cattle, and encumbered by ruins of palaces, which he will hardly mock at himself by calling 'his own.'

From *Unto this Last*, Essay II, § 29

¶ 279
PRACTICAL ECONOMY

Capitalists, when they do not know what to do with their money, persuade the peasants, in various countries, that the said peasants want guns to shoot each other with. The peasants accordingly borrow guns, out of the manufacture of which the capitalists get a percentage, and men of science much amusement and credit. Then the peasants shoot a certain number of each other, until they get tired; and burn each other's homes down in various places. Then they put the guns back into towers, arsenals, etc., in ornamental patterns; (and the victorious party put also some ragged flags in churches). And then the capitalists tax both, annually, ever afterwards, to pay interest on the loan of the guns and gunpowder. This is what capitalists call 'knowing what to do with their money'; and what commercial men in general call 'practical' as opposed to 'sentimental' Political Economy.

From *Munera Pulveris*, Preface, § 19

¶ 280
MODERN WARFARE

If war is to be made by money and machinery, the nation which is the largest and most covetous multitude will win. You may be as scientific as you choose; the mob that can pay more for sulphuric acid and gunpowder will at last poison its bullets, throw acid in your faces, and make an end of you; – of itself, also, in good time, but of you first. And to the English people the choice of its fate is very near now. It may spasmodically defend its property with iron walls a fathom thick, a few years longer – a very few. No walls will defend either it, or its havings, against the multitude that is breeding and spreading, faster than the clouds, over the habitable earth. We shall be allowed to live by small pedlar's business, and ironmongery – since we have chosen those for our line of life – as long as we are found useful black servants to the Americans; and are content to dig coals and sit in the cinders; and have still coals to dig, – they once exhausted, or got cheaper elsewhere, we shall be abolished.

From *The Queen of the Air*, Lecture III, § 116

THE WISDOM OF THE JEW MERCHANT

Some centuries before the Christian era, a Jew merchant, largely engaged in business on the Gold Coast, and reported to have made one of the largest fortunes of his time (held also in repute for much practical sagacity), left among his ledgers some general maxims concerning wealth, which have been preserved, strangely enough, even to our own days. They were held in considerable respect by the most active traders of the Middle Ages, especially by the Venetians, who even went so far in their admiration as to place a statue of the old Jew on the angle of one of their principal public buildings. Of late years these writings have fallen into disrepute, being opposed in every particular to the spirit of modern commerce. Nevertheless I shall reproduce a passage or two from them here, partly because they may interest the reader by their novelty; and chiefly because they will show him that it is possible for a very practical and acquisitive tradesman to hold, through a not unsuccessful career, that principle of distinction between well-gotten and ill-gotten wealth, which, partially insisted on in my last paper, it must be our work more completely to examine in this.

He says, for instance, in one place: 'The getting of treasures by a lying tongue is a vanity tossed to and fro of them that seek death'; adding in another, with the same meaning (he has a curious way of doubling his sayings): 'Treasures of wickedness profit nothing: but justice delivers from death.' Both these passages are notable for their assertion of death as the only real issue and sum of attainment by any unjust scheme of wealth. If we read, instead of 'lying tongue,' 'lying label, title, pretence, or advertisement,' we shall more clearly perceive the bearing of the words on modern business. The seeking of death is a grand expression of the true course of men's toil in such business. We usually speak as if death pursued us, and we fled from him; but that is only so in rare instances. Ordinarily, he masks himself – makes himself beautiful – all-glorious; not like the King's daughter, all-glorious, within, but outwardly: his clothing of wrought gold. We pursue him frantically all our days, he flying or hiding from us. Our crowning success at three-score and ten is

utterly and perfectly to seize, and hold him in his eternal integrity –
robes, ashes and sting.

From *Unto this Last*, Essay III, §§ 42–3

¶ 282

WEALTH

When, in the winter of 1851, I was collecting materials for my
work on Venetian architecture, three of the pictures of Tintoret on
the roof of the School of St Roch were hanging down in ragged
fragments, mixed with lath and plaster, round the apertures made
by the fall of three Austrian heavy shot. The city of Venice was not,
it appeared, rich enough to repair the damage that winter; and
buckets were set on the floor of the upper room of the school to
catch the rain, which not only fell directly through the shot holes,
but found its way, owing to the generally pervious state of the roof,
through many of the canvases of Tintoret in other parts of the
ceiling.

It was a lesson to me, as I have just said, no less direct than severe;
for I knew already at that time (though I have not ventured to
assert, until recently at Oxford,) that the pictures of Tintoret in
Venice were accurately the most precious articles of wealth in
Europe, being the best existing productions of human industry.
Now at the time that three of them were thus fluttering in moist
rags from the roof they had adorned, the shops of the Rue Rivoli at
Paris were, in obedience to a steadily-increasing public Demand,
beginning to show a steadily-increasing Supply of elaborately
finished and coloured lithographs, representing the modern dances
of delight, among which the cancan has since taken a distinguished
place.

The labour employed on the stone of one of these lithographs
is very much more than Tintoret was in the habit of giving to a
picture of average size. Considering labour as the origin of value,
therefore, the stone so highly wrought would be of greater value
than the picture; and since also it is capable of producing a large
number of immediately saleable or exchangeable impressions, for
which the 'demand' is constant, the city of Paris naturally supposed

itself, and on all hitherto believed or stated principles of political economy, was, infinitely richer in the possession of a large number of these lithographic stones, . . . than Venice in the possession of those rags of mildewed canvas, flaunting in the south wind and its salt rain. And, accordingly, Paris provided (without thought of the expense) lofty arcades of shops, and rich recesses of innumerable private apartments, for the protection of these better treasures of hers from the weather.

Yet, all the while, Paris was not the richer for these possessions. Intrinsically, the delightful lithographs were not wealth, but polar contraries of wealth. She was, by the exact quantity of labour she had given to produce these, sunk below, instead of above, absolute Poverty. They not only were false Riches – they were true *Debt* which had to be paid at last – and the present aspect of the Rue Rivoli shows in what manner.

And the faded stains of the Venetian ceiling, all the while, were absolute and inestimable wealth. Useless to their possessors as forgotten treasure in a buried city, they had in them, nevertheless, the intrinsic and eternal nature of wealth; and Venice, still possessing the ruins of them, was a rich city; only, the Venetians had *not* a notion sufficiently correct even for the very common purpose of inducing them to put slates on a roof, of what was 'meant by wealth.'

From *Munera Pulveris*, Preface, §§ 3–6

¶ 283

SCHOOLS AND PRISONS

If you examine into the history of rogues, you will find they are as truly manufactured articles as anything else, and it is just because our present system of political economy gives so large a stimulus to that manufacture that you may know it to be a false one. We had better seek for a system which will develop honest men, than for one which will deal cunningly with vagabonds. Let us reform our schools, and we shall find little reform needed in our prisons.

From *Unto this Last*, Essay II, n. to § 31

¶ 284
LABOUR

Labour is the contest of the life of man with an opposite; – the term 'life' including his intellect, soul, and physical power, contending with question, difficulty, trial, or material force.

Labour is of a higher or lower order, as it includes more or fewer of the elements of life: and labour of good quality, in any kind, includes always as much intellect and feeling as will fully and harmoniously regulate the physical force.

From Unto this Last, Essay IV, § 70

¶ 285
CAPITAL

The best and simplest general type of capital is a well-made ploughshare. Now, if that ploughshare did nothing but beget other ploughshares, in a polypous manner, – however the great cluster of polypous plough might glitter in the sun, it would have lost its function of capital. It becomes true capital only by another kind of splendour, – when it is seen 'splendescere sulco,' to grow bright in the furrow; rather with diminution of its substance, than addition, by the noble friction. And the true home question, to every capitalist and to every nation, is not, 'how many ploughs have you?' but, 'where are your furrows?' not – 'how quickly will this capital reproduce itself?' – but, 'what will it do during reproduction?' What substance will it furnish, good for life? what work construct, protective of life? if none, its own reproduction is useless – if worse than none, – (for capital may destroy life as well as support it), its own reproduction is worse than useless; it is merely an advance from Tisiphone, on mortgage – not a profit by any means.

From Unto this Last, Essay IV, § 73

¶ 286

PRICE

Three-fourths of the demands existing in the world are romantic; founded on visions, idealisms, hopes and affections; and the regulation of the purse is, in its essence, regulation of the imagination and the heart. Hence, the right discussion of the nature of price is a very high metaphysical and psychical problem; sometimes to be solved only in a passionate manner, as by David in his counting the price of the water of the well by the gate of Bethlehem.

From *Unto this Last*, Essay IV, § 69

¶ 287

THE MERCHANT

The fact is, that people never have had clearly explained to them the true functions of a merchant with respect to other people. I should like the reader to be very clear about this.

Five great intellectual professions, relating to daily necessities of life, have hitherto existed – three exist necessarily, in every civilized nation:

The Soldier's profession is to *defend* it.
The Pastor's, to *teach* it.
The Physician's, to *keep it in health*.
The Lawyer's, to *enforce justice* in it.
The Merchant's, to *provide* for it.

And the duty of all these men is, on due occasion to *die* for it. 'On due occasion,' namely: –

The Soldier, rather than leave his post in battle.
The Physician, rather than leave his post in plague.
The Pastor, rather than teach Falsehood.
The Lawyer, rather than countenance Injustice.
The Merchant – what is *his* 'due occasion' of death?

It is the main question for the merchant, as for all of us. For truly, the man who does not know when to die, does not know how to live.

Observe, the merchant's function (or manufacturer's, for in the broad sense in which it is here used the word must be understood to include both) is to provide for the nation. It is no more his function to get profit for himself out of that provision than it is a clergyman's function to get his stipend. The stipend is a due and necessary adjunct, but not the object of his life, if he be a true clergyman, any more than his fee (or honorarium) is the object of life to a true physician. Neither is his fee the object of life to a true merchant. All three, if true men, have a work to be done irrespective of fee – to be done even at any cost, or for quite the contrary of fee; the pastor's function being to teach, the physician's to heal, and the merchant's, as I have said, to provide. That is to say, he has to understand to their very root the qualities of the thing he deals in, and the means of obtaining or producing it; and he has to apply all his sagacity and energy to the producing or obtaining it in perfect state, and distributing it at the cheapest possible price, where it is most needed.

And because the production or obtaining of any commodity involves necessarily the agency of many lives and hands, the merchant becomes in the course of his business the master and governor of large masses of men in a more direct, though less confessed way, than a military officer or pastor; so that on him falls, in great part, the responsibility for the kind of life they lead: and it becomes his duty, not only to be always considering how to produce what he sells in the purest and cheapest forms, but how to make the various employments involved in the production, or transference of it, most beneficial to the men employed.

And as into these two functions, requiring for their right exercise the highest intelligence, as well as patience, kindness, and tact, the merchant is bound to put all his energy, so for their just discharge he is bound, as soldier or physician is bound, to give up, if need be, his life, in such way as it may be demanded of him. Two main points he has in his providing function to maintain: first, his engagements (faithfulness to engagements being the real root of all possibilities in commerce); and, secondly, the perfectness and purity of the thing provided; so that, rather than fail in any engagement, or consent to any deterioration, adulteration, or unjust and exorbitant price of that which he provides, he is bound to meet fearlessly any

form of distress, poverty, or labour, which may, through mainten-
ance of these points, come upon him.

From Unto this Last, Essay I, §§ 21-3

¶ 288
NASTY PLAY

First, then, of the distinction between the classes who work and the
classes who play. Of course we must agree upon a definition of these
terms, – work and play, before going farther. Now, roughly, not
with vain subtlety of definition, but for plain use of the words,
'play' is an exertion of body or mind, made to please ourselves, and
with no determined end; and work is a thing done because it ought
to be done, and with a determined end. You play, as you call it, at
cricket, for instance. That is as hard work as anything else; but it
amuses you, and it has no result but the amusement. If it were done
as an ordered form of exercise, for health's sake, it would become
work directly. So, in like manner, whatever we do to please ourselves, and only for the sake of the pleasure, not for an ultimate
object, is 'play,' the 'pleasing thing,' not the useful thing. Play may
be useful, in a secondary sense; (nothing is indeed more useful or
necessary); but the use of it depends on its being spontaneous.

Let us, then, enquire together what sort of games the playing
class in England spend their lives playing at.

The first of all English games is making money. That is an all-
absorbing game; and we knock each other down oftener in playing
at that, than at football, or any other roughest sport: and it is
absolutely without purpose; no one who engages heartily in that
game ever knows why. Ask a great money-maker what he wants to
do with his money, – he never knows. He doesn't make it to do
anything with it. He gets it only that he *may* get it. 'What will you
make of what you have got?' you ask. 'Well, I'll get more,' he says.
Just as at cricket, you get more runs. There's no use in the runs,
but to get more of them than other people is the game. So all that
great foul city of London there, – rattling, growling, smoking,
stinking, – a ghastly heap of fermenting brickwork, pouring out
poison at every pore, – you fancy it is a city of work? Not a street

of it! It is a great city of play; very nasty play and very hard play,
but still play.

From The Crown of Wild Olive, Lecture i, §§ 23–4

¶ 289
USURY

The idea that money could beget money, though more absurd than
alchemy, had yet an apparently practical and irresistibly tempting
confirmation in the wealth of villains, and the success of fools.
Alchemy, in its day, led to pure chemistry; and calmly yielded to
the science it had fostered. But all wholesome indignation against
usurers was prevented, in the Christian mind, by wicked and cruel
religious hatred of the race of Christ. In the end, Shakespeare himself, in his fierce effort against the madness, suffered himself to miss
his mark by making his usurer a Jew: the Franciscan institution of
the Mount of Pity failed before the lust of Lombardy, and the
logic of Augsburg; and, to this day, the worship of the Immaculate
Virginity of Money, mother of the Omnipotence of Money, is the
Protestant form of Madonna worship.

From Val d'Arno, Lecture x, § 277

¶ 290
PROPHECY

'Was the leisure of the Greeks not owing to the hard work of
the helots and slaves they had?' asked my old friend, Thomas Dixon,
in his letter given last month.

Yes, truly, good labourer; nor the Greeks' leisure only, but also –
if we are to call it leisure – that of the rich and powerful of this
world, since this world began. And more and more I perceive, as
my old age opens to me the deeper secrets of human life, that the
true story and strength of that world are the story and strength of
these helots and slaves; and only its fiction and feebleness in the
idleness of those who feed on them; – which fiction and feebleness,
with all their cruelty and sensuality, filling the cup of the fornication
of the kings of the earth now to the lip, must be, in no long time

now, poured out upon the earth; and the cause of the poor judged by the King who shall reign in righteousness. For all these petty struggles of the past, of which you write to me, are but the scudding clouds and first wailing winds, of the storm which must be as the sheet lightning – from one part of heaven to the other, – 'So also shall the coming of the Son of Man be.'

Only the first scudding clouds, I say, – these hitherto seditions; for, as yet, they have only been of the ambitious, or the ignorant; and only against tyrannous men: so that they ended, if successful, in mere ruinous license; and if they failed, were trampled out in blood: but *now*, the ranks are gathering, on the one side, of men rightly informed, and meaning to seek redress by lawful and honourable means only; and, on the other, of men capable of compassion, and open to reason, but with personal interests at stake so vast, and with all the gear and mechanism of their acts so involved in the web of past iniquity, that the best of them are helpless, and the wisest blind.

From *Fors Clavigera*, Vol. VII, Letter LXXXIII, § 1, November 1877

¶ 291
ASCETICISM

Three principal forms of asceticism have existed in this weak world. Religious asceticism, being the refusal of pleasure and knowledge for the sake (as supposed) of religion; seen chiefly in the Middle Ages. Military asceticism, being the refusal of pleasure and knowledge for the sake of power; seen chiefly in the early days of Sparta and Rome. And monetary asceticism, consisting in the refusal of pleasure and knowledge for the sake of money; seen in the present days of London and Manchester.

'We do not come here to look at the mountains,' said the Carthusian to me at the Grande Chartreuse. 'We do not come here to look at the mountains,' the Austrian generals would say, encamping by the shores of Garda. 'We do not come here to look at the mountains,' so the thriving manufacturers tell me, between Rochdale and Halifax. . . .

Perhaps, it may be well that this England should become the furnace of the world; so that the smoke of the island, rising out of the sea, should be seen from a hundred leagues away, as if it were a field of fierce volcanoes; and every kind of sordid, foul or venomous work which, in other countries, men dreaded or disdained, it should become England's duty to do, – becoming thus the offscourer of the earth, and taking the hyena instead of the lion upon her shield. I do not, for a moment, deny this; but, looking broadly, not at the destiny of England, nor of any country in particular, but of the world, this is certain – that men exclusively occupied either in spiritual reverie, mechanical destruction, or mechanical productiveness, fall below the proper standard of their race, and enter into a lower form of being.

From *Modern Painters*, Vol. V, Part IX, ch. XI, §§ 17–18

¶ 292

ENGLAND'S GREATNESS

Do you know what, by this beautiful division of labour (her brave men fighting, and her cowards thinking), she has come at last to think? Here is a paper in my hand, a good one too, and an honest one; quite representative of the best common public thought of England at this moment; and it is holding forth in one of its leaders upon our 'social welfare,' – upon our 'vivid life' – upon the 'political supremacy of Great Britain.' And what do you think all these are owing to? To what our English sires have done for us, and taught us, age after age? No: not to that. To our honesty of heart, or coolness of head, or steadiness of will? No: not to these. To our thinkers, or our statesmen, or our poets, or our captains, or our martyrs, or the patient labour of our poor? No: not to these; or at least not to these in any chief measure. Nay, says the journal, 'more than any agency, it is the cheapness and abundance of our coal which have made us what we are.' If it be so, then 'ashes to ashes' be our epitaph! and the sooner the better.

Gentlemen of England, if ever you would have your country breathe the pure breath of heaven again, and receive again a soul into her body, instead of rotting into a carcase, blown up in the belly with carbonic acid (and great *that* way), you must think, and feel, for your England, as well as fight for her: you must teach her that all the true greatness she ever had, she won while her fields were green, and her faces ruddy; and that greatness is still possible for Englishmen, even though the ground be not hollow under their feet, nor the sky black over their heads.

From *The Crown of Wild Olive*, Lecture III, §§ 123-4

¶ 293

THE FREE FLY

I believe we can nowhere find a better type of a perfectly free creature than in the common house fly. Nor free only, but brave; and irreverent to a degree which I think no human republican could by any philosophy exalt himself to. There is no courtesy in him; he does not care whether it is king or clown whom he teases; and in every step of his swift mechanical march, and in every pause of his resolute observation, there is one and the same expression of perfect egotism, perfect independence and self-confidence, and conviction of the world's having been made for flies. Strike at him with your hand; and to him, the mechanical fact and external aspect of the matter is, what to you it would be, if an acre of red clay, ten feet thick, tore itself up from the ground in one massive field, hovered over you in the air for a second, and came crashing down with an aim. That is the external aspect of it; the inner aspect, to his fly's mind, is of quite natural and unimportant occurrence – one of the momentary conditions of his active life. He steps out of the way of your hand, and alights on the back of it. You cannot terrify him, nor govern him, nor persuade him, nor convince him. He has his own positive opinion on all matters; not an unwise one, usually, for his own ends; and will ask no advice of yours. He has no work to do – no tyrannical instinct to obey. The earthworm has his digging; the bee her gathering and building; the spider her cunning network; the ant her treasury and accounts. All these are comparatively slaves, or people of vulgar business. But your fly, free in the air, free in the chamber – a black incarnation of caprice – wandering, investigating, flitting, flirting, feasting at his will, with rich variety of choice in feast, from the heaped sweets in the grocer's window to those of the butcher's back-yard, and from the galled place on your cab-horse's back, to the brown spot in the road, from which, as the hoof disturbs him, he rises with angry republican buzz – what freedom is like his?

From *The Cestus of Aglaia*, ch. VI, § 74

¶ 294
INDEPENDENCE

The true strength of every human soul is to be dependent on as many nobler as it can discern, and to be depended upon, by as many inferior as it can reach.

From *The Eagle's Nest*, ch. V, § 77

¶ 295
SATIETY

What do you suppose makes all men look back to the time of childhood with so much regret (if their childhood has been, in any moderate degree, healthy or peaceful)? That rich charm, which the least possession had for us, was in consequence of the poorness of our treasures. That miraculous aspect of the nature around us, was because we had seen little, and knew less. Every increased possession loads us with a new weariness; every piece of new knowledge diminishes the faculty of admiration; and Death is at last appointed to take us from a scene in which, if we were to stay longer, no gift could satisfy us, and no miracle surprise.

From *The Eagle's Nest*, ch. V, § 82

¶ 296
CARPACCIO'S PRINCESS AND THE AMERICAN GIRLS

The bed is a broad four-poster, the posts being beautifully wrought golden or gilded rods, variously wreathed and branched, carrying a canopy of warm red. The princess's shield is at the head of it, and the feet are raised entirely above the floor of the room, on a dais which projects at the lower end so as to form a seat, on which the child has laid her crown. Her little blue slippers lie at the side of the bed, – her white dog beside them. The coverlid is scarlet, the white sheet folded half-way back over it; the young girl lies straight, bending neither at the waist or knee, the sheet rising and falling over her in a narrow unbroken wave, like the shape of the coverlid of the last sleep, when the turf scarcely rises. She is some seventeen or eighteen years old, her head is turned towards us on the pillow, the cheek resting on her hand, as if she were thinking, yet utterly calm in sleep, and almost colourless. Her hair is tied with a narrow riband, and divided into two wreaths, which encircle her head like a double crown. The white nightgown hides the arm raised on the pillow, down to the wrist.

At the door of the room an angel enters (the little dog, though lying awake, vigilant, takes no notice). He is a very small angel, his head just rises a little above the shelf round the room, and would only reach as high as the princess's chin, if she were standing up. He has soft grey wings, lustreless; and his dress, of subdued blue, has violet sleeves, open above the elbow, and showing white sleeves below. He comes in without haste, his body, like a mortal one, casting shadow from the light through the door behind, his face perfectly quiet; a palm-branch in his right hand – a scroll in his left.

So dreams the princess, with blessed eyes, that need no earthly dawn. It is very pretty of Carpaccio to make her dream out the angel's dress so particularly, and notice the slashed sleeves; and to dream so little an angel – very nearly a doll angel,[1] – bringing her the branch of palm, and message. But the lovely characteristic of all is the evident delight of her continual life. Royal power over herself, and happiness in her flowers, her books, her sleeping, and waking, her prayers, her dreams, her earth, her heaven.

After I had spent my morning over this picture, I had to go to Verona by the afternoon train. In the carriage with me were two American girls with their father and mother, people of the class which has lately made so much money, suddenly, and does not know what to do with it: and these two girls, of about fifteen and eighteen,

---

1. The angel is not exceptionally small. Ruskin thought that the shelf running round the room was at 'about the height of the elbow', but it is quite clearly at about the height of the chin.

had evidently been indulged in everything (since they had had the means) which western civilization could imagine. And here they were, specimens of the utmost which the money and invention of the nineteenth century could produce in maidenhood, – children of its most progressive race, – enjoying the full advantages of political liberty, of enlightened philosophical education, of cheap pilfered literature, and of luxury at any cost. Whatever money, machinery, or freedom of thought could do for these two children, had been done. No superstition had deceived, no restraint degraded them: – types, they could not but be, of maidenly wisdom and felicity, as conceived by the forwardest intellects of our time.

And they were travelling through a district which, if any in the world, should touch the hearts and delight the eyes of young girls. Between Venice and Verona! Portia's villa perhaps in sight upon the Brenta, Juliet's tomb to be visited in the evening, – blue against the southern sky, the hills of Petrarch's home. Exquisite midsummer sunshine, with low rays, glanced through the vine-leaves; all the Alps were clear, from the Lake of Garda to Cadore, and to farthest Tyrol. What a princess's chamber, this, if these are princesses, and what dreams might they not dream, therein!

But the two American girls were neither princesses, nor seers, nor dreamers. By infinite self-indulgence, they had reduced themselves simply to two pieces of white putty that could feel pain. The flies and the dust stuck to them as to clay, and they perceived, between Venice and Verona, nothing but the flies and the dust. They pulled down the blinds the moment they entered the carriage, and then sprawled, and writhed, and tossed among the cushions of it, in vain contest, during the whole fifty miles, with every miserable sensation of bodily affliction that could make time intolerable.

From *Fors Clavigera*, Letter xx, §§ 15–18, August 1872

§ 297

THE STUPIDITY OF JUDAS

However in every nation there are, and must always be, a certain number of these Fiend's servants, who have it principally for the object of their lives to make money. They are always, as I said, more or less stupid, and cannot conceive of anything else so nice as money. Stupidity is always the basis of the Judas bargain. We do great injustice to Iscariot, in thinking him wicked above all common wickedness. He was only a common money-lover, and, like all money-lovers, did not understand Christ; – could not make out the worth of Him, or meaning of Him. He never thought He would be killed. He was horror-struck when he found that Christ would be killed; threw his money away instantly, and hanged himself. How many of our present money-seekers, think you, would have the grace to hang themselves, whoever was killed? But Judas was a common, selfish, muddle-headed, pilfering fellow; his hand always in the bag of the poor, not caring for them. Helpless to understand Christ, he yet believed in Him, much more than most of us do; had seen Him do miracles, thought He was quite strong enough to shift for Himself, and he, Judas, might as well make his own little bye-perquisites out of the affair. Christ would come out of it well enough, and he have his thirty pieces.

From *The Crown of Wild Olive*, Lecture I, § 33

¶ 298

THE PUBLIC AND THE CRYSTAL PALACE

The British lower public has no very clear notion of the way to amuse itself – does so at present in a very dismal and panic-struck manner; it has a notion of improving its manners and getting useful information at the same time, and so makes its way to the Crystal Palace, and, with its own instincts principally tending towards ginger-beer, hopes also to have its mind enlarged by the assistance of Greek sculpture, always supposing the enlargement of its mind is to tend somehow to the enlargement of pockets, wages, and other substantialities. It relaxes, indeed, towards Christmas-time in these economical views, but becomes in outer aspect even more dismally pensive than at any other period. I went up to the Crystal Palace this last year on Boxing Day to contemplate the recreations, and perhaps some of my audience may remember the strenuous efforts made to obtain at least recreative effect in the interior. In my old studies of architecture I always used to have great regard to the apse of a cathedral, and whatever else failed, looked always to the close of the great aisled vista as the principal joy of one's heart. . . . So one has a natural tendency to look also to the apse of this cathedral of modern faith to see the symbol of it, as one used to look to the concha of the Cathedral of Pisa for the face of Christ, or to the apse of Torcello for the figure of the Madonna. Well, do you recollect what occupied the place of these – in the apse of the Crystal Palace? The head of a Pantomime clown, some twelve feet broad, with a mouth opening from ear to ear, opening and shutting by machinery, its eyes squinting alternately, and collapsing by machinery, its humour in general provided for by machinery, with the recognised utterance of English Wisdom inscribed above – 'Here we are again.' But the striking thing of all was that, though as I said the humour of the thing could not but have been perfect – being provided for by machinery – nobody laughed at it. Few even had consistency of comparative observation enough to find out that it moved. When they did, they touched their neighbour's elbow, looked up with a frightened expression for a minute, and passed on, with an appearance of discomfort, knowing that it was their duty to laugh, and failing signally when they tried.

From *Modern Art*, § 25

§ 299

THE NINETEENTH CENTURY

Yes, believe me, in spite of our political liberality, and poetical philanthropy; in spite of our almshouses, hospitals, and Sunday-schools; in spite of our missionary endeavours to preach abroad what we cannot get believed at home; and in spite of our wars against slavery, indemnified by the presentation of ingenious bills, – we shall be remembered in history as the most cruel, and therefore the most unwise, generation of men that ever yet troubled the earth: – the most cruel in proportion to their sensibility, – the most unwise in proportion to their science. No people, understanding pain, ever inflicted so much: no people, understanding facts, ever acted on them so little.

From *The Eagle's Nest*, Lecture II, § 35

THE GREAT MYTHS

The great myths; that is to say, myths made by great people. For the first plain fact about myth-making is one which has been most strangely lost sight of, – that you cannot make a myth unless you have something to make it of. You cannot tell a secret which you don't know. If the myth is about the sky, it must have been made by somebody who had looked at the sky. If the myth is about justice and fortitude, it must have been made by some one who knew what it was to be just or patient. According to the quantity of understanding in the person will be the quantity of significance in his fable; and the myth of a simple and ignorant race must necessarily mean little, because a simple and ignorant race have little to mean. So the great question in reading a story is always, not what wild hunter dreamed, or what childish race first dreaded it; but what wise man first perfectly told, and what strong people first perfectly lived by it. And the real meaning of any myth is that which it has at the noblest age of the nation among whom it is current. The farther back you pierce, the less significance you will find, until you come to the first narrow thought, which, indeed, contains the germ of the accomplished tradition; but only as the seed contains the flower. As the intelligence and passion of the race develop, they cling to and nourish their beloved and sacred legend; leaf by leaf, it expands, under the touch of more pure affections, and more delicate imagination, until at last the perfect fable burgeons out into symmetry of milky stem, and honeyed bell.

But through whatever changes it may pass, remember that our right reading of it is wholly dependent on the materials we have in our own minds for an intelligent answering sympathy. If it first arose among a people who dwelt under stainless skies, and measured their journeys by ascending and declining stars, we certainly cannot read their story, if we have never seen anything above us in the day but smoke; nor anything round us in the night but candles. If the tale goes on to change clouds or planets into living creatures, – to invest them with fair forms – and inflame them with mighty passions, we can only understand the story of the human-hearted things, in so far as we ourselves take pleasure in the perfectness of visible form, or can sympathise, by an effort of imagination, with the strange people who had other loves than that of wealth, and other interests than those of commerce. And lastly, if the myth complete itself to the fulfilled thoughts of the nation, by attributing to the gods, whom they have carved out of their fantasy, continual presence with their own souls; and their every effort for good is finally guided by the sense of the companionship, the praise, and the pure will of Immortals, we shall be able to follow them into this last circle of their faith only in the degree in which the better parts of our own beings have been also stirred by the aspects of nature, or strengthened by her laws. It may be easy to prove that the ascent of Apollo in his chariot signifies nothing but the rising of the sun. But what does the sunrise itself signify to us? If only languid return to frivolous amusement, or fruitless labour, it will, indeed, not be easy for us to conceive the power, over a Greek, of the name of Apollo. But if, for us also, as for the Greek, the sunrise means daily restoration to the sense of passionate gladness, and of perfect life – if it means the thrilling of new strength through every nerve, – the shedding over us of a better peace than the peace of night, in the power of the dawn, – and the purging of evil vision and fear by the baptism of its dew; if the sun itself is an influence, to us also, of spiritual good – and becomes thus in reality, not in imagination, to us also, a spiritual power, – we may then soon over-pass the narrow limit of conception which kept that power impersonal, and rise with Greek to the thought of an angel who rejoiced as a strong man to run his course, whose voice, calling to life and to labour, rang round the earth, and whose going forth was to the ends of heaven.

From *The Queen of the Air*, Lecture I, §§ 7–8

¶ 301

DESTRUCTIVE MAN

Fancy what Europe would be now, if the delicate statues and temples of the Greeks – if the broad roads and massy walls of the Romans – if the noble and pathetic architecture of the Middle Ages, had not been ground to dust by mere human rage. You talk of the

scythe of Time, and the tooth of Time: I tell you, Time is scytheless
and toothless; it is we who gnaw like the worm – we who smite like
the scythe. It is ourselves who abolish – ourselves who consume: we
are the mildew, and the flame; and the soul of man is to its own work
as the moth that frets when it cannot fly, and as the hidden flame
that blasts where it cannot illuminate. All these lost treasures of
human intellect have been wholly destroyed by human industry of
destruction; the marble would have stood its two thousand years as
well in the polished statue as in the Parian cliff; but we men have
ground it to powder, and mixed it with our own ashes. The walls
and the ways would have stood – it is we who have left not one
stone upon another, and restored its pathlessness to the desert; the
great cathedrals of old religion would have stood – it is we who have
dashed down the carved work with axes and hammers, and bid the
mountain-grass bloom upon the pavement, and the sea-winds chant
in the galleries.

From *A Joy for Ever*, Lecture II, § 74

§ 302

ANCIENT GREECE

Defied, the betraying and accusing shadows shrank back; the
mysterious horror subdued itself to majestic sorrow. Death was
swallowed up in victory. Their blood, which seemed to be poured
out upon the ground, rose into hyacinthine flowers. All the beauty
of earth opened to them; they had ploughed into its darkness, and
they reaped its gold; the gods, in whom they had trusted through all
semblance of oppression, came down to love them and be their help-
mates. All nature round them became divine, – one harmony of
power and peace. The sun hurt them not by day, nor the moon by
night; the earth opened no more her jaws into the pit; the sea
whitened no more against them the teeth of his devouring waves.
Sun, and moon, and earth, and sea, – all melted into grace and love;
the fatal arrows rang not now at the shoulders of Apollo, the healer;
lord of life, and of the three great spirits of life – Care, Memory and
Melody. Great Artemis guarded their flocks by night; Selene kissed
in love the eyes of those who slept. And from all came the help of

heaven to body and soul; a strange spirit lifting the lovely limbs; strange light glowing on the golden hair; and strangest comfort filling the trustful heart, so that they could put off their armour, and lie down to sleep, – their work well done, whether at the gates of their temples or of their mountains; accepting the death they once thought terrible, as the gift of Him who knew and granted what was best.

From *Modern Painters*, Vol. V, Part IX, ch. III, § 20

¶ 303

CHEMISTRY AND THEOLOGY

It is not, I know, in your modern system, the general practice to put chemistry, the science of atoms, lowest, and theology, the science of Deity, highest: nay, many of us have ceased to think of theology as a science at all, but rather as a speculative pursuit, in subject, separate from science; and in temper, opposed to her.

Yet it can scarcely be necessary for me to point out to you, in so many terms, that what we call theology, if true, is a science; and if false, is not theology; or that the distinction even between natural science and theology is illogical: for you might distinguish indeed between natural and unnatural science, but not between natural and spiritual, unless you had determined first that a spirit had no nature. You will find the facts to be, that entirely true knowledge is both possible and necessary – first of facts relating to matter, and then of the forces and passions that act on or in matter; – that, of all these forces, the noblest we can know is the energy which either imagines, or perceives, the existence of a living power greater than its own; and that the study of the relations which exist between this energy, and the resultant action of men, are as much subjects of pure science as the curve of a projectile. The effect, for instance, upon your temper, intellect, and conduct during the day, of your going to chapel with or without belief in the efficacy of prayer, is just as much a subject of definite science, as the effect of your breakfast on the coats of your stomach. Which is the higher knowledge, I have, with confidence, told you; and am not afraid of any test to which you may submit my assertion.

From *The Eagle's Nest*, ch. IV, § 67

¶ 304

HUMANISM PREFERRED TO SCIENCE

We may assume the attraction of the spectacle of the heavens to be equal in degree, and yet, in the minds of the two girls, it may be entirely different in kind. Supposing the one versed somewhat in abstract Science, and more or less acquainted with the laws by which what she now sees may be explained; she will probably take interest chiefly in questions of distance and magnitude, in varieties of orbit, and proportions of light. Supposing the other not versed in any science of this kind, but acquainted with the traditions attached by the religion of dead nations to the figures they discerned in the sky: she will care little for arithmetical or geometrical matters, but will probably receive a much deeper emotion, from witnessing in clearness what has been the amazement of so many eyes long closed; and recognizing the same lights, through the same darkness, with innocent shepherds and husbandmen, who knew only the risings and settings of the immeasurable vault, as its lights shone on their own fields or mountains; yet saw true miracle in them, thankful that none but the Supreme Ruler could bind the sweet influences of Pleiades, or loose the bands of Orion. I need not surely tell you, that in this exertion of the intellect and the heart, there would be a far nobler sophia than any concerned with the analysis of matter, or the measurement of space.

From *The Eagle's Nest*, Lecture II, § 28

¶ 305

POINT OF A UNIVERSITY

The object of University teaching is to form your conceptions; – not to acquaint you with arts, nor sciences. It is to give you a notion of what is meant by smith's work, for instance; – but not to make you blacksmiths. It is to give you a notion of what is meant by medicine, but not to make you physicians. The proper academy for black-smiths is a blacksmith's forge; the proper academy for physicians is an hospital. Here you are to be taken away from the forge, out of the hospital, out of all special and limited labour and thought, into the 'Universitas' of labour and thought, that you may in peace, in leisure, in calm of disinterested contemplation, be enabled to conceive rightly the laws of nature, and the destinies of Man.

From *The Eagle's Nest*, Lecture 1, § 18

¶ 306
INFIDELITY

No nation ever before declared boldly, by print and word of mouth, that its religion was good for show, but 'would not work.' Over and over again it has happened that nations have denied their gods, but they denied them bravely. The Greeks in their decline jested at their religion, and frittered it away in flatteries and fine arts; the French refused theirs fiercely, tore down their altars and brake their carven images. The question about God with both these nations was still, even in their decline, fairly put, though falsely answered. 'Either there is or is not a Supreme Ruler; we consider of it, declare there is not, and proceed accordingly.' But we English have put the matter in an entirely new light: 'There *is* a Supreme Ruler, no question of it, only He cannot rule. His orders won't work. He will be quite satisfied with euphonious and respectful repetition of them. Execution would be too dangerous under existing circumstances, which He certainly never contemplated.'

I had no conception of the absolute darkness which has covered the national mind in this respect, until I began to come into collision with persons engaged in the study of economical and political questions. The entire naïveté and undisturbed imbecility with which I found them declare that the laws of the Devil were the only practicable ones, and that the laws of God were merely a form of poetical language, passed all that I had ever before heard or read of mortal infidelity. I knew the fool had often said in his heart, there was *no* God; but to hear him say clearly out with his lips, 'There is a foolish God,' was something which my art studies had not prepared me for. The French had indeed, for a considerable time, hinted much of the meaning in the delicate and compassionate blasphemy of their phrase '*le bon Dieu*,' but had never ventured to put it into more precise terms.

From *Modern Painters*, Vol. v, Part ix, ch. xii, § 5

¶ 307
THE REFORMATION

The Reformation succeeded in proclaiming that existing Christianity was a lie; but substituted no theory of it which could be more rationally or credibly sustained; and ever since, the religion of educated persons throughout Europe has been dishonest or ineffectual; it is only among the labouring peasantry that the grace of a pure Catholicism, and the patient simplicities of the Puritan, maintain their imaginative dignity, or assert their practical use.

From *Val d'Arno*, Lecture iii, § 75

¶ 308
LUDGATE HILL

I had occasion only the other day to wait for half-an-hour at the bottom of Ludgate Hill. Standing as much out of the way as I could, under the shadow of the railroad bridge, I watched the faces, all eager, many anxious, and some intensely gloomy, of the hurried passers by; and listened to the ceaseless crashing, whistling, and thundering sounds which mingled with the murmur of their steps and voices. And in the midst of the continuous roar, which differed only from that of the wildest sea in storm by its complexity and its discordance, I was wondering, if the sum of what all these people were doing, or trying to do, in the course of the day, could be made manifest, what it would come to.

The sum of it would be, I suppose, that they had all contrived to live through the day in that exceedingly unpleasant manner, and that nothing serious had occurred to prevent them from passing the following day likewise. Nay, I knew also that what appeared in their way of life painful to me, might be agreeable to them; and it chanced, indeed, a little while afterwards, that an active and prosperous man of business, speaking to one of my friends of the disappointment he had felt in a visit to Italy, remarked, especially, that he was not able to endure more than three days at Venice, because there was no noise there.

But, granting the contentment of the inhabitants of London in consistently producing these sounds, how shall we say this vocal and instrumental art of theirs may compare, in the scheme of Nature, with the vocal art of lower animals? We may indeed rank the danger-whistle of the engines on the bridge as an excruciating human improvement on that of the marmot; and the trampling of feet and grinding of wheels, as the human accentuation of the sounds produced by insects, by the friction of their wings or thighs against their sides: but, even in this comparison, it may cause us some humiliation to note that the cicada and the cricket, when pleased to sing in their vibratory manner, have leisure to rest in their delight; and that the flight of the firefly is silent. But how will the sounds we produce compare with the song of birds? This London is the principal nest of men in the world; and I was standing in the centre of it. In the shops of Fleet Street and Ludgate Hill, on each side of me, I do not doubt I could have bought any quantity of books for children, which by way of giving them religious, as opposed to secular, instruction, informed them that birds praised God in their songs. Now, though, on the one hand, you may be very certain that birds are not machines, on the other hand it is just as certain that they have not the smallest intention of praising God in their songs; and that we cannot prevent the religious education of our children more utterly than by beginning it in lies. But it might be expected of *ourselves* that we should do so, in the songs we send up from our principal nest! And although, under the dome at the top of Ludgate Hill, some attempt of the kind may be made every seventh day, by a limited number of persons, we may again reflect, with humiliation, that the birds, for better or worse, sing all, and every day; and I could not but ask myself, with momentarily increasing curiosity, as I endeavoured to trace the emotions and occupations of the persons who passed by me, in the expression of their faces – what would be the effect on them, if any creatures of higher order were suddenly to appear in the midst of them with any such message of peace, and invitation to rejoicing, as they had all been professing to commemorate at Christmas.

Perhaps you recollect, in the lectures given on landscape during the spring of this year, my directing your attention to a picture of [Botticelli's][1] in the loan exhibition, representing a flight of twelve angels in blue sky, singing that Christmas song. I ought to tell you, however, that one of our English artists of good position dissented from my opinion about the picture; and remarked that in England 'we wanted good art, and not funny art.' Whereas, to me, it is this vocal and architectural art of Ludgate Hill which appears funny art; and not [Botticelli's]. But I am compelled to admit that could [Botticelli's] picture have been realized, the result would, in the eyes of most men, have been funnier still. For suppose that over Ludgate Hill the sky had indeed suddenly become blue instead of black; and that a flight of twelve angels, 'covered with silver wings, and their feathers with gold,' had alighted on the cornice of the railroad bridge, as the doves alight on the cornices of St Mark's at Venice; and had invited the eager men of business below, in the centre of the city confessedly the most prosperous in the world, to join them for five minutes in singing the first five verses of such a psalm as the 103rd – 'Bless the Lord, oh my soul, and *all that is within me*,' (the opportunity now being given for the expression of their most hidden feelings) 'all that is within me, bless His holy name, and forget not all His benefits.' Do you not even thus, in mere suggestion, feel shocked at the thought, and as if my now reading the words were profane? And cannot you fancy that the sensation of the crowd at so violent and strange an interruption of traffic, might be somewhat akin to that which I had occasion in my first lecture on sculpture to remind you of, – the feeling attributed by Goethe to Mephistopheles, at the song of the angels: 'Discord I hear, and intolerable jingling'?

From *The Eagle's Nest*, ch. III, §§ 59–62

1. The picture referred to is Botticelli's *Mystic Nativity* now in the National Gallery, no. 1034, which was then on loan in the South Kensington Museum. In the original text Ruskin refers to it as a Mantegna, but this must be a slip of the pen as it is signed by Botticelli and is in fact his only signed work.

¶ 309
IMMORTALITY

And the more I thought over what I had got to say, the less I found I could say it, without some reference to this intangible or intractable question [of belief in Eternal Life]. It made all the difference, in asserting any principle of war, whether one assumed that a discharge of artillery would merely knead down a certain quantity of once living clay into a level line, as in a brickfield; or whether, out of every separately Christian-named portion of the ruinous heap, there went out, into the smoke and dead-fallen air of battle, some astonished condition of soul, unwillingly released. It made all the difference, in speaking of the possible range of commerce, whether one assumed that all bargains related only to visible property – or whether property, for the present invisible, but nevertheless real, was elsewhere purchasable on other terms. It made all the difference, in addressing a body of men subject to considerable hardship, and having to find some way out of it – whether one could confidently say to them, 'My friends, – you have only to die, and all will be right,' or whether one had any secret misgiving that such advice was more blessed to him that gave it than to him that took it.

From *The Crown of Wild Olive*, Introduction, § 11

¶ 310
WHAT IS MAN?

Through the glass, darkly. But, except through the glass, in no wise.

A tremulous crystal, waved as water, poured out upon the ground; – you may defile it, despise it, pollute it, at your pleasure and at your peril; for on the peace of those weak waves must all the heaven you shall ever gain be first seen; and through such purity as you can win for those dark waves, must all the light of the risen Sun of righteousness be bent down, by faint refraction. . . .

Therefore it is that all the power of nature depends on subjection to the human soul. Man is the sun of the world; more than the real sun. The fire of his wonderful heart is the only light and heat worth gauge or measure. Where he is, are the tropics; where he is not, the ice-world.

From *Modern Painters*, Vol. v, Part ix, ch. i, § 15

6

POETIC DESCRIPTION

NOONDAY IN THE CAMPAGNA

The noonday sun came slanting down the rocky slopes of La Riccia, and their masses of entangled and tall foliage, whose autumnal tints were mixed with the wet verdure of a thousand evergreens, were penetrated with it as with rain. I cannot call it colour, it was conflagration. Purple, and crimson, and scarlet, like the curtains of God's Tabernacle, the rejoicing trees sank into the valley in showers of light, every separate leaf quivering with buoyant and burning life; each, as it turned to reflect or to transmit the sunbeam, first a torch and then an emerald. Far up into the recesses of the valley, the green vistas arched like the hollows of mighty waves of some crystalline sea, with the arbutus flowers dashed along their flanks for foam, and silver flakes of orange spray tossed into the air around them, breaking over the grey walls of rock into a thousand separate stars, fading and kindling alternately as the weak wind lifted and let them fall. Every glade of grass burned like the golden floor of heaven, opening in sudden gleams as the foliage broke and closed above it, as sheet-lighting opens in a cloud at sunset; the motionless masses of dark rock – dark though flushed with scarlet lichen, casting their quiet shadows across its restless radiance, the fountain underneath them filling its marble hollow with blue mist and fitful sound; and over all, the multitudinous bars of amber and rose, the sacred clouds that have no darkness, and only exist to illumine, were seen in fathomless intervals between the solemn and orbed repose of the stone pines, passing to lose themselves in the last, white, blinding lustre of the measureless line where the Campagna melted into the blaze of the sea.[1]

From *Modern Painters*, Vol. I, Part II, Sec. II, ch. II, § 2

1. This famous passage follows a tame description of a once famous painting of Ariccia in the National Gallery, no. 98 by Gaspard Poussin, and ends with the question 'Tell me who is likest, the Poussin or Turner?'

EVENING IN THE CAMPAGNA

Perhaps there is no more impressive scene on earth than the solitary extent of the Campagna of Rome under evening light. Let the reader imagine himself for a moment withdrawn from the sounds and motion of the living world, and sent forth alone into this wild and wasted plain. The earth yields and crumbles beneath his foot, tread he never so lightly, for its substance is white, hollow, and carious, like the dusty wreck of the bones of men. The long knotted grass waves and tosses feebly in the evening wind, and the shadows of its motion shake feverishly along the banks of ruin that lift themselves to the sunlight. Hillocks of mouldering earth heave around him, as if the dead beneath were struggling in their sleep; scattered blocks of black stone, four-square, remnants of mighty edifices, not one left upon another, lie upon them to keep them down. A dull purple poisonous haze stretches level along the desert, veiling its spectral wrecks of massy ruins, on whose rents the red light rests, like dying fire on defiled altars. The blue ridge of the Alban Mount lifts itself against a solemn space of green, clear, quiet sky. Watch-towers of dark clouds stand steadfastly along the promontories of the Apennines. From the plain to the mountains, the shattered aqueducts, pier beyond pier, melt into the darkness, like shadowy and countless troops of funeral mourners, passing from a nation's grave.

From *Modern Painters*, Vol. I, Preface to the 2nd ed., § 37

THE FALL OF SCHAFFHAUSEN

Stand for half an hour beside the Fall of Schaffhausen, on the north side where the rapids are long, and watch how the vault of water first bends, unbroken, in pure polished velocity, over the arching rocks at the brow of the cataract, covering them with a dome of crystal twenty feet thick, so swift that its motion is unseen except when a foam-globe from above darts over it like a falling star; and how the trees are lighted above it under all their leaves, at the instant that it breaks into foam; and how all the hollows of that foam burn with green fire like so much shattering chrysoprase; and how, ever and anon, startling you with its white flash, a jet of spray leaps hissing out of the fall, like a rocket, bursting in the wind and driven away in dust, filling the air with light; and how, through the curdling wreaths of the restless crashing abyss below, the blue of the water, paled by the foam in its body, shows purer than the sky through white rain-cloud; while the shuddering iris stoops in tremulous stillness over all, fading and flushing alternately through the choking spray and shattered sunshine, hiding itself at last among the thick golden leaves which toss to and fro in sympathy with the wild water; their dripping masses lifted at intervals, like sheaves of loaded corn, by some stronger gush from the cataract, and bowed again upon the mossy rocks as its roar dies away; the dew gushing from their thick branches through drooping clusters of emerald herbage, and sparkling in white threads along the dark rocks of the shore, feeding the lichens which chase and chequer them with purple and silver.

From *Modern Painters*, Vol. I, Part II, Sec. V, ch. II, § 2

¶ 314
CALAIS CHURCH

I cannot find words to express the intense pleasure I have always in first finding myself, after some prolonged stay in England, at the foot of the old tower of Calais church. The large neglect, the noble unsightliness of it; the record of its years written so visibly, yet without sign of weakness or decay; its stern wasteness and gloom, eaten away by the Channel winds, and overgrown with the bitter sea grasses; its slates and tiles all shaken and rent, and yet not falling; its desert of brickwork full of bolts, and holes, and ugly fissures, and yet strong, like a bare brown rock; its carelessness of what any one thinks or feels about it, putting forth no claim, having no beauty or desirableness, pride, nor grace; yet neither asking for pity; not, as ruins are, useless and piteous, feebly or fondly garrulous of better days; but useful still, going through its own daily work, – as some old fisherman beaten grey by storm, yet drawing his daily nets: so it stands, with no complaint about its past youth, in blanched and meagre massiveness and serviceableness, gathering human souls together underneath it; the sound of its bells for prayer still rolling through its rents; and the grey peak of it seen far across the sea, principal of the three that rise above the waste of surfy sand and hillocked shore, – the lighthouse for life, and the belfry for labour, and this for patience and praise.

From *Modern Painters*, Vol. IV, Part v, ch. I, § 2

§ 315
APPROACH TO VENICE

In the olden days of travelling, now to return no more, in which distance could not be vanquished without toil, but in which that toil was rewarded, partly by the power of deliberate survey of the countries through which the journey lay, and partly by the happiness of the evening hours, when from the top of the last hill he had surmounted, the traveller beheld the quiet village where he was to rest, scattered among the meadows beside its valley stream; or, from the long hoped for turn in the dusty perspective of the causeway, saw, for the first time, the towers of some famed city, faint in the rays of sunset – hours of peaceful and thoughtful pleasure, for which the rush of the arrival in the railway station is perhaps not always, or to all men, an equivalent, – in those days, I say, when there was something more to be anticipated and remembered in the first aspect of each successive halting-place, than a new arrangement of glass roofing and iron girder, there were few moments of which the recollection was more fondly cherished by the traveller, than that which, as I endeavoured to describe in the close of the last chapter, brought him within sight of Venice, as his gondola shot into the open lagoon from the canal of Mestre. Not but that the aspect of the city itself was generally the source of some slight disappointment, for, seen in this direction, its buildings are far less characteristic than those of the other great towns of Italy; but this inferiority was partly disguised by distance, and more than atoned for by the strange rising of its walls and towers out of the midst, as it seemed, of the deep sea, for it was impossible that the mind or the eye could at once comprehend the shallowness of the vast sheet of water which stretched away in leagues of rippling lustre to the north and south, or trace the narrow line of islets bounding it to the east. The salt breeze, the white moaning sea-birds, the masses of black weed separating and disappearing gradually, in knots of heaving shoal, under the advance of the steady tide, all proclaimed it to be indeed the ocean on whose bosom the great city rested so calmly; not such blue, soft, lake-like ocean as bathes the Neapolitan promontories, or sleeps beneath the marble rocks of Genoa, but a sea with the bleak power of our own northern waves, yet subdued into a strange spacious rest, and changed from its angry pallor into a field of burnished gold, as the sun declined behind the belfry tower of the lonely island church, fitly named 'St George of the Seaweed.' As the boat drew nearer to the city, the coast which the traveller had just left sank behind him into one long, low, sad-coloured line, tufted irregularly with brushwood and willows: but, at what seemed its northern extremity, the hills of Arqua rose in a dark cluster of purple pyramids, balanced on the bright mirage of the lagoon; two or three smooth surges of inferior hill extended themselves about their roots, and beyond these, beginning with the craggy peaks above Vicenza, the chain of the Alps girded the whole horizon to the north – a wall of jagged blue, here and there showing through its clefts a wilderness of misty precipices, fading far back into the recesses of Cadore, and itself rising and breaking away eastward, where the sun struck opposite upon its snow, into mighty fragments of peaked light, standing up behind the barred clouds of evening, one after another, countless, the crown of the Adrian Sea, until the eye turned back from pursuing them, to rest upon the nearer burning of the campaniles of Murano, and on the great city, where it magnified itself along the waves, as the quick silent pacing of the gondola drew nearer and nearer. And at last, when its walls were reached, and the outmost of its untrodden streets was entered, not through towered gate or guarded rampart, but as a deep inlet between two rocks of coral in the Indian Sea, when first upon the traveller's sight opened the long ranges of columned palaces, – each with its black boat moored at the portal, – each with its image cast down, beneath its feet, upon that green pavement which every breeze broke into new fantasies of rich tessellation; when first, at the extremity of the bright vista, the shadowy Rialto threw its colossal curve slowly forth from behind the palace of the Camerlenghi; that strange curve, so delicate, so adamantine, strong as a mountain cavern, graceful as a bow just bent; when first, before its moonlike circumference was all risen, the gondolier's cry 'Ah! Stali,' struck sharp upon the ear, and the prow turned aside under the mighty cornices that half met over the narrow canal, where the plash of the water followed close and loud, ringing along the marble by the boat's side; and when at last that boat darted forth upon the breadth of silver sea, across which the front of the Ducal palace, flushed with its sanguine veins, looks to the snowy dome of Our Lady of Salvation, it was no marvel that the mind should be so deeply entranced by the visionary charm of a scene so beautiful and so strange, as to forget the darker truths of its history and its being. Well might it seem that such a city had owed her existence rather to the rod of the enchanter, than the fear of the fugitive; that the waters which encircled her had been chosen for the mirror of her state, rather than the shelter of her nakedness; and that all which in nature was wild or merciless, – Time and Decay, as well as the waves and tempests, – had been won to adorn her instead of to destroy, and might still spare, for ages to come, that beauty which seemed to have fixed for its throne the sands of the hour-glass as well as of the sea.

From *The Stones of Venice*, Vol. II, ch. I, § I

¶ 316

VENETIAN CHARACTER

This ocean-work is wholly adverse to any morbid conditions of sentiment. Reverie, above all things, is forbidden by Scylla and Charybdis. By the dogs and the depths, no dreaming! The first thing required of us is presence of mind. Neither love, nor poetry, nor piety, must ever so take up our thoughts as to make us slow or unready. In sweet Val d'Arno it is permissible enough to dream among the orange blossoms, and forget the day in twilight of ilex. But along the avenues of the Adrian waves there can be no careless walking. Vigilance, night and day, required of us besides learning of many practical lessons in severe and humble dexterities. It is enough for the Florentine to know how to use his sword and to ride. We Venetians, also, must be able to use our swords, and on ground which is none of the steadiest; but, besides, we must be able to do nearly everything that hands can turn to – rudders, and yards, and cables, all needing workmanly handling and workmanly knowledge, from captain as well as from men. To drive a nail, lash a spar, reef a sail – rude work this for noble hands; but to be done sometimes, and done well on pain of death. All which not only takes mean pride out of us, and puts nobler pride of power in its stead; but it tends partly to soothe, partly to chasten, partly to employ and direct, the hot Italian temper, and make us every way greater, calmer and happier.

Moreover, it tends to induce in us great respect for the whole human body; for its limbs, as much as for its tongue or its wit. Policy and eloquence are well; and, indeed, we Venetians can be politic enough, and can speak melodiously when we choose; but to put the helm up at the right moment is the beginning of all cunning – and for that we need arm and eye; – not tongue. And with this respect for the body as such, comes also the sailor's preference of massive beauty in bodily form. The landsmen, among their roses and orange-blossoms, and chequered shadows of twisted vine, may well please themselves with pale faces, and finely drawn eyebrows, and fantastic braiding of hair. But from the sweeping glory of the sea we learn to love another kind of beauty; broad-breasted, level-browed, like the horizon; – thighed and shouldered like the billows; footed like their stealing foam; – bathed in cloud of golden hair like their sunsets.

From *Modern Painters*, Vol. v, Part i x, ch. iii, §§ 4–5

¶ 317
TORCELLO

The inlet which runs nearest to the base of the campanile is not that by which Torcello is commonly approached. Another, somewhat broader, and overhung by alder copse, winds out of the main channel of the lagoon up to the very edge of the little meadow which was once the Piazza of the city, and there, stayed by a few grey stones which present some semblance of a quay, forms its boundary at one extremity. Hardly larger than an ordinary English farmyard, and roughly enclosed on each side by broken palings and hedges of honeysuckle and briar, the narrow field retires from the water's edge, traversed by a scarcely traceable footpath, for some forty or fifty paces, and then expanding into the form of a small square, with buildings on three sides of it, the fourth being that which opens to the water. Two of these, that on our left and that in front of us as we approach from the canal, are so small that they might well be taken for the outhouses of the farm, though the first is a conventual building, and the other aspires to the title of the 'Palazzo publico,' both dating as far back as the beginning of the fourteenth century; the third, the octagonal church of Santa Fosca, is far more ancient than either, yet hardly on a larger scale. Though the pillars of the portico which surrounds it are of pure Greek marble, and their capitals are enriched with delicate sculpture, they, and the arches they sustain, together only raise the roof to the height of a cattle-shed; and the first strong impression which the spectator receives from the whole scene is, that whatever sin it may have been which has on this spot been visited with so utter a desolation, it could not at least have been ambition. Nor will this impression be diminished as we approach, or enter, the larger church, to which the whole group of building is subordinate. It has evidently been built by men in flight and distress, who sought in the hurried erection of their island church such a shelter for their earnest and sorrowful worship as, on the one hand, could not attract the eyes of their enemies by its splendour, and yet, on the other, might not awaken too bitter feelings by its contrast with the churches which they had seen destroyed. There is visible everywhere a simple and tender effort to recover some of the form of the temples which they had loved, and to do honour to God by that which they were erecting, while distress and humiliation prevented the desire, and prudence precluded the admission, either of luxury of ornament or magnificence of plan. The exterior is absolutely devoid of decoration, with the exception only of the western entrance and the lateral door, of which the former has carved sideposts and architrave, and the latter, crosses of rich sculpture; while the massy stone shutters of the windows, turning on huge rings of stone, which answer the double purpose of stanchions and brackets, cause the whole building rather to resemble a refuge from Alpine storm than the cathedral of a populous city; and, internally, the two solemn mosaics of the eastern and western extremities, – one representing the Last Judgment, the other the Madonna, her tears falling as her hands are raised to bless, – and the noble range of pillars which enclose the space between, terminated by the high throne for the pastor and the semicircular raised seats for the superior clergy, are expressive at once of the deep sorrow and the sacred courage of men who had no home left them upon earth, but who looked for one to come, of men 'persecuted but not forsaken, cast down but not destroyed.'

From *The Stones of Venice*, Vol. ii, ch. ii, § 3

¶ 318

THE TIDE IN VENICE

The average rise and fall of the tide is about three feet (varying considerably with the seasons); but this fall, on so flat a shore, is enough to cause continual movement in the waters, and in the main canals to produce a reflux which frequently runs like a mill stream. At high water no land is visible for many miles to the north or south of Venice, except in the form of small islands crowned with towers or gleaming with villages: there is a channel, some three miles wide, between the city and the mainland, and some mile and a half wide between it and the sandy breakwater called the Lido, which divides the lagoon from the Adriatic, but which is so low as hardly to disturb the impression of the city's having been built in the midst of the ocean, although the secret of its true position is partly, yet not painfully betrayed by the clusters of piles set to mark the deep-water channels, which undulate far away in spotty chains like the studded backs of huge sea-snakes, and by the quick glittering of the crisped and crowded waves that flicker and dance before the strong winds upon the uplifted level of the shallow sea. But the scene is widely different at low tide. A fall of eighteen or twenty inches is enough to show ground over the greater part of the lagoon;

and at the complete ebb the city is seen standing in the midst of a dark plain of sea-weed, of gloomy green, except only where the larger branches of the Brenta and its associated streams converge towards the port of the Lido. Through this salt and sombre plain the gondola and the fishing-boat advance by tortuous channels, seldom more than four or five feet deep, and often so choked with slime that the heavier keels furrow the bottom till their crossing tracts are seen through the clear sea water like the ruts upon a wintry road, and the oar leaves blue gashes upon the ground at every stroke, or is entangled among the thick weed that fringes the banks with the weight of its sullen waves, leaning to and fro upon the uncertain sway of the exhausted tide. The scene is often profoundly oppressive, even at this day, when every plot of higher ground bears some fragment of fair building: but, in order to know what it was once, let the traveller follow in his boat at evening the windings of some unfrequented channel far into the midst of the melancholy plain; let him remove, in his imagination, the brightness of the great city that still extends itself in the distance, and the walls and towers from the islands that are near; and so wait, until the bright investiture and sweet warmth of the sunset are withdrawn from the waters, and the black desert of their shore lies in its nakedness beneath the night, pathless, comfortless, infirm, lost in dark languor and fearful silence, except where the salt runlets plash into the tideless pools, or the sea-birds flit from their margins with a questioning cry; and he will be enabled to enter in some sort into the horror of heart with which this solitude was anciently chosen by man for his habitation. They little thought, who first drove the stakes into the sand, and strewed the ocean reeds for their rest, that their children were to be the princes of that ocean, and their palaces its pride; and yet, in the great natural laws that rule that sorrowful wilderness, let it be remembered what strange preparation had been made for the things which no human imagination could have foretold, and how the whole existence and fortune of the Venetian nation were anticipated or compelled, by the setting of those bars and doors to the rivers and the sea. Had deeper currents divided their islands, hostile navies would again and again have reduced the rising city into servitude; had stronger surges beaten their shores, all the richness and refinement of the Venetian architecture must have been exchanged for the walls and bulwarks of an ordinary seaport. Had there been no tide, as in other parts of the Mediterranean, the narrow canals of the city would have become noisome, and the marsh in which it was built pestiferous. Had the tide been only a foot or eighteen inches higher in its rise, the water-access to the doors of the palaces would have been impossible: even as it is, there is sometimes a little difficulty, at the ebb, in landing without setting foot upon the lower and slippery steps; and the highest tides sometimes enter the courtyards, and overflow the entrance halls. Eighteen inches more of differences between the level of the flood and ebb would have rendered the doorsteps of every palace, at low water, a treacherous mass of weeds and limpets, and the entire system of water-carriage for the higher classes, in their easy and daily intercourse, must have been done away with. The streets of the city would have been widened, its network of canals filled up, and all the peculiar character of the place and the people destroyed.

From *The Stones of Venice*, Vol. II, ch. I, § 6

¶ 319

CONTRASTED CATHEDRALS

And now I wish that the reader, before I bring him into St Mark's Place, would imagine himself for a little time in a quiet English cathedral town, and walk with me to the west front of its cathedral. Let us go together up the more retired street, at the end of which we can see the pinnacles of one of the towers, and then through the low grey gateway, with its battlemented top and small latticed window in the centre, into the inner private-looking road or close, where nothing goes in but the carts of the tradesmen who supply the bishop and the chapter, and where there are little shaven grass-plots, fenced in by neat rails, before old-fashioned groups of somewhat diminutive and excessively trim houses, with little oriel and bay windows jutting out here and there, and deep wooden cornices and eaves painted cream colour and white, and small porches to their doors in the shape of cockle-shells, or little, crooked, thick, indescribable wooden gables warped a little on one side; and so forward till we come to larger houses, also old-fashioned, but of red brick, and with garden behind them, and fruit walls, which show here and there, among the nectarines, the vestiges of an old cloister arch or shaft, and looking in front on the cathedral square itself, laid out in rigid divisions of smooth grass and gravel walk, yet not un-cheerful, especially on the sunny side, where the canon's children are walking with their nurserymaids. And so, taking care not to tread on the grass, we will go along the straight walk to the west front, and there stand for a time, looking up at its deep-pointed porches and the dark places between their pillars where there were statues once, and where the fragments, here and there, of a stately figure are still left, which has in it the likeness of a king, perhaps indeed a king on earth, perhaps a saintly king long ago in heaven; and so higher and higher up to the great mouldering wall of rugged sculpture and confused arcades, shattered, and grey, and grisly with heads of dragons and mocking fiends, worn by the rain and swirling winds into yet unseemlier shape, and coloured on their stony scales by the deep russet-orange lichen, melancholy gold; and so, higher still, to the bleak towers, so far above that the eye loses itself among the bosses of their traceries, though they are rude and strong, and only sees like a drift of eddying black points, now closing, now scattering, and now settling suddenly into invisible places among the bosses and flowers, the crowd of restless birds that fill the whole square with that strange clangour of theirs, so harsh and yet so soothing, like the cries of birds on a solitary coast between the cliffs and sea.

Think for a little while of that scene, and the meaning of all its small formalisms, mixed with its serene sublimity. Estimate its secluded, continuous, drowsy felicities, and its evidence of the sense and steady performance of such kind of duties as can be regulated by the cathedral clock; and weigh the influence of those dark towers on all who have passed through the lonely square at their feet for centuries, and on all who have seen them rising far away over the wooden plain, or catching on their square masses the last rays of the sunset, when the city at their feet was indicated only by the mist at the bend of the river. And then let us quickly recollect that we are in Venice, and land at the extremity of the Calle Lunga San Moisè, which may be considered as there answering to the secluded street that led us to our English cathedral gateway.

We find ourselves in a paved alley, some seven feet wide where it is widest, full of people, and resonant with cries of itinerant salesmen, – a shriek in their beginning, and dying away into a kind of brazen ringing, all the worse for its confinement between the high houses of the passage along which we have to make our way. Overhead, an inextricable confusion of rugged shutters, and iron balconies and chimney flues, pushed out on brackets to save room, and arched windows with projecting sills of Istrian stone, and gleams of green leaves here and there where a fig-tree branch escapes over a lower wall from some inner cortile, leading the eye up to the narrow stream of blue sky high over all. On each side, a row of shops, as densely set as may be, occupying, in fact, intervals between the square stone shafts, about eight feet high, which carry the first floors: intervals of which one is narrow and serves as a door; the other is, in the more respectable shops, wainscotted to the height of the counter and glazed above, but in those of the poorer tradesmen left open to the ground, and the wares laid on benches and tables in the open air, the light in all cases entering at the front only, and fading away in a few feet from the threshold into a gloom which the eye from without cannot penetrate, but which is generally broken by a ray or two from a feeble lamp at the back of the shop, suspended before a print of the Virgin. The less pious shopkeeper sometimes leaves his lamp unlighted, and is contented with a penny print; the more religious one has his print coloured and set in a little shrine with a gilded or figured fringe, with perhaps a faded flower or two on each side, and his lamp burning brilliantly. Here at the fruiterer's, where the dark-green water-melons are heaped upon the counter like cannon balls, the Madonna has a tabernacle of fresh laurel leaves; but the pewterer next door has let his lamp out, and there is nothing to be seen in his shop but the dull gleam of the studded patterns on the copper pans, hanging from his roof in the darkness. Next comes a 'Vendita Frittole e Liquori,' where the Virgin, enthroned in a very humble manner beside a tallow candle on a back shelf, presides over certain ambrosial morsels of a nature too ambiguous to be defined or enumerated. But a few steps farther on, at the regular wine-shop of the calle, where we are offered 'Vino Nostrani a Soldi 28·32,' the Madonna is in great glory, enthroned above ten or a dozen large red casks of three-year-old vintage, and flanked by goodly ranks of bottles of Maraschino, and two crimson lamps; and for the evening, when the gondoliers will come to drink out, under her auspices, the money they have gained during the day, she will have a whole chandelier.

A yard or two farther, we pass the hostelry of the Black Eagle, and glancing as we pass through the square door of marble, deeply moulded, in the outer wall, we see the shadows of its pergola of vines resting on an ancient well, with a pointed shield carved on its side; and so presently emerge on the bridge and Campo San Moisè, whence to the entrance into St Mark's Place, called the Bocca di Piazza (mouth of the square), the Venetian character is nearly destroyed, first by the frightful façade of San Moisè, which we will pause at another time to examine, and then by the modernizing of the shops as they near the piazza, and the mingling with the lower Venetian populace of lounging groups of English and Austrians. We will push fast through them into the shadow of the pillars at the end of the 'Bocca di Piazza,' and then we forget them all; for between those pillars there opens a great light, and, in the midst of it, as we advance slowly, the vast tower of St Mark seems to lift itself visibly forth from the level field of chequered stones; and, on each side, the countless arches prolong themselves into ranged symmetry, as if the rugged and irregular houses that pressed together above us in the dark alley had been struck back into sudden obedience and lovely order, and all their rude casements and broken walls had been transformed into arches charged with goodly sculpture, and fluted shafts of delicate stone.

And well may they fall back, for beyond those troops of ordered arches there rises a vision out of the earth, and all the great square seems to have opened from it in a kind of awe, that we may see it far away; – a multitude of pillars and white domes, clustered into a long low pyramid of coloured light; a treasure-heap, it seems, partly of gold, and partly of opal and mother-of-pearl, hollowed beneath into five great vaulted porches, ceiled with fair mosaic, and beset with sculpture of alabaster, clear as amber and delicate as ivory, – sculpture fantastic and involved, of palm leaves and lilies, and grapes and pomegranates, and birds clinging and fluttering among the branches, all twined together into an endless network of buds and plumes; and in the midst of it, the solemn forms of angels, sceptred, and robed to the feet, and leaning to each other across the gates, their figures indistinct among the gleaming of the golden ground through the leaves beside them, interrupted and dim, like the morning light as it faded back among the branches of Eden, when first its gates were angel-guarded long ago. And round the walls of the porches there are set pillars of variegated stones, jasper and porphyry, and deep-green serpentine spotted with flakes of snow, and marbles, that half refuse and half yield to the sunshine, Cleopatra-like, 'their bluest veins to kiss' – the shadow, as it steals back from them, revealing line after line of azure undulation, as a receding tide leaves the waved sand; their capitals rich with interwoven tracery, rooted knots of herbage, and drifting leaves of acanthus and vine, and mystical signs, all beginning and ending in the Cross; and above them, in the broad archivolts, a continuous chain of language and of life – angels, and the signs of heaven, and the labours of men, each in its appointed season upon the earth; and above these, another range of glittering pinnacles, mixed with white arches edged with scarlet flowers, – a confusion of delight, amidst which the breasts of the Greek horses are seen blazing in their breadth of golden strength, and the St Mark's lion, lifted on a blue field covered with stars, until at last, as if in ecstasy, the crests of the arches break into a marble foam, and toss themselves far into the blue sky in flashes and wreaths of sculptured spray, as if the breakers on the Lido shore had been frost-bound before they fell, and the sea-nymphs had inlaid them with coral and amethyst.

Between that grim cathedral of England and this, what an interval! There is a type of it in the very birds that haunt them; for, instead of the restless crowd, hoarse-voiced and sable-winged, drifting on the bleak upper air, the St Mark's porches are full of doves, that nestle among the marble foliage, and mingle the soft iridescence of their living plumes, changing at every motion, with the tints, hardly less lovely, that have stood unchanged for seven hundred years.

And what effect has this splendour on those who pass beneath it?

You may walk from sunrise to sunset, to and fro, before the gateway of St Mark's, and you will not see an eye lifted to it, nor a countenance brightened by it. Priest and layman, soldier and civilian, rich and poor, pass by it alike regardlessly. Up to the very recesses of the porches, the meanest tradesmen of the city push their counters; nay, the foundations of its pillars are themselves the seats – not 'of them that sell doves' for sacrifice, but of the vendors of toys and caricatures. Round the whole square in front of the church there is almost a continuous line of cafés, where the idle Venetians of the middle classes lounge, and read empty journals; in its centre the Austrian bands play during the time of vespers, their martial music jarring with the organ notes, – the march drowning the miserere, and the sullen crowd thickening round them, – a crowd, which, if it had its will, would stiletto every soldier that pipes to it. And in the recesses of the porches, all day long, knots of men of the lowest classes, unemployed and listless, lie basking in the sun like lizards; and unregarded children, – every heavy glance of their young eyes full of desperation and stony depravity, and their throats hoarse with cursing, – gamble and fight, and snarl, and sleep, hour after hour, clashing their bruised centesimi upon the marble ledges of the church porch. And the images of Christ and His angels look down upon it continually.

From *The Stones of Venice*, Vol. II, ch. IV, §§ 10–15

¶ 320

ST MARK'S

Through the heavy door whose bronze network closes the place of his rest, let us enter the church itself. It is lost in still deeper twilight, to which the eye must be accustomed for some moments before the form of the building can be traced; and then there opens before us a vast cave, hewn out into the form of a Cross, and divided into shadowy aisles by many pillars. Round the domes of its roof the light enters only through narrow apertures like large stars; and here and there a ray or two from some far-away casement wanders into the darkness, and casts a narrow phosphoric stream upon the waves of marble that heave and fall in a thousand colours along the floor.

What else there is of light is from torches, or silver lamps, burning
ceaselessly in the recesses of the chapels; the roof sheeted with gold,
and the polished walls covered with alabaster, give back at every
curve and angle some feeble gleaming to the flames; and the glories
round the heads of the sculptured saints flash out upon us as we pass
them, and sink again into the gloom. Under foot and over head, a
continual succession of crowded imagery, one picture passing into
another, as in a dream; forms beautiful and terrible mixed together;
dragons and serpents, and ravening beasts of prey, and graceful
birds that in the midst of them drink from running fountains and
feed from vases of crystal; the passions and the pleasures of human
life symbolized together, and the mystery of its redemption; for the
mazes of interwoven lines and changeful pictures lead always at last
to the Cross, lifted and carved in every place and upon every stone;
sometimes with the serpent of eternity wrapt round it, sometimes
with doves beneath its arms, and sweet herbage growing forth from
its feet; but conspicuous most of all on the great rood that crosses the
church before the altar, raised in bright blazonry against the shadow
of the apse.

From *The Stones of Venice*, Vol. II, ch. IV, § 18

THE TWO BOYHOODS

§ 1. Born half-way between the mountains and the sea – that young George of Castelfranco – of the Brave Castle: – Stout George they called him, George of Georges, so goodly a boy he was – Giorgione.

Have you ever thought what a world his eyes opened on – fair, searching eyes of youth? What a world of mighty life, from those mountain roots to the shore; – of loveliest life, when he went down, yet so young, to the marble city – and became himself as a fiery heart to it?

A city of marble, did I say? nay, rather a golden city, paved with emerald. For truly, every pinnacle and turret glanced or glowed, overlaid with gold, or bossed with jasper. Beneath, the unsullied sea drew in deep breathing, to and fro, its eddies of green wave. Deep-hearted, majestic, terrible as the sea, – the men of Venice moved in sway of power and war; pure as her pillars of alabaster, stood her mothers and maidens; from foot to brow, all noble, walked her knights; the low bronzed gleaming of sea-rusted armour shot angrily under their blood-red mantle-folds. Fearless, faithful, patient, impenetrable, implacable, – every word a fate – sate her senate. In hope and honour, lulled by flowing of wave around their isles of sacred sand, each with his name written and the cross graved at his side, lay her dead. A wonderful piece of world. Rather, itself a world. It lay along the face of the waters, no larger, as its captains saw it from their masts at evening, than a bar of sunset that could not pass away; but for its power, it must have seemed to them as if they were sailing in the expanse of heaven, and this a great planet, whose orient edge widened through ether. A world from which all ignoble care and petty thoughts were banished, with all the common and poor elements of life. No foulness, nor tumult, in those tremulous streets, that filled, or fell, beneath the moon; but rippled music of majestic change, or thrilling silence. No weak walls could rise above them; no low-roofed cottage, nor straw-built shed. Only the strength as of rock, and the finished setting of stones most precious. And around them, far as the eye could reach, still the soft moving of stainless waters, proudly pure; as not the flower, so neither the thorn nor the thistle, could grow in the glancing fields. Ethereal strength of Alps, dreamlike, vanishing in high procession beyond the Torcellan shore; blue islands of Paduan hills, poised in the golden west. Above, free winds and fiery clouds ranging at their will; – brightness out of the north, and balm from the south, and the stars of the evening and morning clear in the limitless light of arched heaven and circling sea.

Such was Giorgione's school – such Titian's home.

§ 2. Near the south-west corner of Covent Garden, a square brick pit or well is formed by a close-set block of houses, to the back windows of which it admits a few rays of light. Access to the bottom of it is obtained out of Maiden Lane, through a low archway and an iron gate; and if you stand long enough under the archway to accustom your eyes to the darkness you may see on the left hand a narrow door, which formerly gave quiet access to a respectable barber's shop, of which the front window, looking into Maiden Lane, is still extant, filled, in this year (1860), with a row of bottles, connected, in some defunct manner, with a brewer's business. A more fashionable neighbourhood, it is said, eighty years ago than now – never certainly a cheerful one – wherein a boy being born on St George's day, 1775, began soon after to take interest in the world of Covent Garden, and put to service such spectacles of life as it afforded.

§ 3. No knights to be seen there, nor, I imagine, many beautiful ladies; their costume at least disadvantageous, depending much on incumbency of hat and feather, and short waists; the majesty of men founded similarly on shoebuckles and wigs; – impressive enough when Reynolds will do his best for it; but not suggestive of much ideal delight to a boy.

'Bello ovile dov' io dormii agnello;' of things beautiful, besides men and women, dusty sunbeams up or down the street on summer mornings; deep furrowed cabbage-leaves at the greengrocer's; magnificence of oranges in wheel-barrows round the corner; and Thames' shore within three minutes' race.

§ 4. None of these things very glorious; the best, however, that England, it seems, was then able to provide for a boy of gift: who, such as they are, loves them – never, indeed, forgets them. The short waists modify to the last his visions of Greek ideal. His foregrounds had always a succulent cluster or two of greengrocery at the corners. Enchanted oranges gleam in Covent Gardens of the Hesperides; and great ships go to pieces in order to scatter chests of them on the waves. That mist of early sunbeams in the London dawn crosses, many and many a time, the clearness of Italian air; and by Thames' shore, with its stranded barges and glidings of red sail, dearer to us than Lucerne lake or Venetian lagoon, – by Thames' shore we will die.

§ 5. With such circumstances round him in youth, let us note what necessary effects followed upon the boy. I assume him to have had Giorgione's sensibility (and more than Giorgione's, if that be possible) to colour and form. I tell you farther, and this fact you may receive trustfully, that his sensibility to human affection and distress was no less keen than even his sense for natural beauty – heart-sight deep as eyesight.

Consequently, he attaches himself with the faithfullest child-love to everything that bears an image of the place he was born in. No matter how ugly it is, – has it anything about it like Maiden Lane, or like Thames' shore? If so, it shall be painted for their sake. Hence, to the very close of life, Turner could endure ugliness which no one else, of the same sensibility, would have borne with for an instant. Dead brick walls, blank square windows, old clothes, market-womanly types of humanity – anything fishy and muddy, like Billingsgate or Hungerford Market, had great attraction for him; black barges, patched sails, and every possible condition of fog.

§ 6. You will find these tolerations and affections guiding or sustaining him to the last hour of his life; the notablest of all such endurances being that of dirt. No Venetian ever draws anything foul; but Turner devoted picture after picture to the illustration of effects of dinginess, smoke, soot, dust, and dusty texture; old sides of boats, weedy roadside vegetation, dung-hills, straw-yards, and all the soilings and stains of every common labour.

And more than this, he not only could endure, but enjoyed and looked for *litter*, like Covent Garden wreck after the market. His pictures are often full of it, from side to side; their foregrounds differ from all others in the natural way that things have of lying about in them. Even his richest vegetation, in ideal work, is confused; and he delights in shingle, débris, and heaps of fallen stones. The last words he ever spoke to me about a picture were in gentle exultation about his St Gothard: 'that *litter* of stones which I endeavoured to represent.'

§ 7. The second great result of this Covent Garden training was, understanding of and regard for the poor, whom the Venetians, we saw, despised; whom, contrarily, Turner loved, and more than loved – understood. He got no romantic sight of them, but an infallible one, as he prowled about the end of his lane, watching night effects in the wintry streets; nor sight of the poor alone, but of the poor in direct relations with the rich. He knew, in good and evil, what both classes thought of, and how they dealt with, each other.

Reynolds and Gainsborough, bred in country villages, learned there the country boy's reverential theory of 'the squire,' and kept it. They painted the squire and the squire's lady as centres of the movements of the universe, to the end of their lives. But Turner perceived the younger squire in other aspects about his lane, occurring prominently in its night scenery, as a dark figure, or one of two, against the moonlight. He saw also the working of city commerce, from endless warehouse, towering over Thames, to the back shop in the lane, with its stale herrings – highly interesting these last; one of his father's best friends, whom he often afterwards visited affectionately at Bristol, being a fishmonger and glue-boiler; which gives us a friendly turn of mind towards herring-fishing, whaling, Calais poissardes, and many other of our choicest subjects in after-life; all this being connected with that mysterious forest below London Bridge on one side; and, on the other, with these masses of human power and national wealth which weigh upon us, at Covent Garden here, with strange compression, and crush us into narrow Hand Court.

§ 8. 'That mysterious forest below London Bridge' – better for the boy than wood of pine, or grove of myrtle. How he must have tormented the watermen, beseeching them to let him crouch anywhere in the bows, quiet as a log, so only that he might get floated down there among the ships, and round and round the ships, and with the ships, and by the ships,' and under the ships, staring, and clambering; – these the only quite beautiful things he can see in all the world, except the sky; but these, when the sun is on their sails, filling or falling, endlessly disordered by sway of tide and stress of anchorage, beautiful unspeakably; which ships also are inhabited by glorious creatures – red-faced sailors, with pipes, appearing over the gunwhales, true knights, over their castle parapets – the most angelic beings in the whole compass of London world. And Trafalgar happening long before we can draw ships, we, nevertheless, coax all current stories out of the wounded sailors, do our best at present to show Nelson's funeral streaming up the Thames; and vow that Trafalgar shall have its tribute of memory some day. Which, accordingly, is accomplished – once, with all our might, for its death; twice, with all our might, for its victory; thrice, in pensive farewell to the old *Téméraire*, and with it, to that order of things.

§ 9. Now this fond companying with sailors must have divided his time, it appears to me, pretty equally between Covent Garden and Wapping (allowing for incidental excursions to Chelsea on one side, and Greenwich on the other), which time he would spend pleasantly, but not magnificently, being limited in pocket-money, and leading a kind of 'Poor-Jack' life on the river.

In some respects, no life could be better for a lad. But it was not calculated to make his ear fine to the niceties of language, nor form his moralities on an entirely regular standard. Picking up his first scraps of vigorous English chiefly at Deptford and in the markets, and his first ideas of female tenderness and beauty among nymphs of the barge and the barrow, – another boy might, perhaps, have become what people usually term 'vulgar.' But the original make and frame of Turner's mind being not vulgar, but as nearly as possible a combination of the minds of Keats and Dante, joining capricious waywardness, and intense openness to every fine pleasure of sense, and hot defiance of formal precedent, with a quite infinite tenderness, generosity, and desire of justice and truth – this kind of mind did not become vulgar, but very tolerant of vulgarity, even fond of it in some forms; and on the outside, visibly infected by it, deeply enough; the curious result, in its combination of elements, being to most people wholly incomprehensible. It was as if a cable had been woven of blood-crimson silk, and then tarred on the outside. People handled it, and the tar came off on their hands; red gleams were seen through the black underneath, at the places where it had been strained. Was it ochre? – said the world – or red lead?

§ 10. Schooled thus in manners, literature, and general moral principles at Chelsea and Wapping, we have finally to inquire concerning the most important point of all. We have seen the principal differences between this boy and Giorgione, as respects sight of the beautiful, understanding of poverty, of commerce, and of order of battle; then follows another cause of difference in our training – not slight, – the aspect of religion, namely, in the neighbourhood of Covent Garden. I say the aspect; for that was all the lad could judge by, Disposed, for the most part, to learn chiefly by his eyes, in this special matter he finds there is really no other way of learning. His father taught him 'to lay one penny upon another.' Of mother's teaching, we hear of none; of parish pastoral teaching, the reader may guess how much.

§ 11. I chose Giorgione rather than Veronese to help me in carrying out this parallel; because I do not find in Giorgione's work any of the early Venetian monarchist element. He seems to me to have belonged more to an abstract contemplative school. I may be wrong in this; it is no matter; – suppose it were so, and that he came down to Venice somewhat recusant or insentient, concerning the usual priestly doctrines of his day, how would the Venetian religion, from an outer intellectual standing-point, have *looked* to him?

§ 12. He would have seen it to be a religion indisputably powerful in human affairs; often very harmfully so; sometimes devouring widows' houses, and consuming the strongest and fairest from among the young: freezing into merciless bigotry the policy of the old: also, on the other hand, animating national courage, and raising souls, otherwise sordid, into heroism: on the whole, always a real and great power; served with daily sacrifice of gold, time, and thought; putting forth its claims, if hypocritically, at least in bold hypocrisy, not waiving any atom of them in doubt or fear; and, assuredly, in large measure, sincere, believing in itself, and believed: a goodly system, moreover, in aspect; gorgeous, harmonious, mysterious; – a thing which had either to be obeyed or combated, but could not be scorned. A religion towering over all the city –

many-buttressed – luminous in marble stateliness, as the dome of our Lady of Safety shines over the sea; many-voiced, also, giving, over all the eastern seas, to the sentinel his watchword, to the soldier his war-cry; and, on the lips of all who died for Venice, shaping the whisper of death.

§ 13. I suppose the boy Turner to have regarded the religion of his city also from an external intellectual standing-point.

What did he see in Maiden Lane?

Let not the reader be offended with me: I am willing to let him describe, at his own pleasure, what Turner saw there; but to me, it seems to have been this. A religion maintained occasionally, even the whole length of the lane, at point of constable's staff; but, at other times, placed under the custody of the beadle, within certain black and unstately iron railings of St Paul's Covent Garden. Among the wheelbarrows and over the vegetables, no perceptible dominance of religion; in the narrow, disquieted streets, none; in the tongues, deeds, daily ways of Maiden Lane, little. Some honesty, indeed, and English industry, and kindness of heart, and general idea of justice; but faith, of any national kind, shut up from one Sunday to the next, not artistically beautiful even in those Sabbatical exhibitions; its paraphernalia being chiefly, of high pews, heavy elocution, and cold grimness of behaviour.

What chiaroscuro belongs to it – (dependent mostly on candle-light), – we will, however, draw, considerately; no goodliness of escutcheon, nor other respectability being omitted, and the best of their results confessed, a meek old woman and a child being let into a pew, for whom the reading by candlelight will be beneficial.

§ 14. For the rest, this religion seems to him discreditable – discredited – not believing in itself: putting forth its authority in a cowardly way, watching how far it might be tolerated, continually shrinking, disclaiming, fencing, finessing; divided against itself, not by stormy rents, but by thin fissures, and splittings of plaster from the walls. Not to be either obeyed, or combated, by an ignorant, yet clear-sighted youth! only to be scorned. And scorned not one whit the less, though also the dome dedicated to *it* looms high over distant winding of the Thames; as St Mark's campanile rose, for goodly land-mark, over mirage of lagoon. For St Mark ruled over life; the Saint of London over death; St Mark over St Mark's Place, but St Paul over St Paul's Churchyard.

§ 15. Under these influences pass away the first reflective hours of life, with such conclusion as they can reach. In consequence of a fit of illness, he was taken – I cannot ascertain in what year – to live with an aunt, at Brentford; and here, I believe, received some schooling, which he seems to have snatched vigorously; getting knowledge, at least by translation, of the more picturesque classical authors, which he turned presently to use, as we shall see. Hence also, walks about Putney and Twickenham in the summer time acquainted him with the look of English meadow-ground in its restricted states of paddock and park; and with some round-headed appearances of trees, and stately entrances to houses of mark: the avenue at Bushey, and the iron gates and carved pillars of Hampton, impressing him apparently with great awe and admiration; so that in after-life his little country house is, – of all places in the world, – at Twickenham! Of swans and reedy shores he now learns the soft motion and the green mystery, in a way not to be forgotten.

§ 16. And at last fortune wills that the lad's true life shall begin; and one summer's evening, after various wonderful stage-coach experiences on the north road, which gave him a love of stage-coaches ever after, he finds himself sitting alone among the Yorkshire hills. For the first time, the silence of Nature round him, her freedom sealed to him, her glory opened to him. Peace at last; no roll of cart-wheel, nor mutter of sullen voices in the back shop; but curlew-cry in space of heaven, and welling of bell-toned streamlet by its shadowy rock. Freedom at last. Dead-wall, dark railing, fenced field, gated garden, all passed away like the dream of a prisoner; and behold, far as foot or eye can race or range, the moor, and cloud. Loveliness at last. It is here then, among these deserted vales! Not among men. Those pale, poverty-struck, or cruel faces; – that multitudinous, marred humanity – are not the only things that God has made. Here is something He has made which no one has marred. Pride of purple rocks and river pools of blue, and tender wilderness of glittering trees, and misty lights of evening on immeasurable hills.

§ 17. Beauty, and freedom, and peace; and yet another teacher, graver than these. Sound preaching at last here, in Kirkstall crypt, concerning fate and life. Here, where the dark pool reflects the chancel pillars, and the cattle lie in unhindered rest, the soft sunshine on their dappled bodies, instead of priests' vestments; their white furry hair ruffled a little, fitfully, by the evening wind deep-scented from the meadow thyme.

§ 18. Consider deeply the import to him of this, his first sight of ruin, and compare it with the effect of the architecture that was around Giorgione. There were indeed aged buildings, at Venice, in his time, but none in decay. All ruin was removed, and its place filled as quickly as in our London; but filled always by architecture loftier, and more wonderful than that whose place it took, the boy himself happy to work upon the walls of it; so that the idea of the passing away of the strength of men and beauty of their works never could occur to him sternly. Brighter and brighter the cities of Italy had been rising and broadening on hill and plain, for three hundred years. He saw only strength and immortality, could not but paint both; conceived the form of man as deathless, calm with power, and fiery with life.

§ 19. Turner saw the exact reverse of this. In the present work of men, meanness, aimlessness, unsightliness: thin-walled, lath-divided, narrow-garreted houses of clay; booths of a darksome Vanity Fair, busily base.

But on Whitby Hill, and by Bolton Brook, remained traces of other handiwork. Men who could build had been there; and who also had wrought, not merely for their own days. But to what purpose? Strong faith, and steady hands, and patient souls – can this, then, be all you have left? this the sum of your doing on the earth; – a nest whence the night-owl may whimper to the brook, and a ribbed skeleton of consumed arches, looming above the bleak banks of mist, from its cliff to the sea?

As the strength of men to Giorgione, to Turner their weakness and vileness, were alone visible. They themselves, unworthily or ephemeral; their work, despicable, or decayed. In the Venetian's eyes, all beauty depended on man's presence and pride; in Turner's, on the solitude he had left, and the humiliation he had suffered.

§ 20. And thus the fate and issue of all his work were determined at once. He must be a painter of the strength of nature, there was no beauty elsewhere than in that; he must paint also the labour and sorrow and passing away of men: this was the great human truth visible to him.

Their labour, their sorrow, and their death. Mark the three. Labour; by sea and land, in field and city, at forge and furnace, helm and plough. No pastoral indolence nor classic pride shall stand between him and the troubling of the world; still less between him and the toil of his country, – blind, tormented, unwearied, marvellous England.

§ 21. Also their Sorrow; Ruin of all their glorious work, passing away of their thoughts and their honour, mirage of pleasure, FALLACY OF HOPE; gathering of weed on temple step; gaining of wave on deserted strand; weeping of the mother for the children, desolate by her breathless first-born in the streets of the city,* desolate by her last sons slain, among the beasts of the field.†

§ 22. And their Death. That old Greek question again; – yet unanswered. The unconquerable spectre still flitting among the forest trees at twilight; rising ribbed out of the sea-sand; – white, a strange Aphrodite, – out of the sea-foam; stretching its gray, cloven wings among the clouds; turning the light of their sunsets into blood. This has to be looked upon, and in a more terrible shape than ever Salvator or Dürer saw it. The wreck of one guilty country does not infer the ruin of all countries, and need not cause general terror respecting the laws of the universe. Neither did the orderly and narrow succession of domestic joy and sorrow in a small German community bring the question in its breadth, or in any unresolvable shape, before the mind of Dürer. But the English death – the European death of the nineteenth century – was of another range and power; more terrible a thousand-fold in its merely physical grasp and grief; more terrible, incalculably, in its mystery and shame. What were the robber's casual pang, or the range of the flying skirmish, compared to the work of the axe, and the sword, and the famine, which was done during this man's youth on all the hills and plains of the Christian earth, from Moscow to Gibraltar? He was

* 'The Tenth Plague of Egypt.'   † 'Rizpah, the Daughter of Aiah.'

eighteen years old when Napoleon came down on Arcola. Look on the map of Europe and count the blood-stains on it, between Arcola and Waterloo.

§ 23. Not alone those blood-stains on the Alpine snow and the blue of the Lombard plain. The English death was before his eyes also. No decent, calculable, consoled dying; no passing to rest like that of the aged burghers of Nuremberg town. No gentle processions to churchyards among the fields, the bronze crests bossed deep on the memorial tablets, and the skylark singing above them from among the corn. But the life trampled out in the slime of the street, crushed to dust amidst the roaring of the wheel, tossed countlessly away into howling winter wind along five hundred leagues of rock-fanged shore. Or, worst of all, rotted down to forgotten graves through years of ignorant patience, and vain seeking for help from man, for hope in God – infirm, imperfect yearning, as of motherless infants starving at the dawn; oppressed royalties of captive thought, vague ague-fits of bleak, amazed despair.

§ 24. A goodly landscape this, for the lad to paint, and under a goodly light. Wide enough the light was, and clear; no more Salvator's lurid chasm on jagged horizon, nor Dürer's spotted rest of sunny gleam on hedgerow and field; but light over all the world. Full shone now its awful globe, one pallid charnel-house, – a ball strewn bright with human ashes, glaring in poised sway beneath the sun, all blinding-white with death from pole to pole, – death, not of myriads of poor bodies only, but of will, and mercy, and conscience; death, not once inflicted on the flesh, but daily fastening on the spirit; death, not silent or patient, waiting his appointed hour, but voiceful, venomous; death with the taunting word, and burning grasp, and infixed sting.

'Put ye in the sickle, for the harvest is ripe.' The word is spoken in our ears continually to other reapers than the angels, – to the busy skeletons that never tire for stooping. When the measure of iniquity is full, and it seems that another day might bring repentance and redemption, – 'Put ye in the sickle.' When the young life has been wasted all away, and the eyes are just opening upon the tracks of ruin, and faint resolution rising in the heart for nobler things, – 'Put ye in the sickle.' When the roughest blows of fortune have been borne long and bravely, and the hand is just stretched to grasp its goal, – 'Put ye in the sickle.' And when there are but a few in the midst of a nation, to save it, or to teach, or to cherish; and all its life is bound up in those few golden ears, – 'Put ye in the sickle, pale reapers, and pour hemlock for your feast of harvest home.'

This was the sight which opened on the young eyes, this the watchword sounding within the heart of Turner in his youth.

So taught, and prepared for his life's labour, sate the boy at last alone among his fair English hills; and began to paint, with cautious toil, the rocks, and fields, and trickling brooks, and soft white clouds of heaven.

Chapter IX of *Modern Painters*, Vol. V, Part IX

A NOTE ON RUSKIN'S DRAWINGS

In the early nineteenth century all educated people made drawings from nature. It was the equivalent of taking photographs today, and did not imply artistic tastes or ambitions. Ruskin's father drew, and his son followed his example as a matter of course. But the young Ruskin's imitations of Prout showed unusual powers of concentration. He tells us in *Praeterita* that 'the drawings I made in 1835 (age 16) were really interesting, even to artists' and appeared promising enough for his father to arrange a course of lessons with Copley Fielding. There he learnt 'to wash colour smoothly in successive tints, to shade cobalt though pink madder into yellow ochre for skies, to use a broken, scraggy touch for the tops of mountains . . . and to crumble burnt umber with a dry brush for foliage and foreground'. Naturally enough the drawings produced according to this formula are of no interest, and soon ceased to satisfy Ruskin himself; and at this point he began to make copies of the steel engravings after Turner in Roger's *Italy*, developing that mastery of microscopic detail which he was never to lose.

But although he idolized Turner, and was soon to be surrounded by Turner watercolours, Ruskin was too humble and too intelligent to imitate his style. Instead he took as his second model the drawings of David Roberts, and it is in this manner that he executed the records of his visit to Italy in 1840. 'He taught me', Ruskin says, 'of absolute good, the use of fine point instead of the blunt one; attention and indefatigable correctness in detail; and the simplest means of expressing ordinary light and shade on a grey ground.' And he tells us how he showed his parents a drawing he had done in this manner with the words 'Prout would give his ears to make such a drawing as that'. These drawings done in Italy in 1840 and 1841 are indeed skilful and tasteful works; but they are still replete with fashionable tricks. The way in which Ruskin became aware of their deficiencies is beautifully described in two passages in *Praeterita*, quoted in nos. 27 and 28.

These two memories, recorded forty-five years after the event, show the character of Ruskin's best gifts as an artist. He loved what Gerard Manley Hopkins called 'inscape'; not merely detail, that is to say, but inner construction, the rhythms and tensions, which are revealed to a steady penetrating gaze. He had stared fixedly at details all his life, and, as he grew older, to look into something intensively was like re-entering a lost Eden. He also looked into natural objects for a confirmation of his faith. *The Ethics of the Dust*, *The Lamp of Obedience*, *The Law of Help* – these, and a dozen more, of his titles show how he longed for *laws* and hoped to find them revealed in the growth or constitution of plants, rocks, or skies. When the same faith-hungry eye was focused on works of art, the feeling of organic nature was never entirely lost. He loved the marble gryphons of S. Zeno or the crockets on the Scaliger tomb, not only for their design, but on account of every crack and venerable discoloration. If a work of art was too smooth and clean he could not draw it, and his many attempts to record his beloved Ilaria di Careto are all a failure.

Related to this love of organic life was what he called 'an idiosyncrasy which extremely wise people do not share, my love of all kinds of filigree and embroidery, from hoar frost to high cloud'. This is the bias of taste which led him to look at detail rather than mass, ornament rather than proportion, Rouen rather than Durham. Combined with his love of inscape, it meant that he could seldom grasp an object in its totality. His eye focuses on one or two points with such intensity that it seems to be exhausted before it can comprehend the whole, and often a frenzy of emotion ends abruptly, like a piece of oriental music. Sometimes the points of excitement are disconnected from one another with dream-like inconsequence, as in the beautiful drawing of the walls of Lucerne, where his eye, starting soberly enough with the left-hand tower, skips down the battlements, pausing at cracks and crannies with a rapturous suggestion of bonfires beyond them, is almost blinded by the light on the central tower, and passes with relief to the little gazebo in half-shadow, where for a minute the irregular form of an iron railing is irresistible; is off again in rapture along the sunny wall with its espalier fruit trees, and finally drops rather sadly to the potting-shed in the bottom corner.

This inability to resist or to relate the delights of detail is one reason why Ruskin's landscapes are so seldom convincing, the large watercolour of Bonneville being one of the few exceptions. But when he came to the architecture of his favourite towns, love and discipline could be combined. 'I should like to draw all St Mark's and all this Verona stone by stone, to eat it all up in my mind, touch by touch' (no. 35). This appetite allows him to include an incredible quantity of detail without dryness or formalization. His drawings of Venice, Abbeville, and Verona are some of the most beautiful records of architecture ever made, for Ruskin is able to combine knowledge and love, sensibility and precision in a way that is extremely rare. Beside them the ordinary skilful architectural drawing looks tricky and self-conscious. Those who know him chiefly through his writings may be surprised to see how humbly and peacefully this arrogant and angry man has made himself into a kind of *camera lucida*; and it is touching to learn that the self-effacing drawing of Lucca was done only a short time before indignation and despair brought on his first attack of madness.

Ruskin drew almost every day of his life. He drew, as he said, from sheer love and appetite. He also drew to teach himself the laws of nature: every morning after breakfast he followed in a fine pen outline the mode of growth of a leaf or a handful of grasses; and he drew to preserve some record of the works of art, particularly architectural detail, which he saw daily destroyed by neglect or restoration. This daily discipline was the foundation of all his judgements, and before questioning his criticism of a building or an ornament we should think of the precise and active observation, and the acute comparison with living organisms, on which his best criticism is based.

A SHORT LIST OF BOOKS
ABOUT RUSKIN

Far the best account of Ruskin's life is to be found in the introductions to the Library Edition (C. & W.), which make full use of his letters and journals. The journals themselves are now in course of publication – *The Diaries of John Ruskin* edited by Joan Evans and John Howard Whitehouse.

Other books, in chronological order, are:

W. J. Collingwood, *The Life and Works of John Ruskin*, 2 vols., 1893.
W. M. Rossetti, *Ruskin: Rossetti: Pre-Raphaelitism*, 1899.
Letters of John Ruskin to Charles Eliot Norton, 2 vols., 1905.
Frederick Harrison, *John Ruskin*, 1907.
Alice Meynell, *John Ruskin*, 1910.
E. T. Cook, *Life of John Ruskin*, 2 vols., 1911.
Marcel Proust, *Pastiches et Mélanges*, 1927.
A. Williams Ellis, *The Tragedy of John Ruskin*, 1928.
George Macdonald, *Reminiscences of a Specialist*, 1932.
R. H. Wilenski, *John Ruskin: an Introduction to Further Study of his Life and Work*, 1933.
Sydney Cockerell, *Friends of a Lifetime*, 1940.
W. James, *The Order of Release*, 1948.
Peter Quennell, *John Ruskin, the Portrait of a Prophet*, 1949.
Joan Evans, *John Ruskin*, 1954.

Since compiling this list there has appeared the English edition of *The Darkening Glass, a Portrait of Ruskin's Genius* by John D. Rosenberg. It is far the best short book on Ruskin and had I read it before writing the introductions to this anthology it would certainly have influenced my judgement.

THE DATES OF RUSKIN'S WRITINGS
QUOTED IN THIS SELECTION

The principle I have tried to follow is that when a piece of writing appears as a magazine article I give the volume in which it can be found, and if it is published under several titles I give the C. & W. volume.

1837–8   *The Poetry of Architecture*; a series of articles (*Loudon's Architectural Magazine*), reprinted 1892.

1843   *Modern Painters*, Vol. I.

1846   *Modern Painters*, Vol. II.

1847   'Lord Lindsay's *Christian Art*' (*Quarterly Review* for June), reprinted with *Lectures on Architecture and Painting* (C. & W., Vol. XII).

1848   'Eastlake's *History of Oil Painting*' (*Quarterly Review* for March), reprinted with *Lectures on Architecture and Painting* (C. & W., Vol. XII).

1849   *The Seven Lamps of Architecture*.

1851   'The King of the Golden River' (a fairy tale written 1841).

1851   'Pre-Raphaelitism', reprinted with *Lectures on Architecture and Painting* (C. & W., Vol. XII).

1853   *The Stones of Venice*, Vols. II and III.

1853–60 Giotto and his Works in Padua, in three parts.

1854   *Lectures on Architecture and Painting* (Edinburgh, November 1853).

1854   'The Opening of the Crystal Palace', reprinted with *Lectures on Architecture and Painting* (C. & W., Vol. XII).

1855   *Notes on some of the Principal Pictures in . . . the Royal Academy.*

1856   *Notes on . . . the Royal Academy*, etc., no. II.

1856   *Modern Painters*, Vols. III and IV.

1856   *The Harbours of England.*

1857   *Notes on . . . the Royal Academy*, etc., no. III.

1857   *Notes on the Turner Gallery at Marlborough House.*

1857   *The Elements of Drawing.*

1857   'The Political Economy of Art', reprinted as *A Joy for Ever* (*and its Price in the Market*).

1858   *Notes on . . . the Royal Academy*, etc., no. IV (Smith Elder).

1875-7   *Mornings in Florence.*

1875-86 *Proserpina.*

1875-83 *Deucalion.*

1877   *Guide to the Principal Pictures in the Academy of Fine Arts at Venice.*

1877-84 *St Mark's Rest*, in three parts.

1877-8   *The Laws of Fésole*, in four parts.

1878   'My First Editor' (*University Magazine* for April), reprinted in *On the Old Road.*

1878   *Notes on the Turner Exhibition at the Fine Art Society's Galleries.*

1878   'The Three Colours of Pre-Raphaelitism' (*Nineteenth Century* for November and December), reprinted in *On the Old Road.*

1880   *Arrows of the Chace*: letters to newspapers collected by A. D. O. Wedderburn, 2 vols.

1880-5   *The Bible of Amiens.*

1883   *The Art of England.*

1884   *The Storm Cloud of the Nineteenth Century.*

1884-5   *The Pleasures of England.*

1885   *On the Old Road* (reprint of magazine articles), edited by A. D. O. Wedderburn.

1885-9   *Praeterita*: twenty-eight parts, of which twenty-four were collected into two volumes.

INDEX OF NAMES